"Fantastic! CAUGHT IN THE WEB moves with such intensity I couldn't put it down!"

B.R. Christensen, President
Sacramento Publishers Association

"A fast-paced roller coaster of a story that leaves you holding your breath and turning the pages ever faster."

Jodi Wyner-Holmes, Owner
The Bookplace by C. & H.
Elk Grove, CA

"I thought ALWAYS IN A FOREIGN LAND was the best I've ever read, but I was wrong. CAUGHT IN THE WEB is even better!"

Mark F. Brewster, D.C.
Rancho Cordova, CA

"CAUGHT IN THE WEB is a gripping tale of action, mystery and adventure!"

Al Canton, Vice-President
ADAMS-BLAKE PUBLISHING
Fair Oaks, CA

"Adventure/mystery at its best!"

Bruce Merrell
Longview, WA

Other Books by

Barbara A. Scott

ALWAYS IN A FOREIGN LAND

CAUGHT IN THE WEB

By Barbara A. Scott

ZENAR BOOKS

Jean-Marc Rouillan was the leader of the Action Directe group that terrorized France in the 1980s. All other characters in this book are factitious, and any resemblance to actual persons, living or dead, is purely coincidental.

Published by:

> *Zenar Books*
> P.O. Box 686
> Rancho Cordova, CA 95741-0860

Library of Congress Number 96-090041

ISBN 0-9637134-1-8

Manufactured in the United States of America

I would like to thank the firefighters of the Sacramento Fire Department, Engine Company 1 for educating me about firefighting equipment and techniques; the staff at the Ministere De L'Interieur in Paris for their help with my research about the Action Directe group; the staff of the Swiss Embassy in San Francisco for their assistance with other research for this book; the many kind souls at the California Department of Health Services who reviewed and commented on the manuscript; Arlene F. McClung who always knows the right word; and Bob who also works on the team.

Team Members and Friends

Bradley Cover-Rollins: Brad - team leader - British

Mary Cover-Rollins: Brad's wife - British

Paul Artier: Second in command - Working on assignment as Paul Martel - Thai-American

Peter Kononellos: Known to his friends as Kon - Working on assignment as Emile Breaux - Greek

Geilla Kononellos: Kon's wife and member of the team - Italian

Jack Barrons: Team member - American

Nea Cortlin: Dress designer, artist, and business partner to Mary - British

Edgar Marneé: Bank owner and manager - Mentor and father figure to Peter - Swiss

Charlotte Marneé: Edgar's wife who hired Peter as a handyman, but raised him as her son - Swiss

Dr. Carlin La Monde: Family physician to the Marneés and long-time friend and counselor to Peter - Swiss

GIGN: Groupe d'Intervention de la Gendarmerie Nationale - French counter terrorist organization

Chapter One

Kon pulled his aluminum briefcase off the seat of the cab and placed it nonchalantly on the pavement beside him. He paid the driver with small bills, handing over enough for a modest, yet not stingy tip. Usually he gave lavish rewards for personal services, but people tend to remember a person who tips generously, and Kon did not want anyone to remember him on this trip.

The driver mumbled a curt "Thanks" in Dutch and drove away. Kon waited at the curb until the driver was out of sight, then turned and retraced his route, walking three blocks back to the address he intended to visit. It had been almost two years since he had been on an assignment in Amsterdam.

Kon approached the door of the narrow four-story building at mid-block. Ignoring the long, brass doorbar, he pressed his shoulder against the heavy glass and slipped inside. It was 10 a.m. and the small lobby was empty. Most of the clients for the collection of forwarding agents housed there conducted their business by phone or by mail.

Kon walked directly toward the elevators opposite the street door and turned down the corridor to his left. Passing through a wide metal door that was jammed open with a bit of heavy corrugated paper, he left the carpeted public entrance and entered the service area. Twelve feet away on his left was the battered wooden grating which closed off the open shaft of the service elevator. The bottom of the elevator cage was visible high overhead.

Slipping on a pair of thin cotton gloves, Kon snapped open his metal briefcase and pulled out a compact canister. He reached over the shoulder-high grating, lowered the canister onto the edge of a concrete support, and quickly lashed it in place with a twist of a wire. He turned a dial mounted on the canister and retreated back to the public area. Passing the elevators, he opened a door and raced to the second floor, taking the stairs two at a time. Activating the timer on another canister, he placed it into a manilla envelope and cautiously opened the door to the hall. He turned right, passed the elevators, and started down the U-shaped corridor. Checking that the hall was still empty, he dropped the envelope into a mail bin sitting on the floor outside an office.

Kon circled down the hall past the far corner of the building and turned right. Opening a door marked "Exit Only" he stepped through and jammed a small piece of plastic into the latch to keep the door from locking behind him. Quickly he removed two canisters from his metal case, set the timers, and placed the cans in the corner of the landing. Still unnoticed, he retreated back through the door and continued around the building to the elevators. The smell of smoke was barely discernable in the hall. He pressed the elevator button and checked his watch. Jack would love this part of the job, he thought and smiled inwardly. Jack was the team's electronics and demolitions expert who had wired the timers on the AN-M8 smoke grenades.

Kon stepped out of the elevator on the third floor. Checking to see that the corridor was empty, he set another dial and tossed a canister into a metal trash container standing outside the elevator. Then he hurried across the hall to the men's room. Pushing on the door with his gloved hand, he suddenly came face to face with a distinguished looking man in a gray business suit.

"Pardon me, sir," Kon said politely in Dutch and stood aside to let the man pass.

The man nodded and Kon slipped through the door. Finding the room empty, Kon removed another canister from the briefcase, set the timer and watched the canister sink into a cylinder half full of crumpled paper towels.

As he left the men's room, Kon spotted two women chatting by the elevators. He walked casually past them and pushed open the door to the stairs. He detected the faint smell of smoke in the stairwell as he dashed to the fourth floor. The buzzing of a fire alarm met him as he opened the door to the corridor. He slipped into the men's room without being seen and stepped into one of the stalls. He pushed the toilet seat up, stepped onto the rim of the bowl, and hunched down on his heels. As the fire alarm continued to blare away noisily, he waited, carefully holding the stall door partly open. Suddenly the door to the men's room swung open.

"Fire monitor! Everyone out!" a man's voice called in Dutch. Kon smelled the smoke from the hall and held his breath. The fire monitor stepped into the room and gave a careless push on the doors of the first two stalls. Satisfied that the room was empty, he left and Kon heard the hall door click. He waited in place for another five minutes, then stepped down. Easing toward the door, he opened it just far enough to watch the last of the employees file down the stairs. Kon moved rapidly down the empty hall heading for room 436 at the far corner of the building. Finding the office suite empty and unlocked, he walked swiftly past the rows of cubicles and turned right, then left into one of the few offices that boasted a real door. Just inside the door was a three-drawer metal file cabinet which had been left unlocked in the confusion of a hasty departure.

Kon pulled out the top drawer and quickly leafed through the files. His time as key man for this job had come. He was the only person on the multi-national team that could read French, Portuguese and Dutch. This was the assignment that Brad, the team leader, had judged critical enough to ask Kon to delay his wedding trip to accomplish. Kon knew that anything that could disturb Brad's cool British reserve was important. Kon had imagined that Geilla had been with the team long enough to understand that the work schedule was unpredictable, but she certainly had been one very outraged bride until he agreed to let her accompany him. On the flight from Geneva Kon had reassessed what having a wife meant. While he enjoyed sharing his bed and his shirts with Geilla, sharing his feelings was decidedly more difficult. He wasn't sure he could handle the change.

Kon began rifling through the files in the second drawer. It was difficult to turn the pages rapidly without disturbing anything. This whole job had been staged to gain access to these files without anyone knowing that their security had been breached. Kon figured he would have about twenty minutes to complete his task. The fire apparatus was no doubt already on its way and it wouldn't take the firemen long to locate all the smoke grenades. The men would be annoyed at the false alarm and would shake their heads, speculating over who would conceive such a prank.

Kon pulled out his miniature camera and began snapping pictures of records of all materials that originated in France, or were destined for South America. He worked rapidly, keeping an eye on the time. He was too far from the hallway to hear any noise, but he could not risk being seen in the office. Finishing the third drawer, he closed the file cabinet. Hours of pouring over these pictures with a magnifying glass will give me a bad case of eye strain, he thought. But Geilla will be there to rub my temples. Her massage techniques might not be as clinically effective as Paul's, but they are far more sensuous and infinitely more enjoyable. Concentrate, Kon! he told himself sharply. Right now you've got to get out of here without being seen.

Kon picked up his briefcase, left the room, and hastened through the outer offices. Stepping cautiously into the hall he hurried toward the main staircase. Having just recovered from a nearly fatal lung infection, he needed to locate a fireman with a face mask to allow him to make his exit by way of the auxiliary stairs. He had purposely contaminated that route with smoke in order to force the occupants of the building to use the front door.

The pungent odor of smoke hit him as he opened the door on the third floor. He suppressed a cough and crept silently down the corridor. He knew the firemen would be making a walk through, searching for additional smoke grenades. Suddenly Kon flattened himself against the wall as a fireman came out of an office less than ten feet away. Pulling a vial from his pocket, he snapped off the neck and poured the contents into a handkerchief. Keeping the cloth at waist level, he stepped up behind the unsuspecting fireman and tapped him lightly on the shoulder.

As the man turned, Kon closed in. With one fluid motion he pulled the mask away from the man's face and pressed the chloroform-soaked cloth over his nose and mouth. The man's eyes opened wide in surprise, but he seemed too shocked to respond. He made only a feeble attempt to push Kon away before his knees buckled and he fell forward against Kon's chest. Immediately Kon snatched the cloth from the man's face and pulled his face mask loose. Laying the man on the floor, Kon removed the man's helmet, air tank, and rubber coat. He had donned the rubber coat and was about to heft the air tank onto his back when he noticed the man's face. He looked ashen and didn't seem to be breathing. Kon leaned closer.

4

"Dio mio! Don't die on me, you fool!" he cried in alarm. He slapped the man's face and noticed how very young he looked. "Come on! Come on! Wake up!"Kon muttered under his breath. "Shit, you're just a kid! Why did they send a kid? Damn the luck!" When the young man did not respond, Kon quickly pinched the man's nose closed, and began puffing breaths into him. "Come on! Come on, kid!" Kon said impatiently. "I'm running out of time. Don't mess me up on this."

Suddenly he shook the man and was rewarded by a faint moan. "Alright, my friend, you'll be fine. You just need a little air. Sorry I made the hall so God damned smokey. You must be as sensitive to this shit as I am to drugs!" Kon muttered and began pulling the man into the nearest office. He lugged the young man toward the window, checking twice to see that he was still breathing. Leaving the man behind a desk, Kon picked up a metal chair and swung it against the window. The glass shattered wildly, and the cool spring air flooded into the room. Kon kicked the glass aside and propped the man against the wall beneath the window. He checked him one more time to be sure he was breathing normally. "Alright! Just keep breathing! I must go."

Kon dashed into the hall, pulled on the tank, and set the helmet on his head. He ran his gloved hand rapidly over the clasp and handle of the metal briefcase to eliminate fingerprints before he abandoned it and ran toward the auxiliary stairs. He heard shouting behind him in the hall as he rounded the corner and escaped through the exit door.

The stairwell was engulfed in smoke, and for a moment the horrible reality of its suffocating presence shocked Kon. He recovered instantly, however, and pulled the mask over his face. The air was there immediately, just as Jack had said it would be; but Kon had not anticipated his own negative reaction to the confinement of the mask. He absolutely detested having anything over his face. Even while he had lain in that shabby Greek hospital struggling to breathe, the team members had found it necessary to hold his hand and talk to him continually to keep him from pulling away from the life sustaining oxygen. A wave of panic swept over him as he stood at the top of the stairs.

"Move, you idiot! Move!"one part of his mind screamed, and suddenly he bolted headlong down the stairs. Movement restored his senses and he had gained partial control of himself by the time he reached the door to the alley. He pushed on the metal bar with more strength than was needed and the door flew open, almost knocking over a police officer who had been watching the door. Kon longed desperately to tear off the mask and draw the cool air deep into his lungs, but he disciplined himself.

"Don't go in! The smoke is terrible!"he shouted to the officer.

For a moment the officer did not seem to understand him. "Did you see anyone on the stairs?" he asked.

"No! No one!" Kon responded shaking his head. "We should prop the door—for ventilation," Kon continued trying to sound official. The policeman only stared at him. "The smoke!" Kon repeated, "We must let the smoke out!"

"Oh . . . yes . . . yes, of course," the officer finally agreed, and while Kon held the door, he went to fetch a trash can. Kon felt his shirt sticking to his back by the time the door was braced open. He avoided looking the officer in the face as he mumbled, "Thanks," and rushed down the alley as if on some official duty.

Once around the corner, Kon ripped the mask from his face with a violent tug. The air tank had become a tremendous burden and he fought to free himself from it. Setting it down, he tore off the rubber coat and the helmet. Only then did he realize that he was hyperventilating. He felt light headed and slightly nauseous, the way he sometimes did after he pushed himself too hard while running. He ignored the urge to sprawl on the ground and gasp, knowing the feeling would pass if he just kept moving. Dio Mio! That was awful! he thought as he slipped quietly into the crowd. I need to practice before I try that again. Maybe Paul can help me. He's so calm he could train an electron to sit still.

Paul was calm, but he was not without feelings. He just didn't let himself explode the way Kon did. It would have gone against his half-Thai inheritance to lose control of his emotions. He let them sink deep beneath the surface, where they appeared to dissolve. Paul never let his feelings rule him, or so everyone, including Paul himself thought. He had steadied Kon over the years, helping him conquer his almost paranoid suspicion of strangers, and bolstering Kon's battered self-esteem. The team members had given Kon the companionship and acceptance that he had been denied by the Swiss bankers with whom he worked. Except for his mentor, Edgar Marneé, none of them ever let him forget that he was the son of an impoverished Greek fisherman.

Kon took a cab to the photography shop Brad had specified. After the pictures were developed, he picked up the camera and the van that had been reserved for him, then drove to the hotel. Geilla was waiting for him and smiled as she let him in. She had gotten over her disappointment about having to delay her wedding trip. She knew Kon took his work very seriously. He always put team business before his own comfort. It was unrealistic of her to expect him to change just because he had acquired a wife. Perhaps his serious nature was what had attracted her when he had first come to work for her father at the theater in Naples. Unlike herself and her older brother, Alonzo, who were well-off and could afford to be fun-loving and irresponsible, Kon had learned early in life that if you wanted to eat, you had to work and work hard. Kon had attained financial success through hard work, and although he was not greedy or covetous, he derived his sense of self-worth from what he could do.

"I missed you," Geilla said in Italian and took him playfully by the arm. They always spoke Italian when they were alone.

"I am both sorry and glad to hear that," he answered. He bent to kiss her and then looked at her, really looked at her. For years he had not permitted himself to react to her, believing that her heart belonged to Paul. Now here she was, wearing one of his shirts and looking so good in it. She was petite, but gently curved and rounded as opposed to his tall sparse angularity. He was grateful for Paul's direction and training that had enabled him to at last graduate from being outright "skinny" to "very slender." Although he suspected he was in better physical condition than anyone at the bank, he secretly envied Paul's splendidly developed physique and Jack's sheer physical mass.

"Where have you been? Your clothes reek like a chemical factory!" Geilla said crinkling her nose.

7

"Ah, I have been wed scarcely a day and I am berated with the classic wifely question. I must ask Giovanni to supply you with a rolling pin," he teased. "How sweet it is to have someone note my absence," he said, kissing her again. "First I must shower, and then, if you insist, I will tell you about the assignment, for you have been very good about not asking."

"What shall I do about these terrible smelling clothes?" she called into the shower a few minutes later. "Do you need them or can I throw them away?"

"See if you can get them cleaned. We'll find someone who needs them."

Geilla knew Kon would never throw anything usable away. He had not forgotten the shame of arriving at the Marneés in a threadbare shirt and worn out shoes. She called the front desk to inquire about the cleaning and ordered a large pot of coffee to be sent to their room. It was waiting for Kon when he came out of the bathroom. He was wearing a robe, and his thick, dark, unruly hair was still wet.

"Now, tell me, what is so Almighty important that we had to rush to Amsterdam right after our wedding?" Geilla demanded, pouring Kon a cup of coffee.

"Well," Kon began, sitting down at the small table in their cozy room. "While I was busy helping Edgar at the bank and trying to find someone willing to marry us, the English have become involved in a bloody stupid war with Argentina over a small, barren piece of rock in the South Atlantic."

"You mean the Falklands?"

"Yes, the Falklands. Damned messy little war. It seems the British have been taking a beating from the Exocet missiles the Argentine Air Force got from France."

"But I thought there was an embargo in effect. The French can't be supplying them with missiles."

"The French have honored the embargo and frozen all shipments, but Brad learned that six missiles are missing from the Société Nationale Industrielle Aérospatiale warehouse in France. The French government would be terribly embarrassed if the press discovered that some of the Exocets have gone missing. It would cause monumental discord in Anglo-French relations."

8

"Dio Mio! No wonder Brad gave this job priority. He was upset that the situation at the Foreign Office was handled so badly. Exactly what are we supposed to do?"

"Brad got a tip about which shipping company might be involved. I went there this morning to look at their files and now I have to study this packet of photos to see if I can connect them with the missiles."

"That's where your ability to read Dutch comes in."

"Yes. I am still the team's paper shuffler. Jack has no patience with this kind of work," Kon responded opening the thick manilla envelope.

"I know, and Paul isn't keen on it either. This is one time I wish you weren't so blasted fluent with languages."

Kon laughed. "I enjoy learning languages and it gives me something to offer the team." After the morning's episode with the face mask, Kon was glad he had language skills and banking expertise to offer, for he doubted that he could ever make a living as a fire fighter.

"Perhaps I can help you sort through the material," Geilla offered. "You'll be looking for shipments coming from France and going to South America, isn't that true?"

"Yes, but we must also check the dates. Brad suspects the export date to be within the next three days."

"Well I can read the French part for you and find some candidates."

"If you wish, but it's terribly boring and tedious."

"Then the sooner we get started the sooner we can get on to Majorica."

Kon smiled gently and put his hand over Geilla's as she reached for a stack of photos. "I know I have neglected you, but I am glad you came with me. This will be the first assignment we have worked together, really together."

Geilla returned his smile. Yes, she thought, I can really help you now that you've stopped fighting me. But you won't like it if I distract you . . . or would you? Perhaps . . . concentrate Geilla! This is important business. Don't get yourself thrown off the team. She went back to shuffling photos without another word.

"Shall I order more coffee?" she asked after several hours.

"Hm?" Kon responded vaguely, still peering through his magnifying glass.

"Would you like more coffee?"

"More what?"

"Coffee! Coffee! The pot is empty."

"What's empty?" he said looking up quizzically.

"Your head, my love," she laughed. "Do you want more coffee? Or some food? Don't you even stop to eat?"

"I'm sorry, did you want to eat? Forgive me. Please, order something if you wish. What time is it?"

"It's after three."

"Already? Then send down for something. I'm getting near the end here."

Kon went back to pouring over the pictures and Geilla dug out the menu for room service and ordered lunch.

"Tell me, what have you discovered?" she asked as they sat down to eat.

"Well, it's quite possible that I missed something important in the files this morning, but sorting through this material, I have three possible candidates. All of the shipments have arrived from France at approximately the right time and all have been placed in transit warehouses. The three shipments I have singled out are destined for Brazil."

"What are the shipments supposed to be?"

"One is listed as ore extraction equipment and two are listed as drilling tubes. The export licenses of two look genuine, but the other one looks suspicious."

"So what's the next step?"

"I've got to get into those warehouses and check the crates myself. I could use your help."

"When?"

"Tonight."

"So soon? I had hoped . . ."

"It has to be tonight. One of the shipments is scheduled to be loaded tomorrow."

"Oh . . . and I suppose we have to check out their security arrangements before you go in."

"Yes. Would you like to take a tour by motorbike? I thought we might pose as two lost tourists."

"And . . . let me guess . . . you will just have to take my picture in front of several warehouses."

Yes, my love . . . telephoto lens and all. You'll have to wear a scarf and glasses."

"Sounds lovely. Must we go right away?"

"No. I need to study these photos again to see if any of these documents have been forged. I wish I had another magnifying glass."

"Perhaps I can look over your shoulder," Geilla said setting down her coffee cup and moving around behind Kon's chair. She put her hands on his shoulders and massaged them quickly before she put her chin on his left shoulder. He continued to be absorbed by the photos in front of him.

"Don't let me distract you, Signor Kononellos," she purred softly. She put her arms around him and tugged at his belt.

"I won't," he answered, pulling his robe closed and retying his belt.

"I know this is very important to the Queen of England, Signor Kononellos, so I mustn't interfere," she said tugging at his belt again. He caught her tiny hand in his own broad one and raised it to his lips.

"Signora Kononellos, you are interfering with a very important international investigation," he said trying to sound stern, but not succeeding.

"Oh! Mi scusi, Signor Kononellos," she continued and began to kiss the back of his neck. "I wouldn't want to do that. It might upset the Queen, or the French. Of course, the Queen has been married a very long time, whereas I . . . but we mustn't upset the French."

"Hmmmm, no, we mustn't. The French take these matters very seriously—their missiles, I mean," he said tossing the photos aside and turning his face to Geilla's.

She began to tease his lips with hers and he responded, growing more passionate with each kiss. "Yes," she murmured "the French know a lot about these things. They have a reputation for getting all the right parts in all the right places . . . at just the right time."

"Signora Kononellos?" he said taking her in his arms.

"Yes . . ."

"I think we must investigate the French methods if we are to judge their merit."

"Yes, yes. We must do as they do if we are to understand how they operate. But what about the Queen?"

He laughed his deep throaty laugh and carried her to the bed. "I suppose she can come if she wants to, but she will have to wait her turn. My bride comes first."

"Kon! What a scandalous thing to say!"

"What? Don't you want to be first?" he said slipping off his robe.

Two shots rang out before Kon managed to scramble over the wire fence and drop to the ground. As he darted across the broad street heading for the shadows, a siren wailed, and he cursed himself for having been discovered. The street was deserted and quiet, except for the buzz of an engine somewhere behind him. He slowed his pace and suddenly a motorbike skidded to a stop beside him. He leaped onto the seat behind Geilla, being careful not to hit her with the tools he still held in his hands. The bike shot up the wide street and swung left two blocks later.

"Hang on!" Geilla called. She bounced the bike over some railroad tracks and sped along between the rails, tucking behind two box cars that were halted for the night. She cut the engine and killed the lights. Kon leaned close against her as they heard a car pass at high speed.

"Are you all right? I heard shots!" Geilla whispered anxiously after the car was gone.

"I'm fine. It went well over my head."

"Are you sure? There was more than one shot."

"Yes, I'm sure. Don't start fussing over me! I can take care of myself."

"That's debatable," she answered lightly and turned toward him. Pulling his coat open, she caressed his chest and slid her hand down his ribs to where he had recently been wounded.

She remembered the first time she had arrived in the nick of time to save Kon from trouble. After much prodding she had managed to persuade Paul to back her bid for a position on the team. Her maneuvering had almost backfired, when Kon threatened to quit, but Brad had played on Kon's closeness to Paul to keep Kon on the team. A short time later when Kon had found himself fleeing from unexpected danger, she had suddenly appeared with a car. Geilla would never forget the look on Kon's face when he yanked open the door and saw that it was her, not Paul sitting behind the wheel. He had jumped back as if he did not trust her any more than the men who were chasing him. "Don't be stupid! Get in or get killed!" she had shouted at him as she heard gunfire close by. He had obeyed, but she knew then how much he resented her presence on the team. From that time onward she hid her true feelings from him so that she could work near him. Over the years, Kon had learned to let her help him when he was sick, or when Paul wasn't there to look out for him; but forgiveness had been slow in coming. Only the shock of learning that she had decided to leave the team had cracked the wall he had built around himself.

"One bad break does not mean I'm incapable or careless," Kon said, breaking into her mood. "Now let's get on to the next warehouse."

"You mean that wasn't the right one?" she said reluctantly straightening up.

"No," he said kissing her lightly on the cheek. "As far as I could tell, everything there was what the shipper claimed it was. The night watchman must have heard me and called the police."

"Oh well. One more try," Geilla answered reluctantly and started the engine. She drove the bike at high speed until she suddenly pulled up behind an older, nondescript van parked by the curb between the widely spaced street lights. Kon leaped off the bike and pulled open the rear doors of the van. He threw his tools inside and hauled out a small wooden ramp. Taking the bike from Geilla, he held the controls and walked the bike up the ramp. Lifting the ramp into the van again, he closed the doors and joined Geilla, who was already in the driver's seat.

Geilla drove to the spot they had chosen near the next warehouse and parked the van. Kon lowered the motorbike to the street and held it for Geilla.

"I'll go the rest of the way on foot. I don't want anyone to hear the bike until I'm ready," he said carefully packing his tools into his backpack.

"O.K., but do be careful."

"I will. I will. Just stay quiet and wait for my signal."

"Don't worry. I'll be there."

"Good," he said and gave her a quick hard kiss, before he took off at a slow run.

Kon knew that security at the second warehouse was tighter and he approached silently on foot. He chose a dark corner well away from the guardhouse at the main entrance and began to scale the fence. The large diameter of the metal post offered good footing as he slipped around the ends of the three strands of barbed wire at the corner. He was glad Geilla had come by earlier in the day to put out the street light on the nearby post. She was small enough to pass for an unruly street urchin, and thanks to her brother Alonzo's bad influence, she was a crack shot with a slingshot.

Kon was not the sure-footed cat that Paul was, nor a mechanical genius like Jack, but he had learned a lot from both of them over the years. His tools were securely wrapped and remained quiet as he slid to the ground. He carefully removed his lock picks from his pocket and tapped the transmitter strapped to his wrist. He waited, straining his ears, and smiled when he heard the sound. It started like a pounding bass and quickly grew into an obnoxious throbbing roar. Kon heard glass breaking and knew that Geilla has scored a direct hit on the guardhouse window with her slingshot. He ventured a quick look and saw the watchman run out of the guardhouse. Kon could not hear anything above the sound of rock music blaring from the oversized speakers lashed to Geilla's bike, but he imagined that Geilla would be turning figure eights in front of the gate and screaming enough obscenities to keep the watchman distracted. He never noticed his electronic switchboard light up as Kon picked the lock on the door of the employee entrance and slipped inside. Kon made a quick search around the door, felt the wire on the alarm and deactivated the circuit.

The warehouse was cavernous and poorly lit, but Kon moved around quickly, trying to discover the order of the storage system. The number of wooden crates was staggering, but most of them were not the right dimensions. The boxes he was looking for needed to be fifteen feet long and just over three and a half feet wide. They would be marked with the name of some French company.

Kon wondered how Geilla was doing with the watchman. If this place was on the up and up, and the watchman called the police, she would have to make a fast retreat. She would lead them on a merry chase, however, for she could perform some incredible stunts on a bike. Many women would have shied away from the instrument that had caused their only brother's death, but not Geilla. Playing the daredevil on her bike had been the only outlet she had been permitted for her youthful energy while she was married to Servio, a man three times her age. Perhaps Servio understood her need for excitement and indulged her in order to keep her. He had loved her, she had never doubted that.

Kon hurried down the aisles until he found a collection of boxes that looked suspicious. There were six of them, each on its own pallet ready for loading. Kon removed his crowbar from his pack. Using a block of wood as a lever, he began to slowly pry up the nails on the corners of the wooden lid of the first box. He inched the nails free gingerly so as not to make a tell-tale squeak. It took him only a few minutes to free two of the corners, but the lid was too heavy to bend upward. He moved around to the other side of the box, inched the nails out and slid the lid aside. There it was, the Exocet, death and destruction à la Française. Kon pushed aside the packing material to reveal the fins, but as he anticipated, the warhead itself was missing. It had been boxed separately for safety in transit. Kon removed a pair of wire cutters from his pack and quickly cut the shanks off the packing nails, leaving only a half inch stub attached to each head. He was careful to collect the tips of the nails and drop them into his pocket. Just before he lowered the wooden lid onto the box again, he drew a bead of wood glue along the top edge of the box and then slipped the abbreviated nails back into their holes. It would not do to have the lid fall off while the box was being loaded. Kon opened several more boxes and then signaled Geilla that he was leaving the warehouse. He slid out the door, locking it behind him and slipped over the fence without being spotted.

Geilla felt Kon's signal as a distinct pulse on the back of her specially-tuned watch. She stopped screaming at the watchman, made

15

one last pass in front of him, and drove away. She picked up Kon two blocks away and enjoyed the sound of his throaty laughter as she told of her encounter with the watchman. She was not surprised when Kon told her that the missiles had been located. She had suspected as much when the watchman had made no attempt to call the police in spite of her outrageous behavior.

"Alright! Let's get some sleep. There's nothing we can do until morning," Kon concluded as they reached the van.

Kon and Geilla were in the van early the next morning. They parked across the street from the warehouse and watched the container truck from the shipping company arrive. The driver backed the huge metal box against one of the loading docks, then unhitched the cab and drove away. There would be nothing further for Geilla and Kon to do until the container was loaded. They passed the time by chatting with Jack who had arrived from France earlier that morning.

"Somebody had to give you two lovebirds a hand," Jack declared in answer to Geilla's question of why he had suddenly shown up. Jack took Geilla's cool reception to mean that she was still a little miffed that her wedding trip had been delayed.

"Paul had to watch Kon's precious Ferrari," Jack continued with a laugh. "The last I saw him he was headed for a drive in the mountains with Nea. I couldn't get a straight answer out of him about when he'll be back. That's not like Paul. He usually likes to schedule everything in advance and have three alternate plans. Maybe she'll help him unwind a bit. He doesn't show it, but he takes this responsibility stuff too seriously. He needs to have more fun."

Since Paul's maternal uncle had died three years ago, Paul was the oldest male in the Artier family, and he bore a moral and financial responsibility for his mother and seven younger brothers. Not that he wasn't used to it, for he had assumed the duties at seventeen when his father had been killed; but his uncle had always been there to counsel him in the old wisdom. Paul had stopped fighting his Thai ancestry after his American father was gone and drew closer to his uncle who advised him in his struggle to keep his family together.

For his part, Kon was glad to have Jack on the job with them. He had never worried about Geilla before, when he had kept her at a distance, but now that she was his wife, he suddenly experienced a resurgence of the protective feeling he had felt for her when he first fell in love with her. He could not let her know how he felt, however, for she was far too independent to appreciate being smothered with concern. With Jack around there would be less chance of Geilla coming to harm.

Jack was easygoing, dependable and extremely rugged. Indeed if he had let his blond hair and beard grow, he could have played the role of a Viking in some epic film. Women might have swooned for him by the thousands, but Jack would have been too shy and too practical to be affected by the adulation. He had been badly burned by a brief marriage and he was still bitter.

Nea's sparkling green eyes and flaming auburn mane might set Paul on his ear, but to Jack, a woman that good looking was not to be trusted. He'd rather fly his airplane than spend more than a few more or less biological hours with any one woman. It was a shame he felt that way, for even without a beard, Jack attracted women everywhere he went. It could have been more than just physical with some of them for there was not an ounce of meanness in him.

Jack had been surprised when Geilla married Kon, for like Kon he had always thought she was in love with Paul. At least that's what he thought until Kon had been hurt on the last job, and Geilla had refused to leave Kon's side for the five days Kon was in the hospital.

Shortly after 10 a.m., the truck driver returned in the cab to pick up the shipment. Kon waited with Geilla while the driver hitched up his load, checked his papers, and cleared the security gate with a wave to the guard. Then he slipped into the rear of the van with Jack.

Geilla started the engine and began to follow the container truck down the wide street of the sparsely built industrial area. She trailed far behind for several blocks, but as the truck approached the fourth intersection, she speeded up and passed it. She slowed her speed again to ensure that the light at the next intersection was red when she arrived. She watched in the mirror as the cargo truck lumbered up behind her and rolled to a stop with the metallic sigh of air brakes. Slipping the van into reverse, Geilla rolled it back toward the truck.

When the light turned green, she switched into third gear and let the van lurch forward and stall. She started the engine again and purposely stalled it.

Then she opened the door and stepped down, being sure that her short skirt slid well up on her shapely thigh as she descended to the ground. As she began walking slowly toward the truck, the driver leaned out the cab window and shouted impatiently to her in Dutch. She didn't understand a word he said and looked at him in confusion.

"I think I ran out of gas," she said in Italian. It was his turn to be confused, and he started to shout even louder. Ignoring him, Geilla turned, walked back to the van, and snapped open the door over the gas cap. She waved her hands excitedly and he finally understood her gestures. In exasperation he climbed down from the truck and walked toward the van.

"Look!" he shouted above the clatter of the engine he had left running. "I've got a job to do! You'll have to move that thing out of the way!"

Geilla shrugged helplessly, then began to pantomime pouring gasoline into the tank.

"Do you have any gas with you?" the driver asked, but evidently she did not understand. He began to pantomime pouring gas and pointing to Geilla, jabbering away all the while in Dutch.

Geilla finally shook her head "yes" and smiled broadly. She indicated with her hands that she had a big can in the back of the van. After more confusion the driver understood that the can was too heavy for her to lift.

"Alright! Alright! I'll get it," he said more calmly, falling under the spell of Geilla's smile. He walked toward the rear of the van and Geilla followed after him talking rapidly in Italian. She put her hands together and then raised them to heaven repeating that he was the answer to her prayers. He didn't catch a word she uttered, but he recognized her gesture of heartfelt gratitude. He suddenly felt pleased with himself. After all, a man was never too busy to help a women in distress, and such a beautiful woman as this did not cross his path every day.

Chattering gaily, Geilla pulled open the right rear door of the van and pointed into the dark windowless interior. The driver stuck his

18

head inside and then staggered backwards as Jack's powerful fist slammed against his chin. Kon winced as he heard the sound of impact and quickly pulled the truck driver into the van. He knew from personal experience how unpleasant it was to be on the receiving end of Jack's fist. Jack helped Kon arrange the driver comfortably on a sleeping bag spread on the floor of the van next to the motorbike. He produced a small hypodermic and eased the needle into the driver's arm. "That will keep him quiet for a while."

Kon nodded and stepped out of the van. He was wearing a dark blue cotton shirt with the shipping company logo stitched above the pocket. He put the driver's cap on his head and closed the door. "You go first, Geilla. I'll make a little detour and be there in a few minutes."

"O.K.," Geilla nodded. "Be careful, Kon."

"Yes, my love—now go!" he answered and hurriedly climbed into the cab of the truck.

Geilla slipped behind the wheel of the old van and had the engine purring a minute later. She finessed the clutch as the light turned green and sped away down the broad street. Kon chopped through the gears on the truck and lumbered after her. Two blocks later he turned left and cursed himself as one of the rear wheels hit the curb. Ten minutes later he began to back the 18 wheeler towards the loading dock of the warehouse the French had designated as a safe resting place for the missiles. He saw Jack leaning against the rear door of the van and was relieved when a workman appeared to wave him into position and spare him the possible embarrassment of hitting the dock. He was an excellent driver, but he had to admit that his Ferrari was considerably more nimble than the container truck.

A representative of the Société Nationale Industrielle Aérospatiale was waiting to supervise the unloading of the missiles and the warheads and make a careful inventory of the boxes. When he was satisfied that the critical items were accounted for, Jack took charge of their security. At Brad's direction the French representative had brought with him six appropriately labeled boxes of scrap metal equal to the weight of the missiles. Now he supervised loading them with great care so as not to alert the warehouse staff that anything other than a mix-up in materials had occurred. While the missiles were

19

being re-loaded into a smaller unmarked truck, Kon went to check on the truck driver. Seeing that he was still out cold, Kon went to make a telephone call.

"See you later, Jack. Be careful with those things," Kon said as the two men shook hands.

"Have a good trip, Kon. Are you sure you don't want me to stick around a while longer?"

"No. We'll be fine, and you've got a long drive ahead of you."

"O.K.! O.K.! I know when I'm not needed. Take care of this guy, Geilla," Jack added as Geilla came up.

"I intend to, and I intend to keep him all to myself for a while," Geilla answered. "Have a nice drive, Jack."

"Yeah sure! Like hell! You two fly off to Majorica, Paul gets to take a red-head for a drive in a Ferrari, and I get stuck with a pickle-faced Frenchman and a truck full of missiles."

Geilla laughed. "Well you'd better complain to Brad before I get back, because there won't be much left of him when I get through."

Jack grinned and bent to give Geilla a quick, brotherly kiss. "See you two later."

Geilla and Kon watched Jack drive away, then she went back to the van, while Kon climbed into the cab of the container truck. They drove directly to the intersection where they had taken the truck. Geilla arrived first, and Kon positioned the truck close behind her. Turning the engine off, Kon climbed out of the truck and hurried into the back of the van. Kneeling in the confined quarters, he struggled out of his cotton shirt, slipped off his shoes, and put on the jacket, boots and helmet of a police officer. He opened both doors of the van, lowered the ramp, and backed the motorbike into the street. He pushed it over to the curb, put the kickstand down, and hoped no one would notice that it was not a regulation police vehicle.

Hurrying back to the van, he climbed in beside Geilla, who was bending over the truck driver. Kon began to shake the driver gently and call to him in Dutch. "Sir! Sir, wake up! Are you all right?" He kept at it until finally the driver moaned softly and opened his eyes. He looked startled to see a policeman leaning over him. "Are you O.K., sir?" Kon asked again. "We were starting to get worried. You've been out for a long time. Have you been drinking, sir?"

20

"Drinking? No. What happened?" the driver asked sitting up and looking around.

Geilla handed Kon a cup of water and he offered it to the driver who sipped it hesitantly.

"This lady says you were trying to help her put gas in her van, but you hit your head on her loading ramp."

"Ramp! That was no ramp! I swear it was a fist. Somebody punched me!"

"Punched you? But who?" Kon answered in Dutch. Without waiting for an answer Kon switched to Italian and held an animated conversation with Geilla.

"She says you must still be dizzy. Who would punch you? She is by herself. She was standing right beside you when you opened the door. Are you sure you haven't been drinking?"

"Yes! I'm sure! What time is it anyway? I've got to get my load delivered or I'll be in trouble with the boss."

"Don't worry about that," Kon reassured him. "I called your company when I first got here."

The driver looked upset. "Why the hell did you do that? They'll be thinking I lost a truck or something! Now I'm in for it for sure! The boss is always on my neck for something."

"Don't get so upset, sir. I explained things to them. I told them I'd bring the truck in myself if you were still out. It didn't look like you were going to be able to drive for a while and I still don't think you're quite right."

The driver looked at Kon and relaxed a bit. "You told them it wasn't my fault that I'm late?"

"Yes. I told them you were being a good citizen trying to assist a lady in an emergency when you got knocked out. I also told them you were a hero in the lady's eyes."

"You told them all that?" the driver responded, his eyes growing wide in astonishment.

"Yes and they seemed quite proud of you."

"They did? Well, I'll be damned! Maybe they'll get off my back for a change."

"Well, you just call me if they give you any trouble," Kon said with a friendly smile. "Are you sure you feel up to driving?"

"Yes, I'll be O.K.," the driver answered, rubbing his jaw. "But I still could swear that somebody punched me."

"Do you want to make a report? I could call for a car to take us down to the station so you could look at some pictures? It shouldn't take more than a few hours."

"Pictures? What for? I never saw a thing! Look, let's just forget about it. Hero or not, the boss'll be on my ass if I don't deliver this load."

"O.K.," Kon drawled. "If you're sure you feel well enough."

"Look, I'm fine. Just let me get back to work."

Kon stepped out of the van and the driver followed him. He started toward his truck, but stopped when Geilla rushed up to him holding his cap in her hands. She smiled and spoke to him in Italian, but he only shook his head. "What did she say?" he called to Kon in Dutch.

"She says you are an angel—a guardian angel!"

The driver grinned and his ears went slightly red. He said something to Geilla, but she didn't understand. He got into the truck, started the engine and backed away from the van. Geilla waved as he drove away.

"Did you catch what he said after he turned red?" Geilla asked.

"Yes," Kon muttered.

"Well, what was it?"

"Never mind."

"Kon! Don't be silly. What did he say?"

"If you must know, he said, 'If you could read my mind . . .'"

"The bastard! We should have let him lose his job. It would serve him right!"

"I'm sorry, Geilla. I hate it when you have to be the bait on these assignments. I should have smashed his face in!"

"No, that would have ruined the game. I'm glad you controlled yourself. It's all part of the job."

"Come, my beautiful bride," Kon said putting his arms around her and stealing a kiss. "Let's go on our wedding trip!"

"Be careful, Kon! What will people think if they see a policeman kissing a motorist?"

"They will think that he is the luckiest man in the world!"

Chapter Two

Kon moved his long legs forward carefully, trying to stretch them without hitting Jack who was seated directly across from him. For once he did not envy Jack his six-foot-four frame. Jack must feel cramped everywhere he goes, Kon thought idly. Jack looked content enough slouched against the window. He did not seem to feel the need to stretch, but an old wound on the back of Kon's left thigh made itself felt if he was forced to sit in one position for long. In order to be completely functional when he arrived in Paris, he would have to shift positions at least three times before the two-hour train trip was over.

It was late September and Kon had been married for almost four months. Geilla was not with him on this assignment because much to his delight she was expecting their first child. While she was not sure she wanted the "house-full-of-children" that Kon dreamed of, she desperately wanted a baby. She had been devastated when her only child from her first marriage had accidently drowned at age three while on an outing with his father. She knew that Servio had doted on the child, but she could not help blaming him for the loss of the one bright spot in their passionless marriage. She had been young and resilient and had recovered, but Servio was an old man, and the death of his son broke him. His health failed within a month of placing the tiny coffin in the ground, and it seemed to Geilla that she had barely returned from burying her son before she was walking behind her husband's coffin.

Geilla had not given Kon an argument about retiring from the team while she was pregnant. She did not want to risk any harm to this child that Kon had wanted for so long. She knew that despite his doubts about his capabilities, he would be a good father. She had seen how the children at the Children's Home in Geneva responded to him. For the past month she had been going to the Home with Charlotte, a long-time patron of the home. Twelve years ago Charlotte Marneé had hired Kon, never dreaming that in addition to acquiring a kitchen helper, she would take on the responsibility of raising him along with her two young sons. It had not been an easy task for Charlotte and her husband Edgar, but despite the trials and heartbreaks they had endured because of Kon, they loved him as a son.

Kon in turn loved and respected Charlotte and Edgar and attributed his success in life to their persistent efforts to discipline and educate him. He felt he never would measure up to their high standards, but he strove to please them. For their sake Kon learned to keep his passionate nature tightly restrained, as if he were a 14K gold, precision watch. Expressing raw emotion was unsuitable in the staid world of Swiss banking.

Kon shifted his position again and cast a glance at Etienne Rubard, the sulky young man of twenty-two, who sat on the seat beside him. The team was escorting young Rubard from his hiding place in Lyons to a secret villa outside Paris where he would be interrogated by agents from the Groupe d'Intervention de la Gendarmerie Nationale (GIGN), the French national counterterrorism organization.

Brad had been contacted by Etienne's father, an extremely wealthy man who wanted to ensure that Etienne would be granted immunity in return for providing evidence to the government. Realizing that Etienne was to be exiled for his own protection, his father had asked that he be brought back to Paris so that he could see him one last time.

Although Etienne had terrorized scores of people with threats of violence, he had never actually killed anyone. Until that last time he had carried off the robberies without seeing anyone get hurt. Even the bombs he had planted had all been in empty buildings. During his last escape from a bank, however, an eight-year-old girl had been killed by a ricocheting bullet. He had stood paralyzed with horror, watching a hole in the girl's face spurt blood onto her frilly pink dress. As the girl's lifeless body slowly sank to the pavement, he felt compelled to catch her in his arms. He stepped forward, but a comrade slapped his face, dragged him backwards, and shoved him into a car. As the car sped away amidst a hail of bullets, he lay on the floor, shaking helplessly and vomiting. By the time his stomach contents had fouled the floor, he discovered that the "high" of risking death for a cause he only vaguely understood had been disgorged also. He returned with the group, but from that moment he felt apart from them. He did not join in when they divided the money and felt no satisfaction when they gave him a cut for his living expenses. What had once seemed easy money now seemed tainted with the blood of an innocent child.

His superiors noted his response and held a conference after he left. They let him sulk for a day, but when he did not report for his next assignment, they sent another "soldier" to see him. He learned that he was to be sent to Germany for special training, which he understood to mean corrective indoctrination. He agreed to go, readily admitting that he needed his ideology reinforced, but he felt he had to flee. He knew too much about the working of Direct Action to be allowed to quit. They would drag him before a revolutionary court, go through a mock trial and then, as always, he would be executed. He had never actually seen an execution, but he had once helped bury a body. He knew he had to run, before the indoctrination gutted his last shred of human compassion.

Now as he sat on the seat next to Kon, watching the French countryside flash by, he felt very old and used up. What had happened? It had all been fun in the beginning. He was no intellectual and any excuse to disrupt class at the university was welcome. He could barely remember how easily he had been led into the group by a girl he was attracted to. Catia was not particularly beautiful, not even pretty really, but she radiated raw vitality. She was older and obviously more street-wise than he and he was flattered by her attention. He was quickly seduced and as quickly replaced by a more seasoned lover.

Stung by rejection, but still fascinated by Catia, Etienne falsely believed he could win her back by adopting her standards and becoming, if not the best of the best, then the worst of the bad. While Catia did not notice the change in him, some of the other girls did, and they more than compensated for the loss of Catia. To test his loyalty as a full-fledged member of Direct Action, and to prove his total disrespect for law and order, he had been required to kill a policeman. His braggadocio had carried him through, however, and no one suspected that he had intentionally fired a wild shot, allowing his target to dive for cover and escape unharmed. In four years,

25

young Etienne Rubard had gone from chanting slogans during student demonstrations to participating in bank robberies. Although the idea of stealing money for personal gain offended his moral sense, taking money from the rich in the name of the oppressed and the disenfranchised seemed a noble cause.

His sense of power and self-importance grew with each job, fed by the fear he inspired in the people he robbed. He mistook their fear for respect and let the approval of his superiors in the group muffle the cries of his conscience. Enmeshed in an exciting world of casual sex and easy money, he felt he had at last escaped the rigid life of work and responsibility his father had laid out for him.

Young Etienne was not close to his father, a quiet, shy man in his eighties. Adrien Rubard had married very late in life and was in his sixties when Etienne was born. He had been surprised and happy to have fathered a child. But when his young wife presented him with a daughter, two years later, he began to doubt his responsibility for either event. When his wife ran off with her lover five months later, Adrien felt his suspicions were confirmed. However, Adrien Rubard was not a man to shirk his duty or expose himself to scandal. He hired a series of nannies and pretended that the children were his own. He ruled the children with rigid discipline, attempting to compensate for the lack of moral fiber he believed they had inherited from their mother. Young Etienne grew up believing that somehow even his baptism had not removed the mark of sin from him. Feeling that he was damned by an accident of nature, Etienne saw little need to try to improve himself.

Etienne was a docile prisoner. He had come away quietly when Brad, Jack, and Kon found him at the pensione in Lyon. Brad saw no need to put handcuffs on him. Indeed, since Rubard had run out of money, Brad had settled his overdue bill with the landlady and chatted amicably with her, letting slip that he had hired Etienne to help him on a research project. If she thought it strange that three men had shown up to escort the young man she knew as Maurice to a new job, she kept her thoughts to herself and was glad to get her money.

Paul had stayed in Paris to coordinate with agents from GIGN and would be waiting with a car when they got off the train. Brad had chosen to bring Rubard back by train in order to avoid security problems at the airport. In addition to leaving the Direct Action group, young Rubard had made off with a sizeable cache of automatic weapons. He indicated that he believed some of them had been used in the August attack on a Jewish restaurant which had left six people dead and thirty injured. Rubard did not have the weapons with him in Lyon, however, and he refused to disclose where he had stashed them until he had talked to his father. Once this formerly naive young man woke up to the reality of what it meant to be involved in the Direct Action group, he had determined to trade some important information for his own freedom. For all his ideological uncertainty, Rubard had managed to make contact with a great many members of the terrorist world. The group had regarded him as a genius for his uncanny ability to raise money for the cause.

When the train reached the Gare de Lyon in Paris, the team got out and surrounded Etienne. He was understandably nervous and tried to hurry through the crowd. Fearing that Etienne would get separated in the crush of passengers, Brad put his hand on the young man's arm and slowed his pace. As the group came out onto Boulevard Diderot, Jack was on Rubard's left, Kon was on his right, and Brad was directly behind him. The crowd had thinned, and with eyes darting in all directions, they began the walk to the curb where Paul was waiting with the car. As they approached, Paul got out and opened the rear door on the passenger's side. The group was nearing the car when suddenly from out of nowhere two vehicles appeared.

One vehicle pulled to the curb in front of the team's car and the other swung in behind it. The cars had barely skidded to a halt before three masked terrorists burst from each vehicle. It was a mass assault, but they carried no automatic weapons and obviously wanted to take Rubard alive. Etienne saw the guns and knew some of the gang despite their masked faces. He recognized Catia instantly by her clothes and her walk. Still believing she cared for him, he called out and stepped forward. Catia hesitated for only a moment before she raised her gun and fired. At the sound of gunfire several women screamed and the crowd of pedestrians ran for cover. In amazement Etienne clutched his arm and saw the blood trickle between his fingers. He stood mindlessly watching the terrorists run towards him until Kon jumped forward and threw him to the ground.

Even as Catia opened fire, Brad drew his gun. Dropping to the ground, he returned her fire, and felled her immediately. Jack rolled to the ground and began firing at the three men who came at him from the car on his left. He hit one of the band whose gun had jammed, and quickly brought down another man. Paul reached for his Walther and began firing at the men who were shooting at Kon.

Kon lay on the ground, shielding Rubard, and firing at the men on his right. He was too occupied to see the three men with automatics who ran out of the station. Paul spotted them and shouted, "Brad! Behind you!" But before Brad could turn and fire, he was hit in the back. Kon heard Brad shout a warning, but he couldn't take his eyes off the men in front of him. He hit one of the men, but before he realized what had happened, he felt a gun barrel pressing against his neck. It flashed through his mind that these men wanted Rubard alive and wouldn't shoot him in the back for fear of hitting Rubard. Kon froze, still holding his gun.

No one spoke, but someone kicked his wrist and the gun dropped from his hand. Suddenly he was grasped by the collar and yanked to his feet. Etienne turned toward the terrorists and a look of sheer panic spread across his face. While two men held Kon, the third lunged toward Etienne. Before he could grab him, a gunshot rang out and the man fell forward spouting blood. Etienne sprang up and began shrieking hysterically, as if released from a trance.

"Run for it, Etienne," Kon shouted and started struggling with the men who were holding him. Once Rubard was in the open Kon knew his protection was gone. He had nothing to lose and Rubard might get away. He flung himself against one of the terrorists and hung on. At close range the man could not get the long barrel of his weapon into position to fire. The other man dare not shoot for fear of hitting his companion. Kon heard more shots and the wail of a siren as he fought with the terrorists. He did not see Rubard go down, but he heard the man behind him growl. "Let him go! We'll finish him later! Get to the car!"

Suddenly Kon felt an arm around his throat, and his arms were pinned behind him. He got only a brief glance at the carnage as he was dragged backwards. The shooting had stopped and the walk was littered with bodies. The windshield of the car behind Paul's was shattered and the driver was slumped over the wheel. Jack was kneeling over Brad who lay silent and bleeding. Paul had managed to pull Rubard to the shelter of the car, but he was still screaming. Paul had his gun up, but he was just holding it. Kon struggled to twist his head away from the men behind him. "Shoot the bastards, Paul! What are you waiting for? Shoot!" Kon screamed in frustration.

But there was no way Paul could fire at the terrorists without the risk of hitting Kon. When the police arrived in force a moment later, Paul shouted a warning, "Don't shoot! They've taken a hostage!" Paul stood stock still, helplessly watching Kon being hauled away and listening to Rubard scream. The terrorists forced Kon into their car and as they pulled away, one of them hurled a grenade out the window.

"Take cover!" Paul shouted and dove behind the open door of the car. The terrorists were out of sight by the time Paul realized that the light-green, smooth-skinned device was not going to explode. In their haste, the terrorists had forgotten to pull the pin. Paul was thankful for their stupidity for he knew they had no mercy.

Kon kept screaming for Paul to shoot, until he found himself staring at the open door of a car. He tried to pull back, but he was held too tightly. Suddenly he knew the terrorists wanted him alive. He was forced into the car and thrown to the floor. As the car jerked away from the curb, something struck him on the back of his head. It hurt, but he did not lose consciousness.

The terrorists did not treat Kon as kindly as the team had treated Rubard. They lost no time in snapping handcuffs on his wrists and pulling a hood over his head. The handcuffs were uncomfortable, but Kon was glad for the hood. It meant there was something he wasn't supposed to see, something they didn't want him to tell later. Hopefully it meant they planned to free him sometime. He lay on the floor wondering if Brad was still alive. Brad had planned this trip so carefully. How did the terrorists know that they were at the station? Was Rubard really as naive as he seemed or was he playing some sort of game?

Kon knew there was someone in the back seat with him, because every time he tried to shift his position or sit up, he got kicked. In spite of the kicks, he kept moving his hands against the cuffs until he was able to activate the transmitter on his watch. He knew it had a very short range, but it was worth a try. He could not be sure of the time, but it seemed like only fifteen minutes had passed before the car stopped.

Kon lay still when he heard the car door open. A moment later he was yanked from the car and heard it pull away. He knew it was not yet noon, but he could see no daylight through the hood. Although there were two men with him and he was hooded and handcuffed, someone forced the muzzle of a gun into his ribs as they shoved him forwards. He heard no other cars pass as he was forced along, and imagined that he was in an alley. The men kept pushing his head down and he guessed they were concerned that someone would see the hood.

After a short walk along the street he heard a door click open. He was shoved forwards, nearly tripping over a low step, and knew immediately from the stale smell that he was inside an old building. Even with the tight-fitting hood over his head, he was aware that someone in the building kept too many cats, and not very well. He was spun around several times before they began to haul him up a narrow wooden staircase.

He slipped on the worn stairs, fell against the wall several times, and wondered that no one questioned the noise. Round and round they went, up three flights of stairs. He kept kicking the riser, or putting his feet too close to the edge of the stairs and pretending to slip. Every time he fell his shins took a beating, but he hoped someone would hear. The man behind him keep shoving him and swore every time he fell, but no one came to help him. He felt an intense desire to turn and kick the man behind him down the stairs, but under the circumstances he considered it wiser to put up with the abuse.

At long last he heard a door open to his right and he was urged forward by the gun in his ribs. He was forced onto a straight-backed chair and without removing the handcuffs, they lashed his wrists to the back of the chair. He felt hands digging into his pockets and knew they were after his wallet. There were enough papers in there to identify him as Emile Breaux, but nothing that listed his occupation. They must have found what they wanted, he thought when the opaque hood was pulled from his head. A hand grabbed his chin as the hood came off, and he found himself blinking at a ski mask animated by a pair of eyes the color of stale coffee, but with even less appeal.

"Now, Monsieur Emile Breaux, I want to know where you were taking Etienne Rubard," a voice that matched the eyes snarled.

So that's it, Kon thought. They want to regroup and try again. Even though Kon was angry that Rubard had obviously been stupid enough to lead them all into a trap, he was not about to tell this viper where Paul and Jack were. Even the men from GIGN hadn't been told where Rubard would be taken.

Kon stared back at the terrorist. He was no student agitator. He was in his late thirties, a true seasoned insurrectionist. Kon could well believe that he could have slain a room full of men and women who were quietly enjoying their dinner. Kon felt only contempt for him, but he said nothing. He continued to say nothing even after the man behind him pressed the gun into his back.

"You will talk, Monsieur Breaux. You will talk," coffee-eyes said, more as a threat than a statement. "Turn on the radio, Nicolas," he commanded.

As the loud pulsing rock music filled the room, Kon continued to stare at those cold eyes. Taking Kon's silent stare as the insult it was meant to be, the leader turned away from Kon. Then suddenly whirling around he struck Kon in the face with his fist backed by his swinging body. The blow hit Kon so hard it knocked him and the chair to the floor. Kon couldn't suppress a groan as his shoulder hit the floor, wrenching his arms and jerking his wrists. The blow only served to make him angry, however, and he was more determined than ever not to say anything.

Kon was pulled upright again. "Where is Etienne Rubard? Where are the weapons?" the terrorist leader shouted into his face. Again he slapped Kon, upsetting the chair.

Kon knew it was a stupid move. He knew it would do no good, but his temper got the best of him. Just as the two men righted the chair, Kon lashed out with his foot and caught the leader in the groin.

Hearing him howl brought Kon a moment of sweet satisfaction before retribution sent him crashing to the floor again. And so on and on it went, first the shouting and then the blows. The leader's knuckles were raw before he would admit to himself that he had captured a man he could not intimidate.

Kon hardly felt the individual blows any more. He concentrated on disassociating his mind from his body. It was a trick he had developed as a child in order to remain silent while his step-father beat him. He knew his step-father would stop sooner if he could keep from crying out. Over the years Kon had had a lot of practice at suppressing his screams. It was only when he slept that they would escape to shame him. Kon tried to focus on Geilla and her love. It saddened him to think how upset she would be when she learned that he had been kidnapped. Perhaps it would not be in the papers. Perhaps Paul could find a way to hide it from her. Kon speculated on his chances of returning alive and regretted that he had been so eager to father a child. Maybe Brad is right, he thought. A man in this business had no right to create children who had a greater than average chance of being left fatherless. He worried about Geilla being left alone to raise his child, and he made up his mind that he was going to be very hard to kill.

"Take over, Nicolas," the leader said, nudging the other man who had brought Kon up the stairs. The leader sucked his swollen knuckles nervously, then lit a cigarette. He sat on the end of the unmade bed inhaling deep, greedy drags on the cigarette and watched Nicolas. Nicolas stood in front of Kon, contemplating where to strike. Kon's lip was split, his nose was running blood and his right eye was already swollen shut.

"Get on with it!" the leader shouted impatiently. Nicolas opted for something softer than Kon's jaw and hit him in the stomach. It was a well-placed blow and it penetrated Kon's mental defenses. He didn't cry out, but the jolt he felt as his spine hit the back of the chair was more than his nervous system could handle. His body sagged forwards and he blacked out.

The leader was furious. "That was smart! That was really smart! You imbecile!" he shouted at Nicolas. "Now we are really wasting time here."

"I couldn't help it. He was already used up before I hit him. My job is weapons. Let me shoot him."

"Shut up!" the leader snapped. "Don't you realize what we have here? This guy's from GIGN. If we kill him, Paris will be crawling with agents. But if we trade him . . . he could be worth a lot, Nicolas. Yes, we've got ourselves a real prize here. Perhaps he will be more valuable than Rubard in the end."

"Well he's not much good while he's out cold. What do you want me to do with him, Michon?"

Michon dropped his cigarette butt and pressed it into the floor with his heel. "Get him off that God damn chair! He's either extremely stubborn, or extremely stupid. We're going to have to use more subtle persuasion on him. We need to get Edouard over here with his little black bag. He might be able to get his hands on something that will make the guy talk. Listen, I'm going out for a while. Put Monsieur Breaux on the floor and keep an eye on him. Better cuff him to the foot of the bed. If he wakes up before I get back, hit him again."

After Michon left, Nicolas switched off the radio and went to unfasten Kon from the chair. He untied the ropes, dragged Kon over to the foot of the bed, then reached into his own pocket for the key to the handcuffs. As he unlocked them he noticed Kon's watch. It was obvious from the large, finely-crafted face that it was valuable. Nicolas had a commercial interest in watches, having stolen a great many of them in his life. He had also used a few to rig bombs and he valued precision workmanship above artistic considerations.

Nicolas unfastened the sturdy buckle on Kon's watch. He held it by the plain leather band and appraised its worth. The case was somewhat thicker than usual, but he judged that to be part of the masculine design. He noted the complicated array of switches, but did not suspect that it contained a tiny transmitter that was pulsing out a signal. Well, if this Breaux is a prize, I intend to have a piece of it, he thought to himself, and slipped the watch into his pocket. He secured Kon's right arm to the metal leg of the bed, and threw himself onto the bare mattress. It didn't look as though Monsieur Breaux was going to wake up for a long time so he might as well make himself comfortable.

It was late afternoon before Michon returned with the young man called Edouard Sabasté. Sabasté had been a medical student at the university before he was swept into the Direct Action group. Even now he maintained the charade of being a student, living in student apartments and registering for classes. He had not attended lectures for months, however, and used the money his father sent to buy drugs.

Edouard had been extremely bright in school and his future had been full of promise until drugs took over his life. It had started innocently enough at a party with other students. Getting "high" on the week-end in order to relax after the stress of classes and competitive exams was very pleasant. Soon young Edouard was seeking the experience at mid-week and then daily. He had to find new friends who could supply him and he gradually drifted away from the more dedicated students.

As his habit grew more expensive, Edouard wrote his parents more and more often. He had no trouble getting money from them. They were delighted that he was studying to be a doctor. His father sent him cash and his mother never failed to send him a shirt or a sweater when she went on one of her frequent shopping excursions. Edouard lost track of how many sweaters he owned. Most convenient of all, his parents never asked for an accounting of his funds, or his grades, or his time, or his friends, or his difficulties. They never embarrassed him by coming to visit, and didn't seem to mind that he never came home on holidays. Edouard's parents were perfectly indulgent, perfectly self-absorbed, and unfortunately for Edouard, perfectly unaware of what was happening to their son.

As time passed, Edouard found it increasingly more difficult to concentrate on the hard work necessary to pass his exams. His grades began to slip, slowly at first and then suddenly he was failing. Edouard Sabasté, the formerly brilliant Edouard Sabasté, was failing his exams and no one seemed to notice or to care. His new friends did not share his goals, his parents never asked, and the university system was indifferent. When he was barred from studying under Dr. Raimond Moulan, an eminent authority on cellular biology, Edouard became disillusioned and blamed the system. How was he supposed to become a doctor if he was not allowed to study with the best?

At that point he had been recruited by members of the Direct Action group. They had been watching him for some time, carefully nurturing his bad habits and drawing him deeper and deeper into his addiction. It was they who suggested that Edouard take a job at the local hospital. He had liked it at first. He talked to the patients and read their charts; and in his mind the importance of his job became magnified.

He really did want to help people. He really did want to be a doctor. It was just so unfair that he wasn't permitted to study. So he mopped floors and grew more and more bitter that others got their degrees while he was held back. When Michon first suggested that Edouard steal drugs from the hospital he was aghast, but Michon pressured him. It was a way to get back at the system, he had told him. Besides, security was lax and no one would miss the stuff he took.

Edouard was not sure he fully approved of what Direct Action believed in, if indeed they believed in anything, but he did not question too deeply. His analytical powers had become cloudy of late and he didn't want to face the reality of the situation he was in. The first time Michon had taken him to an apartment and asked him to treat a young man who had been shot, he had wanted no part in it and threatened to call the police. He was shocked when Michon reminded him that he was a drug addict and a thief. Michon's true colors became apparent when he threatened to tell Edouard's parents and the police about Edouard's habits. Edouard had been frightened of seeing his world turned upside down. He was too weak and perhaps too naive to realize that he was still on the edge and could have pulled back in time to save himself.

Along with his threats, Michon added his full powers of persuasion which were considerable. He stroked Edouard's ego and convinced him that digging a bullet out of the young man was a noble act of medicine. It was more practice of his art than Edouard would have been allowed in legal channels. A few pleas from the suffering man finally tipped the scale and Edouard agreed. It became routine after that. Michon fed Edouard's ego and Edouard did the dirty work. Edouard began to study on his own again and he became proficient at treating wounds and burns. Once his skill had actually saved the life of a man who had blown his own hand off trying to rig a bomb. Edouard had stolen everything from saline to sutures to antibiotics to treat him. Michon had never commented about the incident, but Edouard viewed it as a triumph.

Nicolas heard Michon coming up the stairs and jumped from the bed to a chair, quickly assuming an air of vigilance. Extending his leg he teased Kon's drooping chin with the toe of his boot. Kon had been awake for some time, but he sat quietly observing his surroundings. His senses had told him even before they snatched the hood away that he was not in a tidy apartment, but the filth he saw around him was appalling. Piles of soiled clothing lined the walls like drifting sand, and stacks of dirty dishes choked the sink. A brownish liquid oozing from a paper bag on the floor by the stove gave off an odor of decaying garbage. It had been long forgotten by everyone but the swarm of ants that marched up and down the sides of the bag. Whoever lived here obviously did not feel the need to maintain a facade of normal bourgeoisie behavior. Kon wondered if Etienne had ever lived in a place like this. The room he had rented in Lyon had been kept clean. Was this to be the "new order"? Can these people really hope to make the world a better place when they can't even clean up after themselves? His sense of contempt for the terrorists deepened his resolve to tell them nothing.

Michon came into the room quietly and spared barely a grunt for Nicolas. "Is he awake yet?"

"He's awake. What took you so long?" Nicolas asked.

"We had to make a stop to get a surprise for our friend. Something to take his mind off his troubles. Cover your face, Edouard," he continued tossing Edouard a ski mask and pulling one over his own face.

Edouard eyed the dirty ski mask with distaste. "What's the big secret? Everyone knows who I am."

"Not everyone, Edouard!" Michon snapped. "Just cover your damn face!"

Edouard thought Michon's attitude was strange, but he didn't argue. It did no good to argue with Michon and he was sick of hearing political lectures. He pulled the mask over his head and looked around quickly. "You live like a pig, Nicolas! How can you stand it?"

"It's not my place. I just use it. Why should I clean it?"

"Because it stinks! It turns my stomach to be here!"

"Quite complaining, Edouard," Michon snapped. "Give him the stuff and get out!"

"Alright! Alright! What happened to him? Why is he on the floor? Here, help me get him on the . . . My God! He's handcuffed to the bed! Why is he . . ."

"Shut up, Edouard! Don't ask questions. Just give him the stuff!" Michon ordered coldly.

"You said he was hurt, Michon," Edouard began. "You didn't tell me . . . Who is this guy, Michon? He's not one of the group, is he? Shit! I don't want any part of this." Edouard stepped back from the bed, but Michon grabbed his arm and dug his fingers into Edouard's flesh.

"But you are a part of it, Edouard. You are part of everything we do. You're with us, Edouard, whether you want to be or not."
Edouard looked at him and his mouth fell open. "Now give him the stuff! We want him to answer some questions," Michon shouted.

"Will you let him go if he tells you what you want?" Edouard asked nervously.

Michon smirked. "Yeah, sure. We don't need him!"

Edouard stared into Michon's stale-coffee eyes. Michon is like a machine, he thought. I don't trust him, but he might let this guy go if he talks. What choice do I have?

"You'll have to hold him down," Edouard said at last and Michon let go of his arm.

Kon had heard their discussion and knew they were going to drug him. He readied himself to resist. When Nicolas tried to grab his legs Kon started kicking. He got one good hit on Nicolas's arm before Nicolas backed off. As Kon lashed out with his left hand, Michon suddenly kicked the bed sideways, jerking Kon's right wrist against the handcuffs and sending a shooting pain up his arm.

"Get him!" Michon shouted. Kon turned to strike at Nicolas again, but Michon kicked him in the back. Michon kept kicking first Kon and then the bed until Nicolas was able to get a hold on Kon's legs. Suddenly Michon leaped at him and pinned his left shoulder to the floor. Kon struggled, but it was hopeless.

Edouard had stood watching the struggle until Michon screamed at him, "Stick him, Sabasté! Damn it! Do your job!"

Edouard was shaking. He hadn't seen this kind of brutality before. The others had always pleaded for his help. He pulled his bag open and readied a syringe.

"Damn you, hurry up!" Michon roared as he struggled with Kon.

"Alright! Alright! Stop screaming!" Edouard snapped and knelt by Kon's left arm. Kon lurched, but Edouard grabbed his wrist and forced his knee into Kon's palm.

"Don't do it, Edouard!" Kon said suddenly breaking his silence.

It was a command not a plea, and Edouard jumped and dropped the syringe. He caught it quickly, but made the mistake of looking Kon in the face. It would be so much easier if I hadn't looked, he chided himself. He hesitated, but Michon started screaming at him again. "Damn you, Sabasté, stick him! Stick him or I'll blow your brains out!"

"I'm sorry," Edouard whispered. "I'm sorry. Don't fight me. It's really not painful. Just answer their questions and they won't hurt you anymore." He pushed up Kon's sleeve, and ripped open his shirt.

"Don't do it, Edouard. It's murder!" Kon shouted again.

"It's really not painful," Edouard repeated and jabbed the needle into Kon's arm. He pressed the plunger and stood up quickly.

Kon quit fighting. As soon as the needle struck he knew the game was up. Being drug-sensitive he felt its effect almost immediately. He thought of Geilla and hoped his poor fatherless child would understand that he gave his life resisting what these men stood for. He wished he could have seen his child, just once. He felt himself sinking and derived macabre pleasure from the thought that he had outwitted these men. The drug might kill him, but he sure as hell wouldn't be able to talk. He felt his pain melting and his split lip twisted into a smirk. "You dumb assholes..." he said with sublime contempt.

Michon grabbed Kon by the chin and turned his head upward. He slapped Kon across the face, but there was no response. When he realized that Kon was unconscious he was overcome with frustration. "Jesus Sabasté! Can't you control that stuff? Why did you give him so much?" he screamed. "If I wanted him dead I would have let

Nicolas shoot him! I would have shot him myself! Shit! Shit! Shit!"

Suddenly Michon turned from Kon and slapped Edouard across the mouth with the back of his hand.

"Hey! Cut it out!" Edouard protested. "I gave him a normal dose. He must be allergic to the stuff or something. How am I supposed to know?"

"How am I supposed to know?" Michon mocked. "You're the medicine man," he said and kicked Kon in the ribs. "You're all talk, Edouard! That's what you are—just talk!" He kicked Kon again more savagely. The sight of Kon's limp body infuriated him and he began to rant and kick Kon over and over again.

"This whole job has been screwed up! I should have killed Rubard on the street. I wanted to do it, but no, Rouillan wanted it done proper. A real execution, he said. Set the example."

Edouard saw that Michon was losing control and it frightened him. He bent over Kon and felt for his pulse. He was surprised at how weak and unsteady it was. He should not have reacted this way, he thought. "Michon, stop it!" he pleaded. "He's not dead. He'll just . . . He'll just have to sleep it off."

"What do you know!" Michon screamed. "Go back to pinching nurses' asses. That's all you're good for. Jesus! He's right, I am in charge of a bunch of assholes! How am I supposed to get a job done?"

Michon kicked viciously at Kon several more times striking him on the head.

"Michon, stop! Please," Edouard pleaded again. "Stop kicking him like that! Just stop it!"

Michon finally regained control. "Damn it all, you're right. Rouillan will have my head. He'll be mad enough about the one we hit at the station. He should have let me do it my way!"

Edouard did not like what Michon was doing, but he did not want to know any more about this stranger. He had given aid to the members of the group because he knew they could not go to a real doctor, but he had never treated any of Michon's victims before. He did not want to think about them. He just didn't want to think about that part of it. "Just don't kick him anymore," Edouard said quickly. "Let him sleep the stuff off. I'll come back later if you want."

"What the hell for? You're only good at stealing drugs. You have no idea how to use them. I hope you never get your license, Edouard. You're nothing but a fake! Go on! Get out of here!"

Edouard glared at Michon and resentment grew in him like a gall. He knew he would never get his degree. He hadn't been to class in months. Once he had thought that it was the system that was rotten. Once he had believed Michon's rhetoric, but not now. He realized that he hated Michon for using him the way he did. Worse yet, he hated himself for letting his future slip through his hands. But Michon was wrong about him. He did know about drugs. He had helped that man with the bullet, and the one who had blown his hand off. He had saved that man's life. Michon could not have done that. He never helped anyone. Michon had no right to call him a fake. It was Michon who was the liar. Edouard fled from the room.

"Call an ambulance!" Paul shouted to the police after the terrorists were gone. He looked at Rubard who lay groaning on the ground. He knew he would help him. To do otherwise was against his healer's instinct. But at the moment he had an urge to kick him in the teeth and silence his whimpering. Were they all fools to risk their lives for Rubard? he asked himself. The stupid little shit must have told someone besides his father that he was coming to Paris.

He went to Rubard and stooped over him. "Shut up and tell me where you've been hit," he said harshly.

"My leg! My leg! Oh God, my leg!" Rubard screamed.

Paul saw the blood on Rubard's left leg. He seized the bottom of Rubard's pant leg and tore it open at the seam exposing his shattered leg. No wonder the bastard's screaming, Paul thought, his anger giving way to pity. He tore off his tie and wrapped it tightly around Rubard's leg above the knee. Putting his hand on Rubard's shoulder, he said calmly, "Hang on, Etienne. You'll be O.K. Understand? You'll be O.K."

"My leg! My leg!" Rubard screamed again and struggled to sit up.

"Lie still!" Paul cautioned. "Listen to me, Etienne. You'll be O.K. The ambulance is on its way. Just hold on. O.K.?" Paul patted

Etienne on the shoulder again. "Have courage, Etienne. Have courage."

Etienne nodded his head and sobbed a few times, but he finally stopped screaming.

"Over here!" Paul called to one of the police officers. "Keep this tight," Paul said as the man ran up. The officer nodded and knelt by Rubard, holding the tourniquet around his leg.

Paul dashed to where Jack sat by Brad, holding Brad's head against his chest. He had turned up the edge of Brad's coat and was using it as a compress against Brad's back.

"He's still alive, but it's serious," Jack said before Paul could ask. "It must have hit the lung."

Paul felt for Brad's pulse and listened to his breathing. "Damn!" he said shaking his head. "Are you O.K., Jack? Did you get hit?"

"No. I'm O.K."

"Good. Watch his breathing," Paul said calmly, knowing Jack could be trusted to start mouth-to-mouth if it became necessary. "I'll see if anyone else is alive."

"Sure," Jack mumbled, but Paul had already moved on. Jack watched Paul stoop over each of the terrorists in turn, carefully searching for signs of life. "Come on! Come on! Come on, you shitheads! Hurry up with that God damned ambulance," Jack kept repeating, offering it as his prayer for Brad.

At last an ambulance arrived and Paul signalled for them to load Brad first and start him on oxygen. He hurried to Etienne, but found him unconscious. After he helped load Etienne, the first ambulance pulled away and a second one arrived. "There's one more still alive," Paul told the attendants and directed them to the terrorist.

Before any of the other bodies could be removed, a reporter appeared and started snapping pictures. Paul came up beside him. "No pictures! No story! This is classified," he said, assuming an authority he did not have.

"What do you mean, no story?" the reported replied. "You've got to be kidding. This is news! The police said they took a hostage. Who was it?"

"Who told you that?" Paul demanded taking the reporter by the arm and shoving him away from the area.

"I heard it on the police radio. You can't hide a thing like this. This is too big!"

Suddenly Paul seized the reporter by the throat. "No pictures. No story. Nothing. Do you understand?" he said coldly.

"A total blackout? Who the hell are you to call for that?" the reporter gasped breathlessly.

Paul tightened his grip on the man's throat. "I'm the man who will break your neck if this hits the papers."

"That's good enough for me!" the reporter croaked and Paul loosened his grip. "Show me your I.D.!" Paul barked and the reporter dug out his wallet and showed a card to Paul. "That cheap tabloid, huh," Paul grunted and returned the card.

"Can you tell me anything?" the reporter asked, regaining a spark of his professional manner. Before Paul could answer, Jack came up. "Give me the film," he ordered holding out his hand.

"Wait a minute," the reporter said indignantly. "You can't just take my film. I've got a lot of material there. This is my job. Who are you anyway?"

Paul shot a quick look at Jack before answering in a less menacing tone, "Look, we're with GIGN. This is a top secret operation." Paul flashed a counterfeit identity card in front of the reporter's face. "I'll level with you. It is a hostage situation, but it must be kept quiet."

"But the press always gets involved in these cases. The publicity helps."

"Not always. In this case it would be very damaging."

"Well, even if I agree not to print anything, what about the other papers?"

"There will be pressure on the editors from others at GIGN. You are the only reporter who was actually here."

"Yes, and this would have been a real scoop. I could use one right about now. I'm not exactly popular with the editor."

Paul sized up the man quickly. "Look, there may be a good story developing here and I promise to give you the first crack at it if you'll cooperate with us."

The reporter looked from Paul to Jack and back to Paul. "And if I don't cooperate, you'll wrap my windpipe around my ears," the reporter said with a nervous laugh.

"Something like that," Paul responded without a smile.

"O.K. I'll keep quiet, but I can't guarantee that someone else won't leak the news."

"We'll take care of that," Paul assured him. The reporter offered his hand and Paul took it, pressing firmly on the reporter's fingers as a reminder of his physical strength.

"See you gentlemen later," the reporter said nervously and hurried away, glad to still have his camera and his neck intact.

"We can't let Geilla hear of this in the papers, Jack. She might lose the baby," Paul said, shaking his head sadly. "We're going to have to get some help from GIGN to get Kon back. We're just too short-handed without Brad and Geilla. I got their license plate number, but they'll probably ditch the car. When we know how Brad is, I'll call Mary to stay with him. No . . . I'd better call her right away . . . give her time to get here. Shit! All the times she worried about him going to Timbuktu and he gets hit in Paris. I'd better call Carl. He can get us some help with GIGN and maybe send someone over here. I'll call Carlin to keep an eye on Geilla and get the police started on tracing that . . . "

"I'll call Carlin," Jack interrupted. "You've got enough to do."

"Thanks, Jack. I also want you to question that terrorist we got."

"Gladly. I want to get some answers from Rubard, too."

"Take a number, Jack. I'm not through with that little shit. I'd better get going. I'll meet you at the hospital later."

Chapter Three

Brad was listed as critical, but stable, and Mary was doing her best to keep up a round-the-clock vigil. Mary told herself she was used to worrying after being married to Brad for eight years, but this was one case where practice didn't make it any easier. Mary was calm and practical, however, and tended to focus on the positive. The bullet had gone through Brad's lung cleanly, almost surgically, not tearing up any major blood vessels. He was surrounded by specialists in a clean modern hospital, and there was no sign of infection in the wound.

Altogether it was a much better situation than Kon had been in last spring. She just wished that Brad would wake up. He had been unconscious when she had arrived late yesterday afternoon, and was still out. It was hard to sit there alone and not worry about all the things that could go wrong. It seemed that just when she needed the team she had supported for years, they were unable to help her. Kon had still not been located and Paul was doing his best to keep the news from Geilla.

Paul had stopped by for a few minutes, and thoughtfully brought her some tea. She had refused it at first, suspecting he had slipped one of his mysterious sleeping potions into it; but he had drank some himself and assured her that he relied on her common sense to get enough rest. She took the hint and reclined in a soft chair while he was there. She did not want to add to his worries. Having the leadership of a decimated team thrust upon him, and worrying about Kon was burden enough. He and Jack were both very busy working with the police.

Paul had asked if she wanted Nea to come and stay with her. He had even offered to make the call himself, but she had declined. Whenever she was away, she depended on Nea to manage the dress boutique they ran in London. Nea never became involved in the team's business. Indeed, she had never met anyone on the team except Brad, until she had designed Geilla's wedding dress and been invited to the wedding. Everyone had noticed that Paul had been more than impressed by Nea, and he had spent a good deal of time with her since the wedding. It was unusual for Paul to cultivate the company of any particular woman. If anything, he was more wary than Jack about becoming entangled in a relationship. Perhaps he had allowed himself to get close to Geilla because he knew she was in love with Kon. Thinking over Paul's offer to send for Nea, Mary wondered if perhaps Paul wished she was there to give him moral support. Of course he would never admit it. It would spoil his image as "Mr. Perfect".

Paul came out of Brad's room at the hospital and went down the hall to where Rubard was being kept. Unlike Brad, Rubard seemed to be recuperating fast. However, Paul doubted if Etienne realized yet that he was going to be permanently disabled. Paul shuddered at the thought of being restricted because of a disability. He demanded a lot from his body and kept it honed to perfection. Well, Rubard is lucky to be alive and eventually he will be able to get around without crutches. From the looks of him, he was never very athletic, Paul thought. Perhaps he won't miss playing sports. He will have to find some other amusement besides robbing banks.

Rubard looked up as Paul came into his room and inquired, "How are you, Etienne?"

Etienne understood from the tone of Paul's voice that he was gathering information rather than expressing any personal concern. He wasn't offended. He was used to being ignored. What was he to Paul anyway except a business deal?

"I'm about as well as can be expected," Etienne answered at last.

"Good. Good. I'm glad to know you're not suffering," Paul said with a slight edge to his voice. "If it makes you feel any better, I've arranged for security to be posted outside your door," Paul continued. He pulled up a straight chair and sat backwards on it, resting his arms on the back. He watched Rubard for a few minutes, intentionally letting his silence make Rubard uncomfortable before he asked, "Remember when I told you that you were going to be O.K.?"

"Yes."

"Well, that was conditional, Etienne. Things could change at any time."

"What do you mean?" Rubard asked nervously.

"I mean I think you've been playing games with us, Etienne."

"What games? I told you I wanted out."

"Who else knew we were coming to Paris?"

"No one! I didn't tell anyone, I swear."

"You must have told someone, Etienne. How did they know we were at the station?"

"I don't know! I don't ..."

Before Rubard could finish, Paul had leaped to his feet. Suddenly he whirled around and snap-kicked the chair with such force that it crashed against the wall. "Don't give me that crap!" he growled into Rubard's face. "I don't have time for your games, Rubard. One of my partners is in a coma, and another has been kidnapped. It's like this: either you tell me the truth, or I turn you and your little arsenal over to GIGN. If they don't execute you, some of your friends will catch up with you in prison. Maybe you can amuse them with your lies."

Rubard went white. He knew that kick would have been directed at him, if he wasn't lying in bed. "You can't! I wouldn't stand a chance with . . ."

"Then you'd better try your luck with me. Why did you set us up?"

"I didn't set you up! I swear."

"You're still lying!"

"No! I don't know how the group found out. I swear I only told my family."

"Your family! What family? I thought there was only your father!"

"Yes, but . . ." Rubard hesitated.

"Who else did you tell, Etienne?" Paul growled.

"My sister," Etienne whispered.

"Sister? What sister?"

"I have a younger sister. She doesn't know anything about . . ."

"What's her name?" Paul demanded.

"Trinette."

"When did you tell her?"

"I called her from Lyon. I was . . . I didn't have anyone else. It was she who advised me to call my father for help."

"Does your sister live at home?"

"No . . . she has an apartment. She's going to the university. She wanted to be closer."

"Where is her apartment?"

"I don't know. I've never been there. I didn't want to get her involved with . . . she didn't know about my . . . my . . . "

"Activities?" Paul supplied sarcastically. "Do you have an address?"

"I don't remember it. I memorized the phone number though."

"Well, that's something to go on. How much did you tell your sister when you called her?"

"Not very much, I don't think. I told her I was in trouble."

"Did she know anyone else in the group?"

"No! No! I told you. She didn't have any idea what I was doing."

Paul kept after Rubard until he was convinced that he wasn't holding anything back. He got Trinette's phone number, and pushed Etienne to dictate a list of names and addresses of members of the group. Etienne said he had not recognized the two men who had kidnapped Kon, but Paul knew Etienne had been completely unnerved when they had tried to grab him. Etienne wasn't cut out to be a terrorist, Paul mused. He really was naive and very easy to intimidate.

"You're not going to turn me over to the police, are you?" Etienne inquired mournfully.

Paul sighed. "Not yet, Etienne. But you'd better pray that Kon is still alive."

Paul met Jack as he came out of Etienne's room. "I hope you're having some luck with Rubard," Jack began. "I can't get anything out of that other one. There's no I.D. on him, his prints aren't on file anywhere—nothing. He's obviously afraid of me, but he's trying to protect the rest of them. What a dupe."

"Well, keep after him. We'll find out who he is sooner or later.

47

Rubard is easier to work with. I believe he really is fed up with the group. He just doesn't know who that guy is. He gave me a list of names and addresses though."

"Good. Let's start checking them out."

Kon had been out for twenty-two hours, and Michon had barely been able to contain himself. Although he had no personal interest in Kon's health, he did not want to lose his only link with Rubard. He had been surprised that there had been no mention of the attack in the morning papers. He had hoped to learn the name of the hospital where Rubard was being treated. Fortunately Carl, the team's group chief in London, had foiled him by bringing his mycelial influence to bear on the press.

Driven by impatience and frustration, Michon began to kick at Kon again. This time was different, however. This time he heard a low moan in response. "Hey, Nicolas! Cover your face. I think our friend, Monsieur Breaux, is finally waking up."

Michon did not realize what a miracle it was that Kon was still alive. Perhaps his strong desire to live to see his child had kept his heart going, or perhaps it was the fact that some of the drug had leaked out of the syringe when Edouard dropped it. The drug had a powerful effect on Kon, but the dose had been too small to be lethal.

Kon awoke slowly, feeling as though he was swimming in a deep pool of pain. Everything hurt; his back, his ribs, his legs, but mostly his head. The sensation of being submerged was enhanced by the fact that his right ear seemed to be full of water. He tried to get his right hand to his ear, but it was hooked on something and wouldn't move.

His left eye wasn't working either, and he was not aware that Michon was hunched over him until he felt a slap. He looked toward Michon, but saw only a blur of the black ski mask. Where am I? he wondered. What is this strange creature? He tried to speak, but only a muted groan came out. He felt more blows on his face, and finally realized it was the creature with the hideous black face that was hitting him. He tried to pull away, but he was on his back, and the creature seemed to be on top of him. The creature was shouting at him, but it was a long time before he could make out the words.

"Where is Etienne Rubard? Where are the weapons?" Michon kept screaming, growing furious that Kon was still holding out.

Finally Nicolas spoke up. "He still looks groggy, Michon. Maybe you should give him some coffee or something."

"What for? He's fine! He's just being stubborn!" Michon snapped.

"I don't know, Michon. He doesn't look too good. You're only going to knock him out again if you don't let up on him."

"What's it to you if I do?"

"Look, Michon. I don't give a damn about him, but I'm getting sick of being cooped up in here waiting for him to snap out of it. Maybe if you let up a bit he'll tell you something."

"All right! Bring me some of that shit you call coffee!"

"It's not shit! I made it fresh. At least I made it. You never do."

"Shut up! I'm tired of your whining."

Nicholas shot Michon an angry look, but poured some of the hot, dark coffee into a cup and handed it to Michon.

Michon held the cup in front of Kon. "Would it please your grace to take some coffee?" he jeered.

Kon smelled the coffee and realized he was desperately thirsty. He reached for the cup, but Michon pulled it away.

"You're right, Nicholas. He does want coffee. Well, well," Michon gloated. He held the cup out to Kon again, but when Kon reached for it, he snatched it away again. Kon stared at the cup, and unconsciously wet his lips. Michon saw Kon's longing and turned it on him like a weapon. "Tell me where Etienne Rubard is and I'll let you have the coffee."

Kon hesitated. He craved the coffee, but he had no idea who Etienne Rubard was. Then, as if his desire for the coffee had focused his mind, he realized he had no recollection of who he was either. It was a very unsettling realization.

"Where is Etienne Rubard? Where are the weapons?" Michon screamed again, breaking into Kon's thoughts.

Kon stared at the cup of coffee in Michon's hand, trying without success to bring the double images together. He rubbed the back of his free hand across his eye, but it did not help. This thing with the black face talks like a man, but why does he look so strange? Kon wondered. And why does he think I know were Etienne Rubard is?

"I don't know." Kon finally whispered, feeling a sense of mental defeat.

Michon took Kon's answer as a sign of continued resistance. "Damn you, Breaux!" he shouted and flung the hot coffee in Kon's face.

Kon winced and drew back. He had not expected that response. It didn't make sense. Nothing made any sense. He licked at the coffee as it rolled down his face, but it did nothing for his thirst. He suddenly felt angry that the coffee had been wasted. When Michon slapped him again, he lunged forward to strike; but Michon was too fast for him, and knocked his hand aside. "I'll break you yet, Breaux!" he vowed and gave the bed a vicious kick. Kon felt his wrist jerk, and he sank back into the dark pool of pain.

It was a struggle to hear Michon's curses, and he didn't bother to make the effort. He lay still, trying to build an identity around the name Breaux, but nothing came save hatred for this strange animal-like man. He had a primitive feeling that something terrible would happen if he told him anything. He sensed that the creature meant to harm Etienne Rubard, and he did not want to cooperate. He determined not to confess his mental confusion.

Mary stood outside the science building at the university, waiting for Trinette to come for an early morning lecture. The night before Paul had asked her to pay a visit to Trinette, and had obtained Trinette's schedule from her father. Paul thought Trinette might respond more openly to Mary than to Jack or himself. It also might appear less suspicious to anyone watching Trinette if she was contacted by a woman.

Mary had not been eager to leave Brad, but now that he was conscious again, she was less anxious about him. She had changed her mind about asking Nea to come. Mary knew Brad would want her to do all she could to help locate Kon. If she had to work with the team, she needed someone she could trust to look after Brad. She wondered how long the team would be able to hide the kidnapping from Geilla. Geilla certainly knew that the team worked undercover, but like any new bride, she would be expecting her husband to contact her.

As Mary was getting ready to leave that morning, Paul had appeared at her door with a collection of theatrical makeup. With almost professional skill he had proceeded to grey her dark hair and wrinkle her skin, taking special care with her hands. He warned her to be extremely careful if she found it necessary to wash them. Paul had also brought her a pair of thick nylon stockings complete with artificial spider-veins, a pair of low-heeled shoes, and a long strand of pearls.

Sensing that she was a bit nervous in her new role, Paul had joked that he should snap her picture and force her to pay him not to show it to Brad. She had laughed and was glad to see Paul smile, for she knew that despite his calm exterior, he was extremely distressed about Kon. He was berating himself for not having checked out Trinette earlier, forgetting that Brad had been in charge of the operation, and that neither Etienne, nor his father had ever mentioned Trinette. Paul knew that as dangerous as an opponent could be, a client who withheld information could be even more deadly.

Mary was able to identify Trinette in the throng of approaching students from the photo Trinette's father had given Paul. Mary stepped up and greeted Trinette, in French, calling her by name. Trinette hesitated and looked questioningly at Mary.

"I have news of Etienne," Mary said quickly.

"Oh! How is . . .?"

"Smile and pretend I am your Aunt Cellia," Mary whispered. Trinette was startled, but accepted a warm embrace from Mary.

"I have something serious to discuss with you, Trinette. We must talk privately."

"Oh . . . er . . . all right."

"I'll call a cab and we can go to a café," Mary said, taking Trinette by the arm and patting her hand. "Keep smiling, Trinette," Mary cautioned. "Remember I'm your aunt."

"Oh yes, of course."

Mary led Trinette away from the university and hailed a cab. "Do you have a favorite café?" Mary asked as she followed Trinette into the cab.

"Well, yes . . . but it's not very elegant."

"That's fine," Mary answered, hoping that Trinette would feel more relaxed in familiar surroundings.

The cab driver was annoyed that he had been saddled with so short a drive, but Mary compensated him with an overly generous tip. She didn't have time to listen to the grumblings of a Paris cab driver.

"Are you with the police?" Trinette asked, after they were seated at a small table in the rear of the café.

"No," Mary began slowly. "I am working with a group that your father hired to help Etienne. Perhaps you would like to call your father. He knows that I was coming to see you."

"Would you mind?" Trinette responded eagerly. "I really would feel better about this if I checked with him first."

"Not at all, but please be careful of what you say. We're not sure his phone line is secure."

"Oh my God!" Trinette said, becoming deadly serious. "How can I possibly ask him a question?"

"Just ask him if he knew Aunt Cellia was in town? When he says 'yes', ask him to join us for lunch. He will tell you he can't make it, but will invite me for dinner." Mary thought Trinette looked nervous as she headed to the pay phone. She was impressed that in addition to displaying a physical attractiveness that was wholly lacking in Etienne, Trinette possessed more good sense than her older brother.

Trinette's combination of beauty and brains had endeared her to Adrien Rubard, whereas Etienne's irregular features and lack of grace had not attracted the elder Rubard's favor. Whatever the reason, Trinette seemed to wear her social stigma more lightly than Etienne.

"Please tell me about Etienne," Trinette begged, as she came back to the table. "I haven't seen him for months, and he was absolutely distraught when he called. I know he's in some kind of trouble with the police. Father won't tell me anything. If you've come to ask me where he is, I honestly don't know, but I will do anything I can to help him."

Mary was relieved to see that Trinette was so eager to cooperate, but Paul had cautioned her not to reveal where Etienne was.

"I can only tell you that Etienne is in Paris and that he is safe," Mary answered.

52

"So, he has returned at last from Lyon. I am so glad. When can I see him?" Trinette asked excitedly.

"Not just yet, I'm afraid. There are a lot of people looking for Etienne, and many of them do not have friendly intentions."

"Oh," Trinette said, becoming more subdued. "I imagine you have not come in secret just to tell me that Etienne is well."

"No. I am trying to determine who else besides yourself and your father knew that Etienne was coming to Paris."

"Well, I certainly didn't tell anyone! Nor did my father," Trinette responded indignently.

"I realize you wouldn't be so foolish as to intentionally tell anyone," Mary assured her quickly, "but can you think of anyone who might have found out accidently."

"No, I have been very careful," Trinette insisted.

"Have you made any new friends lately? Has anyone at school asked you about Etienne, or your family in general?"

"Not that I can think of. I'm always meeting new people, of course."

"No one has taken a sudden interest in you?"

"No."

"Would you mind giving me the names and addresses of some of your friends?"

"I'll list them all if you think it will help, but I assure you I haven't mentioned Etienne to any of them . . . "

"Yes?" Mary inquired when she saw Trinette hesitate.

"Well, I might have talked about Etienne to one of my friends. But that was long before he called."

"I see. What is your friend's name?"

"Lorelle Chalandon."

"Where does she live?"

"I don't know exactly. We always met at the university, or she would come to my apartment. She has a place somewhere, but I gather it's not very nice and she was embarrassed to have me see it."

"Have you known Lorelle long?"

"Why yes. I've known her for months."

"Is she in the same classes with you?"

"No. She's somewhat older than I. We met on campus though."

"When did you meet her?"

"Oh sometime last spring."

"Was it before, or after Etienne disappeared?"

"Oh, way before . . . well no, actually it was shortly after. I remember we went to see a film, and I told her how much Etienne would have enjoyed the film. I guess I was feeling lonely for him. We used to be very close, you know; growing up the way we did, and all. Father never took us anywhere, so we would go together. Etienne was very sweet. He would take me to the films, and afterward we would eat mountains of ice cream. Poor Etienne, it was hard for him in school. I think father convinced Etienne that he would never amount to anything, and he was defeated before he even started."

"Did Lorelle ask many questions about your brother?"

"Come to think of it, she did. She is an only child. I think she envied my having an older brother."

"And did you tell her much about Etienne?"

"Well . . . I suppose I did. She told me about her family's problems, and we shared some secrets as girls will do."

"And when was the last time you saw Lorelle?"

"It was just a few . . . no, it's been over a week, which is strange. Lorelle makes a habit of coming to see me quite often. Oh you don't think Lorelle has anything to do with Etienne's disappearance, do you?"

"I can't be sure, Trinette. At this stage I'm just snooping around. Tell me more about Lorelle. You mentioned her family problems. What are they?"

"Lorelle's father ran off with some Englishwoman when Lorelle was just a baby. Lorelle's mother was very bitter, and so is Lorelle. I guess that's when I told her about my mother."

"Did you ever meet Lorelle's mother?"

"No. Lorelle was a bit ashamed of her, I think. She works in a factory somewhere."

"Do you have any idea where?"

"Lorelle did tell me once. Yes, she works for Renault. The idea seemed to bother Lorelle. She said the workers were being exploited, and that it was a national scandal."

"Would you have a photo of Lorelle?"

"No, we never exchanged pictures."

"Could I visit your apartment, Trinette?"

"If you think it will help Etienne, you are more than welcome."

Mary paid the bill and took Trinette's arm again as they headed into the street. Mary was about to hail a cab, when Trinette mentioned that it was only a short walk to her apartment. Since the weather was still warm, Mary was willing to consent, but she remembered that she was supposed to be more than seventy years old. Deciding that it was better to appear rich and lazy than give herself away by her gait, she asked Trinette to hail a cab. Mary felt a new admiration for the team members who had to slide in and out of identities at will. She was thankful her French was fluent. She could not have carried out her role, if she had been called upon to speak Italian or German.

Trinette's second-floor apartment was simple, yet inviting, and Trinette showed Mary around the few rooms without hesitation.

"Do you have any pictures of your brother?" Mary asked, noticing that Etienne's likeness was missing from the shelf which was overflowing with photos of young men and women.

"Yes," Trinette answered hesitantly.

"May I see them?"

Trinette was suddenly suspicious. "Why? I thought you were hired to help him. Surely you know what he looks like!"

"Yes. I do," Mary answered calmly. "That's why I know his picture is missing from your collection."

"Oh. Well, it used to be there, but ever since he called, I have tried to keep his very existence a secret."

"That's very sensible. What did you do with your pictures of him?"

"I couldn't bear to take them home, so I put them in this," Trinette answered, pulling out a well-worn, leather-bound photo album. Trinette fingered the album lovingly, and sliding her fingers along the edge, she opened it. She suddenly looked perturbed.

"What's wrong?" Mary asked quickly.

"Well, I treasure all of these photos, but the edge of this one has been torn. I can't imagine how it could have happened."

Mary looked closely at the open book. "Did you take it from

behind the plastic to arrange it?" she asked.

"No. I spent a lot of time arranging all these photos just the way I want them. Someone removed this one."

"Did Lorelle ever ask to have a key to your apartment?"

"No, but I often left it laying about while she was here."

"I see," Mary said, and scanned through the pictures. "Is anything else out of order?"

Trinette turned the pages quickly. "No. It's only that one. That's the most recent one I have of Etienne."

"Did any of your other friends know Lorelle?"

"I don't believe so. Whenever I would have a little gathering, she always made excuses. I thought perhaps it was because she was older, and didn't want to bother with silly chatter. Now I am beginning to wonder. Oh Cellia, what am I to say when I see her again?"

"You mustn't say anything about your suspicions. After all, they are only just that, and I don't mean to spoil your friendship."

"You are probably right, but this whole business has me on edge. I am so worried about Etienne."

Mary was glad to see that despite his many flaws, Etienne had one loyal supporter. She wondered what Trinette would think of her sweet brother when she learned how many banks he had robbed.

Mary looked around Trinette's apartment again, and remembered that Paul had instructed her to check the phone. She was not certain what she was looking for, and did not find anything suspicious in the phone itself. She followed the phone wire into the wall plug next to the desk, then got down on her hands and knees. Using a small screw driver that Paul had given her, she started unscrewing the fixture from the wall.

"Whatever are you doing?" Trinette demanded.

"I'm just looking," Mary answered innocently.

"Looking? Looking for what?"

Mary smiled. "I'm really not sure, Trinette. Will you hand me my handbag?" she called from her knees.

Trinette's curiosity was aroused. She hurried to the sofa and fetched Mary's bag.

"Oh, thank you," Mary said. She opened the bag and pulled out a pencil-size flashlight attached to a key chain. Turning on the light, she put her head close to the wall and peered into the opening behind the phone box. "Hello. What do we have here? I'm not sure just how this gadget works, Trinette, but I do believe someone has been recording your telephone calls!"

"What? Are you sure?"

"I'm afraid so, Trinette."

"Well, pull that thing out of there this very minute!"

"No," Mary cautioned. "We mustn't disturb anything, or whoever has been tampering with your line will know that they have been discovered."

"But what am I to do?"

"I am going to put the cover back in place and you must carry on as if you don't know anyone is listening."

Trinette looked startled. "I don't know if I can do that. I . . . I'm frightened, Cellia. I wish Etienne were here."

"Well, that's not possible, but I won't leave you to worry alone. I shall have to arrange for a friend to stay with you for a few days."

"What friend? How can I possibly trust anyone, now that I know someone has been spying on me?"

"Don't worry, Trinette. I'm sure we can find someone trustworthy to stay with you. But right now you must come with me. I won't hear of your staying here alone."

"But where are we going?"

"To lunch, of course, while I locate a dependable friend to stay with you."

"Oh."

Mary quickly screwed the phone plate back in place and stood up.

"Cellia?" Trinette began hesitantly, as Mary was leading her out the door a few minutes later.

"Yes?"

"You're not really as old as you pretend, are you?"

"No, dear, but don't let on."

"Oh I wouldn't dream of it, but I do feel safer just knowing that you could run if we had to."

Mary smiled. "Yes, I can still run. But I'm not about to."

Mary took Trinette to a small, but elegant restaurant, and put in a call to Paul. She told him she would stay with Trinette until he could find a capable young policewoman to pose as a friend. She also gave him the information about Lorelle Chalandon and her mother.

There were five people by the name of Chalandon listed in Renault's current employee file. Two were males, one was a single woman of twenty-six, and two were older women, who had listed one or two dependents.

It was early evening by the time Paul had tracked down the information and given the names and addresses to Mary. After what seemed like an all too brief visit with Brad, Mary switched roles again, and took a cab to the first address. She had thought about calling to make an appointment, but Paul advised her that she might gain more information if she paid a surprise visit. That proved to be the case at the first apartment when a fat man in oil-stained overalls answered the door.

"Is Madame Chalandon in?" Mary inquired politely.

"No," the man replied curtly.

"I see. Will she be back later?" Mary inquired further.

"She'd better be. She hasn't made my dinner yet. Why do you want to know?"

"My name is Alison Blackwell," Mary said. "I'm an attorney employed by the British firm Hunt, Nelson and Crenshaw. I am trying to trace the former wife of a client of ours by the name of Chalandon."

"Former wife?" the man asked in confusion.

"Yes. We have reason to believe she was married to Mr. Chalandon about twenty years ago."

"Oh," the man smiled with relief. "That can't be my Detta. We haven't been married but ten years."

"I see. Are you Monsieur Chalandon?"

"Yes, that's right. What's this all about? Did this Chalandon fellow make off with the crown jewels?"

"Oh nothing like that. We are just trying to track down possible beneficiaries for his estate."

"Beneficiary? You mean you're looking to give money away?"

"I suppose you could say that."

"Oh. This other Chalandon chap . . . he didn't have a brother, or a cousin, did he?" the man said, leering at Mary.

"I'm afraid not. We're just looking for a former wife."

"Oh. Well, I guess my Detta's still got me so she don't qualify."

"I'm afraid not, but it's been a pleasure talking with you," Mary said, thinking how easily a lie could roll off the tongue in French.

"Yes, a real pleasure," Monsieur Chalandon agreed, looking Mary up and down.

Ugh, Mary thought as she hurried out of the apartment building. How can Geilla stand to do this kind of work? I guess she wanted very badly to be near Kon. Well, Geilla, I'll do my best to find a way to get him back to you.

Mary had more success at the second address and found Madame Chalandon at home. "Yes, I'm Madame Chalandon," the woman said nervously, when she saw Mary standing outside her door looking very official in her dark-blue suit. "If you've come to pry money out of me, I won't have any until the end of the month."

"I haven't come to collect anything," Mary assured her quickly, fearing the woman was about to slam the door in her face. "It's about your daughter."

"Oh. She's over eighteen, you know, and I am not responsible for her anymore. Not that I ever could do much . . . is she in trouble?"

"Oh no. It's nothing like that. Madame Chalandon, my name is Alison Blackwell, and I'm an attorney from the British firm of Nelson, Hunt and Crenshaw. We are trying to trace possible beneficiaries of the Chalandon estate. I understand that you were once married to the late Monsieur Chalandon. Is that true?"

"The late Monsieur Chalandon, is it? Well, forgive me for speaking ill of the dead, but nobody deserves to be 'late' more than that bastard Henri. Beneficiaries you say. Well, please come in."

"Thank you," Mary responded and carried her small briefcase inside. Madame Chalandon showed her to a chair in a plain, but tidy apartment. There was no sign of frivolity in either the apartment or Madame Chalandon, but she appeared neatly dressed and in reasonably good health.

As Mary settled into the well-worn arm chair, she noticed some light blue yarn, a pair of knitting needles, and an almost completed sleeve in a basket beside the chair.

"What a beautiful color!" she exclaimed with professional interest. "Is it for yourself?"

"On no! It's for Lorelle. The yarn was rather dear, but she needs a bit of elegance now and then. She don't seem to pay no attention to clothes, like other girls, but . . . " Madame Chalandon shrugged.

"Have you heard from Monsieur Chalandon since he . . . er . . . left?" Mary began cautiously.

"Not a word. Never so much as a word or a penny for the child either," Madame Chalandon said bitterly.

Mary sighed inwardly. This was not going to be as difficult as she had feared. Madame Chalandon obviously did not know if her former husband was alive or dead. "I see," Mary began. "Well, Monsieur Chalandon came to England after he left Paris and did rather well. He never had any other children, and according to his will, his daughter, Lorelle, I believe her name is, will inherit a sizeable sum."

"You mean to tell me that scoundrel finally made something of himself? Good grief! Who would have thought it?"

"I don't suppose you kept your marriage certificate, or any other proof of your marriage?"

"Oh now, you can't get out of giving us the money on that account. I still have the certificate. I didn't want Lorelle growing up thinking that she was the result of some casual . . . Well, I realize it wasn't much, and people looked down on us anyway, but . . ."

"I understand," Mary said with genuine sympathy. "And do you have Lorelle's birth certificate?"

"Oh yes. I didn't want anyone to try to take her away, or make her life any more difficult than it has been. I never was able to give her material things, but I wanted her to have respectability. Perhaps I should have lied that her father had died, but I couldn't bring myself to make up a fairy-tale for her. I wanted to teach her how deceitful men can be. She's a very bright girl, you know. No one is going to take advantage of her."

"Can you tell me where Lorelle lives?"

"It may sound strange, but I really don't know. She moves around a lot. I will be sure to tell her that you are trying to contact her though."

"Well, I am disappointed. I will be in Paris only a few days and I did want to conclude this case."

"Please give her a chance to call you. I don't want her to miss this opportunity."

"Of course. Here is my card. I'm staying at Le Dauphine Hotel, but I'm in and out. Do ask her to call and leave a message. I would love to meet her. You don't happen to have a photo of her, do you?"

"Well, yes, but I wouldn't want to part with it."

"Oh, I don't need it for my file. I was just curious as to what the lucky young lady looks like."

"In that case . . . " Madam Chalandon said before getting up and going into the bedroom. She returned a few minutes later and handed Mary a wrinkled black and white photo. There were several young girls in the picture, which appeared from their attire to be a record of a holiday excursion.

"That's Lorelle on the right," Madam Chalandon explained.

Mary detected nothing sinister in the smiling face in the photo. "Was this taken recently?" Mary inquired.

"Almost two years ago. She and her school friends took a little trip. Lorelle's cut her hair short now. It's a pity really. It was so pretty."

"Yes," Mary agreed, trying to imagine Lorelle without her curls. I'm sure there will be no problem transferring the money."

"That would be wonderful. Just how much will she get?"

"I'm afraid I can't reveal the amount, but it will bring a major change for her."

"Well, Miss, don't go running back to England before Lorelle has a chance to contact you!"

"I will do my best, but please tell her she must act quickly or lose the money."

If that doesn't draw her out, nothing will, Mary thought, as she left the apartment. All in all, my little masquerade as Alison Blackwell has been very successful. A few chats with students at the campus tomorrow to expand the net, and we shall see what sort of bird we can catch.

Chapter Four

Edouard stiffened when he saw Michon come into the ward. He didn't like to be seen with Michon, and he felt trapped every time he talked to him.

"You've got to come, Edouard. Breaux isn't talking," Michon began.

"I can't, Michon," Edouard answered.

"He doesn't look good, Edouard. Maybe if you took a look at him you could help him along. You could give him something to . . ."

"No! I can't keep taking stuff, Michon. Someone is going to miss it. I'll lose my job."

"Well, you're the one who gave him the wrong stuff. He was fine before you messed with him," Michon said.

"It wasn't the wrong stuff!" Edouard insisted. "It should not have hurt him. You said you wanted him to answer some questions. Look, I admit I've never used the stuff before, but . . ."

"Listen, Edouard," Michon said, growing angry. "Do I have to remind you that you wouldn't have your damn job at all if I told certain people what I know about you?"

Edouard stared at Michon, his hatred growing deeper and more bitter, but he said nothing. There was no way to get away from Michon.

"Now get your little black bag and bring something for Monsieur Breaux."

Edouard felt sick, but he obeyed.

As soon as Edouard arrived, he saw that Michon was right about Kon not looking alert.

"How long has he been lying there?" Edouard asked. Michon didn't answer.

"How long?" Edouard demanded.

"Since yesterday."

"Yesterday! Christ! Has he been awake at all?"

"Just for a few minutes."

"Damn it, Michon, how could you do such a thing?"

Edouard bent over Kon. "Monsieur Breaux?" he called. Kon didn't even turn toward him. "Monsieur Breaux? Can you hear me? Monsieur Breaux, it's Edouard. Can you sit up?" Edouard continued. He put his hand on Kon's shoulder, but Kon pulled away. "I'm not going to hurt you, Monsieur Breaux. I just want to look at you. He's not responding, Michon. What's his first name?"

"Look, Edouard, this is not a social visit! I told you he wasn't talking. Just give him something to wake him up."

"You asked me to help him, Michon. I'm just trying to find out what's wrong with him. What is his name?"

"Screw it, Edouard! You'll be all night playing doctor! I'll find someone else to stick him!" Michon said as he turned and stalked across the room.

"What's the big deal, Michon?" Nicolas asked suddenly. "The guy's name is Emile."

Michon turned and glared at Nicolas, but remained silent.

Edouard bent over Kon again. "Emile? Emile, talk to me. Tell me how you feel."

Kon did not speak, but he turned his head in Edouard's direction. Suddenly, dry words from pages Edouard had memorized came to life and combined with what he saw in Kon's eyes. He knew what was wrong with him.

"You've been kicking him, haven't you? Jesus, Michon! I told you not to kick him! No wonder he's not talking. I'm amazed he's got any brains left!"

"What do you mean?" Michon snarled.

"I mean he's got a concussion. Look at him! He doesn't know whether he's coming or going. The poor bastard's been lying there so long he's wet himself. Damn you, Michon, I told you not to kick him. I'm not sure I can help him. Take the handcuffs off him!"

"What for?"

"Take the handcuffs off, and help me get him into the bathroom!"

Michon did not respond, but Nicolas stood up and came over to the bed. "Here! Take them off yourself," he said and tossed a key onto the floor beside Edouard.

Edouard snatched the key and freed Kon's right hand from the bed. Instinctively Kon pulled his arm toward his chest, but Edouard took hold of it. Kon's wrist was cut and swollen from being jerked against the handcuff and his hand was dark purple from lack of circulation. He winced when Edouard took hold of it.

"It's O.K., Emile. I'm just going to look at it," Edouard said, and began to rub Kon's hand. "Damn it, Michon, didn't you notice this? I think it might be broken."

"I don't care if it is!" Michon snapped. "Just fix him up so I can ask him some questions!"

Edouard took a closer look at Kon's left eye and shook his head. "Come on Emile," he said, and tried to pull Kon into a sitting position. Kon gave a low moan and pulled away. "He's worse than I thought, Michon. I need to get him into the bathroom."

Michon just scowled and Edouard turned to Nicolas.

"Give me a hand, Nicolas. I can't lift him by myself. He doesn't understand that I'm trying to help him."

Nicolas watched Edouard struggle with Kon, then bent to help, grumbling, "This whole operation is getting out of hand. I hate sitting around watching this guy. There must be scores of people looking for him by now. Nothing has been set up to hold a hostage."

"Shut up, Nicolas!" Michon growled.

"What is Rouillan going to say when he finds out you've damaged the one link . . ."

"I said shut up!"

Nicolas gave a disgusted grunt. Together he and Edouard overpowered Kon and hauled him into the bathroom. While Nicolas held Kon upright by the toilet, Edouard began to pull Kon's clothes down. Kon started to struggle, but Nicolas pinned his arms. When Edouard ran water in the sink and coaxed softly, "Come on, Emile. This is the place. Let it out," Kon gave in and let nature take over.

Nicolas shot Edouard a questioning look.

"Yes, it's blood," Edouard said in answer to the look. "Kidney damage—from being kicked."

"Well . . . so you've learned a few things, school boy" Nicolas sneered.

"Yeah, I'm a real whiz at water pipes. I should have been a plumber," Edouard responded bitterly. "Sit him down against the wall, Nicolas."

"Aren't you going to take him back in the other room?"

"No. Michon will only handcuff him again."

"Yeah. Being put in charge of this job has really gone to his head."

Edouard shot a quick glance at Nicolas, but ignored the remark. He did not really trust Nicolas. "Besides, if I leave him here he might be able to make it to the toilet himself. O.K., Emile, let's get your wet clothes off," Edouard continued as he began to pull Kon's trousers and underwear off. Kon started to struggle again, but Nicolas held him down. "It's all right, Emile. It's all right," Edouard repeated softly. "This is just part of my job."

"And you want to make your living doing this kind of stuff? You're a fool!" Nicolas scoffed.

Edouard looked at the dirty floor and the mildewed walls and longed for the sanitary atmosphere of the hospital. With a sigh of resignation, he tossed Kon's clothes onto the pile of damp towels fermenting in the corner of the room. "Well, I believe they let you do a few more interesting things once you get your license, Nicolas. But I guess I'll never find out. I don't suppose there's a clean glass in this place."

"I told you, I don't clean," Nicolas responded.

"Yeah, yeah. So I noticed. Maybe I can find some soap. He needs some water."

Leaving Kon slumped against the wall, Edouard went into the main room and began to search the kitchen area. Noticing a pot of ragout that had been left sitting on the counter, he cautioned Nicolas, who had followed him out. "I wouldn't eat that stuff, if I were you. How long has it been sitting there?"

"Just from last night?"

"That's too long. Why didn't you . . . oh never mind. Leave it for the ants, Nicolas. It's not safe to eat."

Edouard found a nearly empty can of cleanser under the sink and slammed it against the edge of the counter several times to loosen the last bit of powder. He chose the cup with the fewest chips from the pile in the sink and scoured it clean. Filling it with water, he carried it in to Kon.

Kon was hesitant to reach for the cup when Edouard offered it to him, but when Edouard pressed the cup into his left hand he accepted it. Seeing how difficult it was for Kon to get the water past his swollen lips, Edouard shook his head sadly.

"I hate to leave you in this filthy pit, Emile, but Michon would never allow me to take you away," Edouard whispered. "I don't know what he hopes to learn, but it would be easier if you would just tell him."

Kon could barely hear Edouard, and he did not respond.

"I wonder if you understand anything I am saying," Edouard continued. He put his hand on Kon's shoulder, but removed it quickly when Kon winced. "Look, Emile, I have to get back to the hospital. I'll come by later and bring you something to eat. O.K.? Maybe some soup—whatever the patients are getting. And I'll see if I can find a blanket for you. I don't know who you are, Emile, but nobody should be treated this way—nobody!" Edouard refilled the cup with water for Kon and went back into the main room.

"He isn't going to talk, is he?" Michon muttered as Edouard came out.

Edouard glared at him. "Jesus! Is that all you can think about? I don't know who he is, or what you plan to do with him, but that man in there should be in the hospital."

"It's none of your business who he is, Edouard. You're just supposed to patch him up so he can talk. You've let me down, Edouard. I won't forget that."

Edouard was used to hearing threats from Michon, but he didn't like the tone in Michon's voice. He shuddered to think what Michon would do to him if he felt he were no longer useful. "Breaux is in bad shape, Michon. I don't dare give him any drugs. Just leave him alone. I'll come back later with some food for him. Just leave him alone for now."

"Get out, Sabasté! You're no good to me!"

Maybe not, Edouard thought, but Emile needs help and no one else is going to give it to him. He left without another word.

Michon smoked nervously for several minutes, then suddenly

snubbed out his cigarette and announced, "I'm going out!"

"What? Again?" Nicolas replied, letting his annoyance show.

"Yes. I've got an idea. Keep your eye on Breaux."

"He's not about to escape, Michon. He can hardly stand."

"We'll see about that! Just watch him."

"O.K.! O.K.! Bring something to eat when you come back."

"Quit thinking about your stomach, Nicolas. I'm still determined to find Rubard."

"Rubard's probably dead. We're just causing ourselves a lot of trouble holding Breaux," Nicolas answered.

Michon clenched his fist. "Damn you, Nicolas! This job is going to come out right if I have to do it without you and Edouard!"

Nicolas did not answer and Michon left in an angry mood. After he was gone, Nicolas checked in the bathroom to satisfy himself that Breaux hadn't moved, then turned on the radio. There was still no news of the attack at the railroad station or the kidnapping.

About an hour later Michon returned with a henchman of Rouillan whom Nicolas knew only as Gérard. Ignoring Nicolas completely, the two men hurried into the bathroom. Gérard straddled Kon's legs, took hold of his collar with both hands, and yanked him upright. Kon felt the hands at his throat and instinctively began to struggle. He gripped Gérard's arm and tried to pull it loose from his collar, but Gérard slapped him across the face. When Kon attempted to back away, Gérard hit him again.

"Listen to me, Breaux! Where is Etienne Rubard? Where are the weapons?" he shouted.

Kon recognized the questions, but he still did not have any answers. Gérard hit him again. The pain focused Kon's senses for a moment and he realized that there were two men in front of him. He tried to lash out with his legs, but his left leg was stiff from sitting on the cold tile. He couldn't seem to move fast enough to avoid getting kicked.

"See what I mean?" Michon said as Kon struggled. "I still think he's holding out!"

"I'm not so sure," Gérard answered slowly and released his grip on Kon's collar. "Let's try one more thing."

Straightening up, Gérard reached into his pocket and pulled out a pack of cigarettes. Tapping one free, he lit it and pulled a few quick puffs to start it. Then quite deliberately he pressed the burning end against Kon's swollen wrist. Kon jerked his arm and an uncontrollable shudder rippled through his body.

"Where is Etienne Rubard?" Gérard demanded.

Kon said nothing, and in an act of cruelty that made even Michon wince, Gérard pressed the burning cigarette against Kon's swollen eyelid. Kon drew in his breath, and only partially succeeded in stifling a cry of agony. Only his intense desire to thwart these men kept him from screaming that he didn't know where Etienne was. He felt the cigarette a third time, and just when he felt he could endure no more, they stopped.

"It's useless," Gérard declared. "I think he's too addled to remember anything. You shouldn't have kicked him in the head. Rouillan won't be happy."

Michon offered no excuse and Gérard turned away. "Forget about Rubard for now. Perhaps we can swap Breaux for some prisoners. I'll talk to Rouillan." Gérard looked at his watch. "It's seven o'clock. You've had him almost a day and a half . . . better feed him something. It's going to be difficult enough to negotiate for him in the state he's in."

Michon nodded. Without a word he followed Gérard out to the main room.

"Call Bernon in two hours. I'll leave word about how Rouillan wants to proceed," Gérard said as he headed out the door.

Nicolas watched Michon's hands shake as he lit a cigarette and pulled a few drags. "What did he say?"

"The bastard's going to report me to Rouillan. I know it. I should have killed Rubard when I had the chance. Damn!" He sat in silence for a moment before suddenly commanding, "Give Breaux some food!"

"What am I supposed to feed him? You didn't bother to bring anything!"

"I'm not your waiter! Where's that stuff we ate last night? Give him some of that!"

"Edouard said it wasn't safe to eat."

"Screw Edouard! He doesn't know what he's talking about. You ate it, didn't you?"

"Yes, but . . ."

"Who are you working for, Edouard or me?"

"You damn it! But Edouard makes more sense about some things!"

"Well, you can just take your ass on out of here if you prefer to mop floors like Edouard."

Nicolas scowled, but he held his tongue. He went to the stove and got the pot of ragout. He ran some cold water into the pot, but it didn't mix with the congealed mass on the bottom. "Shit!" he grumbled and turned on the flame. As the ragout warmed, it gave off a meaty aroma that was not unappealing. "It doesn't smell bad. Maybe Edouard is wrong," he muttered to himself. Looking at the consistency of the watered-down ragout, Nicolas chose a spoon from the pile of dirty dishes. He carried the food into the bathroom and found Kon lying on the floor. As he pulled him upright, he noticed the marks on his face.

"My God! You've got guts, Breaux!" he said with true admiration. "No sense, but . . . my God! Well, here . . . eat!"

Kon could smell the food as Nicolas set the pot down next to him, but he didn't move. He hurt too much to have an appetite.

Nicolas jammed the spoon into the ragout and held it to Kon's mouth. "Come on, eat! We need you in better shape!"

When Kon turned his head aside and ignored the food, Nicolas gave up. "I'm not a God damned nursemaid! When you want it, it will still be here!" he said and stomped out.

"He's not hungry," Nicolas muttered as he went back into the main room. "Let Edouard take care of him. He'll be back later."

"I decide when he eats, not Edouard!" Michon snapped.

"Then feed him yourself! I'm going out!" Nicolas roared.

Michon shouted a few curses at Nicolas' back as he left, but Nicolas did not stop. Michon kicked the door in frustration, then stormed into the bathroom. Kon had slid down the wall again and Michon yanked him upright. "Damn it, Breaux! I said you had to eat and you're going to eat!" He grabbed the spoon in his right hand and seized Kon's swollen jaw with his left.

Kon tried to move away, but he was backed against the wall. He locked his teeth together for a moment, but the pressure on his chin was too much for him. Michon forced a few spoonfuls of ragout into Kon's mouth, and then grew impatient. Noticing the cup sitting on the floor, he dumped its contents into the pot. Dipping the cup into the thinned ragout, he held the cup against Kon's swollen lips and poured. Kon got down one cupful of the cold, greasy liquid, but began to choke on the second ration. Michon gave up and flung the remainder of the cup in Kon's face. He stalked out, leaving the pot beside Kon. Kon slid sideways down the wall until his shoulder hit the floor. He felt better lying flat against the cold tile.

Michon barely looked up when Nicolas returned over an hour later. "It's about time you showed up," he growled and snubbed out his cigarette. "Keep track of Breaux. I've got to see what Rouillan wants to do with him."

"Get Rouillan to take him. I'm sick of being cooped up in here with him," Nicolas grumbled.

"What are you complaining about? You're getting paid!"

"Is Rouillan going to pay if Breaux can't talk? You . . ."

"Shut up, Nicolas! I'm still in charge! Remember that!"

"Sure, sure. Just so long as I get paid."

"Where's your loyalty to the group? I don't know why I pay you."

"Because I can get a job done. I'm not one of your young idealists. You left them lying in the street. Don't talk to me about loyalty."

"They knew what they were getting into."

"Did they?"

"Shut up! Just shut up! Look after Breaux. I'm going out!"

Nicolas sat on the unmade bed, lit a cigarette, and thumbed carelessly through the evening newspaper he had brought back with him. He finished his cigarette and went to use the bathroom. "Oh shit," he said with disgust as he opened the door. Kon was still lying on the floor, but he was doubled over and vomiting. "Now what's the matter with you?" Nicolas demanded. "Where the hell is Edouard? This is his job. I'm not going to clean up after you."

As Nicolas stood watching, Kon continued to retch helplessly, adding to the mess on the floor. "Damn it, Breaux, this place is filthy enough as is!" Nicolas snapped. Suddenly he grabbed Kon by his arms and dragged him over the low edge of the shower stall. He gave a sharp twist on the grimy handle and ducked as a spray of cold water spurted from the shower head. "Christ! I hope Rouillan takes charge of you soon. This is just not worth the money." He watched as Kon huddled against the wet tile and continue to heave. Then with a look of disgust he turned and left, slamming the door behind him.

Edouard was held up at the hospital, and couldn't quit working until after nine o'clock. Earlier that evening, he had been asked to help restrain a drunk who had been brought to the emergency room. After the doctor in charge had filled the drunk with tranquilizers, Edouard slid a bottle of the drug into his own pocket. The emergency room was a very busy place and the staff didn't always have time for a careful inventory of supplies. Edouard found working there very useful. As he gathered his things together, he poured some soup into a clean thermos. He had snatched the soup from the patients' food cart as it sat unattended in a hall.

When Edouard arrived at the apartment, Michon still had not returned and Nicolas was lounging on the bed listening to the radio.

"What took you so long?" Nicolas grunted as he opened the door.

"I got hung up at work. Where's Michon?"

"He went to make a phone call. Your friend Breaux threw up all over the bathroom. I figured since you were the medicine man you could clean it up. I put him in the shower."

"Michon didn't kick him again, did he?"

"No, but . . . well, you'll see."

"See what? What happened?"

"Go look for yourself," Nicolas said, shrugging as if he was annoyed to have to explain himself to Edouard.

Edouard hurried toward the bathroom and saw water seeping under the door.

"What's this? Did the . . ." he stopped abruptly as he opened the door and watched a flood of water stream across his shoes.

Nicolas lost his languor immediately and leaped off the bed spitting out, "Holy shit!"

"You're flooding the place, Nicolas! What the hell did you do?"

"It's the damn shower! The drain must be clogged."

Nicolas stood back while Edouard waded into the room and turned off the water. Edouard gasped as he noticed Kon slumped over against the wall. Grabbing the back of Kon's jacket, he pulled him upright, and sighed with relief that Kon was still breathing. "Jesus, Nicolas! He might have drowned. Didn't you check on him?"

Before Nicolas could offer excuses, Michon appeared in the doorway behind him. "What the hell happened? What's he doing in the shower? Christ, water must be running down the wall!" he shouted. Suddenly he turned on Nicolas and slapped him. "You stupid idiot! The landlord will be up here any minute!"

"Quit it, Michon!" Nicolas growled. "I'm not one of your dumb little students. I admit I screwed up, but there's nobody downstairs right now. When we left this morning Georges said that the apartment below us was empty. Nobody will know until morning."

"Well, that's just great! That makes everything just perfect, doesn't it?" Michon snapped. "You idiot! You stupid idiot!" Michon turned to Edouard who was still holding Kon's jacket. "Get him out of there! We've got to clear out fast!"

Edouard shook his head in disbelief. "You're both crazy. You can't just haul him around. He's sick." Suddenly Edouard spotted the pot of ragout. "Oh Christ! You gave him that filthy food, didn't you? I told you it was no good! I told you I would bring something for him."

"It was Michon's idea," Nicolas objected heatedly.

"Shut up, both of you!" Michon hissed with such fury that Edouard drew back. When he looked down he saw that Kon was shivering. Turning his back to the others, he took hold of Kon's arms and pulled. Kon did not struggle and his extreme lassitude worried Edouard.

"Come on, Emile. I'll get you dried off."

"There's no time for that! We've got to get out of here," Michon shouted.

"But he's wringing wet, Michon!"

"I don't care. We've got to move fast. We've got to . . ."

"Listen, Michon!" Nicolas said, raising his voice. "Don't panic!

I told you nobody will be here until morning . . ."

"I don't care! I say we go now!" Michon shouted.

"Make sense, Michon," Nicolas countered loudly.

"I am making sense. Are you telling me I'm not making sense? I'm in charge of this operation, not you."

Kon could hear loud voices, but he didn't understand what the argument was about. He was thankful that the cold water was no longer falling on him. He was confused as to why he had felt the rain when he seemed to be inside a tiny room. He had been too weak to crawl out of the rain, and now he could not stop shivering. When he felt hands pulling on his coat, he tried to shout that he needed it in the rain, but no one would listen. He tried to hold on to the coat, but there were so many hands he lost his grip. When at last he was completely naked and shaking from the cold, he felt something soft being pressed around him.

Someone was talking in his ear, "Emile? Stop fighting me, Emile. I just want to get you dry." He realized that it was Edouard, the one who had promised him food. He had to warn Edouard about the men with the black faces who had burned him and forced him to drink poison. He had to make him listen.

"Shhh, Emile, be quiet. Shhh please . . . please be quiet," he heard Edouard plead. He tried to make Edouard understand, but he wouldn't listen. "Forgive me, Emile," Edouard whispered. "I don't want to hurt you, but I have to take the risk." Kon felt a sting on his thigh and soon he was drifting away from all the shouting. His body gradually stopped shaking and the fire in his stomach went out. He still ached all over, but he was too tired to care. "Shh, Emile . . . please, be quiet," Edouard kept repeating. He tried again to tell Edouard about the rain, but he wouldn't listen. "Shhh, Emile, please . . . if you make one more sound, Michon will kill us both."

Kon heard the fear in Edouard's voice and it seemed out of place. What was Edouard afraid of? he wondered dreamily. Then he remembered . . . the creatures! They must be after Edouard. He must warn him. He tried to sit up, but his body would not respond. "Watch out, Edouard! Watch out!" he mumbled and he was out.

Paul and Jack were working with the police, systematically checking out the information Rubard had supplied, when suddenly one of the addresses was moved to the top of the list. The landlord had called the police to report a tenant who had trashed one of his apartments and skipped out without paying.

Jack and Paul arrived on the scene only minutes after the police. The door was open and they could smell the rotting garbage as they came down the hall.

"Are you sure this is the right address?" Jack asked as he spied the filth in the room.

"This is it," Paul answered. "God, what a mess! They sure weren't planning on having company. We'll need a shovel to find any leads in this place."

Just then a police officer and another man came out of the bathroom. Before the police officer could ask, Paul flashed his GIGN I.D.

"What's the story?" Paul inquired.

"They trashed my place, that's what! Look at it—garbage all over!" the man blurted angrily, throwing his hands into the air.

"Are you the landlord?" Paul asked.

"Yes. I just bought the place and I've been trying to fix it up. Early this morning I came to do some work on the apartment down below and discovered that water has been running down the wall. How am I supposed to make any money if they wreck the place faster than I can fix it?"

While Paul continued to talk to the landlord, Jack stuck his head into the bathroom. He looked around quickly and was about to retreat when he spotted the pile of wet, dirty laundry in the corner. He picked up a pair of trousers with a growing sense of apprehension and went through the pockets. His heart sank when he pulled out a soggy receipt from a dry cleaners with a Paris address. It was identical to the one he had placed in his own pocket, on the morning that part of the team had set out for Lyon. It was meant to add an authentic detail to their disguises as members of GIGN. Jack searched, but there was nothing else in the trouser pockets. With a sense of helpless fury, he carried the trousers out to Paul and handed him the crumpled receipt.

"Damn! Anything else?" Paul asked, abruptly breaking off his conversation with the landlord.

"Nothing yet, but I'll keep looking."

Paul took the wet trousers from Jack and noticed what appeared to be a blood stain. "The bloody bastards! This is more than vandalism," he said turning to the police officer. "This is kidnapping, maybe even . . ."

Just then Jack found Kon's suit coat, tie, and shirt. There was some blood on the shirt, but no sign that Kon had been shot or stabbed. He showed his findings to Paul, who guessed immediately what the torn sleeve meant. What the hell had they been doing to Kon? he wondered. From somewhere deep inside him one hopeful thought rose to his mind and he seized upon it.

"He must still be alive, Jack," he muttered. "Why would they strip him if he were dead? They would just dump the body somewhere. No, I think the bastards are holding Kon as a hostage! It's standard procedure to strip a hostage."

"God, I hope you're right, Paul, but why haven't we heard from them?"

"I don't know. They were probably trying to get information from him at first. That's why they drugged him."

"Drugged him? How . . . ? Oh shit, the sleeve."

"Yeah."

"Dumb bastards! Drugs won't work on Kon. Nothing works on Kon once he makes up his mind. God damn! I wonder what they're doing to him."

"I bet they're still trying to get organized. They didn't plan to take a hostage, so nothing was set up. This flood might have been an accident."

"Or maybe Kon did it to attract attention."

"Oh God, I hope not. It will only make things worse for him. Shit! I should have shot the bastards. I should have risked it. Damn it! I should have risked it."

"There was no way to do it, Paul. No way at all. If there was I would have done it myself!" Jack said firmly.

Paul turned away from Jack for a moment, then said calmly, "Let's talk to the neighbors. We need a description of the guy who's been renting this apartment."

"Sure. I'll start next door."

The landlord willingly gave a description of his ex-tenant and agreed to come to the police station to look through photo files. Jack and Paul questioned the other tenants, but only Mademoiselle Bouterie, the young woman in the apartment next door was able to supply anything interesting.

"Did you see or hear anything unusual last night?" Jack began after he had introduced himself.

"Well, there has been a bit more noise coming from next door lately."

"Noise? What kind of noise?"

"Oh, loud playing of the radio and some shouting. I didn't want to complain because the young man who lives there has always been quiet."

"When did you last hear the noise?"

"I think it was about ten o'clock last night. It sounded like an argument or something. My boyfriend, Marc, was here. We were having a few drinks and listening to some music. He commented on the noise, because it had never happened before. This isn't exactly a classy neighborhood, but . . . well, I'm a student right now, and it's all I can afford. Anyway there was this row going on about ten and then everything quieted down again and we forgot about it."

"Did you see or hear anything else last night?"

"Well, my boyfriend felt ill later in the evening and left about midnight. I tried to convince him to stay and lie down, but he said he wanted to go home. His place is closer to his work. Anyway, a few minutes after he left I heard a noise in the hall. I thought that maybe Marc had decided he was too sick to drive home and had come back. I opened the door and looked out, but it wasn't Marc in the hall."

"Who was it?"

"I don't know who they were, but there were three of them. They were carrying a bundle of laundry down the stairs."

"Laundry? Are you sure it was laundry?"

"Well, I didn't have a good look, you know. I thought it was laundry but . . . they did seem to be having a hard time with it. You know . . . like it was not just bulky, but heavy."

"Did the men see you?"

"Oh I'm sure they didn't. They never even turned around."

"Do you think your boyfriend might have seen anything?"

"I don't know. I haven't talked to him today."

"Could you give us his name and address please?"

"Sure, if you think it will help."

When Jack talked to Marc, he confirmed that he had left the apartment about midnight.

"Yes, I went out the back way. My motor scooter was in the alley."

"Did you see anything unusual?"

"To tell the truth, Elyette and I had been drinking quite a bit and I wasn't feeling very well when I left her place. I sort of tripped coming out the door and then I stumbled around the corner and was sick to my stomach. A few minutes later I came back around the corner and saw three men come out of the apartment building. They were carrying a bundle of laundry."

"What did they do with it?"

"Two of the men dumped the stuff into the trunk of a car that was parked in the alley. The third guy seemed very upset about it. He kept yelling for them to be more careful."

"Then what happened?"

"One of the men hit the guy who was yelling and the other guy pushed him into the car."

"Did you try to interfere?"

"No, I didn't. I wasn't feeling very good and I was moving kind of slow. I was crossing the street, when all of a sudden the guys in the car backed out and ran right into my motor scooter. Smashed the front end—just like that 'boom'! Bent the fender all to hell!"

"Did you do anything about it?"

"What the hell could I do? They were gone before I could even yell. I got their license number though. Well . . . part of it. Like I said, I was kind of fuzzy."

The license number and the description of the car fit the one used in the kidnapping. The information didn't do Jack much good, though. He already knew that the dark blue Renault had been stolen.

Chapter Five

Kon awoke with the awareness of a throbbing pain in his right hand. He tried to bend his fingers, but they would not move. He struggled to sit up and groaned as he felt a sharp pain in his side. Looking at his right hand, he saw that something was stuck to his arm. When he reached to pull it off, someone grabbed his left hand.

"Leave it, Emile," he heard a voice say, and he realized that Edouard was beside him.

Fearing that Kon's wrist was broken, Edouard had fashioned a crude splint for it, using a roll of paper and some surgical tape. It took Kon a long time to focus, but he finally saw Edouard clearly. His pleasant features could have been attractive, but at the moment, he looked disheveled and distraught.

Kon noticed that he was lying on a concrete floor in some kind of warehouse. On either side of him were row after row of steel shelves loaded with boxes. He wanted to ask Edouard where they were, but his mouth was so dry he could not get the words out. Edouard had pulled him into a sitting position and adjusted the blanket around him before he saw that two other people were in the room. Kon had only a brief glimpse of them before their faces disappeared behind black masks.

So it was just a trick, he thought. Those creatures with the hideous faces were ordinary men wearing masks. Did I imagine it all? he wondered. Then he noticed the marks on his hand. No, it was real. Whoever they were, they had burned me. He looked more carefully at the figures in front of him and saw that they were holding weapons. Skorpions! My God, there are two Skorpions pointed straight at me. The thought was frightening enough in itself, but the realization that he recognized the small, Czech-made machine pistols troubled him further. Who are these people? Are they soldiers? What do they want from me? Am I a soldier? He looked at Edouard and noticed that he was sweating and seemed extremely nervous. He must not like the Skorpions either. When he looked back at the two who were wearing masks, he saw that one of them was drinking something. He suddenly was aware of how thirsty he was.

Edouard saw Kon lick his lips and it dawned on him how dehydrated he must be. His own mouth was dry.

"Could we have something to drink?" he asked the people with the Skorpions.

"No," the man on the right answered curtly. "You'll have to wait."

"Please," Edouard persisted. "I can hold out, but he's in poor shape. It's been hours since . . ."

"I said no!" the man growled.

Edouard turned to the one on the left. "Please, Lorelle . . . I brought that soup for Emile. I don't know what you want from him, but he won't be worth anything if he dies."

"What do you care, Edouard?" the girl answered harshly.

"I don't want to be responsible for . . . Please, Lorelle . . ."

"No!"

"Please, Lorelle. For God's sake, can't you be human just once?"

"Oh all right! But only for him. I want to see you sweat, Edouard. Give him the soup, Georges."

"No!" the man snapped. "I'm hungry. I haven't eaten all day."

"But we can't risk letting Breaux die."

"He's not going to die. Edouard doesn't know what he's talking about."

"But what if he's right about this?"

"Shut up, Lorelle! Look at him. He's worthless." Georges took another drink from the thermos. "I used to think you were smart, Sabasté. Always at the top of the list, always the best in everything. Look at you now! You're nothing! A parasite sucking off your parents."

Edouard glared at him but kept silent.

"Our great healer," Georges taunted, starting in again. "Look at your hands shake. Are you going to surgery this morning, Doctor Sabasté?"

Edouard had become accustomed to insults from Michon, but he could not endure taunting from Georges. "No, I'm not," he answered bitterly. "Not today or ever! I threw all that away. I know it and it's my shame, but I still try to help people. I still care, God damn it!"

"Shut up Sabasté! You disgust me with your great humanitarianism."

"I won't be quiet. I can't sit and watch a man suffer. I don't enjoy it like you do, Georges."

Edouard suddenly jumped to his feet. Georges drew back, but glared at Edouard and raised his weapon.

"Go ahead! Shoot me!" Edouard heard himself roar. "Shoot everybody that disagrees with you. That's all you stand for! Beating and killing. I'm sick to death of it! Go ahead! Shoot me!"

Lorelle was alarmed by Edouard's behavior. He had always been so mild. "Sit down, Edouard. Someone might hear you!"

"I don't care! I'm fed up!" Edouard shouted, suddenly immune to fear. "Go ahead! Kill me. I don't care. I brought that soup for Emile. He's the one who needs it, not you, you filthy . . . !"

Edouard lunged for the thermos, but before he reached it, Kon threw himself against Edouard's knees forcing out a raspy, "Don't!"

Edouard fell just as Georges fired. After the explosive noise stopped, Kon heard Edouard sobbing hysterically. He put his arm on Edouard's shoulder.

"Were you hit, Edouard? Were you hit?"

"No," Edouard sobbed. Kon thought Edouard was trembling, but he felt so shaky himself, he couldn't be sure.

"Don't provoke them, Edouard. Those weapons are deadly."

"What do they want from you, Emile? Can't you just tell them and get it over with?"

"I don't know, Edouard," Kon whispered. "It's all so crazy . . . I can't figure it out."

"Shut up you two," Lorelle shouted, suddenly getting up. "Move away from him, Edouard."

Edouard inched slowly away from Kon and a few minutes later he started retching. Kon crawled toward Edouard, but Lorelle kicked him in the back. He cried out in agony.

"Stop it, Lorelle!" Edouard pleaded wretchedly. "Can't you see he's hurt!"

"Shut up!" Lorelle shrieked. "Look, I'm sorry! I only meant it as a warning. I don't enjoy hurting people. I just . . . for Christ sake, Edouard! Can't you stop making those horrible sounds?"

"I'm not doing this to annoy you, Lorelle," Edouard snarled.

Lorelle watched Edouard double over and retch again. "What the hell's wrong with you, Edouard?"

"He's off his feed, Lorelle," Georges snapped. "Michon carried off his pills and he can't survive without them."

"Pills? What pills . . . oh shit! What are you hooked on, Edouard?"

"Demerol."

"Did you know about this Georges?"

"Of course," Georges sneered, "I'm the one who brought him into the fold."

Lorelle stared at Georges. "That's not the way we operate, Georges. No wonder he . . ."

"Shut up, Lorelle. Where do you get those patrician ideals? You're the dust off the factory floor. This is the revolution. I do whatever is necessary!"

"I've got to get out of here!" Edouard said, suddenly pulling himself upright. "I've got to get . . ."

"Sit down, Sabasté!" Georges roared. "You too, Lorelle. One move and I'll shoot. And I won't miss this time."

Edouard staggered forward, but Lorelle turned her weapon on him. "Edouard, please . . . I know you're sick, but you can't leave until Michon gets back."

Edouard watched her for a few seconds, but he didn't move.

"Please, Edouard. Do what he says," Lorelle pleaded.

Edouard sat down and leaned against the shelves for a minute before he doubled over and started heaving again.

Lorelle sat down also, but clutched her weapon nervously. Their prisoners suddenly looked weak and vulnerable, very much in need of help. She glanced at Georges out of the corner of her eye and realized with a shiver that she had more to fear from him than from the men she was guarding. She would have to let Michon know that Georges had threatened her. Using a weapon against another member of the group was a serious offence.

A short while later Michon and Nicolas came in. "You're coming with us, Edouard. We've got a job for you," Michon said in place of a greeting.

Edouard did not respond. He didn't even look up. "Get a move on, Sabasté! We need you!"

"He can't help you, Michon," Lorelle answered. "You should get rid of him. He's a real risk."

"Shut up! He's useful from time to time," Michon said, going over to where Edouard lay quivering on the floor. "Get up, Sabasté!" he shouted and prodded him with his foot.

Edouard groaned, but did not get up.

"I said get up!" Michon growled again. He bent to grab Edouard by the collar, but saw that he was covered with vomit. "Shit! How long has he been like this?"

"About an hour. He got hysterical and . . . Georges started shooting. I thought . . ."

"You were firing? In here?" Nicholas suddenly demanded, turning to Georges. "You stupid ass! If there had been anything but paper in these boxes, you could have killed yourself. What if somebody heard the shots? We've got to get out of here, Michon. Your recruits really screwed up this time!"

"Alright! Alright! That's enough. Get Edouard out of here, Nicolas! Give him his damn pills. As soon as he stops shaking, get him to work on Bernon."

"Where am I supposed to take him?"

"I don't care! Just get him out of my sight!"

"Jesus! I don't get paid enough for this kind of shit," Nicolas grumbled as he came forward. He took hold of Edouard, but as he started to lift him, Kon hauled himself to his knees, grabbed the back of Nicolas's coat, and gasped, "Leave him . . . !"

Before Nicolas could turn, Georges jumped at Kon and began beating him on the head and shoulders with his Skorpion.

"Emile! Emile! Stay back!" Edouard screamed when he saw what was happening. Kon went down, but Edouard kept screaming until Nicolas hit him in the mouth.

"Call him off, Michon!" Nicolas growled. "The guy's already a hopeless idiot. We won't get anything if your recruits kill him!"

"Get back!" Michon shouted at Georges. "Damn it! I left you in charge of him. Help Nicolas get Sabasté in the car!"

Georges frowned, but he helped Nicolas lug Edouard out the door and over to the dark blue Renault parked in the alley. Edouard vomited again as they were putting him into the car.

"Jesus, Edouard, I thought you were brighter than this," Nicolas remarked as he handed Edouard his black bag. "The money is in selling the shit. You're not supposed to get hooked."

"Don't lecture me, Nicolas!" Edouard gasped. "For God's sake, don't lecture me!" He dug frantically in the bag and quickly swallowed two tablets.

"Alright, alright . . . but hell . . ."

"What do you care? You sell the God damned stuff!"

"Not any more! Not since . . . never mind. Use your head! Get off it."

"Shut up, Nicolas! Just shut up about it!"

"O.K. O.K."

Edouard lay on the back seat anxiously waiting for the drug to take effect, but instead of the longed for relief, the tablets turned his stomach acid and came up again in short order.

"Oh shit! Now what?" Nicolas asked.

"I don't know. This has never happened . . ."

"Have you got anything else in that bag?"

"No! I'm not a dealer, Nicolas. It's just my own stuff. Oh God!" Edouard moaned and doubled over.

"Christ! Look at you. How the hell are you going to fix Bernon?"

Edouard didn't answer. He only moaned again.

"Jesus! You stink, Edouard. Roll down the window!"

"I'm sorry. I can't help myself. I should have let Georges shoot me. I'm finished, Nicolas. I'm . . ."

"Oh shut up!" Nicolas said testily. He got out of the car, opened the rear door and rolled the window down. "You're not going to die! You just shit yourself, that's all."

Nicolas got back in the car and started the engine. "We need to keep you out of sight for a while."

"Shoot me, Nicolas," Edouard sobbed. "Get it over with."

"Shut up, Edouard. God, what a baby you are! Now your friend Breaux—there's a man with guts!"

Edouard looked as bad as he felt by the time Nicolas stopped the car and yanked open the door. "Come on, Edouard. On your feet!"

"I can't . . ."

"Yes you can! Now get up!" Nicolas hissed. He grabbed Edouard by the arm and hauled him off the seat. Supported by Nicolas, Edouard took a few faltering steps. "Shoot me! Just . . ."

"Shut up, Edouard! I just might do it to get some peace."

Nicolas hauled Edouard into a building and all but carried him up two flights of stairs. He stopped in front of one of the apartments and knocked loudly on the door.

"Méline! Méline, open up!" he called. Edouard moaned and clawed at his arm, and he pounded harder on the door. "Méline, open up! It's Nick!"

A woman's voice answered and a moment later the door opened the width of a chain lock.

"Nick! What a surprise!" she started, then quickly put her hand to her face. "Nickie, mon cher, you stink. Are you drunk?"

"No! Let me in, Méline! I've got a kid who needs your help."

Nicolas pushed Edouard forward so that Méline could see him.

"He doesn't need a woman, Nickie. He needs a bath!"

"Come on, Méline, open up. Don't leave me standing out here holding this piece of shit! I need a favor!"

"Oh all right, mon cher," Méline answered reluctantly and opened the door.

"How come you never bring me flowers, Nickie?" she said, giving Nicolas a quick peck on the cheek. "I'd like that better than . . . Oh, he really is ripe! Put him in the tub, cherie."

"Thanks, Méline. You're a sweetheart!"

"I'm a fool for flattery, Nickie, but don't push it! What's his problem?"

"He runs on Demerol, but he hit empty and now he can't keep it down long enough to charge up again. I thought a little dream powder might fix him up."

"Did you bring any?"

"Not this time, baby, but I will. You know I will."

Méline looked him over critically and shook her head. "Yes, you will, Nickie. You don't forget a girl in need. O.K. I'll give him sweet dreams."

"Thanks, Méline. I knew I could count on you."

Edouard didn't object when Méline pulled his shirt off and stuck him in the arm, but his burden of self-loathing shot up as the needle went in. What next? he wondered. How soon before I hit bottom?

Méline opened the window, doused herself liberally with perfume and began to take Edouard's shoes off. She set the plug in place, turned the taps and watched the tub slowly fill with warm water. She put a towel behind Edouard and pushed his head back against it. "Relax, mon cher. Sweet dreams will follow."

Edouard looked up at Méline's double chin and hussy-red hair. She's old enough to be my mother, he thought. Hell, she looks old enough to be Nicolas's mother. But she is kind. My mother would never let me in the house if I stunk this bad. She doesn't like anything dirty. I wonder how she ever managed something so messy as giving birth to me. She must have hired someone to do it.

He thought about the time he had fallen in the pond and his mother had locked him out of the house. He had stood outside crying for hours before Gaston, the gardener, had discovered him and taken him to his cottage. He had liked Gaston. He was big and friendly and took time to talk to him and show him things. Poor Gaston had a wooden leg. He had lost the real one during the war. His leg didn't fit very well and Edouard felt bad about that. He determined that when he grew up he was going to make Gaston a new one so that he could walk without dragging his leg.

Edouard was dreamily aware that Méline was pulling his clothes off and thought it strange that he didn't feel anxious about being naked in front of her the way he always did with girls his own age. He laughed giddily when she thrust a washcloth between his legs. He imagined for a moment that it was Lorelle who was caressing him so gently, but the image didn't last. Lorelle had only contempt for him and he was too shy and awkward to be relaxed with girls. It was true that he had had a turn with Catia, but that didn't really count. Everyone at the university had slept with Catia. She had led him through the motions so well, he imagined he had pleased her, until she began to ridicule him. Maybe she did that with everyone too, but it had spoiled an otherwise enjoyable experience. He felt giddy again and smiled what he hoped was a wicked grin at Méline. She smiled back and kissed him lightly on the forehead. "That's better, mon cher. Give me a smile, my pet."

Edouard not only smiled, he started to laugh. It was pleasant at first, but he couldn't seen to control himself. That frightened him and he started to sob. He was sobbing his heart out as Nicolas lifted him out of the tub. Méline wrapped him in a towel and patted his arm. Then he was on the sofa and Méline was bending over him cooing softly, "Shh, mon cher, go to sleep. You'll feel better soon."

". . . a pretty little thing, Nickie," he heard her say as she and Nicolas went into the bedroom. He stopped sobbing after a moment, but he felt incredibly alone and sad. He wasn't going anywhere, no one cared about him. He hadn't been able to help Gaston. He wasn't helping anyone. As he drifted off, he determined that he had to find a way to help Emile.

Dry toast and weak tea. Méline was holding the plate and coaxing him, but he didn't have an appetite. The smell of her perfume was beginning to suffocate him. He didn't have the heart to complain. The perfume had been her defence against him. After all, she had been kind to him even though he smelled like a sewer.

"What's going to happen to Breaux?" he asked weakly.

"They want to trade him for some prisoners," Nicolas answered.

"He's in bad shape, Nicolas. He really doesn't know what you want from him. Don't let them hit him anymore."

"I don't think they will. Michon knows Rouillan is not happy with the way he handled this job."

"Do you think Rubard is dead?" Edouard asked abruptly.

"What do you know about Rubard?"

"I heard Lorelle and Georges talking last night. I hope he made it. I hope he got free of Michon, and Rouillan and all the rest. This is no way to live."

"Don't worry about it now, you've got to patch up Bernon."

"What happened to him?"

"He got shot trying to rob a bank."

"That was Rubard's job, wasn't it?"

"Yeah, and he was good. I think Roullion is starting to feel the pinch without him."

"Were you with Bernon?"

"No! If I had been, we would have come away with the money."

"Is he badly hurt?"

Nicolas shrugged. "He'll live. You need to dig the bullet out of his arm, and maybe get him some antibiotics."

"You mean steal more stuff. I can't keep . . ."

"Are you ready to go?"

Edouard held out his hands and slowly turned them over. "I guess I can hold them steady now. Thanks for the help, Méline, I . . ."

"That's O.K., pet. I understand. Try to get off it. Don't throw your life away," she said, handing him his clothes which were now dry and freshly pressed. He wondered how she had accomplished so much while entertaining Nicolas. She was obviously a very resourceful woman.

"It's no use, Méline. I already have," he mumbled.

She didn't argue, she just turned to Nicolas. "Come again, Nickie, and remember my dream powder."

"I won't forget."

Nicolas and Edouard were in the car again when Edouard asked, "Is she one of the people you sell drugs to?"

"I told you, I don't sell drugs anymore."

"But she is an addict, isn't she?"

"Well, so are you, but she didn't start on purpose."

"What happened?"

"Her old man and her had a fight one night and he kicked her down the stairs. She hurt her back real bad. I took her to the hospital. She was there for months. By the time she came out, she was hooked on morphine. They won't give her a prescription any more, so I keep her supplied."

"Then she is still a customer. What happened to her husband?"

"She is not a customer, you little shit! She's a friend, a loyal, stick-with-you friend. Her old man was my partner. He got killed while she was in the hospital."

"Your partner? Did you have a business? How did he get killed?"

"We tried to rob a bank and he got shot. She never told the police about me, not once. They badgered her and told the doctors not to give her any more pain killers, but she never told. Not one word."

Chapter Six

Michon was not in a good mood when Georges came back from putting Edouard in the Renault. "I don't appreciate you getting trigger happy on me, Georges! Damn it! Now we have to find some other place to keep Breaux."

"It was Edouard's fault! He made a grab for my gun. He's so damned righteous he makes me sick! Why do you keep the little creep around?"

"Quit griping! He has some talents I find useful. If one of your bullets had ricochetted off these shelves, he would be the one who could dig the lead out of your ass! You really put us in a bind, Georges! Where the hell am I going to hide Breaux?"

Georges looked subdued for a moment and then his mouth twisted into a malignant smile. "I know just the place, Michon. My father is going out of town tomorrow. We can hide Breaux in his apartment."

"How long will he be gone?"

"I think he said three weeks. I can call his secretary to check."

"How can you be sure he won't come back sooner and surprise us?"

"That's very unlikely. He and that shrew he lives with really like their holidays. Last year they went to Italy for a month. They let me use the place while they were gone. All I had to do was unpack their stuff after the painters were through. Hey that's it, Michon! Arnot does odd jobs all the time. He has all kinds of equipment—tools, and ladders, and sprayers, everything. He's even got a van. I've got a key to the apartment. It's the perfect set up."

"Are you sure your father won't come back suddenly and . . ."

"Don't worry! I know the secretary at my father's office. I'll call her every few days. She'll keep me posted on my father's schedule!"

"For once you're thinking, Georges. How soon can you find Arnot? We need to clear out of here."

"Two hours maximum! He's probably in class. I'll be back as soon as I can."

"Make it quick." Michon said to Georges's back as Georges disappeared. Michon sat down wearily on the floor next to Lorelle and pulled out a hardpack of cigarettes. He took one himself, and as an afterthought, he offered the pack to Lorelle. She took one, but he did not light it for her. Instead he tossed her his lighter after he had lit his own. "You'll have to go with Georges when he gets back."

"Why me? I'm beat, Michon. I didn't get any sleep last night. Get somebody else to go!"

"I don't have anybody else right now, Lorelle. We lost a lot of people in that mess at the railroad station. You can sleep in the van."

"Sleep! Are you kidding? I don't trust Georges enough to close my eyes while he's around. He threatened to shoot me and Edouard just before you got here. Did you know he's got Edouard hooked on drugs? I don't like working with him."

"Quit whining, Lorelle. I'm tired of hearing people bitch. Georges doesn't like Edouard and you don't like Georges. This isn't a damn nursery school. We've got work to do. Catia got along with everyone and you'd better learn how."

"I'm not like Catia, Michon!"

"O.K. O.K. Sorry. She was a slut. But she did what she was told. Look, Lorelle, you'll just have to put up with Georges. I don't trust him either. That's why I need you to keep an eye on him. I want to know where he takes that van. I can't risk having the police find Breaux."

"Alright. I'll go."

"Good. Why don't you stretch out until Georges gets back. I'll watch Breaux." He looked around at the concrete floor. "Go over to the other area. There's a pile of cardboard boxes. Here, take my coat. Just quit whining."

"Thanks, Michon," Lorelle said in genuine surprise. She took the coat and disappeared behind the shelves.

Georges appeared extremely animated when he came into the room about three hours later. His demeanor seemed due to more than high spirits, however.

"Where the hell have you been?" Michon demanded immediately.

"Hey what's the big deal? I got the van, didn't I?"

"What else did you get?" Michon asked, stepping closer to Georges.

"Don't crowd me, Michon," Georges responded angrily.

"I'm watching you, Georges," Michon growled, putting his hand on George's throat. "Don't screw up on this job again."

"Has that little bitch been squealing on me? Is that it, Michon?"

"I've been hearing a lot of things about you, Georges. Some of them aren't too good. Just watch yourself!" he finished and took his hand away. "Where's the van?"

"In the alley!"

"O.K. I'll open the bay door and you drive it in. I don't want anyone to see what we're loading."

"O.K. O.K. Hey, stay cool, Michon. I won't screw up!"

"Just get the damn van!"

Once the van was inside, Michon closed the bay door and opened the rear doors of the van. "What's all this junk, Georges? Where the hell are you going to put Breaux?"

"I'll just push it to one side. All this stuff will look authentic when I spread it out in the apartment. We can be there for days and no one will ask questions. Give me a hand with it."

"O.K." Michon agreed, "but I still don't know if I like this idea." Michon helped Georges move some of the equipment aside and then went to bring Kon. Michon had handcuffed Kon to the steel shelves, but it hardly seemed necessary. Kon had his eyes open, but he was just lying silently on the floor. Michon unfastened the handcuffs, and tried to get Kon to stand up, but Kon just moaned.

"We'll have to carry him," Michon said. As he and Georges lifted Kon, the blanket Edouard had wrapped around him slid to the floor. Kon arched his back and twisted as he was being handled, but it did no good. The men laid him on the bare metal floor behind the driver's seat and Michon snapped the handcuffs to the seat track.

"I'm going to tie his legs, just to be sure," Michon said. "He's real good with his feet. Hand me that roll of tape!"

"That's masking tape," Georges objected. "It's not very strong."

"It'll work if you twist it around enough times. Hold his ankles. That ought to hold him," Michon concluded when he was finished. "He's been pretty quiet, but put a gag on him if you have to."

Georges showed his twisted grin.

"I want him alive, Georges. Do you understand? No games and

no funny stuff!"

Lorelle came around the corner as they were closing the rear doors of the van. She looked half-asleep and was carrying Michon's jacket. Georges looked at her and his lips formed into an ugly smile. Lorelle glared at him, but remained silent.

"Remember what I said, Georges," Michon warned. "Keep your mind on your job." Michon looked at his watch. "It's after five. Get yourselves some food, and eat in the van. Don't park in the same place all night. Keep it moving. I'll be at Bernon's. Don't forget to call in."

"Yeah, yeah. I won't screw up, Michon," Georges answered, but it didn't seem like a promise.

It was after dark and Lorelle was having trouble staying awake despite the fact that it was starting to get chilly in the van. She stretched a few times and shook her head. "Damn! I wish I had some coffee. Would you like some? If you drive, I'll go get it."

"Who needs coffee," Georges answered, leering at her. "I've got these," he continued, holding out his hand.

Lorelle looked and then turned away. "Shit, you're as bad as Edouard. No, you're worse. Edouard is just a worm, but you, you're a real snake."

"Shut up! Do you want some or not?" Georges snarled.

"No!" Lorelle shouted and they lapsed into angry silence. She saw Georges swallow several of the tablets.

Kon had been quiet except for an occasional faint moan, but gradually his moans became more audible and more frequent. Suddenly he started to roll around and Georges went into the back of the van. He felt for the flashlight fastened to the wall, and pulling it free he shone the light in Kon's face. "Shut up!" Georges hissed and slapped Kon across the mouth. Kon closed his eyes against the light and was silent for a moment; but before Georges moved away he moaned again, very softly, very feebly.

Lorelle heard the sound as Georges slapped Kon again. "Stop hitting him, Georges. It isn't doing any good. Maybe he's thirsty. Here, give him a drink," Lorelle said. She reached between the seats and handed Georges a small paper carton of juice.

Georges set the light down and opened the carton. "Hey! Are you thirsty?" he asked gruffly. When he saw Kon looking at him, he took a drink from the carton, and held it out to Kon. Kon reached for it with his free hand, which was wrapped with Edouard's splint. Georges saw that there was no way for Kon to hold the carton. "You're in a bit of a spot, aren't you?" he gloated. He took another drink from the carton and held it in front of Kon's face. Kon licked his lips and then started to shake. "He really is thirsty, Lorelle. He'll be whining like a dog in a minute. Come on, Monsieur Breaux, government agent, let's see you beg!" Georges held the carton out again, but suddenly Lorelle stepped between the seats and knocked his hand. "Stop it, Georges! There's no need to treat him like that. Can't you see he's helpless?"

"Stay out of this, Lorelle. I'm in charge of this operation."

"By whose authority? Michon wants him alive and you're not following orders. Leave him alone!"

"Are you going to squeal on me again, you little slut?"

"I will report you to Michon if you don't leave him alone."

Georges turned and spat at Kon, but he moved toward the back of the van. Lorelle picked up the flashlight and shone it on Kon. She was embarrassed that he was lying naked on the floor, but she could not take her eyes off him. She was horrified at how severely bruised he was. "My God, Edouard was right! You're in terrible shape."

Finally Lorelle turned the light aside. She reached between the seats and grabbed a plastic bag. Pulling out a fresh carton of juice, she opened the top. "I don't know exactly how to do this, Monsieur Breaux, but you need to get this down."

Kon made no effort to move or reach for the juice and Lorelle sighed. "Shit, where is Edouard when you need him? Come on, Monsieur Breaux, drink!"

Lorelle slid in close to Kon and sat on the floor on his left. She forced her right arm under his head and managed to lift it slightly. Then she held the carton to his mouth. "Come on. I'm not going to tease you with it. Drink!"

Kon was barely conscious, but he drank. He was sorely in need of nourishment, and he was grateful for even a few ounces of liquid.

"That's all there is!" Lorelle said when the carton was empty. She raised the flashlight and looked closely at Kon's battered face. "You must have been a good looking bastard before they started in on you," she said softly and brushed the hair off Kon's forehead. He looked at her and mumbled softly, "Geilla? Geilla? Where are we?"

"Geilla? No, I'm not Geilla. You don't understand any of this, do you?" Lorelle asked. "It's just a phase, Monsieur Breaux," she continued wearily. "We have to make it worse in order to make it get better. I'll tell you a secret, Monsieur Breaux. I'm sick of it. I don't like to hurt people. I don't like it at all, but I have to do it. It's nothing personal. It's for the revolution. You'll see, it will all be better someday. Once we win, you'll see we are right and come over to our side."

Lorelle nodded drowsily, but suddenly caught herself. She jerked herself upright. Looking down at Kon, she saw that he was shivering. She realized that her own hands were cold. "What happened to the blanket he had?" she asked Georges.

"What blanket?"

"He was in a white blanket at the store. What happened to it?"

"I don't know and I don't care. Damn it, he's just a prisoner."

"I know, but we're always protesting about how our people are treated in prison. We're treating Breaux much worse." She took the flashlight and looked around the van. Suddenly she saw that Georges was sitting on several heavy drop cloths.

"Those will do. Get up, Georges. Help me put one of those over Breaux."

"No! What are you thinking? He's a God damn GIGN agent!"

"I don't care. Look at him! He's a human being and he's cold. Edouard said he could die if we weren't careful!" Lorelle set the light down, and began to pull on one end of the drop cloth, trying to pull it out from underneath Georges. She was on her feet, stooping over and pulling as hard as she could when without warning Georges stood up. Lorelle stumbled backwards and suddenly Georges was on top of her, tearing at her clothes.

"Get off me, Georges! What are you doing?" Lorelle said, trying desperately to push him away. As she shoved her hands against him, she realized that he had stripped his shirt off.

"You know what I'm doing! I saw you looking at Breaux. You like naked men, don't you? They really turn you on."

"Get off me!" Lorelle shouted. "What are you talking about?"

"Don't play stupid with me, you little bitch. I know what you and Michon were doing while I was gone!"

"You're crazy, Georges. Get off me or you'll be sorry!"

"What are you going to do, Lorelle? You don't dare scream."

Lorelle imagined that she saw Georges's twisted smile even in the dark. She forgot her fatigue and began to fight with all her strength. She had told Michon the truth when she said that she was not like Catia. She was very particular about whom she allowed to touch her and she had faced this situation before.

As Georges brought his face close to hers, she tucked her chin and rammed her head against his nose. He swore, but he let go of her right wrist and began to claw on her jeans. She twisted her right leg under her and seized a knife from the sheath strapped to her lower leg. As Georges yanked again on her jeans, tearing them open, she raked the tip of her knife down his back. It was not intended as a mortal wound. It was only meant to be bloody and painful and success was instant. To Georges's credit, he choked back his scream, but he let go of Lorelle. She wriggled out from under him and slid between the seats before he could recover.

"I warned you, Georges," she said without a trace of remorse.

"You bitch! You stinking bitch!" he snarled. He staggered after her, but he stumbled over Kon's arm. Realizing that Kon had intentionally tripped him, he leaped at Kon and clutched him by the throat. Kon gasped. Even in his extreme condition he could not endure a hand on his throat.

Despite the pain, Kon tried to push Georges away with his injured hand. Georges seized Kon's hand and slammed it against the side of the van. When Kon let out a cry, Georges panicked. Grabbing his shirt, he jumped on top of Kon and shoved the cloth against Kon's face, forcing it into his mouth. In a vengeful frenzy, he pulled out his cigarette lighter, turned up the wick, and tried to set the shirt on fire.

Kon was cringing on the floor, staring wide-eyed and terrified at the jet of flame shooting from the cigarette lighter when the rear doors of the van were suddenly yanked open.

"What the hell are you doing?" Nicolas demanded as he vaulted into the van.

Georges looked up, but did not answer as Nicolas came up behind him.

"Get off him, Georges!" Nicolas ordered, but again Georges ignored him. "I said, get off him! Are you crazy? What are you trying to do?"

Georges turned and Nicolas saw his wild-eyed expression. He grabbed Georges by the arm, yanked him off Kon, and smacked him in the face with his fist. The flame went out, the lighter went flying, and Georges sank onto the pile of drop cloths.

"Jesus, Georges! You're a maniac!" Nicolas sputtered in disgust.

Edouard pushed past Nicolas and bent over Kon. "Emile, are you O.K.?" He felt for Kon's shoulder and heard him draw in his breath. Edouard found the flashlight and turned it on for a moment before Nicolas hissed, "Shut that off! Close the doors!"

Edouard grunted a half-audible protest, but he scrambled over Georges and pulled the rear doors closed. Quickly he flicked on the light and shone it on Kon. Kon recoiled from the light and raised his splinted hand to protect his head.

"It's O.K., Emile. It's Edouard," Edouard said, and pulled the shirt away from Kon's face.

Kon was panting and shaking, either from the cold or from fear or a combination of both. "Stay away from her," Kon gasped and then he began to mumble incoherently.

"Calm down, Emile. She got away," Edouard said, but Kon remained agitated and kept mumbling.

"Can't you keep him quiet?" Nicolas snapped.

"No! I think he's in shock. Look at him. Georges had that flame so close, he singed part of his hair. Damn it! Nobody is safe around him!"

"Put him to sleep like you did before."

"I think I'll have to. My stuff's in the car."

"Hurry up and get it! I want to move the van. Bring something for Georges's back. Lorelle did quite a job on him."

"He deserves whatever he got!" Edouard said as he slipped between the seats and went out the passenger door.

Edouard realized that Kon was very weak and gave him only a small dose of tranquilizer. Then he removed the fake-fur seat cover from the passenger seat, and worked it under Kon's head and shoulders. He spoke soothingly to Kon, but he saw that touching him only increased his anxiety. After Kon was quiet, Edouard held the light and examined him more closely. He shook his head when he saw the tape fastened around Kon's ankles and used his scissors to cut it off. "Does Georges have the key to these handcuffs?" he asked Nicolas.

"I don't know. I'll take a look," Nicolas said and started going through Georges's pockets. "I can't find it. Michon must have it. He'll never know the difference. He's really out."

"I know, but his wrist is getting chaffed. I'd better stay with him, Nicolas. He's in bad shape."

"You can't stay. You've got to take the car back to Bernon's."

"Who's going to take care of him? He needs some food and water. He hasn't had anything for days! Doesn't anybody understand that? You're treating him like . . ."

"I'll give him some water as soon as he wakes up. O.K.?"

"That's not enough. He needs some food. He doesn't even have a God damn blanket anymore."

"That's not my fault! Where am I supposed to come up with . . . here put one of these over him," Nicolas said, pulling one of the drop cloths free.

"No! That's dirty and . . ."

"Jesus, Edouard, quit griping! It's all we've got. What's he to you anyway?"

"He's a man, Nicolas—a living, breathing person, and he's hurt!"

"O.K.! O.K.! Look, I'll let you know where he is and you can bring him something later. Bring him silk sheets and a God damn seven course meal if you want. Let's just get him somewhere secure before the police are on our backs. Alright?"

"Alright, I'll take the car back, but don't forget to let me know where you take him."

"I won't! I won't! Now see what you can do for Georges."

"O.K. I'll bandage him. I'm sure he's got his own pain pills."

Chapter Seven

Geilla was disappointed that she had not heard from Kon. He hadn't given her a definite idea of how long he would be gone, but he had promised to call her from Paris. She had gone to the Children's Home with Charlotte the first day and had enjoyed playing with the youngsters, but she missed her husband.

She and Kon had moved to a larger apartment as soon as she learned that she was pregnant, and she wanted his opinion about some of the designs she was planning for the nursery. She had discovered that as long as everything in the apartment was functional, Kon didn't voice any objections about what style or color decorations she chose.

Three days after Kon left, Carlin had invited her to lunch. She thought it strange, but she had agreed to go. Carlin was always very polite to her, but Geilla knew he did not approve of Kon's marriage to her. Their relations had been strained at first, but had improved suddenly when Carlin had confirmed her pregnancy. She had begun to see some of the warmth that had so endeared him to Kon.

Carlin had made excuses that he could not take her as a patient and had referred her to a very competent young obstetrician. Kon had been stung by Carlin's attitude. As a rule, he did not trust doctors and did not want a stranger looking after his wife. He was relieved, however, when Carlin assured him that he would personally review everything Dr. Brekke did. Geilla came to see that Carlin had been wise to put someone else in charge of her case, lest his feelings towards her cloud his professional judgment.

When they met for lunch, she could tell from the many questions Carlin asked that he was looking over Dr. Brekke's shoulder. She was experiencing more morning sickness with this child than she had with her first, but so far everything was proceeding normally. Carlin assured her that Peter was probably very busy on his assignment and that she should not take it amiss that he hadn't called. That was just his way, and they had all gotten used to it. She wondered how Carlin knew that Kon had not called, but imagined that he had anticipated Kon's behavior and was trying to make excuses for him.

She enjoyed the lunch, but declined when Carlin suggested that if she was lonely she could go to stay with Charlotte and Edgar. She hoped that Kon would be calling soon and she didn't want him to be greeted by an answering machine. She did call Charlotte, who sympathized with her, but assured her that it was quite normal for Peter to go off and leave everyone in the dark about his whereabouts. Charlotte invited her to come and stay with her and Edgar, but again she declined. She just knew Kon would call soon. Brad always found time to call Mary, no matter how trying the circumstances.

Geilla waited all night for a call, but it never came. In the morning she decided to call Mary and ask as casually as possible if she had heard from Brad. She invented several flip answers to give to Mary to cover her disappointment that Kon had not called. "Kon was obviously not as well trained as Brad", or "Show a man the bright lights of Paris and he soon forgets he has a wife at home." There was no need to cover her disappointment, however, for she never got through to Mary. The woman at the answering service could give Geilla no details other than Mary's stock answer that she was out of town on business and would return the call as soon as possible.

Why had Mary gone on a business trip while Brad was away? Geilla wondered. Mary usually left the buying chores to Nea. Geilla made herself some toast, puttered listlessly around the nursery for a while, and then dashed to deposit her half-digested breakfast in the toilet. The imported red current jelly didn't look as appetizing floating in the bowl as it had when gracing her toast. Here I am alone, throwing up in Geneva, while Kon is running around Paris, she thought. We are going to have to discuss his "house-full-of-children" idea when he gets back.

As soon as her stomach settled down, Geilla put in a call to Nea hoping that she might know where Mary had gone. Nea was not at the shop and the phone was answered by a clerk that Geilla had not met.

"I'm sorry but . . . er . . . Ms. Cortlin isn't here," the clerk stammered. She seemed a bit confused and Geilla became suspicious.

"Can you tell me when she will be back?"

"I don't really know. She left in a hurry."

"Can you tell me where she is? I really must speak to her," Geilla answered in English.

"She had to go to Paris to handle some emergency. She left . . ."

Suddenly the conversation broke off and another voice came on the line, "Who's calling, please?"

Geilla's mind clicked into high gear. "This is the French police calling," she answered, adding a heavy French accent to her voice. "I need to speak to Mademoiselle Cortlin immediately. It's about Monsieur Artier."

"Oh dear, now what? I'm terribly sorry, but Ms. Cortlin has gone to Paris for some emergency."

"Yes, I know about that, but we need to contact Monsieur Artier. Do you know where Mademoiselle Cortlin went in Paris?"

"Oh dear, I'm not supposed to tell anyone."

"Madame!" Geilla responded with official indignation, "I am calling on government business involving Monsieur Cover-Rollins. Please cooperate. Where is Mademoiselle Cortlin?"

"Oh my, just a minute. She left an address is case of an emergency."

"This is that very emergency, Madame. Mademoiselle could be in grave danger."

"Oh my Lord! She is staying at Le Dauphine Hotel, Room 561."

"Thank you, Madame. Please don't tell anyone other than Scotland Yard about this call."

"Oh, of course. Is there anything else I can do to help?"

"No. Just don't mention this call to anyone."

"Oh, I won't. I won't. I promise."

Geilla's hand trembled as she hung up the phone. What's going on in Paris? she wondered. Is there really an emergency? Nea isn't even on the team. I'm going to find out for myself. Maybe I should telephone Carlin and ask if he knows what is going on. No, he probably won't tell me anything and I'll look foolish. I expected Kon to be more open with me, but maybe I am wrong.

She took a shower, which made her feel a little better, then got dressed and packed a bag. She decided to take the train to Paris rather than trust her stomach to behave on an airplane. It was an easy two-hour ride to Paris and many wealthy women in Geneva took the trip just for a day of shopping.

Geilla was not feeling well by the time she arrived at the hotel in Paris. She checked in, casually asking for a room on the fifth floor. She freshened up a bit, called the front desk to verify that Nea actually was registered in Room 561, and asked to be connected. She was not surprised when there was no answer. Adding a crisp British accent to her voice, she called down a second time to complain that the drain in Room 561 was not working properly. About twenty minutes later, she strolled by Room 561 and found the door open. She walked in boldly, holding her fifth floor key in her hand. "Have you located the problem?" she asked the repairman who was bending over the tub.

"No, Mademoiselle, I haven't. I pulled a little bit of hair out of the drain, and it seems to be working fine."

"Well, perhaps I overreacted when the water was slow to go down. I just didn't want to cause a flood at some inconvenient time."

"It's working fine now, so there's nothing to worry about."

"Thank you, Monsieur, you are most kind," Geilla gushed and pressed a tip into the repairman's hand. He looked surprised for a moment, but he took the money and smiled back. She closed the door behind him and sat in the soft chair by the bed. It was almost four o'clock.

It was after nine o'clock when Geilla heard a key in the lock. She jumped and realized that she must have fallen asleep. She didn't know the time, but the room was dark and she knew she had been waiting for a long time. The door closed, but no one turned on the light.

"Can you stay?" she heard Nea ask.

"No. I need to check with Jack," Paul answered.

Geilla heard some rustling and felt embarrassed that she was intruding on Nea and Paul's privacy. She wondered briefly if perhaps the sudden emergency was just a romantic interlude. Well, there is no smooth way out of the situation. Might as well get on with it, she thought and reached for the light switch.

"Hello, Nea. How nice to see you again!"

Nea and Paul both jumped at the sound of her voice. She had expected them to be mildly embarrassed, but they stared at her in absolute disbelief. Finally Paul found his tongue. "Hello, Geilla. What brings you here?"

"I'm sorry to interrupt, but everyone seemed to be coming to Paris for some emergency and I wanted to find out what I was missing. Where's Kon?"

"Kon? Well, he's . . ." Paul began. He looked away from Geilla for a minute "Ah . . . did Carlin say anything . . ."

"No. Carlin hasn't told me anything," Geilla said, suddenly guessing that Paul was hiding something. "Where is Kon, Paul?"

Paul let go of Nea's hand reluctantly and came towards her. "Geilla, Kon's . . . Oh God, Geilla there is no gentle way to say this." He suddenly looked distraught and fear gripped at her. "We don't know where he is. They took him," he continued in an unsteady voice.

"Took him? Who took him?"

Paul looked at Nea for help, but she was mute. "The Direct Action group met us at the station."

"Terrorists! When?"

"Three days ago."

"Three days!" She jumped to her feet. "Paul! I don't understand! Why didn't you tell me?"

Paul hesitated. "I couldn't, Geilla. We didn't know until yesterday if Kon was dead or alive."

"Oh my God! Where are they keeping him? What are you doing about it? Why didn't you tell me, Paul? I was so angry when he didn't call. I thought . . . God forgive me . . ."

"I'm sorry, Geilla. Please believe me," Paul said. He went to her and tried to put his arms around her, but she pulled away. "Leave me alone! I can't believe you kept this from me. You, of all people!"

"Geilla, please. I knew you would be upset. I didn't want you to worry. I was concerned about the baby. If anything happens to you or that baby, Kon would never forgive me."

"But he's my husband, Paul! I have a right to know!" She swayed and Paul steadied her.

"I know. I know. I'm sorry. God, I'm sorry. I thought we would find him before you found out. Come on. Sit down here."

He signaled to Nea who was still standing rigidly at attention.

"How did you find me?" Nea asked, coming forward.

"I called the shop. I told them I was with the police."

"I should have known I couldn't fool you, Geilla, but I was only thinking about the baby," Nea apologized.

"The baby's fine! It's Kon I'm worried about. What do they want with him? When are you going to get him back?"

"It's not that easy, Geilla," Paul responded. "The group is demanding the release of some prisoners and the government is very reluctant to give in. Kon is not a French citizen and our work is being touted as interference with internal affairs."

"What is Brad doing? Can't he bring some pressure to bear?"

"Geilla," Paul began softly, "Brad is in the hospital. Mary is here with him."

Geilla suddenly felt the baby flutter and she winced.

"Geilla, are you all right?" Paul asked quickly. "Nea, get some water."

"How critical is Brad?" Geilla asked after she sipped the water.

"He'll be O.K. He's out of intensive care."

"Oh no . . . poor Mary. Was Jack hurt?"

"No. He's fine. Listen, I'm working with Carl to convince the government to cooperate, but I don't have the personal contacts that Brad does. We have a student who left the group and he's given us a lot to go on. We also captured one of the group at the station."

"What can I do?"

Paul wondered how he could make Geilla see the obvious without hurting her feelings. He looked at Nea for help and this time she read his thoughts.

"Geilla, I think your job is to take care of yourself and the baby. Why don't you get some rest and then, if you feel up to it, you can help me look after Mary."

Geilla suddenly felt tired and useless. She knew Nea was right. Kon would blame her if she did anything to jeopardize the baby. If something went wrong, he would never forgive Paul for not taking care of her. She looked at Paul and saw how careworn he looked. He is closer to Kon than I am in some ways. He must be suffering too, if he asked Nea to come.

"All right, Paul. I'll stay out of your way."

A message from Lorelle was waiting for Mary at the front desk of her hotel. She called the number, but it was only a recording telling her that Lorelle was ready to meet with her and instructing her how to get to the meeting place. Lorelle was obviously very independent and organized and unwilling to go out of her way even to claim an inheritance. She had left Mary the option of choosing the time, however, and Mary chose eleven o'clock the following morning. Keeping her voice crisp and businesslike, she left a description of herself and what she would be wearing. She decided on Allison's blue suit and Aunt Cellia's long strand of pearls.

Mary felt confident that she could identify Lorelle, both from the photo her mother had shown her and from snatches of surveillance videos Paul had played for her. It seemed that Miss Chalandon was very busy, for in addition to attending classes and befriending Trinette, she was wanted for questioning concerning a recent car bombing.

When Mary arrived at Café Vivienne the next morning, all the outdoor tables were occupied, but as a waiter approached and asked if she wanted to sit inside, a man suddenly folded his newspaper and left.

"I'd prefer to sit outside," Mary told the waiter. "I'll take that table, if I may."

The waiter nodded and went to clear the table. Mary followed him. "I'll have coffee and a petite brioche, please." Relax, everything is in place, she told herself as she looked around.

Jack, who was wearing a loud sports shirt and a baseball cap, was seated at the table directly to her right; and Paul, who was wearing a suit and tie and hiding his face behind wire-rim glasses, was seated at a table ahead of her and to her left. Mary put her briefcase by her feet, but kept her handbag in her lap. She gazed expectantly over the rows of white chrysanthemums in white wooden planter boxes that separated the tables of the café from the pedestrians on the walk, but she did not spot Lorelle in the crowd. It was only after Lorelle had passed through the lattice arch of the entranceway that Mary recognized her. She was wearing faded jeans, a once elegant, but now dirty, hand-knit sweater and dark glasses. Her pretty blonde curls were gone and her hair was short and straight. She stalked up to Mary, and with no effort at politeness demanded, "Are you the English attorney?"

"Yes, I am Allison Blackwell," Mary replied with dignity. "Do sit down, Miss Chalandon. This will only take a few minutes, but there are some formalities."

"Like what?"

"Well, for one thing, I will need to see some identification. Then we must discuss the terms of payment."

"I want cash."

"Oh, I'm afraid that's not possible. You are still underage. Do sit down, Miss Chalandon."

Lorelle looked around nervously, but she took the chair across from Mary.

"That's better," Mary said and smiled. "Now, did you bring a driver's license or something that identifies you?"

"A birth certificate," Lorelle replied curtly. Reaching into the pocket of her jeans, she extracted a well-creased piece of paper with a plain black border.

Mary took the paper from her and glanced at it briefly. "Miss Chalandon, I am afraid you will have to come along with me."

"Where to? I don't have all day, you know! I want the money."

"Well, you will have to answer some questions first."

"Questions? Why? I am Henri Chalandon's daughter."

"Oh, there is no doubt about that, my dear, but some people would like to ask you about a car bombing and a kidnapping."

Lorelle's expression never changed, but suddenly she jammed the table against Mary and leaped to her feet. She turned to run, but Jack was behind her immediately and caught her by the arm.

"Let go of me, you big ape!" she shrieked.

Paul hurried forward and was about to seize Lorelle's other arm when suddenly Mary jumped to her feet screaming, "Paul! Behind you!"

Paul whirled around with his gun drawn, but it was too late. A shot rang out, several women screamed, and Jack lurched forward. Lorelle tried to pull away from him, but before she succeeded, Mary was beside her, pressing a Beretta between the knits and purls of her sweater. "Don't even think about it, Lorelle. I would hate to ruin this beautiful handiwork."

Meanwhile, Paul fired, hitting the man with the gun in the arm. A moment later four GIGN agents hurdled over the planter boxes and knocked him to the ground. Seeing that he was down, Paul ran to Jack. Blood was streaming down the sleeve of Jack's brightly colored shirt, but he still had a firm grip on Lorelle.

"Jack! How bad is it?" Paul asked anxiously.

"It's nothing, but you'd better get the girl out of here before Mary blows her away."

Paul signaled and two GIGN agents came to lead Lorelle away.

"Are you all right, Mary?" Paul inquired as soon as Lorelle was gone. "I'm sorry things got so rough!"

"I'm fine. I'm just fine, Paul," Mary responded, trying to sound calm although she looked a little shaken.

"Are you sure?" Paul asked again.

"Yes. I'm fine, really," she repeated.

"Good. Glad to hear it. You'd better give me that thing," Paul continued, nodding at the Beretta Mary still held in her hand. "I didn't expect you to use it, you know. We had the place surrounded."

"Well, you should have told me. I was afraid she might get away. These people have hurt . . ." Mary stopped short and bit her lip. She handed Paul the gun.

"You did very well, Mary. Are you sure you are O.K.?" Paul asked putting his arm around Mary and giving her a friendly hug.

Mary shook her head and smiled bravely. "Yes. I'm O.K. now. You know Brad would be very displeased if I let Lorelle get away."

Paul smiled. They all knew there was hell to pay whenever Brad was "displeased" with anyone on the team. "Yeah, right, Mary. You're liable to get fired. Let me see your shoulder, Jack."

"I told you it's nothing."

"I don't care. Let me see it!"

"Jesus! It's just a . . ."

"Look, I'm in charge now . . ."

"Yeah, and it's starting to go to your . . ."

Paul shot Jack a glance and he stopped short. Jack knew better than to contradict Paul when he had that look in his eye. Although he stood a good six inches taller than Paul, he could not match his speed.

"O.K.!" he started, but Paul had his hand inside his shirt before he finished.

"It's more than a scratch, Jack. I want you to go to the hospital and get patched up."

"Shit! Can't you just put a bandaid on it?"

"No! I don't have time and it can't wait. You'd better go with him, Mary, to see that he behaves. Call me at the police station when you're done."

"You're making a mountain out of a molehill, Paul!" Jack objected.

"That may be, but you're my responsibility now, and I want that wound taken care of," Paul said decisively and hurried away to talk to the men from GIGN.

Jack continued to grumble even after Paul left. "Damn! He always treats me like I was his kid brother!"

"You're his mate, Jack," Mary said, exaggerating her British accent.

"Sure we're mates, but why does he have to be such a pain in the ass about it? Why does he suddenly think I need a nursemaid?"

"Because he's the chief now and you're the only indian he's got left. A commander has to take care of his troops. Brad worries about everyone on the team."

"I still think he's playing big brother. I got enough of that at home. I make my own decisions now."

"Don't let it bother you, Jack. He treats Kon the same way."

"Yeah, but Kon didn't grow up being the little brother. He's not sick of it."

"Just play along with Paul. He's worried sick about Kon."

"Well, so am I!"

"I know. We all are, but we can admit it."

Jack smiled. "Jees, you're right, Mary. I'm glad you're here."

Mary patted Jack's massive arm affectionately. "What have you decided about the hospital?"

"Ah hell! Let's go, before Paul becomes displeased with me," Jack said with a laugh.

Chapter Eight

There was no longer any mystery as to how the Direct Action group had known that Etienne Rubard would be at the train station in Paris. The answer was Detlef Berentson, the young man who had shot Jack. He was carrying German identification papers, and a search of his apartment turned up a wealth of terrorist pamphlets. He also had airline schedules and a railroad timetable with all the connections between Paris and Lyon circled. Under questioning he confessed that he had coordinated a group of students who worked in relays, watching for Rubard at the airline terminal and the railroad station.

Later, Detlef broke down and begged forgiveness for having hurt Jack. He had been living a lonely life of seclusion for over a year and seemed positively relieved to have someone to talk to. He poured out his heart to Paul, occasionally weeping as he told how much he missed his country and his parents. He hated the life he was living, and was tired of hiding from the police.

Detlef Berentson was twenty years old, and the second son of a prosperous family in Hannover. From his earliest years he had absolutely idolized his older brother, Lothar, who was ten years his senior and associated with the notorious Baader-Meinhof gang. When Detlef turned eighteen, Lothar recruited him to lead student demonstrations. Instead of studying his books, Detlef learned to wire explosives. He hated lying to his parents about his activities, but he did whatever Lothar told him to do. At Lothar's bidding he gave up his student friends and followed Lothar to secret meetings and political rallies. Lothar demanded total secrecy and absolute obedience.

Detlef never dared question what his brother was involved in, for fear of revealing his own inexperience and inadequacy. When Detlef's father expressed concern about Detlef's grades, Lothar made excuses that Detlef was helping him in his export business. There was no cause for worry, Lothar told his father. Detlef would always have a secure job with him. Indeed, Detlef thought he had found his place in life until the day he had disappointed Lothar and his friends by losing his nerve while trying to fulfill his initiation requirement.

Detlef had mastered hitting tin cans and bottles with a pistol, but when asked to shoot a police officer, his hands shook so violently, he had not been able to pull the trigger. Worse yet, when Lothar became enraged and shouted for him to fire, he had accidently wounded Lothar.

Lothar had been unrestrained in rebuking Detlef in front of the group, and Detlef was devastated. He fell into a deep depression and dropped out of school. In desperation he stole Lothar's gun and attempted suicide. When he botched the job, he brought forth more acrimonious reproaches from Lothar. Much to the family's relief, Lothar managed to patch Detlef and hide the incident from the police.

Detlef's behavior was incomprehensible to his parents. Lothar had always been strong and capable. They agreed readily when Lothar suggested that Detlef be sent to school in France. Fortunately, Detlef was enough of a scholar to be accepted at the university in Paris. He left home reluctantly, but he was determined to prove to Lothar that he could make something of himself. He was scarcely settled in school, however, before he was contacted by members of Direct Action. Lothar had notified them that Detlef would be a likely candidate for a low-level job with the group. Detlef seized the opportunity to prove to Lothar that he could measure up. He began to steal cars, make bombs, and do surveillance on potential kidnap victims. That was how he had met Lorelle.

When Lorelle learned that Detlef had connections with the Baader-Meinhof group, she was impressed. She was fascinated when Detlef parroted Lothar's rhetoric, and she found him a more pleasant working companion than either Georges or Michon. Soon she was spending an occasional evening at his apartment. Detlef had virtually no friends in Paris and relished his contact with Lorelle. Their working relationship gradually developed into a physical union. It would have surprised Edouard, but at least while she was in Detlef's arms, Lorelle could be very human indeed. There was no commitment on either side, but their relationship gave support to both of them.

Lorelle had been taught to be independent and to expect nothing but grief from men. She was aware of the brutality the men in the Direct Action group exhibited, but she told herself that it was necessary to associate with them in order to bring about changes in society. Women did have a certain equality within the group, but she was more reserved than Catia and believed that true emancipation meant more than the license to sleep with anything even remotely masculine. Although she interpreted Edouard's compassion as a sign of weakness, she found Detlef's non-violent side very appealing. She had no idea of the moral dilemma he suffered because of working with the group.

Detlef had not realized the depth of his feelings for Lorelle until he had seen Jack grab her arm at the café. Suddenly a protective urge drove him to fire at a man for the first time in his life. He apologized profusely for the act and was relieved to learn the Jack had not been seriously injured. As Detlef talked, Paul concluded that Lothar was a savage, domineering tyrant. Although Detlef verbalized allegiance to and admiration for his older brother, Paul guessed that in reality he was scared to death of him. Perhaps Detlef's accidental shooting of Lothar was a form of repressed rebellion.

Detlef asked about Lorelle several times during his talk with Paul, but he refused to reveal anything about her role in the Rubard affair. Paul felt stymied. He could not get Lorelle to talk, and he was convinced that she knew where Kon was being held.

Trinette was beginning to be annoyed by all the protective attention she was getting. Vérèna, the young policewoman who was staying with her, was very nice; but living under her watchful eye was rather like having a nanny again. She wished that Cellia would visit her again so she could ask about Etienne. Trinette suspected that Cellia knew a lot more about what was going on than Vérèna did.

It was early morning and Trinette was rushing to get ready for class. Despite the need to hurry, Vérèna was carefully performing her morning ritual of reciting a series of numbers into a tiny radio. As always, the numbers were answered by static, a garbled voice, and then more numbers. Trinette saw no point in it. She gathered up her books and her sweater, and was tempted to open the door and walk out; but she didn't want to upset Vérèna who took the ritual quite seriously.

Apparently Vérèna thought the numbers foretold a propitious day, for she opened the door and peeked into the hall. No one was lying in wait for them so Vérèna stepped out, followed by Trinette who locked the door. More numbers were exchanged as they went down the stairs and Vérèna cautiously opened the street door. Vérèna was not permitted to recite numbers once they were on the street and Trinette was glad. She was impatient with asking permission for every mundane action in her life.

Vérèna walked to the left of Trinette as they started toward the entrance to the Metro. The weather was unusually cool for the end of September, but the sun was out as Trinette stepped along, full of the vigor of youth. They had gone one block and crossed a side street, when Trinette noticed a young man on a bicycle coming down the sidewalk towards them. Thinking that he was inconsiderate to be on the sidewalk, but expecting him to keep to his right as he passed, Trinette continued her lively pace. She was about to remark to Vérèna about the man's rude behavior, when suddenly he swerved sharply to his left and came straight at them. Reacting quickly, Vérèna pushed Trinette aside, but as the bike pressed between them, the front wheel clipped Vérèna on the leg. Vérèna cried out as she fell, but the biker sped away without stopping.

Trinette was appalled. She stared after the young man for a moment then stooped to help Vérèna. Suddenly a heavy-set man wearing a black ski mask sprang from the back of a battered van parked several feet behind her. Running forwards, he seized Trinette from behind, clamped a hand over her mouth, and began to drag her toward the van. Trinette panicked and began to struggle like a frightened animal, kicking and scratching. Her resistance made it so difficult for him to drag her, that he picked her up, turned around, and began to carry her.

He had gone only a few feet before two plainclothes men who had been following the young women appeared. They fired warning shots into the air and shouted for the man to release Trinette. Before they could reach her, however, a blast of automatic weapons fire roared from the back of the van. One of the policemen was hit, and fell into the street. The other one quickly dodged behind a parked car. He fired a few shots at the man with the automatic who was standing in the door of the van, but he was afraid to fire at the man with the mask for fear of hitting Trinette.

Suddenly Vérèna recovered herself and drew her gun. Taking careful aim, she fired low, hitting the leg of the man holding Trinette. The man staggered and Vérèna fired again. As the man fell, Trinette struggled free.

"Run for cover, Trinette!" Vérèna screamed and Trinette obeyed. She dashed towards the nearest building. Bullets zinged past her and ricochetted off the metal railing as she climbed the staircase leading to the front door. Luckily the door was unlocked and she burst inside. In sheer fright she ran up three flights of stairs before she stopped to catch her breath. She stood in the hall panting, expecting to hear footsteps on the stairs behind her at any minute. Instead, all she heard was Vérèna who was excitedly reciting her litany of numbers. Trinette prayed that Vérèna's absurd numerical supplication would be answered by something other than the usual static.

"Vérèna, are you all right?" she called aloud.

"Stay up there, Trinette!" Vérèna shouted back. "Don't come down, do you hear?"

"Are you all right, Vérèna?" Trinette called again. "Come up with me. I'm afraid alone. Vérèna?"

"I can't. Just stay up there . . . just stay," Vérèna responded faintly.

"No. I'm coming down," Trinette insisted. This time there was no answer from Vérèna. A moment later Trinette ran down the stairs and found Vérèna lying on the floor. Her jacket was stained with blood. "No! Oh God! No!" Trinette moaned. Suddenly she began to scream hysterically and pound on doors. "Help! Help! Open up! For the love of God, somebody help us!"

The terrorist who had been captured during the assault on Rubard had finally been identified. After he had missed several classes at the university, one of his professors finally noticed, and took the trouble to call his parents. The parents had been worried by their son's strange absence and had called the police. The police, in turn, noticed that the description Monsieur and Madame Garday gave of their son, Philippe matched that of the captured terrorist. The Gardays had been driven to the hospital where they identified their son. Although they were shocked by the list of charges against Philippe, they expressed their determination to stand by him.

Jack had pleaded with the Gardays to convince Philippe to cooperate with the team in the kidnapping investigation in exchange for leniency from GIGN. However, either from fear or from loyalty, he would not confess any knowledge of the Direct Action group.

"He still won't talk to me," Jack told Paul when he met him at the hospital. "I've asked his parents to work on him, but they're not having much luck either. It's so damned frustrating!"

"I know. I can't get Lorelle to open up either. Detlef told me all about himself and his brother, but he won't say anything about Direct Action. Someone's got them all scared."

"They might be afraid of retaliation after seeing the way the group went after Rubard for daring to leave the fold."

"I think you're right, Jack. They were all involved in tracking him down. If we can get just one of them to crack, they might all fall in line."

Before Jack could answer, a stocky, middle-aged police officer rushed up to them. "I was down in emergency," he puffed breathlessly. "We just got a call about a kidnap attempt on Trinette Rubard. Three officers were killed, and one suspect and another police officer were severely wounded."

"What about Trinette?" Paul asked quickly.

"Apparently she wasn't hurt. The ambulance has already left, but we could catch them if you want."

"Let's go!" Paul answered. He and Jack ran down the hall after the sweating police officer. Fortunately, the officer was faster behind the wheel than he was on foot, and in less than ten minutes the three of them were tearing past Trinette's apartment building with the siren blaring and lights flashing. The car had barely skidded to a stop before Paul and Jack threw open the doors and leaped out. Two ambulances were parked along the curb, and another police car was stopped in the street.

Several police officers were on duty, and Paul flashed his GIGN I.D. at them as he hurried up. "Martel, from GIGN," he said in a no-nonsense voice. "Where is Trinette Rubard?"

"She's inside," one man answered, pointing to a brick apartment building. "We have a man with her, but she won't come out. She's pretty shaken up."

"O.K., Jack, go talk to her. Tell her you're a friend of Etienne's. Maybe we'll have to let her see her brother," he added quietly. "I'll meet you back at the hospital."

Jack nodded and went up the stairs. Paul turned back to the police officer. "Are you the one working this job?"

"Yes. My name's Davout. Officer Netter and I were tailing Rubard."

"What happened?"

"We were following about a half block behind the women when we saw a guy on a bicycle coming down the sidewalk towards them. Then he swerved right into Vérèna. She's the policewoman who was working the detail. Vérèna fell and Rubard bent down to help her. Before Netter and I got any closer, this big guy wearing a ski mask jumped out of a van and grabbed her. She's a spunky girl and she started kicking and squirming like a she-devil. We ran to help and fired warning shots, but another guy stuck his head out of the van and started blasting away with a little foreign-made automatic. Netter got hit, but I ducked behind a car and called for backup. I tried to hit the guy who had Trinette, but I couldn't get close enough.

"Luckily, the guys were ignoring Vérèna—guess they didn't know she was with the police. Anyway, she managed to hit the big guy in the leg and Trinette got free. She and Vérèna ran for the nearest building, but the guy in the van opened up on them. Vérèna got hit in the back. I took a few shots at the guy with the automatic, but the most I could do was to keep him from getting to the guy on the sidewalk. The big guy was screaming for help, when all of a sudden the guy in the van turned and fired on him. Can you believe it, he just cut him to ribbons? Then he pulled away as cool as could be.

"I signalled for the backup to go after him, but he lobbed a grenade at their car. Two good men . . . blown away, just like that! These bastards really play rough," he continued, shaking his head.

"How is Vérèna?"

"She's alive—I just don't know. There was so much blood . . . She's in the ambulance."

"Where is the guy who grabbed Trinette?"

"They loaded what's left of him on a stretcher. I'll take you over," the officer said, and led the way toward the ambulance. "This guy's from GIGN," he told the ambulance attendant who was about to close the door. "Don't get in his way!"

Paul slipped inside the ambulance and the attendant closed the door. As the vehicle pulled away from the curb, Paul leaned over the stretcher and began searching through the suspect's pockets.

"What's your name?" Paul asked evenly.

The suspect sensed immediately that Paul was not part of the ambulance crew, and gasped, "Nicolas, Nicolas Grenelle."

"Who was it, Nicolas. We'll get him."

"Gérard. The bastard . . . anything to save his own skin."

"Gérard who?"

". . . don't know any other name."

"Where is he, Nicolas?"

". . . don't know. Ask Michon."

Suddenly Paul pulled a watch out of Nicolas's pocket. He felt a wave of nausea as he recognized it as Kon's. The dial was still set on transmit, but the battery was totally spent. Paul felt he was holding a symbol of Kon's fruitless cries for help in the palm of his hand. A strange shiver went down his spine as his anger fought to triumph over his healer's instinct.

"Where is Breaux?" Paul demanded, struggling not to scream at the man who was bleeding to death in front of him.

". . . the apartment," Nicolas mumbled softly.

"What apartment, Nicolas? Where?" Paul asked, leaning closer to Nicolas's face.

". . . three flights up," Nicolas mumbled. "Get Edouard. I need him."

"Where is the apartment, Nicolas? Where?" Paul heard himself plead. He put his hand on Nicolas's shoulder. "Where, Nicolas?"

"Get Edouard, please . . . He can still feel . . . The rest are all dead. God have mercy on me," Nicolas gasped and he was gone.

Hearing Nicolas's prayer, Paul suddenly felt his anger dissipate. It's useless to curse a dead man, he thought, fighting off a crushing sense of frustration. "God have mercy on you, Nicolas. You've got a lot to answer for," he whispered and pressed Nicolas's vacant eyes closed. "And God have mercy on Kon, if the rest are like Gérard."

Lorelle looks different in prison garb, more feminine and perhaps a trifle unsure of herself, Paul thought, as the matron brought Lorelle into the room. Lorelle accepted the cigarette he offered, and he lit it for her using Jack's fake-gold lighter.

"Detlef has been asking about you. Do you have a message for him?" Paul began in a conversational tone.

Lorelle started at the name, but was thoughtfully silent for several moments. "Detlef? I don't know any Detlef."

"Come off it, Lorelle, you know as well as I who Detlef is. He tried to kill my partner to defend you. He told us all about you."

"Really," Lorelle responded calmly, taking a drag on her cigarette. "Then why do you bother me?"

"I thought you might be ready to fill in a few details. You and Detlef are in serious trouble, Lorelle. If you ever want to see him again, I suggest you cooperate."

"I told you, I don't know who you are talking about!" she replied, raising her voice slightly.

Paul sighed. "That's too bad, Lorelle. Detlef is really worried about you."

Lorelle looked away impatiently.

"I admire you for trying to protect the group, Lorelle, but they're not all as kind as Detlef. Did you know they tried to kidnap Trinette? Were you a party to that?"

Lorelle looked up in surprise. "Trinette? Er . . . who's Trinette?" she asked, recovering herself.

"Trinette Rubard, the young girl you befriended. Nicholas is dead, Lorelle! Gérard shot him! Did you know they were planning to kidnap Trinette? Did you betray her friendship? Is that what Direct Action practices, deceit and betrayal?"

"No!" Lorelle objected heatedly. She began puffing furiously on her cigarette. "There is loyalty in the group."

"Loyalty to what? Gérard shot Nicolas to save his own slimy skin!"

"I can't believe anyone would send Gérard to kidnap Trinette. Gérard is . . ."

"Gérard is what? Cruel? Heartless? Do you trust him with a girl like Trinette? Trinette was your friend, Lorelle. She looked up to you. How could you send Gérard after her?"

"I didn't send Gérard! I didn't send anybody after her!"

"Who did, Lorelle? Who wanted to hurt Trinette?"

"I don't know? Why would anyone hurt Trinette? She's just a dupe . . . an innocent little dupe."

"Maybe they wanted to hurt her brother. Maybe they wanted to bring him out of hiding."

"Did they hurt her?"

"What do you care? You don't care about anybody, do you? You didn't care what happened to Etienne. He's in the hospital, Lorelle. I saw what was left of him after your friends got through with him. He nearly bled to death, and he's never going to walk again. Your friends shot my partner in the back! What do you care what Gérard does to Trinette?"

"Stop it!" Lorelle shouted, casting the end of her cigarette to the floor. "I didn't do those things! I didn't know they were going to kidnap Trinette. I swear I would have warned her."

"Warnings aren't enough, Lorelle. You have to take action. Someone called to warn the police to hurry the negotiations for Emile. They said he wasn't going to make it if we didn't hurry. Who called, Lorelle? Who in your organization has even a spark of mercy?"

"You're wrong about us! We don't all like to hurt people. I don't like to hurt people. I tried . . . I tried to help Breaux. I gave him a drink."

"You saw him? When?" Paul asked quickly.

Lorelle suddenly turned away. Paul moved his chair closer to Lorelle's. "Listen to me, Lorelle," he began softly. "I have to negotiate for Breaux. How can I be effective if I don't know whether he is dead or alive?"

116

"You figure it out! That's your job!" Lorelle snapped.

"It's more than my job, Lorelle" Paul said softly. "Breaux is a friend of mine, a very close friend."

Lorelle made no response and Paul leaned closer to her. "I don't think you and Detlef are like the others, Lorelle. I don't believe you like to hurt people. Did you know that Emile Breaux was recently married?"

Lorelle shot Paul a quick glance and then turned away again.

"The wedding was in May. I was his best man."

"I don't care what you were!"

"Maybe not, but it was important to me. I've known Emile and his bride a long time. Did you know she is expecting their first child? Yeah, Emile was so excited about it. She's worried about him, Lorelle. She can't eat. She can't sleep. All the worrying is bad for the baby. She might lose it if we can't find Emile. Is that what you want, Lorelle?"

"No! Stop it!" Lorelle shouted. She put her hand to her face and lowered her voice, "Tell Geilla he's alive. He was calling for her."

"Calling for her? When?"

Lorelle turned her head away again. Very gently Paul put his hand on her arm to encourage her. "I need to know, Lorelle. What am I going to tell Geilla? When did you see Breaux? Where is he?"

Lorelle did not answer and Paul put his hand over hers. "Does Gérard have him? What are they doing to him? Why did someone call to tell us to hurry if he's O.K.? Why, Lorelle? Someone doesn't think he's doing well. Who would know?"

Lorelle pulled her hand away and put it to her mouth as if to hide her words. "It was probably Edouard. The little worm just keeps harping about Breaux being in poor shape. He made me feel guilty."

"Guilty? Guilty about what? Did you hurt Breaux?"

"No! No! It was Georges! He was hitting him. I tried to help him. He was so bruised."

Paul felt a knot in the pit of his stomach and he struggled to keep his voice calm. "When did you last see him?"

"I don't know. I've lost track of time in this damn place!"

"When, Lorelle? You must remember something!"

"It was the night before I was arrested."

117

"Where was he?"

Lorelle was silent.

"Don't try to protect them, Lorelle. Do you want Breaux's death on your conscience?"

"No! He was still alive. He was in the van."

"Where were they taking him?"

"To some apartment. I don't know where it is. I . . . I left the van before . . ."

Paul sensed Lorelle's hesitation. "Why did you leave? What happened?"

Suddenly Lorelle turned away from Paul, and lowered her head. "What happened, Lorelle? Tell me," he said, gently putting his hand on her back.

"It was Georges. That slimy son of a bitch . . . he jumped on me and tried to rape me! I had to get out of there . . ."

Paul dredged his heart for an ounce of sympathy for this girl he felt held the key to Kon's life. "It's O.K. You're safe now," he said and handed her a tissue. She wiped her eyes. "Who else was with Breaux? Where did they take him?" he asked gently after Lorelle had composed herself a bit.

Lorelle covered her face, as if ignoring Paul would make him go away.

"I need to know, Lorelle," Paul said softly.

"I don't know! I don't know! Georges said it was his father's apartment. He was going out of town. I don't know the address. Nobody knew. Georges is weird. I don't trust him. Nobody trusts him."

"And you left Breaux with him?"

"Yes . . . no! When I jumped out of the van I ran down the street and there was Nicolas. Michon had sent him to watch the van. He and Edouard were there."

"Who is Michon?"

"He heads up several of the groups."

"Where can I find him?"

"I don't know. He's everywhere and nowhere. It's not like he was my friend or anything!"

"What's his last name?"

"I don't know that either. Nobody uses last names. Some of us have code names."

"Who is Edouard?"

"He's just a worm, a nothing."

"If he's a nothing, why did Nicolas ask for him when he knew he was dying?"

"Nicolas asked for him?"

"Yes, several times. What does Edouard do in the group?"

"He patches people up. He used to be a medical student before Georges got him hooked on drugs."

"Where can I find him?"

"I don't know. He works at some hospital . . . sweeping floors or something."

"Does he have a last name?"

"Yes, he's too stupid to hide anything. It's Sabasté."

"Do you think he could be the one who called the police about Breaux?"

"Yes. I think he would. He's too weak to be involved in the revolution. He was upset about Breaux. Georges kept saying Breaux was O.K., but . . . he wasn't, you know. I didn't realize how beat up he was. He was . . . he was just lying there . . . like he didn't really understand what was going on."

"You said he was calling for Geilla. When?"

"In the van. He was so thirsty . . . and Georges . . . I gave him a drink. He must have thought I was Geilla. I didn't know he had a wife and a baby. He was just a prisoner, you know, a GIGN agent. I didn't want to think of him as a person, only Edouard made me feel guilty. I didn't want to be a worm like Edouard. Edouard's afraid of Michon. I told Michon to get rid of Edouard, but Michon said he needs Edouard's skills."

"To patch people up?"

"Yes."

"I don't believe you enjoy hurting people, Lorelle. I think you and Detlef are different from the rest. I have to find Edouard and get to Breaux. Is there anything else you can tell me?"

"No."

Paul sighed. "Do you have a message for Detlef?"

119

"No."

"O.K. You know, I might be able to help you if you would cooperate a little more."

"I can't. I just can't."

"O.K." Paul said and signaled to the matron that he was ready to leave. He stood up and shoved his chair away from Lorelle's. She looked at him as if she realized for the first time that he was leaving.

"Paul?"

"Yes."

"Tell Detlef to have courage. I . . . I think of him."

"Is that all?"

Lorelle hesitated and the matron took her arm. "Tell him . . . tell him that if things had been different I think I could have loved him."

"I'll tell him," Paul promised. I wonder if I should tell Geilla that Kon has been calling for her, he thought. I'd better not mention it. Under the circumstances it might only upset her more.

Chapter Nine

Edouard was busy clearing away lunch trays at the hospital when he heard his name being called. "Edouard! Hey, Edouard! These gentlemen want to talk to you." He turned and saw one of the young doctors from the emergency room standing beside two strangers. One was tall and blonde, the other shorter and dark. Noting their grim, official air, his heart froze. That very morning he had snatched more Demerol and some other drugs from the supply cabinet. The stuff was still sitting in his locker along with the duplicate key he had made. Oh God! Someone must have seen me take it, he thought in alarm. I haven't got a prayer if they get their hands on me. Feeling panic sweeping over him, he turned quickly and ran for the door to the stairs.

Jack and Paul saw Edouard's guilty look and scrambled after him. He was ahead of them down three flights of stairs, and as he bolted through the door to the main lobby. Paul was only two yards behind as he chased Edouard through the lobby, but Edouard dodged around a patient in a wheelchair and headed for the door to the parking garage. Edouard charged headlong through the door, tripped over a concrete tire stop, lurched forward, and found himself staring at the front end of a car that was racing through the garage. With a squeal of tires, the car swerved, and Paul yanked Edouard to safety.

"Slow down!" Jack shouted after the car, but the driver raced around the curve and up the ramp without stopping.

Edouard stood trembling from the shock of a near-fatal accident, and his fear of arrest and exposure. His mind seemed to slip out of gear and race blindly in all directions. His emotions varied wildly as Paul and Jack hauled him towards their car and pushed him into the back. Guilt hit him hard, as he hit the seat, and he gave in to an overwhelming desire to confess and make everything right again.

"I'm sorry! I'm sorry I took it! I needed it. I'm not selling the stuff, honest. I just use it myself and . . . maybe to help some friends. I know I shouldn't have taken it, but . . ."

"It's your friends we want to talk about, Edouard," Jack began.

"My friends? What friends? I don't have any friends. They all deserted me when I left school."

"Your terrorist friends, Edouard, the ones that got you started on drugs," Jack continued.

Edouard blanched, but did not answer. "Yeah. We heard it was Georges. Is that right? Or was it Nicolas?" Paul asked.

Edouard still did not answer. He was beside himself with fear. For months he had dreaded being discovered, but he had never visualized it like this. He had always imagined that one of the doctors would find out and tell him what a disgrace he was to his profession. This was different. These men thought he was a terrorist. They associated him with all the bombs and killing he hated. How did they know about Georges and Nicolas? Edouard sat speechless and sweating with fear until at last Paul spoke up.

"There's no use in pretending, Edouard. We know all about your association with Direct Action. We know you're involved in the kidnapping and murder of Emile Breaux."

"Murder! No! He's still alive!" Edouard blurted.

"But he won't be alive for long if he doesn't get help. That's what you said. It was you who called the police, wasn't it?" Paul continued.

Edouard was amazed. These men seemed to know everything about him. They didn't even give him time to confess and save himself. And their version of his involvement with the group made him out to be much worse than he really was.

"What are they doing to Breaux, Edouard? Are they beating him? Was that how he got so bruised?" Jack asked.

"How do you know he's bruised? I never said he was bruised! I only said . . ."

"Did you hit him, Edouard? Is that how he got bruised," Jack asked again.

"No! I didn't hit him!" Edouard objected excitedly. "I didn't hurt him. I didn't mean to. I just gave him some sodium pentothal so he would answer some questions."

"You gave him what!" Jack shouted, grabbing Edouard's arm. "Do you realize you could have killed him? He's drug sensitive, you bastard! Did you even care?"

"Stop! You're breaking my arm!" Edouard wailed. "I didn't want to hurt him, I swear!"

"Shut up! That's what you all say," Jack snapped. "If you're all such God damned pacifists, how come my partner got shot in the back? How come two police officers got blown to kingdom come this morning? How come a young woman . . ."

"I don't know!" Edouard screamed. "I never killed anyone! I was trying to be a doctor. I was trying to help people!"

"Sure, you help people, Edouard. Right into the grave! Christ you make me sick!" Jack snarled and tightened his grip on Edouard's arm.

Edouard cried out, and suddenly Paul put his hand on Jack's arm.

"Let up, Jack. You'll hurt him. Go take a walk around the hospital."

"No! I want to find out what else this little creep . . ."

"Not that way. Get out of the car, Jack," Paul insisted quietly.

Jack shot Paul an angry look. "Jesus, Paul! Don't you care what he did to . . ."

"Get out of the car, Jack. Now," Paul repeated, without raising his voice.

Jack jerked his hand away from Edouard. "What's with you, Paul? I thought you cared about . . ."

"For Christ's sake, Jack!" Paul suddenly hissed. "Don't make this any harder for me. Get out of here until you cool down."

Jack clenched and unclenched his fist twice. "Damn! I'm sorry. You didn't see the look on Trinette's face . . . I'm sorry," he said and stepped out of the car.

Paul put his hand on Edouard's arm and quickly rubbed the area that Jack had been squeezing. Edouard was rigid. "Relax, Edouard. Look, I didn't come here to beat up on you. My name is Paul and I'm with GIGN. I need your help to get Emile back."

"I don't know where he is, I swear."

"Lorelle said you were with him in the van. Where did you take him?"

"I didn't take him anywhere. I had to take the car back."

"Back? Back where?"

Edouard hesitated. He couldn't remember if Paul or Jack had

123

mentioned Michon. They seemed to know everything, but maybe they didn't, he thought. He was torn between his hatred of Michon and his fear of reprisal if he betrayed him.

"Back where?" Paul prodded again. "Did you leave Emile alone in the van with Georges? You know Georges can't be trusted! How could you leave Emile alone with him?"

"I didn't leave him alone."

"Did you know that Nicolas is dead?" Paul asked, abruptly changing the subject.

"Nicolas . . . dead? How?"

"Gérard shot him."

"Gérard? Who is Gérard?"

"You tell me, Edouard. You seem to know a lot of people in the group."

"I don't know those people! I just work on them! I can't believe that Nicolas is dead. He was supposed to call me about Breaux. He said I could come and take care of him. He promised to call me, but he never did."

"So you got worried and called the police."

"Yes. Emile was so weak. I wanted to stay with him, but Nicolas insisted that I take the car back."

"Back where?"

Edouard paused for a moment then shrugged. "Back to Bernon's. I had been working on him."

"Where did Nicolas take the van?"

"I don't know. Nicolas didn't know either. It's Georges' father's apartment. Only Georges knows where it is."

"What's Georges' last name?"

"I don't know. I don't even know if Georges is his real name."

"Listen, Edouard. You've got to help me find that apartment. Emile is still in trouble."

"I don't know where it is! I'm not really part of the group. Nobody tells me anything. They all think I'm a worm! They just call me to patch them up when they get hurt. I tried to help them, but they're killers. I should have refused to help them. I should have let them die!" Edouard sobbed.

Paul put his hand on Edouard's shoulder. "I don't think you could do that, Edouard. I don't think you could refuse to help them."

"They all thought I was weak because I couldn't stand to see them hitting Emile. I should never have helped them. So many of them just went on to hurt more people. I should have let them die."

"It's not your place to judge, Edouard. Doctors are sworn to help people, no matter who they are, or what they have done. You were just doing your duty."

"But I'm not a doctor," Edouard said, looking at Paul and biting his lip. "I didn't finish school. I . . . I. . . I'll never get my license."

"You may not have the papers, Edouard, but you are a healer. I can see it. You care about people. Even Nicolas knew that. He called for you when he realized he was dying."

"Nicolas called for me?"

"Yes."

"Well, why not?" Edouard answered with self-deprecation. "None of them could dare go to a real doctor. They just badgered me to steal things for them."

"It was more than that, Edouard. Nicolas wanted you there for your compassion. He said you were the only one who still had any feelings."

"Huh. That's strange. Nicolas always made fun of me. He acted like I was stupid to want to help people."

"Not at the end, Edouard. He wanted you there because you are still human. You're not a heartless machine like the others. You had the heart to see Emile as a man, not a GIGN agent. I need your help, Edouard. We've got to get Emile out of that apartment before it's too late."

"I can't help you! I told you I don't know where the apartment is. I swear it!"

"O.K.! I believe you. Listen, Edouard. I've got a plan. The next time the kidnappers call to negotiate for Emile, I am going to tell them I want some proof that he is still alive. I'll ask for a tape of him answering some questions."

Edouard shook his head. "It won't work. Emile won't talk to them. They've tried everything. They'll only hurt him."

"That's where you come in, Edouard. Do you think he will talk to you?"

"I'm not sure. He was so far gone when he was in the van he was babbling."

Paul clenched his fist for a moment and then released it. "Babbling? How bad is he, Edouard?"

Edouard looked around nervously.

"I've got to know, Edouard," Paul pressed. "Do you think you can get him to talk?"

"I don't know. I'm not sure. I'm not sure of anything. I'm . . . I'm afraid. If they suspect anything, they'll kill me."

"You've got to try, Edouard. You're Emile's only hope. How does Michon usually contact you?"

Edouard started at the name. So they did know about Michon. What was left to hide?

"He always comes in person. I never really want to go with him, but . . . he threatens me, and I always give in."

"Threatens you? How? What does he say?"

Edouard put his hand to his mouth and bit his knuckles.

"Tell me, Edouard. We have to be ready. I don't want him to hurt you."

Edouard hung his head. He couldn't seem to get away from Paul any more than he could get away from Michon.

Paul sighed. "Tell me, Edouard. I can find out some other way, but I'd rather you told me."

"He threatens to tell my parents that . . . that I'm hooked on drugs. He says he'll tell the police that I steal . . . I don't sell it. Honestly, I don't. I only take what I need for myself and to fix up the ones who get hurt. They beg me for help. I can't stand to see them . . . I only take what I need, honestly."

"How long has this been going on?" Paul asked softly.

"Months. I don't remember. It seems like forever. It's all over now. My parents think I am still in school. I was able to fool them about that, but my father will have a fit when he finds out I've been arrested for stealing drugs."

Edouard suddenly put his head in his hands and his shoulders began to shake. "Oh God! It's the end of everything! I'll never be able to work in a hospital again. I've ruined my life!"

"Listen, Edouard. I can help you with this. I'll get you into a treatment center."

"No. I can't. I just can't face it. I missed a couple of doses once and it was terrible. I thought I was going to die. I can't go through that again."

"It won't be the same next time, Edouard. You won't be alone. I'll help you. If you help me get Emile out, I'll see you through this. If you help me, I can help you. I can work a deal with GIGN for you. I've got the power, Edouard."

"Why? What makes Emile so important to GIGN?"

"This is more than GIGN business, Edouard. Emile is like a brother to me. I'll do whatever it takes to get him out, and I won't forget you if you help me."

Edouard was impressed by Paul's earnestness. He had no doubt that Paul's concern for Emile was genuine, but somehow he was surprised a GIGN agent could have such deep feelings.

"What about my parents?"

"I'll make up a story for them if you can't face them."

"It's too late. My life is ruined."

"It's not too late, Edouard. You're still young. You can start over. Rubard is starting over. He's getting out. You can do it too!"

"Rubard is alive? He made it?"

"Yes. He's got problems, but he's out."

"I'm glad! I'm so glad! I wondered about him. Nobody ever gets out. Nobody!"

"Rubard did it, so can you. I can help you, but we have to get Emile out first."

"O.K. I'll try, but what about my job? How is Michon going to find me?"

"You'll have to keep your job for the time being. I'll tell your boss that you're not the man I'm looking for. Just don't steal any more drugs. Tell Michon you can't risk it for a while."

"How will I know where to contact you if Michon comes?"

"We'll be here, Edouard. We'll be watching you night and day, to see that you don't get hurt."

"You mean, spying on me!"

"It's for your own protection, Edouard. Does Michon know where you live?"

"I don't think so. He's never tracked me down at my apartment, and I moved recently to save money. I don't even have a phone anymore."

"Well, that's one less worry."

Edouard hung his head. At least I no longer have to worry about getting caught by the police, he thought. I hope Paul comes through about talking to my parents. I just can't face them right now.

Paul got out of the car and looked around. Before he could even signal to Jack, who was pacing up and down the walk several car lengths away, Jack had dropped his cigarette and hurried over.

"I'm sorry. I wasn't much help on that one," he offered contritely. "And I'm the one who ribs Kon about having a short fuse."

"It's O.K.," Paul said, looking directly at Jack. "You just softened him up for me to make my pitch. He's nervous, but he has agreed to help us."

"Good. Are you ready to go back in?"

"Yeah. I said I'd tell his boss that he wasn't the guy I was looking for, but I'll have to make up some story if we're going to be hanging around here for a few days."

"Maybe you can get Edouard assigned to the emergency room. I noticed that there's always a lot of people waiting around down there. Nobody would notice one more."

"Good idea, Jack. Let's walk him back in."

A few minutes later, as Jack and Paul accompanied Edouard into the lobby of the hospital, they stepped aside for a nurse who was pushing an elderly man in a wheelchair. Suddenly the man recognized Edouard and called out to him, "Edouard! Hey, Edouard! Guess what? The graft is finally taking! I'm going home today!"

Edouard halted and then smiled weakly. "That's great, Monsieur Le Conté. That's just great!"

"Right, Edouard. I bet you'll get a lot more done with me out of your hair."

"You were no trouble, Monsieur Le Conté. I'm just glad you're feeling better."

The old man smiled up at Edouard then looked at Jack and Paul. "Edouard's a good kid. He's the only one who managed to bring me really hot coffee. The rest of them were either too slow or too damned lazy to bother. Where are you off to, Edouard? Some big medical meeting?"

Edouard was speechless. He stared from Monsieur Le Conté's smiling face to the grim looks on Jack's and Paul's faces, and it was all he could do not to burst into tears. His job wasn't much, but it was the one thing he really liked to do.

Sensing Edouard's mood, Paul finally broke the silence. "That's right, Monsieur Le Conté. Edouard's late for a very important meeting."

"Oh sure . . . didn't mean to hold you up. Well, take care, Edouard."

"Take care, Monsieur Le Conté," Edouard mumbled.

While Jack kept his eye on Edouard, Paul went back to the GIGN office to wait for a call from the kidnappers. He had left instructions that he was to be contacted directly if any calls came, but he was not positive that he could trust the GIGN agents not to try a little negotiating on their own. Although he was putting on a show of confidence in front of Jack, Paul suspected that he was being by-passed by some of the GIGN agents who were aware that he was second in command.

Several of his calls had not been returned, and the GIGN high command was not pressuring the French government to swap Direct Action prisoners for Kon. The fact that he did not know many of the key people on the French team the way Brad did, was a definite handicap. He had promised Edouard that he could arrange a deal with GIGN for him, but he knew he could not deliver it without Brad's influence.

When at last the call came, Paul was surprised that in addition to demanding the release of Direct Action prisoners, the kidnappers were now demanding money. Paul wondered if the kidnappers had found out that Emile was no ordinary GIGN agent. Under other circumstances, Kon's personal wealth alone could make him a target for kidnappers. If Kon had indeed been reduced to babbling, what was he saying? Paul did not betray his fears, however, and stalled the caller by insisting that the kidnappers produce some proof that Emile Breaux was still alive. Paul turned down the caller's offer to send a photograph, and coolly requested a tape of Breaux responding to some personal questions.

Evidently, the caller was upset by Paul's request. He hung up in anger, and Paul was left to pace the room, wondering if he had pushed too hard. He found it hard to keep his voice steady when the kidnapper called back two hours later and agreed to provide a tape.

Paul dictated a series of questions that only Kon could answer and said he would wait to hear when and where he could pick up the tape. He felt drained as he hung up the phone and was glad he was alone in the room. He closed his eyes for a moment and did some deep breathing exercises to relax. He tried to send positive energy to Kon and visualized him surrounded by a powerful protective force, but it wasn't easy to drive out the thought that Kon's life might depend on the courage of a weak-willed, pill-popping kid.

Once the request for a tape had been made, Paul knew that Michon might show up at the hospital at any time, and he needed to arrange more surveillance of Edouard. Although the GIGN high command had rebuffed several of Paul's requests for help, the local police had been very cooperative. It was their ranks that had to bear the brunt of most of the terrorist attacks, and the two men they had lost that morning were not their first casualties. Police headquarters quickly agreed to put two unmarked cars with crews on surveillance detail at the hospital. Initially, they were eager to nab Michon as soon as he showed up; but after some persuasion from Paul, they agreed to hold out for more arrests.

After Paul talked to the police, he drove back to the hospital to coordinate schedules with Jack and Edouard. In an effort to make it easier for Michon to find Edouard, Paul had persuaded the hospital administrator to keep Edouard on the day shift in the emergency room until further notice. Paul hung around at the hospital with Jack, but by the time Edouard's shift ended, Michon had not shown up.

Jack looked tired, so Paul sent him back to the hotel to get some rest, while he drove Edouard home, stopping only to pick up a few groceries. He was glad to see the unmarked police car following at a discreet distance behind them. Aware that his energy reserve was hitting empty, he was grateful for some fresh bodies on the scene.

Edouard lived alone in a small, but clean apartment on the third floor of a building whose glory had long ago passed into history. The tiny rooms might have felt cramped if Edouard had not hung the walls with oil paintings, watercolors, and cheap posters of pastoral scenes. Everywhere the eye looked there were snatches of brightly colored flowers peeping from under bushes, expanses of water, or forests of painted trees. One could almost smell the images of clean earth rather than the reality of moldy wallpaper. The effect was soothing, and Paul let his tired senses soak it in, thinking how artistic and personal the apartment was compared to the filth of the one where Kon had been held.

"You have an interesting collection, Edouard. Did you do any of these?"

"Me? No. I just picked them up at flea markets and such. I guess they remind me of home. I didn't grow up in the city, and I have a hard time adjusting to it. I'm used to more space, but what the hell, it's cheap. Look them over while I get some food started."

"Can I give you a hand with anything? I didn't mean to make you do all the work."

"I guess not," Edouard responded. "This kitchenette is hardly big enough for me."

After a few minutes, Paul thought he heard Edouard talking to someone, and his attention was drawn away from the paintings. He looked in the kitchenette and saw three cats of mixed breeds circling persistently around Edouard's legs. Paul grinned. "Did you pick them up at the flea market too?"

"No. They just sort of came with the place. I left my window open one night and they wandered in off the fire escape. Come on, you guys, let me get to the stove," Edouard concluded in exasperation as he stepped over a grey cat.

Paul stooped and tried to attract the cats' attention, but they ignored him. "Do they have names?" he asked.

"You mean other than 'kitty'? No, but here," Edouard said, handing Paul a large can of cat food and a can opener, "if you put some of this in their bowls under the counter there, they'll be your friends for life."

"O.K.," Paul answered, starting to work on the can. "Here, kitty, kitty, and kitty—leave the chef alone so he can fix dinner."

The cats were stretched out, looking fat and content by the time

Edouard carried the meal for Paul and himself out to the coffee table by the couch. Paul felt too played out to eat, but he toyed with his food and complimented Edouard on his cooking.

"I guess you're set on guarding me tonight, huh?" Edouard asked, after they had finished eating.

Paul nodded. "I've got a lot riding on you, Edouard."

"Well, if I'm stuck with you, don't get in my way," Edouard said gruffly. Then remembering that Paul was a GIGN agent who could haul him off to prison, he added, "You can sleep here on the couch if you want."

"Thanks," Paul responded, ignoring Edouard's rudeness.

Edouard sighed. "You know, I'm not really looking forward to dealing with Michon tomorrow. He's sneaky, you know what I mean? Every time he comes, he starts by telling me how much he needs my help, then he starts with the threats, and then he makes me feel bad that people are suffering. I wish I'd never gotten involved with him. I wish I'd never listened to his lies. Shit! I sound like a jilted lover or something. I sure have made a mess of my life."

"Don't worry about it now, Edouard. Let's just take it one step at a time."

"That's what Nicolas said, and look what happened to him! When the hell will it be time to stop and think? I can't go on like this. I don't know where I'm heading. I'll never make it in prison."

"Stop worrying about prison. I told you I can work a deal for you. After we get Emile out, we can discuss it. Just don't make any changes in your routine right now that might alert Michon or the others."

"O.K. O.K. Say, I could use a glass of wine. How about you?"

Paul knew that the last thing his stomach needed right then was alcohol, but he didn't want to discourage Edouard's friendliness.

"Sounds great! What have you got?" he asked with forced eagerness.

"Not a very big selection," Edouard said, going into the kitchen. He rummaged in the cupboard and came back with a bottle of red wine and two elegant long-stemmed glasses.

"My mother sent me these. She must think I'm some sort of Romeo. What girl wants to go out with a guy who sweeps floors?

132

That's all anyone thinks I do. They don't understand . . ."

Edouard poured wine for Paul and himself and sat back on the couch. "This wine's not great, but hell, I can't afford to be a connoisseur like my father. He's got a cellar you could get lost in. Christ! I hope you can deal with him. He and I . . ."

Paul took up his glass, but as he sat back and crossed his legs, his foot knocked over a plate that had been sitting perilously close to the edge. He sat up abruptly.

"Shit! I'm sorry, Edouard!" he apologized. "How clumsy can you get? Have you got a sponge or a cloth I can use?" He leaned over the table and picked up the plate.

"Right!" Edouard answered and shot into the kitchen leaving his wine goblet on the coffee table.

Paul straightened up as Edouard returned with a wet cloth. "Jees! What a slob I am. Here, let me do that!" Paul said, grabbing the cloth from Edouard and dabbing at an imaginary stain on the rug. "Gee, I feel bad about this! How about if I clean the dishes to make it up. You just sit and drink your wine."

"It's no big deal, but O.K." Edouard agreed.

Edouard settled back on the couch and sipped his wine, and Paul gathered the remaining plates and carried them into the kitchenette.

"Is it hot in here?" Edouard called a few minutes later. "I'd better open . . ." He tried to rise from the couch, but slipped quietly to the floor. Paul hurried from the kitchenette.

"Edouard? Are you O.K.?" he asked for effect, already knowing the answer. He leaned over and confirmed that Edouard was out.

"Sorry to end the evening so early, Edouard, but I've got a lot to do; and I don't trust the locals to keep tabs on you tonight."

Paul felt his muscles quivering from fatigue as he lifted Edouard and carried him into the one tiny bedroom. He laid Edouard on the bed, searched his pockets as he undressed him, and carefully hung his clothes. Edouard didn't make a sound as Paul rolled him under the covers. "Sleep tight, Edouard. I'll be needing you tomorrow," Paul mumbled.

Paul made a quick search of Edouard's bedroom and turned up a half dozen full bottles of Demerol, and stashes of partly-used bottles of other drugs that Edouard had stolen. He has a varied collection,

Paul thought, but he's strictly small time. It's a shame he let himself be pulled in deeper and deeper over such a stupid habit. If only he had been given a little help earlier on, he would never have gotten so messed up. Edouard's just one more kid with nowhere to turn.

Paul glanced at his watch and saw that it was almost eight o'clock. I'd better hurry, he thought. I wish Edouard had wanted coffee instead of wine. Paul hurried out of the apartment locking the door with Edouard's key. He stopped at the unmarked police car just long enough to tell the police to keep an eye on the fire escape. He did not want Edouard to be trapped if the old building caught on fire while he was gone. It's stupid to worry about such things, Paul told himself, but I can't afford to have anyone else get hurt.

Paul drove to the hospital to check on Brad. He knew Mary would be there, but damn it, he was in charge and it was his duty to keep everyone cheerful and calm. When he arrived, he was disappointed to learn that Brad was already asleep. He felt the need to discuss the recent developments of the kidnapping with him and get his advice. Brad always used the members of his team as a sounding board before making decisions. Unfortunately, the team was in disarray at the moment and Paul was forced to make critical decisions without their input. Well, Mary has not criticized the way I am handling things and neither has Jack, he thought. Jack knows how to follow orders, but you can count on him to speak up if he thinks you're doing something stupid.

Although Paul had not intended to stay at the hospital for long, he found himself following Mary to the visitor's lounge where she brewed him some tea, apologizing for the lack of milk. Then he sat and patiently answered all her questions, truthfully or otherwise. Yes, I have eaten. No, I'm not really tired. Yes, Jack is O.K. I sent him back to the hotel to rest. Yes, we finally got some information out of Lorelle. Yes, we are definitely getting close to finding Kon. Yes, I will get some rest. Yes, soon. Yes, I would appreciate it if you would call Geilla and tell her I am coming over.

He was glad to see that Mary's confidence in him was not waning, and hoped Brad would agree.

Paul's next drive was back to the hotel to visit Geilla. She had been so upset about Kon being kidnapped that she was having increased problems with her pregnancy. When she refused to return to Geneva to see her own doctor, Mary had notified Carlin. He admitted that he knew Kon was missing, and insisted on coming to Paris immediately. When he arrived, he diagnosed Geilla's cramping and spotting as serious problems and ordered complete bed rest.

Paul was not particularly eager to face her now, but he felt it was his duty to keep her posted. He rapped quietly on Geilla's door and was surprised when she opened it herself.

"I'm sorry to get you out of bed, Geilla. I . . . er . . . I thought Nea was staying with you."

"She was, but I sent her to get some rest. Come in, Paul."

"Oh," Paul answered, trying not to let the tone of his voice betray the keen disappointment he felt.

"Nea has been running herself ragged trying to look after me and keep Mary company. Where's Jack tonight?"

"I sent him back to get some sleep. I think his arm was bothering him. He was really dragging."

"You look tired too. Shall I send for some tea?"

"No thanks. I had some with Mary."

"How is she holding up? She didn't say much when she called."

"She's fine. Mary's always fine. Brad is doing much better. He was asleep when I got there. How are you?"

"Still a bit tired. I . . . I just can't sleep, Paul," she said, suddenly letting her feelings show. "Have there been any new developments?"

"Yes. I think we are definitely getting closer. I talked to someone who saw Kon recently," he said trying to sound hopeful.

"Someone saw him! Where? Who was it? Can I talk to them? How is Kon?"

"I can't tell you much, only that he is alive," Paul answered evasively. He did not believe it would be wise to let Geilla talk to Lorelle. He was doing his best to make Lorelle see Kon as a person, but he did not want to lay too much guilt on her. She was quite vulnerable now that she was isolated, and too much guilt might drive her to desperation. She was a backup if the situation with Edouard did not work out, and he did not want to lose her.

"But where is Kon?" Geilla blurted.

"We still don't know," Paul confessed.

"How much longer, Paul?"

"I'm sorry, Geilla. I just don't know."

She was silent and he felt powerless. He went to her and put his hands on her shoulders. He wished desperately that he could find words to tell her he understood exactly how she felt. He began to massage her back, using his hands to express what he could not put into words. He leaned to kiss her, and suddenly he realized that things had changed. All those years, when Kon was off chasing some other woman, Geilla had come to him for consolation. He had been able to give it then. He had comforted her, and caressed her, and yes, he had made love to her, gently, tenderly. He had been close to her without barriers, because he had no fear of involvement. He was just a substitute. She was in love with Kon.

Now she was Kon's wife. It would not be right for him to touch her that way. He had fooled everyone into thinking that he did not need anyone. He had almost convinced himself. He disciplined himself to be strong and give to others, but he had not realized that his giving was a circle. Comforting and helping others was a way of receiving. Now that he could no longer do that for Geilla, he would never be as close to her. He felt apart from her and it saddened him. If he could not comfort her, how would he release the pain he felt, fearing that Kon was being brutalized by Gérard. It was a struggle, but he settled on giving Geilla a fatherly kiss on her forehead. It was a gesture of support and he would not be ashamed to do it in Kon's presence.

"I'll get him back, Geilla," he assured her. "No matter what it takes, I swear I'll get him back."

"I know you will, Paul. I'm sorry. I didn't mean to burden you. You really should get some rest."

"I will. I will. I just have one more stop."

Geilla took his hand in hers. "What would we do without you, Paul? You give us all strength and courage."

The glare from the headlights of oncoming cars was bothering Paul's eyes. He was driving slowly, carefully, trying not to lose his way as he searched for the hospital where Vérèna had been taken. If this run of bad luck keeps up, I'll know the layout of every hospital in Paris, he thought bitterly as he pulled into the parking lot.

The hospital seemed quiet and deserted as he rode up in the elevator. He flashed his GIGN identification at the nurse in the intensive care unit, but she wasn't very cooperative. He wondered if anyone from GIGN had been in earlier. There was no telling what they were doing behind his back. He thought of pushing his way past the nurse, but he didn't know exactly where Vérèna was. He was spared from causing a row by the timely arrival of Officer Davout who had been at the scene of the shooting early that morning.

"It's Martel, isn't it?" Davout asked as he recognized Paul.

"Yes. How is Vérèna?"

Davout wiped his face and shook his head wearily. "I don't know. Nobody knows. She's plugged into all these machines . . . The poor kid, she's just lying there."

"Can I see her?"

"You want to go in? Sure. Some people can't . . . Well, I guess you've seen a few things in your business. Come on. Her mother's with her."

Davout turned and Paul followed him into Vérèna's room. Paul took one quick look and froze. The pale, lifeless figure on the bed was a graphic reminder of Gérard's brutality and it sickened him. He forced himself to go closer. He didn't want Vérèna's mother or Davout to think the sight repulsed him. It was only his feeling of helplessness that weighed on him. He said a mental prayer, realizing his calm emotional shield was wearing dangerously thin. He turned, wanting to rush away, but he saw that Vérèna's mother was watching him.

"Do you work with Vérèna?" she asked quietly.

Paul felt a lump in his throat. He stooped over the woman in the chair and impulsively took her right hand in his. "Yes," he lied. "She is very smart and very brave. You can be proud."

He prayed she would not ask him anything else, or notice how unsteady his hands were.

She placed her left hand over his hand and he felt her maternal kindness wash over him. "I'm glad Vérèna works with such caring people. The work is so rough. I worry she might . . ."

"It hasn't hardened her. She was defending another young girl."

The woman nodded her head. "Thank you. I'll stay with her. You must have a lot to do."

"Yes," Paul mumbled, and withdrawing his hand, he turned and left.

As he came into the hall Officer Davout glanced at him for a moment, then held out a roll of stomach tablets. "Help yourself."

Paul shook his head vaguely.

"Go ahead," Davout encouraged.

"Thanks," Paul muttered, taking the roll and counting out three tablets. "I've been on the run so much . . ." his voice trailed off.

"It's too hard, you know," Davout responded.

"What's that?" Paul asked absently.

"It's too hard to pretend it doesn't get to you . . . a young girl like that, all shot up. Makes a man want to cry."

"Yeah. Well that won't help her, will it?"

"I guess not, but it's not good to keep it all bottled up. Did you get anything out of that guy in the ambulance?"

"A couple of names."

"There's more to this than that kidnap attempt this morning, isn't there?"

"Yes. A lot more."

"How could anyone shoot a young girl like that? Those people are animals!"

"The bastards kidnapped my partner!" Paul blurted suddenly.

"No! Where are they holding him?"

"I wish to God I knew," Paul answered and immediately felt ashamed that he had let a total stranger see his anguish.

"It's rough. Believe me, I know," Davout responded sincerely. "Say, do you need a ride home or anything?"

"No, thanks," Paul answered numbly. "I've got a car."

"Why don't you go on home? Her mother is here. We can't really do anything for her."

"You're right. I can't seem to do anything for anyone tonight. Thanks for the tablets."

"Get some sleep, Martel!" Officer Davout called as Paul tread slowly down the hall.

Paul drove back to Edouard's apartment in a mental fog, circling past the building three times before he spotted the number. As he got out of the car, he noticed the unmarked police car, and wondered how he could have missed it so many times. At least the place hasn't burned down while I was gone, he thought as he went in. Taking the rickety lift to Edouard's floor, he let himself into the apartment and found Edouard sound asleep as he had left him.

Paul closed the door of Edouard's bedroom and went into the kitchen. He gave the counter a perfunctory wipe, piled the dishes in the sink, squirted in some dish soap, and filled the sink with hot water. He reached into the soapy water, and suddenly felt the room sway. He clutched the edge of the sink to steady himself. To hell with this, he thought. I've got to get flat right now. He stumbled toward the couch, startled two cats, and sank into the softness without removing his coat or his holster. I hope this place doesn't come with roaches as well as cats, he thought as sleep overcame him.

Paul awoke early the next morning. He no longer was as dead tired; but as he pulled himself off the couch, he felt a crick in his back and questioned whether the sleep had been worth the pain. He staggered into the kitchenette and searched the cupboards for coffee. As the dark liquid dripped slowly through the filter, Paul rinsed the soap from the well-soaked dishes. He opened the window and leaned out. He could not see the police car and wondered if they were still on duty.

Then he sat quietly, focusing his mind inward. Moments of calmness had been few and far between lately, and he relished this brief break. Mentally he repeated an affirmation that Kon was alive and well and then went to wake Edouard.

As soon as Edouard saw Paul standing by his bed, he guessed what had happened, and he was angry. "You sneaky son of a bitch!" he growled. "Is that what they teach you at GIGN?"

Paul grinned. He had been given that appellation more than once. "No. It's something I developed on my own. It's quick and safe, with no groggy after effect."

"I don't feel groggy, I feel manipulated! Are you trying to get back at me for giving Emile pentothal? I told you I didn't want to do it! How was I to know . . ."

"Hey, calm down, Edouard. It was a necessary precaution."

"Necessary? From whose point of view? You're as bad as Michon! You're just using me the way he does. Why should I cooperate with you? I agreed to help you. I let you in here . . . Shit! I even fixed you a meal and you tricked me."

"Oh, come on, Edouard. No harm was done. I was just too damned tired to watch you last night. You know, I could have locked you in a cell at the police station so I could get a good night's sleep. I'm trying to get you out of this mess, Edouard. You'll just have to trust me."

Edouard looked uncertain, but Paul continued to smile at him. "Come on, Edouard. I made some coffee. You said you wanted to help Emile. Well, this is your opportunity. If you'll help him, I'll help you."

"And if I don't help you, I'll go to prison. Some choice!"

"That's life, Edouard. You're in serious trouble, and I'm offering you a way out."

"All right. I'll do it your way."

"Good! How do you like your coffee?"

"Light . . . no sugar."

Paul drank coffee with Edouard then waited while Edouard showered and got ready for work.

"Are you going to clean up?" Edouard asked after he was dressed.

"Maybe later. I've got to get you to work and check in at GIGN. What's the matter?" Paul asked, when Edouard shook his head.

Edouard shrugged. "Nothing. You just look kind of rumpled, that's all."

Paul gave a half-hearted brush to his suit coat. "It will have to do," he grunted. "Let's go."

Although it was still early, Jack was already on duty when Paul arrived at the hospital with Edouard. He looked wide awake and fresh in his clean white uniform.

"Hey, Jack! You look great in that outfit," Paul commented. "Where did you come up with one that was big enough?"

Jack grinned. "Mary got it at the hospital where Brad is. I should have asked her to find something for you. You look awful, Paul. Did you spend the night under a rock?"

"That's about the way I feel. I've got the worst kink in my back," Paul responded. "I guess I don't look very fresh either."

"Fresh! Hell! You could scare Wolfman with that beard."

"O.K.! O.K.! I get the message. Can you handle things while I get cleaned up?"

"Sure. Take your time. The police are here in force and I plan to be Edouard's assistant today. I won't let him out of my sight."

"Great! I'll go back to the hotel."

Paul drove back to the hotel, thinking about letting hot water pelt on his stiff back. As he stepped out of the elevator, he was surprised to see Nea in the hall.

Suddenly he felt embarrassed about how grubby he looked. Why should that bother me now? he wondered. "Er . . . Good morning, Nea. How are you? Mary and Geilla aren't keeping you too busy, are they?" he asked.

"Good morning, Paul," Nea responded with a laugh. "It is Paul, isn't it, behind that beard?"

Paul ran his hand across his chin. "Come on, I don't look that bad, do I?"

"Have you checked in the mirror? You look as though you slept in a doorway."

"It wasn't a doorway. It was a dilapidated couch. I think some cats sleep there when I'm not in residence."

"So, am I to believe that all that hair on your suit is feline? In that case, could you use some help cleaning it off? I have a lint brush in my room." Nea reached out and gently brushed Paul's jacket letting her fingers linger lightly on the sleeve.

"That sounds like fun, but I'm in a hurry. I don't want to leave Jack alone on the job."

"Jack will call if he needs you," Nea answered stepping closer to him. She put her hand on his chest. "Maybe I could help you find a clean shirt."

Paul smiled and hesitated. "Well . . . er . . . you could come in and talk to me while I'm getting ready."

Nea sat on Paul's bed while he stripped off his crumpled suit. "Can

141

you spare a few minutes, if I have some coffee sent up?"

Paul hesitated. "Sure," he drawled. "I'm sorry, Nea. I'm always running out on you, but . . ."

"I understand. Go ahead. Take your shower. Need someone to wash your back?"

Shit! Paul thought. I must really be out of sync. Why can't this happen when I have more time? "I . . . er . . . I'm afraid it could end up taking longer if you helped," he answered.

"O.K. I'll just order coffee then."

"Fine. Fine," he said aloud. Damn, what a poor second choice! I must have rocks in my head, he mused.

Paul turned and stepped into the bathroom, and a moment later Nea heard the buzz of an electric shaver. She picked up the phone and made sounds as if she was ordering coffee. As she heard the water running in the shower, she slipped off her shoes.

When Paul stepped out of the shower a short time later, he could not suppress a smile. There stood Nea draped in a towel, her glorious auburn mane flowing down onto her creamy smooth shoulders. Her smile silently offered him much more than the snowy white towel she held out to him. "Well, I sure can't fault this place for poor room service!" he remarked with obvious admiration.

"I know you want to check on Jack, but I'm just following orders," Nea purred.

"Orders?" Paul said in surprise. "From whom?"

"From your one last indian."

"My what?"

"Your one last indian. He said to tell you he was sorry he screwed up yesterday. I'm not supposed to let you out of here until the kink in your back is gone."

Paul laughed. "That son of a bitch! So it wasn't a coincidence that you were coming down the hall when I arrived!"

"That's right, big brother."

"Big brother? Wait 'til . . ."

"Uh ah, not now! Face down on the bed! Show me this notorious kink!"

"All right, I guess Jack can watch Edouard as well as I can," Paul laughed and threw himself on the bed. "It's right here," he said, trying to reach the area below his right shoulder. "Does all of Paris know my ailments?"

"Only those who care," Nea said softly, pressing her long fingers into his back.

Care? As in worry about? he thought, his mind focusing on her choice of words. His mental alarm went off. Uh oh! Attachment! This is getting out of hand. I don't want involvement. Nea understands that. She's very independent. I just want . . . a back rub . . . God, that feels good! Nea has the most wonderful hands! Must be from all that work with clay. Lucky little pots, to have Nea working on them, shaping them, caressing them, kissing them. Kissing them? Oh this is good. This is way beyond clinical. This is so good, it could become a habit.

I'll have to back off from Nea. Even Jack is starting to notice how often I've been seeing her, and he can be pretty dense sometimes. I can't afford to get carried away. I don't want to get trapped into any more emotional responsibilities. Falling in love is for men like Kon, who want stability and children and all that other stuff. Not me! Hell! I have enough to worry about. I'll have to keep my distance from Nea, sort of taper off.

Suddenly Nea leaned to kiss the area she had been massaging, and he felt her breasts, soft as clouds against his back. Oh God, why does she have to be so damn good at this. Nobody ever did this for me—nobody. Women always want me to make them feel good . . . all that crap about my strong hands. This is just too good.

"I see you got your training at the old 'Kiss it and make it better school'," he said dreamily.

"Any objections?"

"None at all. Absolutely none at all."

"How's the kink?"

"What kink?"

He turned and gently pulled her down against him, his energy restored by the pleasure of her closeness. This is all I want, he thought, this wonderful sensation of being totally alive. No attachments. She understands that. That's why we get along. Even when we're not in bed, we get along. She doesn't draw energy from me. She has so much of her own. Boy, does she ever!

Chapter Ten

Despite the temptation, Paul did not linger long with Nea. He appreciated the fact that she understood that his job and his responsibilities came first. She didn't need to be catered to. That was a definite plus in her favor.

Jack did not comment, but he noticed that Paul looked less harried when he appeared in the emergency room. Paul maintained such a cool exterior, it was hard to tell when he was feeling stressed. Jack had learned to read the signs, however, a less fluid walk and a few tiny lines around Paul's mouth. You had to tread very carefully in order to help Paul. He would feel like a failure if anyone noticed he was not totally self-contained.

Paul was sitting in the patient waiting area, and Jack was helping Edouard dispose of some bloody dressing when a nervous-looking man, with thin, slicked-back hair approached. Edouard shot Jack a worried look, and Jack guessed that the stranger was Michon.

"I need to see you," the man said in a voice that allowed no argument.

Jack knew that for better or worse, the time had come for Edouard to play his part. "Go ahead, Edouard. I'll see you after lunch," he said quickly. He took the plastic tray from Edouard and turned away as if being interrupted was an everyday occurrence.

"You've got to stop coming here," Edouard began, but Michon grabbed his arm and pulled him into the hall.

"I need you, Edouard. Now, shut up and get your little bag!" Michon hissed.

"It's about Breaux, isn't it? What's happened? Where is he? Nicolas never called me."

"Never mind! Just get your stuff!" Michon ordered.

"O.K.! O.K.!" Edouard answered, torn between his fear of Michon and his concern for Emile. "I should bring some juice. Did you feed him anything?"

Michon didn't answer.

"I knew it! None of you give a damn about Emile! He's just a pawn. You . . ."

"Shut up, Edouard! Hurry up and get your stuff together!"

"All right. We can go through the kitchen on our way out."

Edouard stopped by his locker and gathered a few things. Now that he knew Emile was drug sensitive, he was afraid to give him anything. He didn't have much left in his locker anyway, since Paul had confiscated all the stuff he had stolen the day before. He felt squeezed between Paul and Michon. They were both forceful and strong-willed, and he felt like a puppet. After he got his bag, Edouard led Michon through the hospital kitchen where he slipped a few small cartons of juice into his bag.

Edouard's anxiety increased as he left the hospital. He wondered if Paul would be able to fulfill his promise of protection. Michon led him several blocks away from the hospital and he scanned the curb for Georges' dark blue Renault. He was surprised when Michon unlocked the door to a sleek, white Mercedes.

"Where did you get this?"

Michon smirked at Edouard's surprised look. "Georges' father. Get in the back, on the floor."

Edouard was alarmed. "What's up, Michon. Where are we going?"

"Never mind. Just get in!"

"Why the secrecy? You never . . ."

"Things have changed, Edouard," Michon answered coldly.

Lorelle must have said something to Michon about me, Edouard thought wildly. He looked over his shoulder nervously as he got in, and was disheartened that he did not see Paul. Maybe Paul was all talk, he thought fleetingly.

"Lorelle has disappeared," Michon said as he started the car. "Have you seen her?"

"Not since she ran out of the van."

"Did she mention where she was going?"

"No. Why would she tell me anything? She can't stand me."

"I don't like it when people disappear," Michon concluded.

Michon seemed to be driving for a long time, and Edouard felt nervous. He tried to remember the turns, but he soon got confused. Several times it seemed to him that Michon was deliberately driving in circles. He worried that he would not be able to tell Paul where the apartment was located. He worried that Michon had spotted Paul following them and was trying to throw him off, and he worried that Paul wasn't following at all. He lay face down on the floor, clutching his bag with both hands. Michon saw me with Jack, he thought. Maybe he suspects something. Oh my God! Maybe we're not going to Georges' father's apartment. Someone killed Nicolas. Maybe I'm next! He felt his anxiety rising to the level of panic.

After what seemed like an eternity, the car made a sharp right turn and a moment later it stopped. When Edouard got out as ordered, he saw that they were in an underground parking garage. He felt more vulnerable than ever as he followed Michon from the car. Well, Michon had said he needed him, that was some protection. Looking around quickly, he did not see the battered green van, but decided he'd better not ask where it was.

Michon opened the door next to the elevator and led the way to the third floor. No one else was using the stairs, and Edouard figured it was highly probable that no one ever did. This building was definitely not cheap student housing. Michon paused cautiously as he opened the door to the wide hall, but the elegantly-carpeted corridor was empty. Suddenly Edouard realized how conspicuous he looked in his crisp white uniform. No one who can afford to live in this building has to do the type of work I do, he thought.

Leaving Edouard concealed on the landing, Michon slipped down the hall and rapped quickly on one of the doors. It opened a crack, and Michon beckoned to Edouard. Edouard took a quick glance up and down the hall and hurried forward. As he reached the apartment, someone yanked him inside. The door closed and Edouard stood face-to-face with Georges' malicious smile.

"So our great white healer has arrived!" Georges jeered.

"Back off, Georges!" Michon ordered. "You haven't produced anything for all your efforts."

Suddenly Edouard wished he had taken something to calm himself. "Where is Breaux?" he heard himself ask in a strained voice.

"He's over here," Michon answered then added curtly, "Get out of his way, Georges! Let him get on with it!"

Michon shoved Georges aside, and Edouard got his first glimpse of the apartment. He realized that the three of them were standing in a large, wood-panelled entrance way. An ornate wrought iron chandelier, hanging from the high ceiling, was only partially successful in dispelling the somber atmosphere of the windowless room. Edouard wondered if the gloom was intended to contrast with the beautiful, bright room that appeared like a vision on the other side of a wide archway. The effect certainly made him want to rush forward, but as he moved, Michon caught his arm. "Over here, Sabasté."

Edouard looked down and noticed that the tiled floor was strewn with the same dirty drop cloths he had seen in the van. Taking a step forward, he saw Kon lying half-covered by a pile of the cloths. His left wrist was handcuffed to the leg of a huge, marble-topped table.

"Oh my God!" Edouard gasped.

"What's the matter, Sabasté? Got no stomach for the job?" Georges yelled. "You're the medicine man. Do something!"

Michon seemed unmoved. "We're trying to swap him for three of our men, but now some guy at GIGN wants to hear him on tape. We've tried and tried, but we can't get anything sensible out of him."

"What happened? Nicolas was supposed to call me!" Edouard asked, trying to confirm what Paul had told him.

"Shut up about Nicolas! See what you can get out of Breaux!"

Edouard strained to control himself and leaned over Kon. As he got closer, he saw dried blood on Kon's face, and some new burn marks on his shoulder. He was horrified by this new evidence of brutality. He felt sick and ashamed that he had ever helped the group. Paul is wrong, he thought. I should never have helped them, never.

Edouard knelt by Kon and set his bag down. With trembling hands, he pulled the stiff cloths aside.

"Emile?" he whispered, fearing that Emile had escaped into the peace of death. Edouard had seen suffering before, but he was appalled that anyone could intentionally inflict such cruelty on another human being. Kon did not respond when Edouard touched him, but he was still warm. In fact, his skin was dry and hot with fever. The healer in Edouard awoke, and he made up his mind that, come what may, he was going to save Emile from the group. Freeing Emile was the only way he could free himself from his own guilt and shame.

"Emile?" he called again. "Emile. It's Edouard."

He tried to pull Kon into a sitting position, but Kon only moaned.

"Why is he handcuffed? Can't you see he's helpless!" Edouard demanded suddenly.

"Gérard said . . ." Michon started.

"I don't care what anyone said. If you want him to talk, you'll do this my way. Give me the key," Edouard said coldly, looking Michon in the eye.

No one was more surprised by Edouard's audacity than Edouard himself, but Michon handed him the key. Edouard felt oddly detached from his surroundings. He recognized the feeling, but he was too upset to connect it to the drugs he was taking. He knew his emotions had been harder to control lately, but he would have denied it if anyone had diagnosed his erratic behavior as severe mood swings. He felt a momentary sense of triumph as he unlocked the cuffs.

"Emile?" he called again, but Kon did not respond. He didn't even open his eyes.

"Why did you leave him by the door? There must be some place better than this for him. Don't you have an extra bed?"

"He's a filthy mess!" Georges objected.

"And whose fault is that?" Edouard snapped. "You've been treating him like an animal. Where's the bathroom? There must be at least one in a place like this."

"He'll mess up the apartment. I don't want my father complaining . . ."

"Look, Michon," Edouard said with unusual determination. "You beat Breaux half to death, and now you expect me to fix him. I can't work miracles, you know! I've got to clean him up a little and get some fluids into him. You'd better help me get him into a bathroom somewhere, or he's as good as dead!"

"Who do you think you are, coming in here and giving orders?" Michon growled. "I'm still in charge of this operation."

"I'm not giving anybody orders, Michon. I'm a nobody! I'm just a worm who fixes people. Well, if you want Breaux fixed, you'll have to give me a hand."

"All right! All right! There's a bathroom down the hall. Give him a hand, Georges."

"No! I told you . . ."

"That's an order, Georges. Do it!"

"No! What authority does Sabasté have? He's . . ."

"Damn it, Georges! I've had it with you!" Michon snapped. "We don't need people in the group who can't follow orders. Now you give Sabasté a hand or I'll report you to Gérard."

Georges stiffened at the mention of Gérard. "All right! I'll do it, but if Breaux makes a mess, Edouard can clean it up."

Michon glared at Georges, but did not reply. After a moment, Edouard took hold of Kon's shoulders. "Get his feet," he said quietly to Georges.

Georges mumbled a few disgusted grunts and grabbed Kon's legs.

"Be careful with him, Georges," Edouard remonstrated. He began to back through the archway and into the living room, half-dragging, half-carrying Kon along.

Edouard took a curious glance around the room as he stumbled backwards and noticed that clothes were strewn carelessly over the costly furniture. Dirty dishes and magazines were stacked on the coffee table, and several Skorpians were lying on the floor underneath it. Georges is definitely in residence, he concluded in disgust.

Georges dropped Kon's legs as soon as they reached the door to the bathroom, and Edouard had to drag Kon the rest of the way himself. Laying Kon on the bare tile floor, he bent over him. He was alarmed that Kon seemed to be in a torpor. A moment later, Michon stuck his head into the room. "Here's a list of questions the guy from GIGN wants answered," he said, handing Edouard a crumpled piece of paper. "And here's the recorder. Just press that red button on the side. I'll keep Georges occupied, but don't be too long. We need that tape."

"O.K. O.K. You are going to set him free if he answers, aren't you?" Edouard asked plaintively.

"Sure. Sure. He's no use to us. Just get him to talk. Here's your bag. Give him something to wake him up."

Edouard no longer believed anything that Michon said, but he kept his doubts to himself. He turned the ornate tap on the sink and let the water begin to warm while he searched in vain for something more functional than the tiny hand towels that hung on a brass-plated ring beside the sink. Although the room was almost as large as the living room in Edouard's apartment, it was only a wash room. The only decent-sized towels in sight were crumpled, wet ones strewn on the floor. Georges really is a pig, Edouard mused.

He took up one of the small hand towels, folded the monogram to one side, soaked it in warm water, and pressed it gently to Kon's battered face. "Emile?" he called softly. "Can you hear me? Come on, Emile. You've got to talk to me."

Using just one small wet towel and one dry one, Edouard did his best to clean the most obvious signs of abuse and neglect from Kon. He searched in his bag, pulled out two small cartons of juice, and pulled the tops open. Then he attempted to raise Kon into a sitting position. Kon began to struggle weakly, but eventually Edouard worked his way around him. Holding him from behind, Edouard held the carton to Kon's mouth. Immediately Kon locked his jaw. Edouard pulled Kon's head back against his left shoulder and held his arm across his chest in a protective embrace.

"It's all right, Emile. It's all right. Everything's all right," he repeated softly. What if I can't get him to talk? he wondered. Suddenly he wished that Paul *had* locked him in a cell. Then, still holding Kon against his chest, he began to stroke Kon's forehead, pushing the hair from his face. He wished he had remembered to bring some salve for the burn on Emile's eyelid. It looked as though it had become infected.

"Come on, Emile. It's Edouard. I promised I would come. I brought you some juice. Come on, drink."

Edouard held the carton to Kon's mouth again, but Kon resisted. Edouard was about to give up and force Kon's jaw open, when suddenly Kon whispered, "Edouard?"

"Yes, it's Edouard. Come on, you need to drink."

"Where's Geilla?" Kon mumbled. "Did he hurt her?"

For a moment Edouard was taken aback and then he remembered Kon's mumbling in the van. "She's O.K.," he assured Kon. "She got away."

"She got away?"

"Yes. She's O.K. Come on, Emile. Take some juice."

"I'll kill him if he hurt her," Kon mumbled. "I swear I'll . . ."

"Shh, Emile. She's O.K. He didn't hurt her. You must drink . . . please. Aren't you thirsty?"

"Thirsty? Yes."

"Then take some juice. Come on," Edouard coaxed again.

Kon turned his head away. "Don't drink it, Edouard. It's poison. It made me sick. It made you sick. Don't drink!"

Edouard sighed heavily with frustration. "It won't make you sick, Emile. I promise. Come on . . . please."

"What do they want from me, Edouard? I don't understand their questions."

"I'm not sure, Emile. I'm not sure. Come on, take some juice. You'll feel better." Edouard pressed the carton to Kon's lips again and this time he drank. Edouard was about to give Kon the second carton of juice, when Michon stuck his head into the room again. "Did you get him to talk?" he asked sharply.

Edouard felt Kon cringe at the sound of Michon's voice, and he pulled him closer against himself. His anger welled up. He wanted to scream at Michon for his brutality, but he was afraid he would frighten Emile. "Just leave us alone," he forced himself to say quietly, waving Michon away with his hand.

"Be quick about it," Michon said in a threatening tone. "I don't want you here when Gérard gets back."

Edouard started to ask who Gérard was, but Michon turned on his heel and slammed the door shut. Kon jumped at the sound.

"Relax, Emile. He's gone," Edouard said and offered Kon more juice. "Listen, Emile, I'm trying to help you get out of here. Some of your friends want to hear your voice on tape to prove that you are still alive. They want to get you out, but you'll have to answer some questions."

"No more questions, Edouard . . . please. I don't have the answers."

"You must try, Emile. I'll help you."

"No questions, Edouard . . . no more . . . please."

"It's for your own good, Emile. You must try. It's very important."

Edouard reached for the tape recorder. "Come on, Emile. Just repeat what I tell you, O.K.?"

Suddenly Kon tried to pull away, but Edouard held him more

tightly. "It'll be O.K., Emile. Just repeat what I say. My name is Emile Breaux. Come on, Emile, say it."

"No more questions, Edouard," Kon said, becoming agitated.

"Come on, Emile. It's easy. Just repeat. My name is Emile Breaux. Come on, Emile, please," Edouard pleaded. He held the recorder at the ready until at last Kon mumbled, "Emile."

"That's good," Edouard responded. "Now say it again. My name is Emile Breaux. Come on."

"My name," Kon began and paused. "My name is Emile Breaux."

Edouard had pressed the button, but he wasn't sure he had captured everything. "Say it again, Emile—louder this time."

"My name is Emile Breaux," Kon repeated numbly.

"Very good, Emile. Let's go on. What is your wife's name?"

"My name is Emile Breaux! My name is . . ."

"Not your name, Emile, your wife's name. What is your wife's name?"

"My wife? I don't have a wife," Kon mumbled.

"Who is Geilla? Is she your wife?"

"My wife? . . . she was in the van. He tried to hurt her. I'll kill him if he hurt her! I swear I'll kill him!"

"Shh, shh, Emile. Calm down. She's O.K. She's O.K. She got away! Just pretend she is your wife O.K. Just repeat, my wife's name is Geilla."

"Geilla," Kon repeated.

"That's good. Now say it all together. My wife's name is Geilla."

"My wife's name . . . my wife's name . . . I don't remember a wife."

"O.K. O.K. That's good enough."

"Where do you live, Emile?" Edouard asked, with a growing sense of defeat.

"I . . . I don't know."

"Do you live in Paris?"

"No more questions . . . please."

"You probably live somewhere in Paris, Emile. What's your address?"

Before Kon responded the door opened and Michon stepped into the room. "You've run out of time, Edouard. Did you get anything out of him?"

"Not much," Edouard confessed. "He's terribly confused, Michon. He needs to be taken care of. He needs . . ."

"I don't give a damn what he needs! I need that tape! Now shut up and get out of here!"

"You mean you're throwing me out? Just like that?"

"Come on, Sabasté! Quit stalling! Gérard will be back any minute."

"Who's Gérard?"

"Never mind. You don't want to meet him. Now get your stuff and clear out."

Edouard felt let down. He hadn't accomplished anything. "I have to go, Emile," he said softly, and letting go of Kon, he laid him gently on the floor. "Can't you spare a blanket for him, Michon?"

"He doesn't need a blanket!" Michon grumbled and grabbed Edouard by the arm. "I'm not running a hotel. Hurry up!"

"He needs some medicine," Edouard insisted, picking up his bag. I can get a blanket at the hospital. I could come back after work."

"No! don't come back here!"

"He's sick, Michon. He's having trouble breathing," Edouard lied. I could bring him some medicine."

"No!"

"Maybe the GIGN people won't take him when they find out how sick he is. I could . . ."

"I said no!"

"How do you know when Gérard is coming back?"

"That's none of your business. Now get out of here!"

"O.K. O.K." Edouard responded reluctantly and took up his bag. He wanted to say something encouraging to Emile, but he dared not, not in front of Michon.

Edouard followed Michon into the living room. "Now where the hell is Georges?" Michon mumbled. "Wait here!" he ordered curtly and then disappeared down the hall on the far side of the archway.

Edouard looked around the room carefully, estimating its size. Hearing Michon and Georges arguing at the far end of the apartment, he slipped quietly past the bathroom and peeked into the kitchen. He hurried back to the living room just as the other men came in.

"Georges will take you back," Michon announced firmly, and

Edouard guessed from Georges' expression that he wasn't too happy about it.

"Are you ready?" Georges barked.

"Yes," Edouard answered immediately. Without another word, he followed Georges out. Georges opened the door to the stairs and pushed Edouard through. "I don't know why Michon insists on keeping you around. I'd have killed you long ago."

"Michon thinks I'm useful. Who else would patch up you people? I even helped you, Georges. Why do you hate me?"

"Cause you're soft, Sabasté. And you're not loyal."

"What do you mean, I'm not loyal?"

"I don't trust you. You're not really a part of the group. I think you're getting too involved with Breaux."

Edouard started. He wondered if Georges was beginning to suspect something, or if he was just expressing his usual hostility. He pushed open the door at the bottom of the stairs and stepped into the parking garage. He halted suddenly when he spotted a man standing by a car parked near the white Mercedes. The man was puffing furiously on a cigarette, and kept checking his watch, as if he were waiting impatiently for someone. Probably his wife, Edouard guessed. Edouard was about to retreat, when he felt something hard press against his back.

"Just keep moving,"Georges growled. "Act naturally. When we get to the car, walk around and get into the passenger seat."

Naturally! Edouard thought. How can I act naturally with a gun in my back? He started to shake. Michon had threatened to tell the police about him. He had even bloodied his nose once or twice, but he had never held a gun on him. Slowly he began to move, but it was more of a shuffle than a walk. His feet didn't want to obey, and he feared his knees would fail him. He could feel beads of sweat running down the back of his neck. He prayed that the man with the cigarette would not notice how out of place he looked in his white uniform and little black bag. Did people in these fancy apartments know each other any better than the people in his run-down building? He hoped not, for one friendly "Bonjour, Monsieur," might get rewarded by a bullet.

Luckily, the man seemed too preoccupied to take notice of Edouard and Georges as they approached the Mercedes. As Edouard walked stiffly around the car, Georges unlocked the door and got behind the wheel. Edouard could see a pistol lying on the seat as Georges fumbled with buttons to unlock the door for him. Obviously Georges was not familiar with his father's expensive car. Georges placed the Browning high-powered pistol in his lap, muzzle-end pointing towards Edouard, and started the car. At least I'm in the front, Edouard thought, as Georges maneuvered the car up the parking ramp. Maybe I can get my bearings as to what section of town I'm in. As they passed through the security gate, Edouard turned his head to look for a sign identifying the apartment building. Suddenly he felt a sharp pain in the back of his head. He didn't see anything else.

Edouard felt someone shaking him, and he tried to push their hands away. His head hurt, and the movement was making him sick to his stomach. When someone slapped him across his face, he finally succeeded in prying his eyes open. The sight of Georges' malicious grin, only inches from his face, startled him, and he pulled his head back sharply. "What happened? Did we hit something?"

Georges laughed unpleasantly. "Come on! Wake up, you dumb bastard! What do you think happened?"

Edouard put his hand to the back of his head, and then he remembered. "You hit me, didn't you? Jesus, Georges, why . . ."

"Shut up, Sabasté! Get your stuff."

Suddenly Edouard realized that he was in the front seat of the Mercedes. Georges was leaning over him. He couldn't see the pistol, but he figured that Georges still had it. He opened the car door and slid out. He recognized the building in front of him and knew they were still several blocks from the hospital. He was surprised when Georges got out also and came around the car.

"I can find my way back, Georges. You don't have to take any risks on my account."

"You keep telling me how useful you are, Sabasté. I want you to prove it. I want you to give me some stuff."

"What kind of stuff? What are you talking about, Georges?"

"Don't play innocent with me. Bernon said you gave him morphine.

155

You must have a supply."

"I don't, Georges. I swear. Look, Nicolas had . . ."

"Quit stalling, Sabasté," Georges hissed, shoving his pistol into Edouard's back. "I want to see what you've got stashed away."

"This is crazy, Georges. You're taking a terrible risk coming here! What if someone sees you?"

"Shut up! Michon comes all the time."

"But at least he's careful. He doesn't wave a gun around. I don't think this is a good idea. Michon will be mad if he finds out."

"Are you planning to tell him, Sabasté? Is that it? Are you going to snitch on me like Lorelle did?"

Edouard could see that Georges was becoming paranoid, and it frightened him. Georges was vicious enough under the best of circumstances. If he became unstable, there was no telling what he might do.

"I won't tell anyone anything, Georges. I promise, but this is not a good idea."

"Shut up! Stop telling me what to do! Just because you order Michon around, doesn't mean I'm going to take orders from you."

"I'm not giving orders, Georges. I'm just trying . . ."

"Shut up! Just shut up! We'll just go in nice and quiet, and no one will get hurt."

Georges grabbed Edouard by the arm and pulled him in front of himself. "You just take it nice and easy, Sabasté, or I might get nervous and start shooting."

He's really going to do it! Edouard thought in alarm. He's going to make me walk in there and open my locker. What if I meet one of my patients like I did yesterday? I can't do this. Georges might kill somebody. And what's he going to do when he finds out I don't have anything he wants? He'll kill me for sure.

"Get a move on, Sabasté," Georges snapped.

Edouard jumped. He knew he would have to move or Georges would kill him right there on the sidewalk. Slowly, slowly, as if time were standing still, Edouard went towards the hospital. He felt as though he were delivering a bomb that might explode at any minute. He noticed three student nurses coming out the door in their spotless white uniforms. They looked so young to him, so innocent, so full of life. They were completely unaware of the danger he was leading into their midst. Well, if death was following him, he was not going to lead it in through the front door.

"I usually go in by the side door," Edouard said in a shaky voice. "We won't meet as many people that way."

"O.K. Let's do it then."

Edouard kept moving forward. He realized that his legs were working although he felt that his heart was pounding so hard that it would burst. He was relieved that they did not meet anyone on the stairs as he led Georges to the third floor. As he climbed slowly upward, acutely aware of the gun pressed against his back, his once familiar surroundings seemed transformed into a nightmarish landscape. What if someone saw the gun and called the police?

When they reached the third floor, Edouard thought it strange that the corridor was empty; but he was too nervous to analyze the situation. As they moved past the nurses' station, he was surprised that it too was empty. He prayed that his luck would hold until he got to the men's locker room near the end of the hall. He realized how sweaty his palms were when he pressed the chrome plate on the locker room door and left a wet print.

"Which one is yours?" Georges demanded as soon as they were inside.

"Three-sixty-seven," Edouard answered weakly.

"Open it!"

"I told you, I don't have anything, Georges."

"I said open it!" Georges barked, ramming Edouard's shoulder against the lockers.

Edouard did not respond, but turned and began to fumble with the combination lock. His mind was racing wildly, and he had to try three times before the lock finally released. Georges shoved Edouard aside impatiently and stuffed the gun into his coat pocket. He grabbed the locker door and it swung open, hitting the other lockers with a loud clang. Georges began riffling through Edouard's clothes and searching through the few half-empty bottles of Demerol that Paul had not taken.

Edouard was cringing against the lockers, expecting an angry outburst from Georges, when suddenly the locker room door opened, and a man stepped into the room. He was wearing glasses and had a white lab coat over his street clothes. Edouard looked up nervously, but did not recognize Paul until he spoke.

"There you are, Edouard! What's been keeping you? I've been covering for you during lunch and I'm starved."

Edouard's mouth dropped open, but he remained speechless. Suddenly the door opened again and a tall man with a mustache entered. "Excuse me," he said politely, squeezing past Paul. He walked toward the lockers on the other side of Edouard, put his foot on the bench, and calmly began untying his shoe. Meanwhile Paul stepped forward. He put his hand on the locker next to Edouard's and leaned on it forming a barrier between Edouard and Georges.

"Look, Edouard," he said impatiently, "I don't give a damn what you do on your lunch hour, but it's after two. Are you coming back to work, or do I have to tell your boss?"

Ignoring the open door of his locker, Edouard slowly edged away from Georges. "I er . . . I'd better get back to work," Edouard said nervously and stepped toward the door.

"Go back to sweeping floors, Sabasté. That's all you're good for!" Georges sneered and slammed the locker door shut.

Edouard's courage failed at the sound, and he ran for the door. Grasping it with both hands, he gave a mighty pull and dashed into the hall. Immediately someone clamped a hand over his mouth, seized his arm, and spun him into the nearest room. Before he could resist, he was forced into a chair. He was quivering with confusion and fright when Paul slipped into the room and closed the door.

"Let him go," Paul commanded quietly, and the man holding Edouard released him.

Edouard stared at Paul and his fear turned to rage. "Where were you? Where the hell were you?" he screamed. "You said you would help me! You said you would protect me! You . . ."

"We were right behind you, Edouard. I was tracking you every minute."

"You're lying! You never left the hospital!"

Paul stepped closer to Edouard and put his hands on Edouard's shoulders. "Calm down, Edouard. I was there. I had a man in the garage. I followed you back here. We cleared everyone out when you came up the stairs just now. I couldn't get any closer without tipping off the guy who brought you back. Who was he, Edouard?"

"It was Georges. Why didn't you arrest him for Christ's sake? He had a gun on me!"

"I know, Edouard, and I'm sorry, but if we take him in the rest of them will get suspicious. We have to act as though everything is normal."

"Normal! What's normal about having a gun in your back? Georges is crazy! He might have shot me! I was afraid he might kill one of the patients. I just can't deal with him. I can't . . ."

"Calm down, Edouard. You're safe now. Just relax," Paul said reassuringly and began to move his hands skillfully over Edouard's shoulders. "Tell me about the apartment. Is . . . is Emile still alive? Did you talk to him?"

"Yes."

"How is he?" Paul asked, trying not to betray his anxiety.

"Not good. He's confused. I had to prompt him to get him to say his name, and he can't remember where he lives. He kept saying he didn't have a wife. Is he married?"

"Yes, he's married. Where are they keeping him?"

"They had him by the door. He was handcuffed to a table. They didn't even give him a blanket. I asked Michon if I could bring a blanket, but he said no."

"Were you able to get him to drink anything?"

"I gave him some juice. He's so bruised it's . . . it's pitiful. I cleaned him up a little. I hauled him into a bathroom and cleaned him up. Georges didn't want to let me do it, but I told Michon there was no other way to get him to talk."

"You didn't mention me, did you?"

"No. I just told Emile that some of his friends wanted to know that he was alive."

"Who else was in the apartment?"

"Georges and Michon. Michon kept talking about someone named Gérard coming, but I didn't see him."

"Could people have been hiding in the other rooms?"

"There might have been. I only saw the living room and one bathroom. Oh, on the way out I took a quick look into the kitchen."

"Was there a lot of stuff around as if several people were living there?"

"Who knows. There were clothes and dirty dishes scattered all over the place. Georges is a real pig."

"Did you see any weapons?"

"Yes. Skorpians lying on the floor."

"How many?"

"Five."

"Was Emile still in the bathroom when you left?"

"Yes."

"You did very well, Edouard, but you're still shaking. Did you take anything this morning? Do you want something to help you relax?"

Edouard looked up at Paul. "Yes . . . No! No, I don't want to end up like Georges. He came here looking for drugs. I told him it was too risky, but he'll do anything to get them. I don't want to be like that, Paul. Please, you said you would help me. Don't let me get like that. Please . . ."

"O.K.! I'm trying to help you, Edouard. Believe me, I'm trying," Paul said, and stepping around behind Edouard, he slid his hands down Edouard's back, pressing his fingers against his spine. "Look, I know this has been rough. Would you like to go home for a while and rest?"

Edouard felt himself relaxing as Paul's fingers pressed into his back. He longed to yield to Paul's serenity. He longed to let Paul protect him. But suddenly, fearful of falling under Paul's spell, he pulled away. I will not let myself be controlled by Paul, he determined. I let myself be controlled by my father and then by Michon and look where it has led. I have to stand up for myself. I have to get free. I have to get free of them all, but oh God . . . it is so hard.

Edouard jumped to his feet. "No, I don't want to go home! I just want . . . I just want to get back to work. Let me do my job! I just want to do my job. It's all I have left!"

"O.K.!" Paul agreed readily. "Whatever you want to do is fine. I'll walk down with you."

Edouard shot Paul a glance and seemed about to object.

"I'm trying to protect you, Edouard. You don't have to do this alone."

Paul opened the door and as Edouard stepped through, he saw the tall man with the mustach hurrying down the hall. As he came closer, Edouard realized it was Jack.

"Great job, Edouard! You kept it real cool," Jack commented, smiling at Edouard.

Edouard smiled feebly and waited while Paul confered with Jack in a short, whispered conversation. He noticed that two nurses were on duty at the nurses' station and an orderly was pushing an empty gurney down the hall. Everything seemed to be back to normal.

"Hey, would you like some lunch?" Paul asked cheerfully.

The thought of food made Edouard's nervous stomach churn. "No thanks," he muttered and headed for the elevator. He felt his hand shake when he pressed the button for the first floor. As he stepped in followed by Paul and Jack, he wondered why he hadn't taken the stairs. I always take the stairs, unless I am with a patient. Obviously everything is not back to normal.

"Are you sure you feel up to working?" Paul asked, as the elevator door opened on the first floor.

Edouard nodded his head without looking at Paul. I'm not sure of anything, he thought to himself. If I can just do something familiar, maybe everything will seem real again. He started down the hall with Paul and Jack following along. As he passed through the swinging doors into the emergency room, a doctor called out to him. "Hey, Edouard! I'm going to be tied up with this patient for a while. Go see how many others are waiting out there. If there's many, I'll have to call someone in. Who's on call today?"

"Er . . . I don't know," Edouard answered. "I'll see who's out there and check the schedule."

Edouard passed by the treatment rooms and stepped into the waiting room. Glancing around quickly, he counted a young woman with two small children, an old woman with a cane, and a young man holding a bloody handkerchief over one eye. Edouard froze as he spotted a middle-aged man, and a woman in a dark-red suit. They did not notice him until the young man with the handkerchief called out in distress, "How much longer will it be?"

Suddenly everyone looked up and the middle-aged man appeared shocked. "Edouard! What is the meaning of this?" he demanded in a loud voice.

Edouard was galvanized. He whirled on his heels and flew past Paul who had come up behind him.

"Edouard! Come back here!" the man shouted, but Edouard was gone.

Paul glanced briefly at the couple, muttered, "Oh shit! Not now. Keep them occupied, Jack!" and ran after Edouard.

He chased him past the treatment rooms, through the swinging doors, down the hall, and into the lobby. Edouard was in a mindless panic, and didn't even slow down when he bumped into an old woman with a walker. Paul caught the woman as she fell and deposited her safely in an arm chair, before he burst through the glass doors in pursuit of Edouard. He saw Edouard flee down the broad sidewalk and across the lawn heading for the street. Edouard slowed for a moment at the curb then dashed among the oncoming vehicles.

Amidst the cacophony of squealing brakes and blaring horns, Edouard miraculously made his way unscathed across two lanes of traffic. Paul finally caught up to him on the safety island. Edouard screamed in defiance and fought against Paul, until Paul threw him on his back and pinned him down.

"Edouard! Edouard, calm down! It's all right. You don't have to see them."

"Why? Why did you call them?" Edouard shrieked hysterically.

"I didn't call them! I swear it," Paul affirmed quickly.

"You did! You did! Why else would they come?"

"I didn't call them, Edouard. I don't know why they came. Maybe they got worried about you. They're your parents! Have you written to them lately?"

"Yes . . . No . . . I don't remember. I've been making up lies for so long, I can't remember what I said. I can't face them, Paul. I can't. You said you would take care of things. You said . . ."

"You don't have to see them, Edouard. You're still in my custody. I said I would protect you and I will."

Edouard stopped struggling and began to sob, and Paul released his grip on him. "They want me to be a doctor, so they can brag about me. They have no idea how hard it is. They have no idea how lonely it is. I hate the city! I hate the university! I hate my father for sending me here! They never even came to visit me. Never!"

Paul pulled Edouard into a sitting position and put his arm around him. "It'll be all right, Edouard. I'll talk to them. You tried, Edouard. You tried."

"I did try," Edouard sobbed. "They have no idea how hard it was, always trying to be the best. They insisted I always be the best. They don't know how hard it is. My mother never does anything harder than shop for clothes. She can't even remember what size sweater I wear. She doesn't care, Paul. Nobody cares!" Edouard turned and burying his face against Paul's shoulder, he sobbed uncontrollably.

"Edouard, don't! Don't," Paul pleaded, as the poignancy of Edouard's despair pierced his emotional shield. He wrapped both arms around Edouard and held him, patting his head and rocking him. "Shh, shh, Edouard. I'm sure they care. You're their son. They must care. I care. You've been a friend to Emile and I'm grateful. He needs you, Edouard. Don't fall apart on me! Please, don't fall apart on me!"

"I can't help Emile. I can't go back there, Paul. Please don't make me go back there! I was so scared when Georges had that gun!"

"It's all right, Edouard. Everyone is afraid of Georges. You did a great job, a really great job!"

Just then Jack came across to the traffic island, shouting as he ran up. "Paul! Is he hurt? Paul? Paul, are you O.K.?" He grabbed Paul by the arm. "Answer me, damn it! Are you O.K.?"

Paul looked up and bit his lip, struggling with emotion. He nodded his head, even as he continued to rock Edouard. "He's O.K.! He's O.K.! Bring the car!" he gasped and immediately turned back to Edouard. "Listen," he said, regaining control. "I'm going to take you home for a while."

"No!" Edouard sobbed. "No! I don't want to go home. I can't face them."

"Not home to your parents. I'll take you back to your apartment. I won't let them find you. O.K.?"

"Don't tell them where I am, Paul," Edouard begged mournfully. "Please don't tell them!"

"I won't. I won't. Just try to calm down. You're making yourself sick."

Paul sat, holding Edouard in his arms, until Jack arrived a few minutes later with the car. "Come on, Edouard, let me help you," Jack said, gently pulling Edouard away from Paul. Edouard was shaking so badly he could hardly stand, and Jack supported him while Paul got into the back seat. Edouard groped his way into the car, fell onto the seat next to Paul with a moan, and began to vomit. Paul tried to steer Edouard's head toward the floor, but he didn't succeed.

"I'm sorry! I'm sorry!" Edouard moaned. "I can't do anything right. I wish I were dead, Paul. I wish one of those cars had hit me!"

"Shh, shh, Edouard. You'll be O.K. You just waited too long between doses. I'll get you something to make you feel better."

"I don't want anything. I just want to die! Just let me die. I'd rather die than end up like Georges."

"You'll never be like Georges, Edouard. Never. You'll be O.K. I promise. I'll help you get off the stuff."

Edouard vomited again and Paul held his head, and patted his shoulder until they reached the apartment.

Jack helped Paul get Edouard out of the back seat then went to park the car. I hope Paul can get Edouard up to the apartment by himself, he thought. Paul is starting to look a little ragged around the edges. He's becoming too involved in Edouard's personal problems. The last thing he needs is another little brother to worry about.

Paul helped Edouard into his apartment building and into the old-fashioned lift. I should have given Edouard a tranquilizer after I rescued him from Georges, he berated himself. He was a basket case then. I should have recognized it. I could have saved us both a lot of grief. But, damn it, his job means a lot to him.

Edouard was still sweating and shaking as Paul helped him into the bedroom. "Don't tell them where I am, Paul," Edouard muttered, as Paul laid him on the bed.

"I won't, Edouard. Just relax for a while."

"Don't make me face Georges again, please. Just let me die."

"We'll talk when you're feeling better," Paul answered. Then taking Edouard's hand in his own, he reached into the pocket of his lab coat and pulled out a small syringe. "You need to rest for a while, Edouard," he said reassuringly. Swiftly he flicked the cap off the needle, pressed his thumb tightly against the back of Edouard's hand and slipped the needle into a small vein.

Edouard drew in his breath and jumped. His eyes opened wide with fear and he stared at Paul gasping, "I don't really want to die! I don't really want to die, Paul!"

Paul smiled calmly and put his hand on Edouard's shoulder. "Don't worry, Edouard. I knew it all along. You just need to rest. It's my own special brew."

Edouard laughed giddily with relief. Already he could feel his tension slipping away. He was thankful for Paul's help. There was nowhere else to turn, and he was too weak to do anything alone. If I am going to be a puppet, at least I can choose who I want to pull the strings, he thought. Paul is so calm and logical. He doesn't rant and rave at me like Michon and my father. He smiled at Paul and muttered dreamily, "I know where Emile is. I stole a magazine with the address."

"That was very clever, Edouard, very clever," Paul answered instantly.

Edouard laughed drunkenly, buoyed by the warmth of Paul's praise. He had finally done something right. "It's in my bag. It really is. I hid it when no one was looking. Georges doesn't know . . ." Edouard dissolved into silent giggles.

"That was very smart, Edouard, and very brave," Paul responded.

Paul's words sank into Edouard's drifting consciousness. I never thought I could be brave, but maybe I can. If Paul believes in me, maybe I can, he thought and drifted gently into sleep.

Paul removed Edouard's shoes, and then finished undressing him. He pulled the covers over him and was about to leave when he heard a muffled meow. Looking over he saw the grey cat pressing itself against the window and crying. "O.K., kitty," Paul said opening the window a bit. "Come in and keep Edouard company. He could use a friend." As the cat squeezed under the window, Paul caught it and set it on the bed. Kitty seemed to understand what was required and curled up beside Edouard, keeping watch over him, and licking its paws.

Jack was sitting on the couch when Paul came out to the living room. "How is he?" he asked as Paul sank down wearily beside him.

"He's asleep. I should have put him out before. How the hell did his parents find him?"

As if he took Paul's question as rhetorical, Jack made no answer, but pulled a silver flask out of his pocket and handed it to Paul.

"What the hell time is it?" Paul asked.

"It's after three. What difference does it make? This is gay Paree, and you need it."

"Gay Paree, huh. Is that where we are?" Paul answered sarcastically, taking a swig from the flask. "Thanks. I . . . he really got to me out there, Jack. He was trying to get killed. He thought I had let him down."

"I guess seeing his folks was a shock to him. I didn't detect a lot of warmth from them."

"Warmth! They upset him more than Georges did. Why did they have to show up now?"

"Apparently they came to Paris for a shopping trip. They met some people they knew and started bragging about their son, the doctor. When they went to get Edouard, to show him off, they couldn't find him. They were so angry about being embarrassed in front of their friends, they went charging to the university, threatening to bring all kinds of charges against them for losing their son. The school managed to locate someone who remembered that Edouard worked at the hospital. His parents are fit to be tied that he is doing such menial work. They're really out of touch with Edouard. I tried to tell them that Edouard loves his job, but they wouldn't listen. They have some screwy idea that he's already a doctor."

"Shit! He had barely started his second year of med school when he dropped out. They must have been pushing him for years. I checked his personnel file at the hospital yesterday. Edouard has been in several accelerated programs. He's really bright, but the kid's only nineteen. And a country bumpkin to boot!"

"No wonder the group got their fangs in him so easily. Is he going to pull himself together long enough to help get Kon out?"

Paul sighed heavily before answering, "I think so. He actually did pretty well this morning. I think most of his behavior was due to drug withdrawal. He's under so much stress his usual dose didn't hold him."

"Do you think he'll go back to the apartment?"

"I'll work on him. I believe he wants to help Emile."

"Well, we can't wait forever. I got the apartment layout from the manager. If there's only two of them in there with Kon, I say the sooner we go in the better."

"It's too risky," Paul countered. "We don't know for sure how many people are in that apartment. Edouard saw five Skorpians lying around. And don't forget, Georges is in there. The guy's a psycho. There's no way to predict what he will do. From what Edouard says, Kon is completely helpless. They were keeping him right inside the door. We've got to be sure he's out of the line of fire before we go charging in there."

"All right, we wait. How long is Edouard going to be out?"

"I can't be sure. About three hours. I didn't give him much."

"Then what?"

"I honestly don't know. I hope I can talk him into going back, but I honestly don't know."

"Can't you shoot him up with something to make him feel invincible?"

"I've thought about that, but that stuff is too dangerous. Edouard's behavior would be totally unpredictable. He's already tried to kill himself. I can't do that to him."

"O.K., so now what?"

"You can start rounding up equipment for a raid. I've got to check the GIGN offices to see if they've had a call about that tape. We can't stall Michon forever. I'll call for someone to stay with Edouard. I don't want to leave him alone."

"You'd better change clothes before you go to the GIGN offices."

"Why?"

"Have you forgotten that Edouard puked all over your pant leg?"

"So? Are you telling me that vomit is not in style! Does it ruin the crease! Maybe some of those office types need to be reminded what the real world is like!"

"Whoa," Jack said looking up in surprise. "Have another drink, Paul."

"O.K. O.K. I'll change. Anything to get more cooperation from those guys."

Chapter Eleven

Edouard was sitting in the car with Paul. Whatever Paul had given him had really worked. He felt clear headed and had been able to get some food down. He was mildly apprehensive, but supposed that was normal under the circumstances. He knew he had to help Emile. Even before Paul talked to him, he knew. Despite his stupid involvement with drugs, he was a decent person, and he had to prove it to Paul. He didn't know if he could ever please his parents, or if he even wanted to, but he wanted to please Paul. He sensed that Paul cared about him. No one had cared much about him since Gaston.

Paul stopped the car. "It's only three blocks from here, Edouard. Do you have any questions?"

"I don't think so."

"Just do exactly as I told you and you'll be safe. Here's your bag and the blanket. You'd better carry the magazine so you won't have to dig for it."

"I just hope they don't see how nervous I am."

"Don't worry about it. If it becomes an issue, blame it on the drugs."

"I've got to get off them, Paul. I'm losing control."

"You will, Edouard, I promise. You'll do fine. You'll do just fine," Paul smiled with a confidence he did not feel and patted Edouard on the shoulder.

Edouard grinned nervously and got out of the car. His anxiety increased rapidly as he started down the street alone, but as promised he did not look back. After all, coming back to see Emile was supposed to be his own idea. He walked quickly toward the apartment building. It was almost 7:15 p.m., but it was still light. He spotted the number on the building then saw an older woman with a shopping bag coming towards him. As she got closer, he noticed that she was wearing a long strand of pearls. Without looking at Edouard, she turned in at the apartment building directly ahead of him. Edouard pretended to search his pocket for a key, but the woman had hers ready. When she set her shopping bag down to unlock the door, Edouard stepped forward. "Allow me," he said politely.

The woman smiled and he carried her groceries through the door. Once inside, he hesitated and she took the bag from him.

"You'll do fine, Edouard. You're not alone in this," she said warmly and disappeared through the door to the garage. Edouard stood gazing after her. I wish I could follow her, he thought, but I can't let Paul down. He obviously cares a lot about Emile.

Although the lobby was empty and he was not wearing his white uniform, Edouard chose the stairs rather than risk meeting someone in the elevator. He opened the door to the third floor, walked to apartment 3B, and rapped softly on the door. He waited several minutes, but no one answered. He could not hear any sound from inside the apartment. He rapped again more persistently, but still there was no answer. His resolve began to fade as he stood in the silent corridor. Paul had warned him that this might be the most difficult part of the job. He had to gain access to Emile to be of any help, but he had no idea of the mood of the men on the other side of the door. Holding the magazine in one hand, Edouard steeled his nerve and pounded on the door with his fist. The sturdy door never rattled against the jam, but on the fourth blow, it flew open. A hand grabbed his wrist, and he was yanked into the apartment so violently, he feared his arm would snap. He was no sooner inside than he was seized by the throat and shoved against the wall.

"What the hell do you think you're doing here, you stupid asshole?" Michon hissed into his face.

The fury in Michon's voice petrified Edouard, and he cowered against the wall.

"How did you find your way back here?" Michon demanded, slamming Edouard's head against the wall.

Silently Edouard held out the crumpled magazine. Michon snatched it, but didn't understand its meaning. "How did you know where to come?" he screamed at Edouard.

"The address . . . it's got the address . . ." Edouard mumbled weakly.

"Jesus! So now you're a sneak thief. What if someone saw you?" Again Michon slammed Edouard's head into the wall. "Why did you come back here?"

Edouard was terrified. "I brought a blanket for Emile," he offered in a quivering voice.

"A blanket! You risked this whole operation for a God damn blanket? I ought to break your skull!" Michon growled and slammed Edouard's head into the wall a third time.

Edouard was reeling and feared he would black out if Michon knocked him into the wall again. He knew he had to do something drastic if he hoped to survive Michon's wrath.

"I know where Rubard is," he croaked as Michon's fingers tightened against his wind pipe.

Michon's mouth fell open in surprise. "What did you say?" he asked, slamming Edouard's head against the wall for emphasis.

For a moment Edouard saw bright lights swimming in a dark void. Then he was aware that Michon's lips were moving, but he could not make out the words.

Finally he heard Michon scream, "Where is Rubard?" When he didn't answer, Michon slammed him against the wall and repeated the question. Oh God! This is what they did to Emile, Edouard thought. I've got to get him out of here. I've got to save him. He blinked at Michon and forced himself to think. ". . . at the hospital," he heard himself whisper.

Michon tightened his grip on Edouard's throat. "Where?"

Edouard struggled to hang on to consciousness. Lie, Edouard, lie! You're getting good at it, he thought before mumbling, "The orthopedic ward. They brought him in this afternoon."

Michon's eyebrows shot upwards and his eyes gleamed with obsession. "I want that son of a bitch, Edouard, and you're going to take me to him. Do you understand?"

Edouard nodded his head numbly. "I can get you in."

"When?"

"Tomorrow morning when I deliver the breakfast trays."

Michon's evil smirk sent a chill down Edouard's spine. "Good!" Michon barked. "I'm not letting you out of my sight until I get Rubard."

Michon released his grip and Edouard slid down the wall until he hit the floor with a jolt. He wondered if his head was bleeding, but he was too weak to move. He sat blinking up at Michon then he began to retch.

"You're disgusting, Edouard," Michon growled. "You'd better pull yourself together by tomorrow."

Edouard didn't answer. He just vomited again.

"Jesus, Edouard, get in the bathroom before you make a mess of the place."

Edouard struggled to his feet and swayed dizzily.

"And take your God damn blanket with you!" Michon yelled, kicking the blanket towards Edouard.

Edouard fumbled with the blanket and stumbled through the archway into the living room. He staggered a few feet to the right and bumped into Georges who immediately demanded, "What the hell are you doing here?"

Without answering, Edouard turned to get around Georges and ran straight into the wall. Georges laughed in derision. "Jesus, you're an ass, Sabasté." Suddenly he noticed Edouard's unsteady gait as he lurched toward the bathroom. "Christ, you're high on something, aren't you? What is it? Damn! I knew you were holding out on me."

Georges turned and started after Edouard, but Michon shouted after him. "Let up, Georges. He's not high. I think he's running out of whatever he took before. Jesus, I wish you'd never gotten him started. He's becoming useless. He can't hold it together for more than a few hours, and I'll need him tomorrow."

"So that's it!" Georges laughed slyly. "Well, I can fix that. Come on, Sabasté, it's time you graduated to the real stuff!"

Edouard saw Georges start after him and he panicked. He tried to run but he tripped on the end of the blanket and fell to his knees.

"Leave me alone, Georges. I don't want . . ." he gasped.

Georges laughed scornfully, but as he lunged for Edouard, Edouard threw the blanket in his face and slid away. Georges cursed, but Edouard managed to stagger to his feet. In desperation he ran along the wall and threw himself into the bathroom. Fighting his crippling nausea, he pushed the door closed and turned the lock just before Georges got to it. Edouard could hear Georges pounding on the door as he sank to his knees panting. He knew for certain now that his head was bleeding. He turned to check that Emile was locked in the room with him. Feeling weak and sick, he fumbled with the watch Paul had given him. I'm sorry, Paul, I can't do any more, he thought. He tried to crawl away from the door, but slipped to the floor. As he lay on the cold tile, a single thought passed through his mind. I'm sorry, Emile, I tried to bring you a blanket. I really tried.

Jack stood behind the door on the third-floor landing, trying to maintain order over a group of GIGN agents and police officers. They were all dressed in body armor and helmets and eager to charge the apartment.

"Any signal yet from Edouard?" he asked Paul impatiently, using his hand held radio.

"Not yet," Paul answered coolly from the roof.

"What the hell's he doing in there?" Jack shot back.

"Probably taking heat from Michon about coming back. Hold your fire, Jack. Give him a chance to get to Kon."

"All right! All right! But these guys are getting edgy," Jack complained.

"Keep them in line, Jack. It's our man in there and no one moves until I give the signal."

"I read ya," Jack acknowledged and ended his transmission.

He held his hand up and shook his head at Pienaar, the lead GIGN agent, who was directly behind him. Actually the whole transmission had been just for show. Jack's special watch was tuned to the same frequency as Paul's and Edouard's. It was just harder for Jack to be patient than it was for Paul. Paul didn't seem to need to pace or smoke to calm himself. He's probably meditating right now, Jack thought, then changed his mind. Naw, he's probably calmly checking his lines. Christ, I wish I could be up there to see that nothing comes loose on him. I hope that guy from GIGN knows what to do. It's hell being spread so thin.

Jack's reverie was abruptly terminated as he felt Edouard's signal pulsing on his left wrist. Almost simultaneously Paul's transmission came through. "It's a go! Now!"

Michon's mind went into high gear the moment he heard the shouting at the door. He tore into the living room, screaming a warning to Georges as he went. "Clear out! The police are here! Get out a window! Jesus! They must have followed Edouard!" Michon snatched a Skorpian from the stack and tossed one to Georges as he ran up behind him.

"Stop and think, Michon!" Georges growled. "I bet that son of a bitch brought them. I'm not going out the window. We've got hostages!"

"Breaux's no good to us now, Georges. We'd have to carry him."

"Do what you want! I'm going for Sabasté."

"Get out of here, Georges! The police won't give a damn about Sabasté," Michon screamed, but Georges did not hear him.

Georges raced back to the bathroom and started kicking at the door. His curses were drowned out by the thunderous pounding on the apartment door. Michon watched Georges leave, realizing that he had lost the last semblance of his control. He had taken orders, and given orders, but everything had gone wrong. To hell with the group! It's every man for himself now, he thought bitterly.

He turned toward the window, but before he could move, the glass exploded into a million splinters as Paul swung into the room. Instinctively Michon raised his Skorpian and fired, but Paul was moving too fast. He released his line, dropped to the floor, and rolled behind a chair to Michon's right. As Michon turned, Paul opened fire with his automatic. Michon's eyes opened wide in shocked disbelief. He dropped his weapon and fell forward. As Paul came forward to confirm that Michon was dead, he heard the blast of an automatic. He turned, expecting to face a terrorist, and saw that Georges was screaming like a man possessed and firing into the bathroom wall.

Suddenly the apartment door broke under the blows of the four-man steel ram and Jack burst into the entryway followed by what seemed like a small army of police officers and GIGN agents. Seeing Paul holding an Uzi, one of the men in the rear of the band pulled the trigger on his automatic. "Hold your fire!" Jack screamed above the roar. Paul dove for the floor calling out, "On your right, Jack!"

Immediately Jack stormed through the archway in time to see Georges whirl and flee into the dinning room. Jack and the others chased after him. Georges turned once to fire at his pursuers, but when he turned back to struggle with the lock on the high double windows, Jack's force slipped into the room.

"Give it up! You're surrounded!" Jack commanded, in French, but Georges had ceased being rational. He turned to face Jack screaming, "Capitalist pigs!" and raised his Skorpian. His death was swift and violent as suddenly every man in the group opened fire to defend himself and his companions.

While Jack's force was pursuing Georges, Paul signaled to the men who had used the ram to open the door. Arming themselves quickly from the veritable arsenal GIGN had in the corridor, they followed Paul down the hall to the left of the archway. Sending two men to search each of the two large bedrooms, Paul went cautiously down to the far bedroom alone. No one appeared to be in the room, but Paul noticed that the bed was unmade. Circling the room with his light, soundless tread, he saw that the double window was ajar. Flattening himself against the wall for a brief moment, he suddenly raised his weapon and pulled the right window open. To Paul's surprise, there on the railing of the narrow balcony stood a young man with shaggy brown hair. He was unarmed and tottered precariously as he stretched to reach a drain pipe fastened to the side of the building.

"Give up! You'll never make it!" Paul called.

The young man turned and Paul read the desperation in his eyes.

"Don't shoot! Please don't shoot! I swear I didn't know they were going to kill that girl! Gérard's a madman!"

As the young man tried to move farther away from Paul, his foot slipped and he swayed away from the building.

"Hang on!" Paul cautioned. "Come back inside. I won't shoot."

The young man gave Paul a frightened look and glanced down at the street. He stretched again, trying to reach the drain pipe, but it was still too far away.

"You can't make it!" Paul said firmly. Shit! He's scared to death of me, Paul thought suddenly. He stepped back from the window, put his automatic out of sight, and stripped off his helmet. Going to the window again, he slowly extended his hand to the man on the railing.

"Come back inside. I won't hurt you."

The man looked at him pleading, "Don't come any closer! I won't let you put me in prison. I swear I'll jump first!"

"Don't do it. You'll be O.K., Give me your hand," Paul answered, moving closer.

The man stared at Paul, but didn't move. "Don't come any closer. I won't go to prison."

"It won't be that bad. I'll help you."

"No. I can't . . ."

"Yes you can. I'll help you. What's your name?"

"Arnot," the man whispered nervously.

"Come on, Arnot. Give me your hand," Paul coaxed. "Come with me. I promise you won't have to deal with Gérard any more."

"Gérard's a madman. I didn't know. I swear I didn't know . . ."

"It's O.K. You won't have to face him. Come inside."

Arnot looked down again and swayed. "Help me!" he suddenly cried.

Instantly Paul reached forward and grabbed Arnot by the knees. Arnot screamed in terror, "Help me! I'm falling!"

"I've got you! I've got you! Put your hands on my back," Paul said quietly, but Arnot continued to shriek as he teetered on the railing.

"Let go of the wall, Arnot," Paul commanded firmly. "Take hold of me. Anywhere. Grab onto me, Arnot. Now!"

Suddenly Arnot let go of the wall and flung himself at Paul, landing on Paul's back. Paul staggered under Arnot's weight, but managed to roll Arnot safely through the window. "You're O.K." Paul assured Arnot as he patted him on the back. "I'll get someone to stay with you."

Paul grabbed his automatic, and leaping to the door, he bellowed, "Pienaar! Get a man down here!" Turning back to Arnot, he softened his voice. "You'll be O.K., Arnot. Just go with the police. I'll visit you later. No one's going to hurt you."

Just then a GIGN agent dashed in wielding an automatic. "Put that away," Paul said shaking his head. "He's unarmed." Lowering his voice to a whisper, he added, "Keep an eye on him. He's on the verge of hurting himself."

Paul hurried down the hall and past the archway. Jack had managed to complete Georges' job of breaking the bathroom door open and it dangled from the one hinge that still clung to the shattered frame. The door and the nearby wall were riddled with bullet holes. Paul's calmness suffered a severe jolt as he came through the door and spotted Edouard lying face down on the floor. Blood was trickling down the back of his neck.

"Oh my God! Edouard, what happened?" Paul gasped as he dropped to his knees beside Edouard. Paul felt for Edouard's pulse, and picked up a tiny vial laying by Edouard's limp hand. "The poor kid," Paul commented mournfully to Jack who was bending over Kon. "How's Kon?" Paul forced himself to ask.

"He's alive," Jack answered hesitantly. "The bastards beat the shit out of him, but he's still alive. What's keeping that damned ambulance crew?"

Jack rolled Kon onto his back and called to him. For a moment Kon opened his eyes as if he recognized Jack's voice. Then a terrified look passed across his face and he drew in his breath.

"Kon! It's Jack. Take it easy," Jack said touching Kon on the shoulder. Kon winced and pulled away gasping, "No!" He raised his hand to protect his head and then he went limp.

"Jesus! . . . the helmet," Jack cried. Letting go of Kon he unfastened the face mask. "Oh Christ! I scared him, Paul. I scared him! I thought he recognized my voice, but he didn't. Shit! How could I be so damned stupid?"

Instantly, Paul was beside Jack, feeling for Kon's pulse. "Take it easy, Jack. He just fainted. He's so weak it didn't take much to shock his system." Paul glanced quickly at Kon's bruises and visualized the horror Kon had been through. He shuddered inwardly at the images, but did not want to alarm Jack who obviously felt guilty about frightening Kon. "Don't worry, he'll be O.K." Paul mumbled, but his voice broke and he suspected that Jack knew he was just mouthing the words.

Before Jack could respond, two men from the ambulance team arrived. "What took you so long?" Jack grumbled.

"The police couldn't decide whether or not it was safe for us to come in. How many wounded are there?"

"Just one in here. The other one's dead," Paul answered quickly. "Anyone hurt out there?" he asked, looking at Jack.

Jack shook his head. "Georges is dead. Everybody else is O.K."

The men from the ambulance started to step over Edouard's body, but Paul put his hand up. "Stay there. We'll bring him out."

Without being told, Jack took hold of Kon's legs and helped Paul carry him to the waiting stretcher, stepping carefully over Edouard as they went. While the ambulance crew was covering Kon and strapping him down, Paul heard someone shouting his name.

"Hey, Martel! There's a reporter from some scandal sheet downstairs who keeps insisting that you gave him permission to come up. What do you want us to do with him?"

"Send him up," Paul answered.

"What the hell do you . . ."

"I said 'send him up here.' He's been cleared with Pienaar."

Suddenly Jack noticed blood on the front of Paul's pant leg. "What the hell happened to your leg, Paul?"

"Ah, nothing much. I scratched it when I came through the window."

"It sure is bleeding a lot for a scratch. I think you should go to the hospital."

"I'll be O.K. I've got to finish up here."

Paul turned, but Jack blocked his way. "I really think you should go to the hospital, Paul."

"Come on, Jack. Get out of my way. I don't have time to argue."

"Is that an order?"

"Yeah, yeah, come on, Jack!"

"O.K., but it's a stupid order," Jack answered and stepped aside.

"I'm fine, Jack," Paul insisted. "Go down and look after Kon. If he wakes up again, he'll be in a panic about being strapped down. I'll be along in a minute."

Jack nodded and followed the stretcher out through the archway. Just before the ambulance crew got to the door, a man with a camera hurried in. Seeing Kon lying on the stretcher, he immediately raised his camera. Jack was on guard, however, and had his arm over Kon's face before the flash went off. The last thing Geilla needed was to see pictures of Kon's battered face plastered all over the cover of some cheap tabloid. "Get that thing out of here!" Jack snapped as he recognized the reporter who had been at the scene the morning Kon had been kidnaped. Well, Paul had promised that guy a story if he kept the kidnaping quiet, he thought as he continued out the door. I sure as hell wouldn't have bothered with him, but Paul's in charge.

Paul caught the reporter's arm as he came into the living room. "In here," he said, motioning toward the sofa. "You can get pictures, but don't touch anything."

"This is real front page stuff!" the reporter responded eagerly as he snapped several pictures of Michon's body. "My editor will swallow his cigarette!"

"Just shut up and get on with it," Paul snapped. Leaving the reporter absorbed in his work, Paul retrieved the blanket Edouard had dropped and slipped into the bathroom. Hurriedly he searched though Edouard's pockets. He tore off his jacket and laid it over Edouard's body, then he spread the blanket over Edouard covering him from head to toe. "There's one in here," Paul said as he joined the reporter in the living room. Taking the reporter by the arm, he shoved him into the dinning room. He watched in silence as the reporter circled Georges' body, clicking off pictures as rapidly as possible. Suddenly the reporter leaned in for a close-up of Georges' bullet ridden body. Paul seized the reporter's arm and yanked him away.

"Jesus, you're a ghoul! How can you . . .?"

"It sells, Martel. Hey, you guys are the ones who blasted him—not me!"

"O.K.! That's enough!" Paul snapped. He pulled the reporter away from Georges and pushed him toward the bathroom.

"I want you to give this one front page coverage. His name is Edouard Sabasté. He was a stupid kid that started playing with drugs and ended up being controlled by a gang of terrorists. Play up the drug bit. I want kids to see where it leads."

"What's the deal? Are you on the narc squad, or something? I don't write sermons."

"Well, maybe you should start," Paul growled. Leaning down, he carefully pulled back the blanket revealing Edouard's bloody head.

"Nice job, Martel, really nice work," the reporter sneered. "Did you have to shoot the bastard in the head?"

"It's not our work. Georges in there was trying to get at the hostage and shot Edouard by mistake. Go ahead, get your close-up. And be sure to spell his name right. He was a medical student and I want everyone to know what a brilliant career was shattered by drugs."

The reporter leaned toward Edouard's body and quickly snapped several pictures. He was about to step around Edouard, but Paul grabbed his sleeve.

"Leave him in peace! You've got enough material."

"But I can't see his face! Nobody's going to recognize the back of his head!"

"Then take this," Paul snapped, and reaching into his pocket he pulled out Edouard's hospital I.D. card and handed it to the reporter.

"I thought you weren't supposed to touch anything!"

"Just shut up and take it! I want to make this kid an example for all the others who think they can play with fire and not get burned. Blow his picture up as big as a billboard, sell it to the T.V. stations. Get out of my sight!"

"Why did you call me if this bothers you so much? You know perfectly well this is my job."

"None of your business," Paul snapped. "Go on! Get out of here!"

The reporter started out, but turned to snap a picture of Paul's face as he leaned over Edouard's body. "Print that and you're dead," Paul warned icily as the flash went off.

"O.K. O.K. I'll keep it in my private collection—to remind myself that some guys with badges still give a damn."

"Get out of here," Paul responded without emotion. After he was sure that the reporter had left, he gently rolled Edouard unto his back. "I'm sorry I had to destroy your reputation, Edouard, but it's the only way out," Paul said, gently stroking Edouard's face.

A moment later Paul stepped into the hall. Looking around quickly he called to one of the police officers who was taking official photos of Michon's body. "Hey! Send the ambulance crew up here."

"I thought you said that guy was dead!" the officer responded in surprise.

"Well, I thought he was. What the hell do I know! I'm a GIGN agent, not a medic!"

Paul was leaning against the sink when the ambulance crew arrived a few minutes later. It was a different crew and he hoped that the first ambulance had left with Kon. He had been the one to stipulate that two ambulances be on alert for the siege of the apartment. "Has the other ambulance left?" he asked to be certain.

"Yes. We were just waiting to deliver the bodies to the morgue," one of the men answered.

"You'll have to send another team for them," Paul mumbled. "This guy needs help."

Paul waited while the ambulance crew secured Edouard onto a stretcher and followed them when they carried Edouard down the hall. He kept watching Edouard's face for any sign that he had regained consciousness, but Edouard was deathly still. Paul was about to follow the ambulance crew into the elevator when he spotted Pienaar coming out of the apartment. He waved the crew on and went back to talk to the leader of the GIGN agents. "Remember to keep the official record straight, Pienaar. Sabasté died in the shoot out."

"Yes, Monsieur Artier. It will be as you say."

Paul thought he detected a hint of sarcasm in Pienaar's voice, but he wasn't sure. "Thanks," he said aloud and turned toward the elevator. I don't want anything else to get screwed up on this job, he thought as he pressed the elevator button. Suddenly he felt drained and guessed his adrenalin rush had worn off. He waited, wishing the elevator would hurry. He was anxious to get to the jail and see Arnot. Perhaps Arnot could lead him to Gérard. Paul was glad that Kon had been rescued, but bitterly disappointed that Gérard had not been captured.

Paul winced when the elevator stopped abruptly on the first floor. He suddenly realized that his leg was hurting more than a little bit. He limped out of the elevator and noticed that there was a crowd of people in the lobby. Police officers he didn't know, GIGN agents he recognized, and people that he guessed were tenants of the building were all milling around in what seemed to him utter confusion. He made his way unsteadily through the crowd and out the front door. The street was dark now and he was struck by how cold it was.

He wished he had his jacket and vaguely remembered having left it in the apartment. He thought about going back for it, but decided he didn't have the energy to fight his way past the crowd again. He staggered toward the curb and looked around. Where did I leave the car? he wondered. He started toward one of the police cars, intending to ask for a lift to the police station, when suddenly Jack was beside him.

"Where have you been, Paul? I saw the second ambulance crew go up. How did it go?"

"I thought you were with Kon," Paul shot back anxiously. "Didn't you take him to the hospital?"

"Relax, he's gone. I sent Mary with him. How long have you been wandering around out here?" Jack asked, noting how pale and glassy-eyed Paul looked.

"I don't know . . . couldn't find the car and . . . it's really turned cold, Jack. I . . . I left my coat somewhere. I need to get to the police station."

"Here, put this on," Jack said, quickly slipping out of his jacket and putting it over Paul's shoulders. "You're shaking."

"I didn't think it got so cold here this time of year. I don't know why I didn't wear a jacket," Paul mumbled.

Jack shook his head. "Come on, Paul. You need to get inside."

"I have to get to the police station, Jack. We didn't get Gérard. Arnot might know . . ."

"O.K. O.K. We'll go to the police station. I don't remember where the car is either," he lied. "We'll take a police car. Come on, there's one over here." Jack answered. He started to lead Paul toward the curb but Paul was limping badly.

Chapter Twelve

"Are we going the right way, Jack?" Paul asked in confusion.

"Yes. We're almost there."

"I . . . I feel . . . shit!" Paul said, stumbling against Jack. ". . . need a hand, Jack. Don't let those guys from GIGN see me fall on my face . . . stupid idiots . . . shot my leg."

"What! Who?" Jack said, suddenly picking up on what Paul was mumbling.

". . . coming in the door . . . no discipline . . ."

"Jesus! Why didn't you say something? I thought you cut yourself on the glass."

"Pienaar's so damn smug . . . had to finish with Edouard."

"O.K. O.K. Just hold on a minute longer," Jack answered, putting Paul's arm across his shoulder. He half-carried Paul the last few steps to the police car. The two men inside did not notice Jack until he was almost at the door. "Hey! Wake up! My friend's been hurt!" Jack growled in place of a greeting.

"Who the hell . . . ?" a young police officer sputtered in surprise.

"We're with GIGN. Now shut your mouth and open the damn door."

"Oh . . . sure," the officer answered, quickly jumping out of the passenger seat and pulling open the rear door. "What happened up there? We saw some guy go in the window and . . ."

"Look!" Jack said sternly. "This is the guy who went in, and he got cut up doing it. He needs to get to a hospital right now."

"O.K. O.K. I understand!" the young officer replied, suddenly realizing that his curiosity was out of place. "Here, let me help you get him in."

"Don't touch him! I've got things under control," Jack snapped. "Just close the door and get moving. Use your siren and turn up the heat!"

"Oh shit!" the second officer grumbled. He spun the car away from the curb, turned on the siren, switched on the flashing lights, and shoved the accelerator to the floor.

"Are we at the police station?" Paul mumbled when he heard the siren.

"Not yet, Paul. Just hold on, O.K." Jack answered, straining to sound calm. It was dark in the car and he couldn't tell where Paul was bleeding. He could only feel that Paul's pant leg was wringing wet. Damn! he thought to himself. I should have made you go in that ambulance, Paul. I shouldn't have listened to you. You can lie so damn well!

"Give me your coat," Jack said quietly to the young officer in the front seat.

"My coat? What for?"

"Don't they teach you guys anything?" Jack barked, letting his exasperation show. "Just give me your coat!"

The younger man still seemed reluctant, but the older officer reprimanded him. "Give him the damn coat! We don't need anybody from GIGN dying in our vehicle."

"Shut up!" Jack ordered, hoping Paul had not heard the remark. He caught the coat as the officer tossed it over the back of the seat and wrapped it snugly around Paul's leg.

Paul drew in his breath and then began to mumble. "You'll have to go in, Jack. I'll . . . I'll wait here . . . I'm not doing too well."

"What's so damned important about the police station, Paul? Can't it wait?"

"No . . . got to get there right away . . . guy named Arnot . . . I think . . . I think he might know where Gérard is."

"Hell, he's not going anywhere. We can see him later!"

"No . . . no . . . Arnot's scared. He's in over his head . . . has to be handled just right or . . . he might kill himself. He's desperate. I saw it . . . need to get to him right away . . . right away."

"O.K. O.K. I'll go see him just as soon as . . ."

"Be careful, Jack, be careful . . ."

"Alright, alright, just stop worrying. I'll be all sweetness and light. I promise."

"Good, good . . . I'll check . . . I'll check on Kon and Edouard."

"Stop worrying about everybody, Paul! For Christ's sake, will you stop worrying. I'll take care of things."

Paul was still mumbling about checking on everyone when the police car arrived at the hospital. As the car stopped, Jack looked up and read the sign beside the emergency room door. "Where the hell are we?" he bellowed from the back seat.

"We're at the hospital. I thought that was what you asked for," the driver answered defensively.

"You idiots! This is the wrong hospital!"

"But we always bring our men here. It's got the best trauma . . ."

"I don't care what it's got! Jesus! Can anything else get screwed up on this damn job? O.K. O.K. It's too late now! Go get someone to bring a stretcher."

After the young police officer hurried into the building, Jack turned back to Paul. "Everything's going to be O.K., Paul. They've got a good set-up. They'll know what to do. I'll take care of things. Don't worry. I'll take care of things."

Paul was too weak to resist when two men came to help Jack lift him onto the stretcher, but when he realized he was not at the police station, he became angry. "We were supposed to go to the police station, Jack. Damn it! I thought you could follow simple directions. You're as bad as the jerks at GIGN."

"Take it easy, Paul. I'll go, O.K.! I'll go, just as soon . . ."

"You're not giving me any help on this, Jack. Nobody's giving me any help."

Strangely enough, Paul's irrational ranting made Jack upset. He was hurt that Paul could believe he would abandon a friend. Didn't Paul know how much he meant to him? Jack was still feeling guilty about frightening Kon, and he felt it was his duty to comfort and protect Paul. After all, Paul was the one who went out of his way to help people. He took the weight of everyone's problems as his own. Seeing him lying there, bleeding and confused, Jack could not help but think that Paul deserved more attention. He gave so much to others, he was entitled to the comforting presence of a friend in his hour of need.

Jack stood by the stretcher, holding Paul's arm and repeating that he would go to the police station just as soon as he was sure that Paul was O.K. As Jack waited, he grew angry that no one was taking care of Paul. He remembered the sense of helplessness he had experienced as he held Brad in his arms, waiting an eternity for an ambulance. He remembered staring at Kon's battered body and cursing the ambulance crew for their slowness. He remembered his best friend in the military who had bled to death because the helicopter couldn't land. It seemed to him that everyone on the team, everyone he cared about was in need of help, and people were just standing around. Suddenly his anger burst forth in a roar that blasted through the emergency room.

"Jesus Christ! Isn't anyone going to help this man! Are you going to let him bleed to death while you screw around!"

Jack's outburst brought instant response. Heads turned and people ran toward him, trying to calm and reassure him, trying to appease and placate the tall, blonde volcano that had erupted in their midst. The first person to reach him was a short woman with light brown hair. She looked very official in her white pants suit.

"Calm down!" she ordered firmly in English. "You're not helping him with all your shouting. Calm down and tell us what happened."

Gratefully Jack took the hand she extended. She was speaking English. What a relief! He was unaware that he had momentarily lapsed into English to vent his frustration. He struggled to control himself. He knew his size alone intimidated people, and he didn't want to frighten her the way he had frightened Kon.

"He's bleeding!" Jack blurted. "He told me he cut himself . . . I shouldn't have believed him. He's been shot. You've got to help him!"

Several other people were around him now, bending over the stretcher and examining Paul.

"We will take him to the surgery, Monsieur. Please calm down," someone said in French.

"Are you hurt?" the woman asked in English.

"No! I'm fine. Just take care of Paul, please."

"Are you sure you are all right?" she asked again.

"Yes! Yes! I'm fine," Jack insisted impatiently.

"That's not your blood on your pant leg?"

He looked down and saw the stain. "Oh God, it's Paul's. He was bleeding in the car. For Christ's sake, will you hurry up!"

"Calm down, Monsieur. Everything will be fine," he heard again.

"Please! Would you just hurry!" Jack said, trying to calm himself.

He watched anxiously as the stretcher was wheeled away.

"Do you work here?" he asked, turning back to the woman.

"Could you stay with him? I have to check on someone. I hate to leave him like this, but he'll have a fit if I don't go."

"I don't work here," the woman answered. "I'm just here for some training. I don't know if they will allow . . ."

"Please," Jack pleaded. "You are a nurse, aren't you?"

"Yes, but . . ."

"I'll pay you . . . whatever you charge. Please. I can't leave him alone. He doesn't deserve that. You don't know him, but he looks after everybody. He deserves to be taken care of. Please . . ."

"I see you care a lot about him."

"Yes, yes. I can't just leave him. This isn't even the right hospital. They're all at the other one. Please stay with him. I won't be gone long. Please," he begged.

She patted his arm and smiled the most wonderful smile, broad and kind, but with too much mischief in it to qualify as angelic. He knew from her accent that she was British, and he welcomed the chance to express his feelings in his own language. Perhaps he associated her with Mary, for like Mary she seemed so calm and dependable.

"All right, I'll stay . . . but not in any official capacity for I have no standing here . . . only as a friend."

"Thank you! Thank you! You don't know how much this means to me," Jack answered, feeling as though a great weight had been lifted from him. "I hope I didn't scare you with all my shouting. I probably looked like a madman. I . . . I usually don't get so strung out, but this . . . this week . . . this job has been a nightmare. Everyone on the team is down. We all kind of lean on Paul and . . ."

"I understand," she said and smiled again. "You are very worried about your friend."

"Yes," Jack agreed readily. "I'm so glad you're here. Look, if the GIGN people come around, Paul's papers are fake. His real name is Artier, not Martel . . . and . . . it's kind of complicated . . . just tell anyone that asks to call the GIGN headquarters and talk to Pienaar."

"Pienaar. All right, I'll tell them," she said nodding her head.

"Oh, and tell Paul I went to the police station. Make sure he understands that. He's got himself all worked up. I won't be gone long."

"And who shall I say went to the police station?"

"Oh yeah, my name's Jack, Jack Barrons."

"Jack," she repeated with a trace of skepticism in her voice. "Is that your real name or your fake name?"

Jack stopped short. "God, I must sound like a crackpot. Jack is my real name."

"I'm pleased to meet you, Jack. My name is Bridget."

"I'm so glad you're here, Bridget," he said taking her hand. She smiled again and he knew Paul was in good hands. "I've got to go," he said and turned away reluctantly. He noticed that the two police officers were still in the hall. Probably waiting to see if they're going to put a straight jacket on me, he thought wryly.

"Could you give me a lift to the central police station?" he asked sheepishly as he came up to them.

"Sure. What else have we got to do besides drive GIGN agents around?" the older man answered sarcastically and started out.

"Say, don't worry about your friend," the younger man piped up. "They handle this kind of stuff all the time. Just last week . . . well, it's kind of a long story, but they really are good here."

"Thanks," Jack responded. "And thanks for the fast ride."

"Any time! Hey, he was really something going through that window! I'm sorry he got hurt."

Jack looked back to see if Bridget was still there and she was. She smiled and waved. It was a silly little wave, the kind one gives to encourage a child on its first day of school. He should have resented it, but he didn't. He grinned in spite of himself and waved back. It felt good to smile. It seemed a long time since he had felt like it. Well, I've really made a good impression on her, he thought. She must think I've got crumpets or something for a brain. So? Why should I care what she thinks? Why indeed? But he did.

Jack was calmer by the time he reached the police station, but he was angry with himself for losing his temper. It's no wonder Paul treats me like one of his kid brothers. I deserve it, coming apart like that. But Jesus! All that blood and the way Paul was shaking scared the shit out of me. He never says a word until he drops. I shouldn't have believed him about being O.K. What the hell was I thinking? I guess I'm tired and my stupid arm still hurts. Well, I'd better handle Arnot with kid gloves. I promised Paul I'd do a good job. And I'd better call Dr. La Monde right away so he can be here when Kon wakes up.

It was quiet at the police station when Jack arrived. He learned that several agents from GIGN had been questioning Arnot, but apparently he was not in a talkative mood. He looked slightly haggard when he was brought into the interview room and despite an attempt to adopt a "tough-guy" stance, Jack knew Paul was right about Arnot being scared. He couldn't seem to sit still and kept jiggling his leg and looking around nervously. Jack felt no empathy for Arnot, but he made a studied effort to imitate Paul and act like a sympathetic listener. Playing big brother came naturally to Paul, and Jack was determined not to ruin this contact for him.

Jack leaned back in his chair, crossed his legs in a relaxed manner, and lit a cigarette. He pulled a few contemplative drags before offering the pack to Arnot who snatched it from Jack's hand with the eagerness of sheer physical need. Jack noticed Arnot's rugged, workman's hands shake as he lit the cigarette for him with his fake-gold lighter. Arnot was obviously not a pampered intellectual and Jack wondered about his membership in the Direct Action group. Most working-class youngsters were too busy making their way in the world to get involved with radical ideologies.

Doing his best to appear friendly and concerned, or at least neutral but interested, Jack tried to draw information about the group from Arnot in exchange for leniency from the courts. Arnot again expressed his strong desire to stay out of prison, but seemed terrified that Gérard would retaliate if he betrayed the group.

Arnot had witnessed the great lengths to which Rouillan had gone in order to track down and punish Etienne Rubard, and he believed that Rubard was more clever than himself. Although Jack tried to assure Arnot that he would be protected, Arnot insisted that he had no idea where Gérard or Rouillan could be found. The session ended with Arnot giving a detailed description of Gérard and agreeing to try to identify him from GIGN mug shots. Arnot turned down Jack's offer to contact his parents, saying mournfully that the shame of his being arrested would kill his mother. In the end, Jack found himself promising to visit Arnot again, and wondering why he had made the offer. Perhaps it was the desperation with which Arnot had gripped his hand when he stood to say good-bye. For a moment his terrorist facade fell away, revealing a confused lad who felt totally at the mercy of a system he believed was heartless and oppressive. As he left the police station, Jack warned the guards to keep careful watch on Arnot lest he hurt himself.

Rather than bother the police for another ride, Jack took a cab to the hospital where Kon and Edouard had been taken. He was relieved when Mary hurried out to the reception desk in answer to his page.

"Jack! Where have you been? I expected you hours ago. Where is Paul? Good heavens! What happened to your leg? Sit down. Let me call . . ."

"I'm O.K., Mary. Don't get excited. Paul was hurt in the assault. I tried to bring him here, but we ended up at another hospital."

"Is he O.K.?"

"I'm not sure. I think so. He kept insisting that I go to the police station to see one of the terrorists we captured. I found a nurse to stay with him. How's Kon?"

"They're still running tests and taking X-rays. He's so battered. Do you want some coffee or something to eat, Jack? You look exhausted."

"No. I'll be O.K. I need to get back to Paul. I hated to leave him alone like that. Is Nea here? He'd probably like to see her."

"She's here but . . . she's with Geilla."

Tired as he was, Jack caught the slight hesitation in Mary's voice and suspected she was holding something back. "How is Geilla? She didn't see Kon, did she?"

"I'm afraid so. We couldn't keep her away. She's been so worried. It was a shock. She nearly fainted and about an hour ago she started having pains."

"Oh God no," Jack moaned. "Don't tell her about Paul!"

"I won't. Perhaps it would be better if . . ."

"I understand. I'm scaring everybody with these bloody clothes. I called Carlin. He should be here soon."

"Thank God! I'm sorry, Jack. I'll just sneak in and get Nea. I'm sure she would like to see Paul. I'll tell Geilla that you and Paul are still questioning suspects. The doctor gave her a sedative so she isn't really alert."

"O.K. I'll wait here."

"Why don't you sit down, Jack."

"O.K." Jack agreed, but he remained standing.

"Oh, I forgot," Mary added. "Edouard has a concussion. I alerted the doctors to his Demerol addiction. It complicates matters, but they are keeping him under close observation."

"Good. I'm just glad he's alive. We wouldn't have gotten to Kon in time without his help."

"Do sit down, Jack," Mary said in her best no-discussion-allowed voice.

"O.K. O.K.," he answered mechanically, but this time he sat.

Jack knew he had made an impression on the emergency room staff, because as soon as he walked through the door, a woman in a white uniform hurried up to him with the news that Paul had been taken to the fifth floor. She directed Jack and Nea to the elevators, then slid behind a counter, and picked up a telephone receiver.

Bridget was sitting quietly, reading a magazine when Jack and Nea came into the room.

"Oh, you came back," she said, looking relived.

"I told you I wouldn't be gone long."

"Well, yes but . . . when those policemen took you away, I . . ."

"They didn't take me away! I asked for a lift. Jees, you must have thought I was bonkers."

"Oh no! I just . . . I wasn't quite sure what to think, but I felt someone had to see that your friend was taken care of."

"Is he going to be all right?" Jack asked, going towards the bed.

"Oh my God!" Nea blurted when she saw how lifeless Paul looked.

Jack had wondered how she might react to Paul's appearance. He was glad to see she wasn't repulsed, even though at the moment Paul looked very much in need of the unit of blood that was attached to his arm. He didn't respond when Nea touched his hand.

"Don't worry," Bridget offered. "He's not as sick as he looks. The doctor told me that they had to put him to sleep to keep him from climbing off the table. He kept insisting that he had to get to the police station. He certainly has a one-track mind."

Jack grinned. "Yeah, Paul can be pretty determined sometimes."

"Determined?" Nea put in. "I'd say bull-headed is more the word for it. Four of them work as a team and they are all that way!"

Jack laughed. "Bridget, this is Nea, a friend of Paul's."

"Hello, Nea. It's nice to meet you," Bridget said and smiled.

"Hello, Bridget. Thank you for taking care of Paul."

"Oh, I'm really only here as a friend."

"Well, by the looks of things Paul certainly needed a friend. We can take over now if you want to leave."

"Thank you. I really must be . . ."

"You don't have to leave so soon, do you?" Jack asked impulsively. "Let me pay you for your time."

"Oh, that's all right. I was glad to do it."

"At least let me buy you some coffee? I guess it's kind of late for dinner."

"That's not necessary. It's just part of my job."

"But I really want to. You don't know how much I appreciated your being here. We could get some coffee. It's not too late for you, is it?"

"Well, training does start early tomorrow."

"Oh," Jack mumbled. "What are you training for?"

"Rescue transport operations."

"You're kidding! You mean you're in one of those flying medic units?"

"Yes."

"That's great! That's really great! What a lucky break that you were here. Hey, I want to hear about this. Are you sure it's too late?"

Bridget cast a quick look at her watch and her nose crinkled a bit as she considered the time. Then she looked at Jack's eager, expectant face. Nea noticed the look too. "Oh, go ahead, Bridget! Jack needs to take a break. He's been running all over tonight."

"It seems that way. You never did tell me how your friend got hurt."

Jack grinned. "It's a long story. I want to find out how you came to be here."

"That's a long story too."

"Then we'd better get started!" Jack exclaimed.

"All right, coffee it is. Good night, Nea. It was nice to meet you."

"Good night, Bridget. See if you can coax Jack to eat. I don't think he's had supper yet."

Jack started to follow Bridget out, then turned back to Nea. "Are you going to be all right here by yourself?"

"Certainly. Go eat and relax."

"O.K. I won't be too long."

"Take your time," Nea said picking up the magazine Bridget had abandoned. "I'll catch up on my fashion magazines and see if my designs reflect the latest Paris fad."

Jack laughed and hurried after Bridget. "So you're a traveling nurse. That's great! I'm a pilot myself."

"Oh, what do you fly?" she asked, pressing the elevator button and smiling up at him with calm curiosity.

For a fleeting moment Jack suddenly forgot everything he knew about airplanes. She must be one hell of a nurse, he thought. Her smile hits like a double dose of morphine.

"Still worried about your friend?" she asked when he didn't answer.

"Er, no . . . well, yes, but . . . er . . . I have a Piper Arrowstar."

Bridget nodded her head knowingly. "Ah, then you're more than a week-end pilot."

"Yeah. I have my commercial rating."

"Ever fly whirly birds?"

"Occasionally. Don't tell me you fly choppers!"

"How else am I going to get to those blokes who break their legs climbing rocks on the moors?"

"You are something, Bridget! You are really something," Jack exclaimed with more than a little admiration.

Chapter Thirteen

Nea glanced up and smiled as Jack came into Paul's room. "Have a good time?"

Although Nea was not officially part of the team, she had been doing her best to help out during the past week, and Jack noticed how tired she looked.

"Yeah. Bridget likes to fly so we had a lot to talk about. How's Paul?"

"He hasn't moved. He still looks bad, but I guess they're not going to give him any more blood."

"He's probably worn out. I don't think he got much sleep all week."

"He was so worried about Kon. They must be very close."

"They are. But Paul worries about everybody. Say, I retrieved the car. Why don't I drive you back to the hotel. You must be tired."

Nea shrugged. "I thought I'd like to stay with Paul."

"I appreciate that, but I can almost guarantee that he isn't going to wake up until morning. There's nothing you can do for him right now. You should get some rest. Mary is probably going to need your help tomorrow."

"Yes, but . . ."

"Come on, Nea. I'm the last one standing so I must be in charge. You need some rest and I have to get you back to the hotel while I can still see."

"O.K., I'll go, but what about you? You haven't had much sleep either."

"I plan to fix that as soon as I get to the hotel."

"O.K. I won't keep you."

"Good. I'm too tired to argue. I'll tell the night nurse we're leaving and ask her to check on Paul."

When they reached the hotel, Jack escorted Nea to her room before going to his own. He hadn't spent much time there all week, but the freshly-made bed beckoned him now. He phoned the front desk to request an early wake-up call, took a pain pill for his arm, slipped off his clothes, and dropped into bed. God, I hope Kon and Paul are going to be O.K., he thought. And then he was out.

Jack was back at the hospital by 6 a.m., but Paul didn't stir until shortly after eight. Several times he woke long enough to shift positions and then fell asleep again. When Jack saw him looking around the room, he called to him. "Paul? Are you awake?"

Paul turned his head at the sound of Jack's voice. "Jack? What . . . ? What happened?"

"You got hurt in the assault on the apartment."

"Oh . . . right . . . Did you get Kon to the hospital?"

"Yes. Carlin is with him. He's got a good chance to recover."

"Good . . . good. What about Edouard? I was supposed to help him. He must be in a panic," Paul said, shaking his head as if to clear it.

"Don't worry, he's still out. He's got a concussion, but he'll make it."

"There was something else . . . the police station! Did you get to the police station?" Paul asked anxiously.

"Yes. Relax about that. I went to see Arnot, but he either couldn't or wouldn't tell me where Gérard or Roullian are. He did give me a good description of them and agreed to look at mug shots."

"Damn! He must know more than he's telling. I'd better go see him," Paul said, struggling to get up. Suddenly he stifled a cry and went rigid.

"Hey!" Jack yelled, grabbing Paul by the shoulders. "Stop wiggling around! You're not going anywhere, buddy! You lost a lot of blood last night."

Paul didn't answer. He just grimaced and clenched his fist. Jack watched him for a moment before suggesting, "Hold on. I'll get a nurse."

"Don't! Just give me a minute," Paul called hoarsely.

"Forget that mind control bullshit, Paul! You need a shot of something," Jack said decisively and hurried out to the nurses' station.

"Monsieur Artier needs something for pain," he reported to the nurse on duty.

"So, he is awake. We will have to check him first."

"Look," Jack said, fixing the nurse in a steady gaze. "Skip the blood pressure crap. He's hurting right now and my blood pressure will go through the roof if you don't do something about it!"

"Yes, Monsieur," the nurse agreed meekly. "I think the doctor left some orders for medication."

"Find them," Jack answered without a smile.

The nurse grabbed a folder and leafed through it quickly, casting nervous glances at Jack. "Ah yes, here it is. I must get it from the cabinet."

"Fine," Jack said coolly. "I'll wait with Monsieur Artier. I trust it won't take long."

"No, Monsieur. I will be right there."

The nurse was true to her word and Jack had barely returned to Paul's bedside before she hurried in.

"This isn't necessary," Paul objected weakly, but the nurse guessed from Paul's tense posture that he was lying.

"Doctor's orders, Paul," Jack cut in. "Just cooperate with the lady or I'll have to pin you down."

"Don't listen to him," Paul cautioned the nurse. "He thinks he can boss me around because I'm flat on my back."

"I think it is best, Monsieur," the nurse responded. "I do not wish to do battle with your very large friend."

"O.K.! O.K.! The sooner it stops hurting, the sooner I can get out of here."

"Just lay down and be quiet, Paul," Jack said after the nurse left. "You can't do anything right now. Kon's asleep and so is Edouard. Let Carlin do his job."

"O.K.," Paul agreed reluctantly. "I really don't think I could stand up for long."

"Well, use some of your superior oriental wisdom and don't try it."

Jack figured the shot was working when a few minutes later Paul smiled weakly and grumbled, "Stop acting like a drill sergeant."

"Sorry," Jack apologized as he arranged Paul's pillow for him.

"Sometimes you need to be smacked down for your own good. Do you want some breakfast?"

"No. I'm not . . . do you suppose they have any juice?"

"Well, if they don't, I'll get some. What do you want? Orange?"

"Yeah. But don't bother . . ."

"Nothing to it. Stay put!"

Paul nodded and Jack hurried out. The nurse shot Jack a "now-what" look as he arrived at the nurses' station, but relaxed when she learned that all he wanted was orange juice. She didn't need a doctor's order for that.

"Success!" Jack beamed as he came back holding his prize.

"Thanks, Jack," Paul answered, eagerly accepting the juice. "I'm a little vague about what happened after I left the apartment. I remember trying to get to the police station, but people kept getting in the way."

"Yeah. I heard you were trying to get off the table while they were sewing you up."

"They must have thought I was crazy."

"No . . . I told them you got shot by a jealous husband and had to keep moving."

"Oh jees! Thanks pal. What a friend."

"I had to say something to get you some help. I'm afraid I did some yelling. I sure made an impression on one of the nurses. Every time she sees me, she runs behind a counter and picks up a phone, even if it isn't ringing."

"You do have a way with women, Jack."

"Not with all of 'em. One brassy, little English nurse as much as told me to shut up! Very politely, of course."

"Of course. Did you scare her too?"

"As a matter of fact, no. She's very interesting."

"Oh? What's been going on while I was out?"

"Not that way. I mean 'interesting' interesting. She flies helicopters and rescues people off the moors. I'm taking her to dinner."

"You never quit, Jack . . . making dates over my dead body . . ."

"Come on. I got you here, didn't I? And it's not a date! It's just a meal."

"That's how it starts. First you eat and then . . ."

"You're off the beam on this one, Paul. She's not like that. She's just . . . you know . . . interesting. I've never met a female pilot. We'll probably talk about airplanes and gear and stuff. She's got the wildest sense of humor though."

"Enjoy . . ." Paul mumbled wearily. "Forgive . . . forgive me if I don't . . . wait up."

"Get some rest, buddy. I'll be back later," Jack said, seeing that Paul was too tired to talk.

At half past ten, after he had checked on Kon, Jack decided what he was going to do. It probably wasn't the best thing he could do to foster good will with GIGN officials, but damn it, he was angry. It was bad enough that Paul had been seriously hurt by that jerk from GIGN, but because of that guy's stupidity, Paul was unable to be there when Kon needed him. Jack determined that he was going to find out who was responsible and see that he was fired. Jack wasn't positive that Brad and Paul would agree to a head on confrontation with Pienaar, but hiding his anger behind a string of polished verbiage was not Jack's approach. He wondered how Brad had managed to negotiate the initial arrangement with GIGN, because once he was out of the picture, Pienaar had given very little help to Paul. Well, with everyone in the hospital, I'm in charge for the moment, Jack reasoned. And I'm determined to let Pienaar know how I feel.

He drove to the GIGN offices, announced himself, and was shown swiftly to Pienaar's office. Pienaar didn't seem surprised to see him. He extended his hand to Jack as a formality, but there was no warmth in his greeting. Jack had labeled Pienaar aristocratic at first, but suddenly he decided that Paul was right. Pienaar was just plain smug. His thin, dark beard was trimmed to such a point that it looked positively theatrical and he tended to wave his hands nervously when he talked.

"Ah, Monsieur Barrons, good-day," Pienaar began. "It is always a pleasure to see you. Please sit down. How may I be of service?"

He's going to deny all responsibility, Jack thought in disgust. I might as well get to the point. "I've come about Monsieur Artier," he

197

said, ignoring the offer of a chair. "One of your trigger happy agents shot him last night and I want a name."

"Ah yes," Pienaar began calmly and lowered himself stiffly into the chair behind his desk. "A most unfortunate event . . . most unfortunate. I read the report early this morning. How is our friend, Monsieur Artier?"

So he knows, Jack thought, feeling his temper rise at Pienaar's use of the term "our friend." He's no friend of Paul's and his condescending over familiarity is insulting. "He'll live—no thanks to you," Jack stated bluntly. "He was awake for about ten minutes this morning before they had to dope him up again."

"I am truly sorry to hear he is still down. He concealed his injury so well. Last night . . . he was all business. I did not suspect . . . ."

"Paul's no complainer, but I want the guy who did it. I figure it had to be Varenne or Falcon. I want him out. He has no business . . ."

"I am truly sorry, Monsieur Barrons, but what you are asking is very difficult."

"I'm not asking, Pienaar. I'm telling! That guy could have killed my partner. I'll go over your head if I have to, but I want him out."

Pienaar put his hand to his head, as if the very idea of Jack going over his head gave him a headache. Jack noticed that Pienaar no longer looked smugly detached. For a moment he looked almost harried, but he straightened himself quickly. "Please, Monsieur Barrons, you do not understand what you are asking."

"Look, Pienaar, I'm no diplomat, but I know a lousy cop when I see one. He . . ."

"The man is not a lousy cop, as you so rudely imply!" Pienaar objected. "He is one of my best agents."

Jack was startled. "Well, if he's one of your best, you've got problems. He's out of control!"

"Please, Monsieur Barrons, calm yourself. This . . . this is very difficult for me," Pienaar began and Jack saw that he really was distressed. "I apologize for what happened to Monsieur Artier. I am deeply sorry. I am sorry too that I was not able to give him all the help he needed. I have been very short handed, Monsieur Barrons. The men I was able to offer were all junior people. The man that you are so set in condemning is one of my best agents. He is thoroughly experienced in dealing with terrorists, but he has been on medical leave. He has only just now returned to duty. I feel I might have done him a terrible disservice by allowing him to return to work so soon."

"Disservice to him? What about to Paul?" Jack sputtered.

Pienaar looked even more distressed and it seemed to Jack that the last shred of his aristocratic mien fell away. "You do not understand, Monsieur Barrons," he began in a pleading tone. "The man of whom we speak, the man you want to degrade, is, or was, one of my best agents. In fact, he was so zealous in pursuing the Direct Action group that he became a marked man. Six weeks ago his wife and only child were gunned down before his eyes as they left home. He himself was severely wounded trying to defend them."

"Oh God!" Jack gasped as he pictured the incident.

"The man was devastated, as you can well imagine," Pienaar continued. "He has recovered physically and sustains himself with he thought of continuing his work to stamp out the group. It has become a crusade for him. It's all he lives for. I was doubtful that he was stable enough to return to duty, but he begged me and I took a chance. Last night I thought I had handled everything so beautifully. Your friend was rescued alive, my agent was back to work. You see, it is I who am to blame for this disaster."

"Oh jees! What a mess!" Jack exclaimed. "Does the guy even realize that he hit Paul?"

"Yes," Pienaar said slowly. "I knew he was the one who had fired last night. But until I read the police report this morning . . . I brought it to his attention privately. He is overcome with remorse, but if I dismiss him . . . I had hoped that I could approach Monsieur Artier or Monsieur Cover-Rollins, but . . . It was another error on my part to think I could hide such a thing."

Oh shit! What have I done? Jack asked himself. If only I had been even a little bit diplomatic instead of charging in here kicking open a hornet's nest! Who am I to ruin a man's career? I sure as hell lost it last night, screaming and swearing at everybody. What could I say if someone reported my unprofessional behavior to Brad?

Jack did not respond for a moment and Pienaar interpreted his silence as hardened resolve. "Would you like to talk to the man?" he asked.

"No! Christ no!" Jack answered quickly. "I don't even want to know his name. Look, Paul is the last person who would persecute anyone. He's very forgiving. I was just so damn mad . . . He's like my brother, you know. I'm sorry I came."

"I was a fool to think I could cover up such a thing. Monsieur Artier was relying on me and I let him down."

"What's going to happen to your agent?"

"There will be an inquiry and he will be sent for psychiatric evaluation. He will probably be suspended without pay. I will lose my rank, and I will be unable to help him." Pienaar lowered his head and studied his hands.

Oh great! Brad will have a fit if Pienaar loses his job, Jack thought uneasily. "Does it have to end that way?" he asked tentatively. "You said yourself that if you had talked to Paul . . . Can't we just forget that I came? I never dreamed the situation was so complex."

Pienaar suddenly raised his head and looked slightly less defeated. "You could do that?"

"Well, yeah . . . why not?" Jack answered, shrugging his shoulders. "Nobody else knows I came here."

"What about Monsieur Artier? Will he want satisfaction when he remembers what happened?"

Jack was thoughtfully silent for a moment. "Probably not. If he does, I'll explain the situation to him privately. I'm sure he'll go along. Like I said, Paul is very forgiving," And he doesn't lose control like I do, Jack added to himself. Jees! After all the time I've worked with Paul, you'd think I would have learned something.

"It would save the career of a man with an excellent record," Pienaar replied. "He would be most grateful. I would be most grateful to put the matter behind me."

Jack smiled. "Good. Let's just pretend I came to follow up on last night's joint venture."

"Well put, Monsieur Barrons. Very well put," Pienaar responded with no trace of smugness.

By late afternoon Paul was awake again and insisting that he was ready to leave the hospital. He had almost convinced the young doctor in charge of his case to release him by swearing a solemn oath that he would remain in his bed at the hotel until he was fully recovered. His escape was foiled, however, when Jack arrived with Carlin. During a brief conference with the young doctor, Carlin declared that Monsieur Paul Artier was notorious for disregarding medical advice and could not be trusted to keep his word. To add weight to his argument, Carlin hinted that Paul had a ticket for a 9 p.m. flight to Cairo.

Aghast that he had nearly fallen for Paul's duplicity, the doctor vowed that he would keep a close watch on Monsieur Artier. Carlin mollified Paul's frustration by explaining that he was having trouble keeping Geilla in bed, Mary was exhausted, and Nea was worn out. He stressed that Paul was in no condition to get around by himself and he would only cause everyone to worry if he left the hospital. Carlin concluded his lecture by promising to look after Kon, and to come for Paul early the next morning.

Paul grudgingly admitted that Carlin was right. It had been an exhausting week for everyone and a little rest was needed all around. Before he left, Carlin extracted a pledge from Paul that he would not try to sneak out of the hospital on his own. Paul remarked bitterly that his reputation for deception was overblown if his own friends believed he could escape without their aid.

Thus assured that Paul would stay put for the night, Carlin left to attend to Kon. Jack stayed to visit with Paul, helping him hobble to the bathroom, seeing that he had a palatable evening meal, and providing him the comfort of a forbidden drink from his trusty silver flask. Paul still looked tired, and Jack was not surprised when he fell asleep early.

Bridget was waiting in front of her hotel when Jack pulled up to the curb. He almost didn't recognize her without her uniform, but when she brightened and waved, there could be no mistake. Her spontaneous, silly wave was unique. It made him laugh. He felt relaxed, as if he were meeting an old friend rather than taking a woman to dinner.

It wasn't really a date, he kept telling himself. He didn't date serious women like Bridget, at least not intentionally. He only dated sleek, sophisticated, up-tight women who would settle for a brief no-strings-attached encounter. Most of the time they ended up making him feel like a misplaced farm boy. He never really wanted to get to know any of them. He didn't want to have to explain himself.

Bridget was different. She was genuine. Jack felt he could relax and be himself with her. She was reliable and enjoyed caring for people. It wasn't just a job to her. Jack definitely wanted to know more about her.

Bridget hadn't actually said much when Jack took her for coffee the night before. Rather she had encouraged Jack to talk about all the people he was worried about. She hadn't been able to sort them all out, of course. The cast of characters seemed too large and their problems too numerous for her to fathom. She had just listened and nodded and in the end, Jack seemed to feel better. She was impressed by the depth of his concern for people. Obviously he was extremely loyal to his friends.

Bridget had been surprised when he invited her to dinner. His schedule seemed so impossibly busy, she couldn't imagine how he would work it in. But when he had pressed the invitation, she agreed. As she waited outside her hotel, she realized she was slightly intimidated by Jack. It wasn't his size, for she had seen how gentle he had been with Paul. She just couldn't imagine what she was going to say to such a handsome, adventurous, worldly man as Jack.

She knew from experience that men like Jack weren't interested in her. Oh yes, they all thought she was wonderful when they were flat on their back and she was taking care of them. They all loved her then. But as soon as they were better, they started to notice that she wasn't as tall and long-legged as they had thought. They began to notice that she was a bit hippy too, and that the voice that had comforted them in their pain was not velvety and musical. It was crisp, and her accent betrayed her working-class background. She had been gullible at first, but after a few heartbreaks she got wise. She learned not to take men's pledges of love for anything more than delirious ranting. Still, she was curious as to why Jack had asked to see her again.

Bridget was glad that Jack had not tried to impress her by taking her to one of the extravagantly expensive night clubs Paris boasted. She was nervous enough in her rather plain skirt and blouse combination. She was a bit startled by all his attentive door-opening and chair-holding though. The men she worked and socialized with on the rescue squad had quit treating her as special long ago. To them she was just a handy lass to have in the group. She liked it that way. It kept the jealous gossip down.

Bridget remained self-consciously quiet until she and Jack were seated at the restaurant and had ordered. Then she took the plunge.

"So when did you learn to fly, Jack?"

Jack grinned. "You mean legally?"

She hesitated. "Not necessarily. I mean, how did you get interested?"

Jack toyed with his silverware as if deciding carefully how much he wanted to say. It's almost too late to hold anything back, he reasoned. Bridget already thinks I'm a screaming lunatic.

"I grew up on a farm in Kansas," he began tentatively. "Every year the crop dusters would come by. I would watch them and dream of swooping around like they did. When I was about fourteen, I started riding my bike or hitching rides to the local airport on weekends. It wasn't much of a place. I tagged along behind the pilots and the mechanics, listening to everything they said, trying to pretend I understood. One day one of the pilots asked me if I wanted to go up with him. Did I ever! I was in heaven. After that, I just about lived at the airport. Some of the younger pilots started teaching me things. I soloed in a piper before I was sixteen. I couldn't tell anyone, though. Not even my family. Especially not my family! They didn't want to hear a word about flying. They wanted me to finish school and get on with the business of running the farm."

"Are you from a large family?"

"No. There's just my mom and dad and my two older brothers. What about you?"

"Well, I'm the oldest. I have a sister that's married, and a little brother. He's the baby."

"You've got to stop calling him that!" Jack said forcefully. "I bet he hates it! How old is he?"

"You're right, of course. He's ten. He was a bit of a surprise, you see. Ryan's a good lad, though."

"Well, I was no big surprise, but I hated being the baby. My brothers, Frank and Dave, were always bossing me around. I got so sick of it I joined the Marine Corps right after high school. I wanted so badly to be tough—tougher than Frank or Dave. That's why I picked the Marines. Jees, I was dumb! I was only seventeen. My mother cried buckets about losing her 'baby'. Dad ranted a bit, but in the end he signed for me. He knew there was no use trying to keep me on the farm. My heart wasn't in it. I guess he hoped I'd wash out, come to my senses, and come home. It wasn't a happy parting. Everyone thought I was weird."

Jack interrupted his story when the waiter came with their food. Bridget suddenly realized that she was hungry and was glad they had been served quickly.

"It's hard, isn't it?" she began after the waiter left. "I mean, getting up the nerve to do what you want to do, instead of what your family wants. Going to nursing school was bad enough. At least that meant getting a job. But wanting to fly helicopters! Now that's just plain crazy!"

Jack laughed. "Why did you do it? Was it something you had always dreamed of?"

"Good heavens, no! I'm too feet-on-the-ground for that. I was scared to death to go up in one at first. But they needed some people to take the training and I had a friend who was keen to go. She thought it would be a great adventure. She talked me into signing up with her. Then she failed the entrance exam. I couldn't let everyone down. So there I was, part of the team. Did you quit the Marines?"

"No. I stuck it out. It was hard. God, it was hard. I didn't mind the work. I was strong enough, but all those people giving me orders and inspecting, it was worse than being at home. I sure as hell didn't get treated like a baby anymore. That was the good part."

Jack stopped talking and held his fork in mid-air for a moment.

"Did you get to fly in the Marines?" Bridget asked, sensing that Jack was uncomfortable talking about the bad part.

"Yes. Yes I did," Jack said, starting in on his food again. "I was assigned to an air wing out of boot camp and went to Vietnam. Did a lot of engine work mostly. Then we started using up 'copter pilots pretty quick, so I got to try my hand at it. Got some experience, even made staff sergeant. When my tour was up, I came home for thirty days before my next assignment."

Jack stopped talking again and Bridget ate in silence. She knew he was choosing what he wanted to tell her. She sensed that Jack was being more open with her than he usually was on a date. He was not reciting a well-rehearsed story to impress her.

Indeed Jack was struggling to decide how much to tell Bridget. He wondered what would she think of him if he tried to tell her what he hated about 'Nam? Would she think he was weak? Would she understand why he had married Linda as soon as he got back? Would she grasp that Linda represented everything that was real and lasting. Could she understand how much he had yearned for someone to make it all seem worthwhile?

He often wondered if he had really loved Linda. They hadn't dated much in school. Maybe she was just looking for a meal ticket and had latched onto him when he was vulnerable. He wasn't sure their love was real. True love is supposed to last more than five months, isn't it? The pain he felt when she left was real though. He was sure of that. The hurting just went on and on. Maybe if he could have told someone about it, it would have gone away sooner. But who was there to tell?

Linda had not been happy living in Germany with him. She had gone back to Kansas, supposedly to wait for him on his parent's farm. She told them a pack of lies about him and they believed her. They even gave her money. Then, after she had cleaned out his bank account and left town with some bearded drifter, they acted like it was all his fault. That had ended any chance he had of feeling close to his brothers. Maybe that was why he was so attached to Paul and Kon. They knew him. Hell, they would die for him. They wouldn't have listened to a lying little bitch like Linda.

Suddenly Bridget interrupted Jack's reverie with the fatal question, "What did you do after you got home, Jack?"

This is where things get tricky, he thought, suddenly realizing that he had drifted away from Bridget. Shit! Linda is still screwing up my life, he thought bitterly. He looked at Bridget's clean-scrubbed face, framed by her shining brown hair. She was looking intently at him.

Did she suspect he never told women the whole story? He gazed into her sympathetic brown eyes. How can you lie to eyes like Bridget's?

"I . . . I married my high school sweetheart, but . . . but it didn't work out," he stammered.

"Oh . . . what a terrible disappointment for you," she said with sweet sincerity.

There was no thunderclap, no flash of flame, but suddenly Linda's ghost was gone, dissolved in the warmth of Bridget's clear brown eyes. He felt a profound sense of relief. He had told her the truth and she understood. Amazing! Could he have told any of those other women to free himself? No, they would not have understood why he told them. Not many people have the capacity to absorb other people's problems like Bridget does.

"Yeah, it was kind of bad," he finally continued. "We were in Germany. I was working as a Marine Security Guard at the embassy. She didn't like it there, so she left."

"Did you like Germany?"

"Yes. I really did," he answered wistfully. "I already knew some German. Picked it up from an old guy who had the farm next to ours. It was a good assignment. That's where I met Brad. He's the leader of our group."

"Oh, is he an American too?"

"No, he's a Brit. You'd like him."

"How did you come to meet a Brit in Germany?"

"There was a ruckus at some demonstration and . . . well, anyway I ended up clearing a path to his car and keeping the mob off him and some other folks. He actually came around later on another trip, to tell me what a good job I had done. Told me to look him up if I ever got to London."

"So you went to London."

"Not right away. I went back to the farm when I'd finished doing my thing for the Marine Corps. That didn't work too well either. I knew I was different, but it was like the same old crap from Frank and Dave. I couldn't make them see there was a whole big world out there."

"Yes. I've run into that attitude myself. Where did you go from there?"

"I went to St. Louis. Got a job on the line at an airplane factory. That was about as close as I could get to flying. I didn't have any money saved . . . well, shit! . . . she took it all. I wasn't happy though. I guess I was getting pretty close to burn-out when my supervisor sat me down for a talk. He said I'd better settle down and get some more education if I hoped to get off the line. He actually advanced me some money. Said it was like a scholarship from one former-Marine to another. He told me he'd lost his own son in 'Nam so he had some money set by. I didn't even know if it was true . . . about his son and all, but I enrolled in college. Thought maybe I could be some kind of engineer. I went for two years. It was hard, but I did O.K.

"Then there was a shake up at the factory. I got laid off and so did he. He'd been there over twenty years and he took it hard. I didn't have anything saved and I wasn't popular at home so I sold some gear and took a part-time job so I could eat until the semester ended."

"Did you go home after that?"

"Naw. I figured I couldn't do that. They'd all think I'd screwed up again."

"I think you were being too hard on yourself. They're your family."

Jack smiled. He had never thought of it that way. "Believe it or not, when things looked the worst, they started to get better. I was reading the papers every day looking for job openings. One day I spotted this ad for couriers, you know, the people who hand deliver important papers all over the world. They weren't offering much cash, but the deal included a return ticket to London. I hadn't been out of St. Louis in so long I was antsy, so I signed up. Next thing I know I was in London."

"How did you like it?"

"I loved it. I looked around, visited some pubs, met some girls. In just a few days it was time to go home. Unfortunately, the stupid airline was on strike and I was stuck. I mean really stuck. I'd used up what little money I had. So there I was sitting on the floor in the terminal—people were sitting and sleeping all over the place. I didn't mind too much. It was clean and dry and all, but it was rough for people with kids. Anyway, suddenly I remembered the card Brad had given me. I dug around in my wallet and sure enough it was still there, wrinkled as hell. I could barely make out the number he had written on the back of it.

I dropped my last pocket change into that damn phone and dialed. I knew it was a long shot, but when a woman answered and said Brad wasn't in, I figured I was sunk. She asked if I wanted to call back or leave a message. Before I could answer, the operator was on the line asking for money. I figured it didn't matter, so I admitted I didn't have any more. I apologized to the woman for bothering her and was about to hang up, when all of a sudden, she tells the operator to charge the call to some number she rattled off. Then she starts with the third degree, but very polite and confidential. Where was I calling from? Could I give my name?

"I thought, this is strange. I'm a total stranger just passing through. What does it matter? But she sounded so concerned, like it was a matter of life or death or something. So I told her where I was and about meeting Brad. Next thing I know she's transferring me around to different numbers. Nobody was answering, but she kept trying. Finally, this guy comes on the line. I don't know what she told him, but he was really friendly. I knew right away he was an American and it surprised me. Well, he didn't ask many questions except, 'What are you wearing? Can you find your way to such and such exit? And can you be there in twenty minutes?'

"Well, what else have I got to do? So I described myself. It's hard to miss something as big as I am and I say, 'Sure I'll be there.'

"Exactly, I mean exactly, twenty minutes later, a dark blue sedan pulls up and out jumps this guy with jet black hair and slanted eyes. 'Welcome to London, Jack. I'm Paul,' he says with this American accent. Well, I don't know, maybe it was some kind of defensive reaction. But all I could think of was, 'He's not American. He's Vietnamese!' I just wasn't expecting it, you know, right smack in the middle of London. I sort of froze when he put out his hand. He picked up on my reaction right away, but he didn't make as issue of it. He just said something like, 'You look like you could use a beer, Jack.'

"Before I could even nod, he whipped open the rear door, hefted my bag onto the seat and opened the front door for me. 'Brad's out of town until tomorrow, but you can stay at my place,' he said. He made it seem as though Brad was expecting me. Hell, I was tired, and American or not, a beer sounded good. So I got in.

"I found out later that the number Brad had given me was his home phone number. He doesn't give that to many people. So when I called and got his wife, Mary, she knew I was someone Brad had an interest in. Mary had asked Paul to take care of me until Brad came back. Apparently, taking care of people was part of Paul's job. He's good at it. He's still looks after me. Sometimes I get annoyed, but hell . . . I guess that's why I blew up at the hospital last night when nobody came to help him. Anyway, I found out later that Paul isn't Vietnamese. He's half-Thai. He runs into a lot of people who react the way I did, but he deals with it."

"So you ended up joining the group".

"Yeah. It happened kind of fast really. Paul took me to an apartment he said was his, but I knew it wasn't. I mean, the place was nice, but it wasn't personal. There wasn't anything lying around. Nobody's that neat. I figured maybe it was a place he used for business guests. Anyway, after I stowed my stuff and got cleaned up, Paul took me to dinner. He didn't say much about himself other than that he was from Chicago. It was a great meal with a different wine showing up for every dish. I thought to myself, this guy really knows how to live. I don't know, maybe I had too much to drink or maybe it's just the way Paul is, but I ended up telling him my life history. Kind of like the way I've been chewing your ear off. I'm sorry. I'm probably boring you to death."

"Oh, please don't apologize. It's a very interesting story, Jack. I'm glad you told me. Paul sounds like a wonderful person."

"He's really a great guy," Jack responded with enthusiasm. "I told him about you. He . . ." he hesitated and looked a bit embarrassed.

"Oh? What did he say?" Bridget enquired, picking up on Jack's look.

"Well . . . he kind of teased me . . . said I was making dates over his dead body."

Bridget laughed. "Sounds like he was feeling better."

"Yeah. I think he'll be O.K. He was just exhausted from worrying about Kon and being in charge of things. Maybe you could meet him tomorrow."

"I would like that, but I can't. Training ends tomorrow and I'm due back in London straightaway."

"Tomorrow," Jack said with obvious disappointment. "Do you have to go back so soon?"

"I'm afraid so. Moving around is part of my job."

"I can relate to that," Jack agreed sadly. Then he brightened. "Well, here I am talking my head off and you never did tell me how you went from being a part of the team to being a pilot. You must have gotten over your fear of flying."

"Yes, I got used to it. I was so busy I forgot to be afraid. Then one day, a call came to pick up an accident victim out on the moors. A little girl had been thrown from a pony. A winter storm was predicted and the authorities thought we could get there and back before a ground crew. I was ready, but the pilot I was supposed to go with was drunk. I was furious. He was totally unreliable. He'd been drunk before, but we were always short of pilots so they kept him on. It was hours before we found another pilot and I vowed I would learn how to manage that bird myself."

"Obviously you did. What happened to the little girl?"

"We got to her, but she ended up with pneumonia. It gave us all a scare. She came out O.K. in the end though."

"That's good. It's hard to lose people you're trying to help."

"Yes it is. It's difficult to deal with sometimes, especially the little ones. But you have to polish your skills and go on. That's why I'm here for training."

"I'm glad you were here, Bridget, but I'm sorry you're leaving so soon. I really would like to see you again. Maybe some time when we both have more time."

Bridget smiled and tossed her head. "Well, we'll probably run into each other again. I mean, in your line of work, you must spend a lot of time in emergency rooms."

Jack laughed and then became serious again. "That's true, but I've been working in London for years and our paths have never crossed. I can't exactly set an appointment now, with everyone on the team in the hospital, but I don't want to run all over London hoping I'll bump into you. Can't we be a little more definite?"

Bridget looked uncertain. "You're not likely to run into me in London, Jack. I work out of Devon."

"See, that's exactly what I mean. I don't even know where to look for you. Can't we be more specific? Unless there's someone else . . . Jees, I never even asked if you were engaged or married or . . ."

Bridget laughed, crinkling her nose. "I'm not married, or engaged. It's just . . . well, I don't see how you are going to find time . . ."

"I'll make time, Bridget. I've got a plane for God's sake! Devon is not the moon. I know I can't promise when I'll be back in London, but I would like to see you again."

"Devon's not like London, Jack. There's not a lot to do really and . . . ."

"It's got to be a great place. The prettiest helicopter pilot I've ever met lives there. Hey! What do I have to do to get a date with you, Bridget? Crash my plane on the moors and hope you'll be on the rescue team that day?"

Bridget laughed. "You really mean it, don't you?"

"Of course I mean it. I know you probably think I'm bonkers or something but . . . I don't know many people in England, aside from the team members. I don't have a regular schedule—hell I don't live by anything you could call a schedule—and I'm a loud-mouth American and all, but couldn't we be friends?"

Bridget was surprised by his persistence. He is so good looking and smart, she thought. Surely he must have lots of women to call in London—beautiful women who have every hair curled just right, the kind that know about all those wines he was talking about, gorgeous women like Paul's friend Nea, who designs dresses and oozes sophistication. Does he think I'm naïve and will be an easy conquest? I hope not. He seems too honest. Well, it wouldn't hurt to give him my work number. He probably won't call anyway, and I can always say I'm busy.

Chapter Fourteen

Paul was at his wit's end. Kon had been rescued and conveyed to the safety of a hospital, but the nightmare of being kidnaped seemed to have no end for him. Each time he regained consciousness, he was so suspicious and truculent that it had been necessary to sedate him to prevent him from hurting himself.

The first time he came to, before anyone even realized that he was awake, he lunged for the IV tube. He managed to pull the needle out, tearing up his arm in the process. Jack's mad dash to stem the flow of blood running down Kon's arm had sent Kon into a near panic. He obviously viewed the sudden attention as an attack and he struggled valiantly, although ineffectively, until he was pumped full of drugs.

The second time Kon awoke, he didn't seem to notice Geilla who was sitting by his bed. All he saw was the IV needle taped to the back of his left hand, and he didn't like the idea. Before Geilla could offer assurances or explanations, he tried to remove the needle. Since his right hand was splinted and secured to the bed rail, he attempted to use his feet. It caused him considerable pain to twist and kick so violently, but he kept at it until, once again, Carlin judged it best to sedate him. Geilla kept repeating, "Kon, it's me. Kon, it's me. Take it easy! No one's going to hurt you." But even as Kon sank limply against the pillows, he kept up his mental resistance.

Despite Paul's words of comfort, it was hard for Geilla not to be hurt by the look of utter hatred and contempt that glinted in Kon's one unbandaged eye. Even Paul hadn't seen that kind of venom from Kon since the day the team had taken him into protective custody more than five years ago. He tried his best to keep Geilla away from Kon, but she stubbornly refused to leave his bedside until finally Carlin ordered her back to her bed. He was worried that continual stress was harming Geilla's unborn child. He feared that Kon was fighting his wife and his friends because he did not recognize them. Kon was not suffering from fever or drug induced delirium. He had amnesia and Carlin dreaded the task of discovering how extensive it was.

Physically Kon had been treated and although he had been severely brutalized, the prognosis was that he would recover. Before Carlin even arrived, the doctors had discovered that Kon had three cracked ribs and a fractured wrist. His kidneys had suffered some damage, his left eye was battered, and his eyelid was burned. Two of his teeth were chipped, but amazingly his jaw was still intact. Not understanding that the reason he could not hear was because his left eardrum was perforated, Kon had repeatedly scratched and poked his ear until it was raw and infected. He had been extremely dehydrated when they brought him in, and there was hardly a spot on his body that was not black and blue.

Carlin had taken the first flight to Paris as soon as Jack had notified him that Kon had been freed and taken to the hospital. Jumping on a plane and flying off to take care of Kon had become a part of Carlin's life and he never complained. He believed in the work the team did, and keeping Kon healthy was his contribution to their efforts. Brad had pulled himself out of bed long enough to call Carl requesting that he extend the mantle of his influence and give Dr. Carlin La Monde full authority over Kon's treatment. Carlin had run a battery of tests on Kon ranging from blood chemistry and X-rays to MRI and CAT scans. Kon obviously had a severe concussion, but a full assessment of his mental condition could not be made until he was awake and reactive. Unfortunately, his initial response to his environment had not been promising.

The third time Kon awoke, Carlin tried a different approach. Seeing that Kon was struggling to free his right arm from the restraints, he unfastened the band and asked Paul to hold Kon's arm while he lowered the bed rail. Then he pulled the sheet tightly over Kon's legs, and sat on the bed beside him. He told Kon softly in French, Italian, and then in English that he was safe and that no one was going to hurt him. Carlin tried to get him to drink some water, but Kon shrank from the glass and cringed when Carlin put his hand on his shoulder. "Peter, it's Carlin. Don't you know me?"

Kon looked warily from Paul to Carlin then made a series of low sounds that resonated with revulsion.

"Did you understand any of that?" Carlin asked Paul.

"Yeah. It's Greek. I can't give an exact translation, but I think he just wished us both a painful death in full view of our loved ones."

Carlin shook his head. "Well, at least he's not ready to admit defeat. That's a good sign. I worry when he gets depressed." Carlin turned back to Kon and began in French, "I don't understand Greek, Peter. You will have to insult me in French the way you usually do. Can you understand me? Speak to me, Peter. Are you thirsty? Would you like some water?"

Carlin offered the glass again, but again Kon drew back. Kon needed the water, but Carlin didn't have the heart to force his swollen jaw open to get him to take it. "I'm not going to hurt you, Peter. I just want to ask you some questions?"

At the word "questions" every muscle in Kon's body tensed and he began to struggle. He twisted beneath the taut sheet and tried to kick Carlin off the bed. Carlin was very disappointed, but he remained calm.

"I'll have to sedate him again. I'll try a tiny dose, but it's almost impossible to gauge the right amount for him."

"I know," Paul responded, and traded places with Carlin on the bed. Carlin got a small syringe and put a dose of tranquilizer into the IV tube. Kon watched Carlin's every move in silence, but he fought against Paul until the drug took effect and his muscles would no longer respond. When Kon at last lay quiet, just staring at him, Paul poured some water on a towel and wiped Kon's forehead. Kon tried to turn away at first, but then he lay still and let Paul wipe his face. Paul spoke softly to him in French, Italian and English, offering assurances that he was safe. Despite Kon's belligerent actions and defiant words, Paul read the fear on Kon's battered face. It tore his heart to see the man who had repeatedly risked his life for him shudder at his touch. For a brief moment he wished that Michon were still alive so that he could have the satisfaction of tearing him limb from limb; but he quickly cast the desire out of his mind. It strained his sense of justice to think that saving a little twerp like Etienne might have destroyed a capable, generous, loyal man like Kon. He hoped that Kon understood how hard he was trying to help him.

"I won't hurt you, Kon, I swear. I won't hurt you," Paul repeated again, but Kon did not respond. He just lay there watching Paul and Carlin and there was no way to know what he was thinking. After a little while, Paul got up from the bed, pulled the end of the sheet from under the mattress and straightened Kon's legs. Then he tucked the sheet loosely under Kon's feet, knowing Kon preferred it that way. Maybe that one little gesture made Kon feel more relaxed, for he fell asleep within minutes.

"He's not doing well here," Carlin remarked.

"I know. I hate to admit it, but I don't think he recognizes us."

"I would like to take him to a special institute in Switzerland."

"Institute? What institute? Kon hates hospitals."

"It's not an ordinary hospital. I'm afraid Peter has serious brain damage. He needs special care."

"You bet he does, but not at some damned institute. What do they know about him?"

"They have an excellent record of treating brain disorders. Peter needs professional help, Paul. He's got a serious affliction."

"I don't agree with your diagnosis, Carlin. Kon's not 'afflicted' with anything. He's been kidnaped, and tortured, and scared shitless. What does your institute know about that?"

"They are experts at treating mental disorders. You can see for yourself how withdrawn he is. They can help him. Believe me, I wouldn't send Peter there if I didn't have full . . ."

"No. Absolutely not." Paul responded quietly. "I won't let you put Kon in a mental institution. He's not crazy."

"I didn't say he was crazy. I said he was withdrawn and . . ."

"That's the way Kon reacts to stress! He's always been suspicious, and uncooperative, and combative. That's part of his personality. If some damned shrink gets a hold of him, he might never get out."

"That's nonsense, Paul. I would never allow that to happen. Believe me, Peter is very dear to me. It breaks my heart to see him behave this way. I would never do anything to hurt him."

"I didn't mean to insinuate . . ." Paul paused and ran his hand across his eyes as if trying to wipe away his fatigue.

Carlin saw the gesture and shook his head. "You should stay off your feet, Paul. You're wearing yourself out trying to look after Peter and Edouard. You've got to start taking care of yourself."

"I'll be O.K. I'm sorry, Carlin," Paul continued more calmly. "I just can't agree to turn Kon over to strangers who have no idea of what he's been through."

"They're highly trained medical people, Paul."

"That's just it. They may know a lot of medicine, but do they have any idea what it's like to be abducted and tortured? Can they even begin to understand what it's like to sit for hours, staring down the barrel of a gun held by some fanatic who would kill you in a second if he thought it would advance his twisted version of some cause? Can they imagine the humiliation of being stripped, and beaten, and made to lie in filth? I doubt that your specialists have any idea of the mental trauma Kon has been subjected to."

Paul paused, but Carlin had no answer.

"I've seen this behavior before, Carlin. Kidnaping is my business. Kon is very fragile right now. He needs to be with people who can understand why he sees every move we make as a threat. He'll come out of it. I know he will. He just needs a little time."

"But what if he doesn't? What if he has suffered actual physical damage. I can't neglect him."

"You have hardly neglected him, Carlin. You've prodded and examined and scanned him from one end to the other several times. You've done everything, but turn him inside out and you haven't found anything you can treat."

"Maybe that's what scares me. What if I've missed something? If he were at the institute he would be under constant observation."

"Oh great! Kon would really love that, wouldn't he! For God's sake, Carlin, the man's been cooped up under constant surveillance for long enough. You saw how he reacted to the word 'questions'. Don't lock him up again. He'll crack. Let me take him out of here. There's too many people and too much noise here. Let me take him somewhere quiet where he won't have to deal with anyone who doesn't know his habits."

"And who is going to take care of him? You? You're stretching yourself too thin."

"Jack can help me and maybe I'll hire a nurse. I'll manage."

Carlin knew that Paul acted as the team's medic. He was well trained and highly skillful at taking care of everyone but himself. Carlin was reluctant, but he realized that Paul was right about keeping Peter secluded for a while. Peter was inherently shy and mistrustful of strangers. Carlin had seen Peter's confidence and self-esteem grow and develop while working on the team. He had chosen Paul and Jack as his friends and he trusted them. Carlin believed that Peter trusted him too, but perhaps at the moment Peter needed to be cared for by people who did know what it was like to be kidnaped.

"All right," Carlin sighed. "I'll let you take him for a week, but if there hasn't been any progress . . ."

"A week! That's not enough time."

"One week," Carlin repeated sternly. "Then perhaps we can negotiate a different set-up. Will you take him to his apartment here in town?"

Paul had not anticipated that Carlin would want to take Kon away. He didn't really have a plan, but he formulated one on the spot. "No, it's too small. I'll take him to the villa where we were going to debrief Rubard. It's quiet and there's plenty of room."

"Are you sure it's safe there?"

"It's safe. I'll push GIGN to send us some men. They owe me that much. We can move Rubard there as planned. It will be easier to keep an eye on him."

"Is he dangerous?"

"No, but Etienne's a nervous wreck and I don't want the GIGN people to get him alone. He might confess to things he knows nothing about. He's not exactly at the top of our popularity list, but his father is still a client and we want to get the best deal possible for him."

"When will you want me to bring Peter?"

Paul glanced at Kon who was lying motionless. "Let's get him there before he wakes up again. I hate to see him tied down like this. I'll arrange for an ambulance."

"All right. May I come along?"

Paul was about to object, but Carlin put up his hand. "I promise to leave before he wakes up, but I want to be able to tell Charlotte and Edgar that Peter is properly settled."

Paul nodded, and Carlin smiled. "How did I get involved with a group that gives so little credence to my medical advice? My patients in Geneva are all more docile and respectful."

"We respect your opinion, Carlin," Paul answered quickly. "That's why we call you. We're just too stubborn to take your advice."

After Peter was moved, Carlin returned to Geneva, all the while worrying, as he had done for years, if he had done the best thing for Peter.

Kon was having a hard time waking up and his eyes felt as if they were stapled shut. Slowly he became aware that whatever he was lying on was warm and soft. He didn't remember all the places he had been kept during the past week, but they had all been cold and hard. He moved and realized he was lying on his right side. Was I only dreaming that I was tied to the bed? he wondered. He struggled again to pry his eyes open, but there definitely was something over his left eye. When he tried to brush it away someone put a hand on his. "Don't do that, Kon. You'll only irritate it." He turned his head and was surprised to see a mountain of a man with blonde hair smiling at him. He struggled to recognize the face, but he didn't. What's happening to me? he wondered. Every time I open my eyes I'm somewhere else and different people are staring at me. I can't seem to tell if I am dreaming or awake. Nothing makes sense—nothing seems real anymore.

"How are you feeling?" the blonde mountain asked.

"Confused" came to his mind, but he decided not to admit it. How *did* he feel? Terrible, weak, sick, why say it? It won't make any difference to the mountain. Kon turned and noticed that his right wrist was in a cast. When he touched it with his left hand, he saw that it too was bandaged at the wrist. What happened to me? he wondered. I remember the beatings and the questions. I don't remember what they were asking. I only remember that something terrible will happen if I tell anyone anything. The questions and the beatings had been terrible . . . but this. How did this happen? Did they cut me or . . . oh my God! I must have tried to kill myself. But I failed! Oh, Christ, I failed! Now what? When they start hitting me again, I won't be able to hold out. They don't even cover their faces anymore. They must have decided to kill me. I wish they would just get it over with. I am so tired of fighting them.

Kon was too sick and too depressed to respond when Paul and Jack began to ask him questions. Was he thirsty? Was he hungry? Was he warm enough? He didn't believe they really cared, and he was determined not to fall into a trap. Paul kept asking the questions, however. He could tell that Kon did not trust him, but he needed to find out if Kon could understand what he was saying. He wanted to draw him out of himself, make him relate to his surroundings. More than that, he wanted to assure Kon that he was safe and that people did care about him. It was difficult. Kon had been abused so often that he was always suspicious and defensive. Now he was convinced that he was absolutely alone in a hostile, dangerous world and he locked the doors of his mind against friendship and caring.

Since Kon would not take any food or medicine from them, Jack and Paul were forced to overpower him, drug him, and continue using IV lines. Unfortunately, the drugs made Kon even more disoriented and nauseous. Paul tried to explain to Kon that they wouldn't have to put needles in him if he would take some fluids, but Kon turned down everything they offered. He struggled when they injected antibiotics and he fought when they put drops in his infected ear. Paul kept explaining in English, that Kon's eardrum was perforated, but that it would heal. He didn't want Kon to think that his deafness was permanent. Paul checked with Carlin as to how to explain the situation in French and in Italian, fearing that if he used the wrong expression, he would upset Kon even more.

Paul had made up his mind that he would not tie Kon to the bed, so he and Jack took turns sitting with him. Kon would stay awake watching them as long as he could force his eyes open and they could rest only while he was asleep or drugged. In between times, they offered him food and hauled him into the bathroom every few hours. Kon balked at entering the bathroom the first time, panicking at the sight of the floor tiles. Paul was mystified, but once he got the idea of covering the tile with a small rug and some towels, Kon relaxed. So many little things seemed to have negative associations for Kon. Even after hours of questioning Edouard, Paul could only piece together what had happened.

Paul was infinitely patient, however, with Kon and with Edouard. As the first born, he had grown up taking care of his seven younger brothers. After his father's untimely death, his role had been impressed upon him by his mother and his uncle and he had accepted it. He was the family's strength, their example, their provider, their healer, their hope for the future.

Paul was torn between bringing Geilla to see Kon and sheltering her from Kon's hostility. Carlin backed his decision to keep Kon's whereabouts from Geilla, but Mary and Nea did not approve. How could he explain to them how painful it was to deal with Kon's paranoid behavior? Geilla was having enough trouble with her pregnancy. He couldn't risk letting her be rejected by her own husband. Paul missed the solace he might have had from Nea, but he felt it was his responsibility to protect Geilla's baby from harm. Kon would expect it from him.

After two days of using patience to get through to Kon, Paul decided to let his frustration show. He reasoned that perhaps he could rouse Kon to anger and get him to open up. "Give me a hand here, Kon," he all but shouted at him one afternoon. "I know you can hear me. I know you understand. Say *something*, for God's sake!"

Kon didn't answer, but Paul sensed that he had his full attention. "If you don't speak up, Kon, they're going to put you in a straight jacket and lock you away somewhere. I won't be able to stop them if you won't talk to me. I don't want that to happen to you. Please, say something, Kon . . . anything . . . please!"

Kon was still confused, but he wanted to put an end to Paul's badgering. He glared at Paul and suddenly blurted in French, "My name is Emile Breaux! My name is Emile Breaux! My name is . . . Stop shouting at me, you bastard! I'm not going to tell you anything!" Kon's words were defiant, but he cringed as he spoke as if expecting Paul to strike him.

Paul only smiled with relief. "Well, I'll be damned! Emile, you sure as hell look and sound like my friend Kon. Maybe you can help me find him."

"No!" Kon shouted. "I won't tell you where he is. I won't tell you anything! Stop asking . . . please . . . stop asking."

"O.K.! O.K.! I won't ask. I just wanted to know if you could speak, that's all. Would you like some water? Are you hungry?"

"Leave me alone! I won't . . ."

"O.K. Relax. Just let us know if you want anything."

220

Kon did not hear them come into the room, he only sensed that they were there. When he looked up, he knew it was true. He watched them warily. The blonde one pressed the light switch and the light dimmed. Then the dark-haired one went to the table in the corner. He kept his back turned and Kon could not see what he was doing. After a moment Kon smelled something burning and his vague apprehensions turned to true fear. They were going to burn him, like the others had.

He gauged his chances of making it to the door, but the blonde mountain was in the way. Before Kon could move he heard the sound of music. It was unfamiliar, but he could make out that it was singing, sweet singing, very soft, very slow, almost like a lullaby. Well, if they mean to drown out my screams the music needs to be louder, he thought bitterly. Then the dark-haired one turned towards the bed.

"Come on, Kon," he said softly. "This has gone on long enough. You need help. You're not connecting."

As Paul began to pull the covers away, Kon felt his heart speed up. The thing he had been dreading had begun. They were going to hit him and ask questions, and he still did not know the answers. For a moment he was almost frozen with fear, then he gasped and lunged toward the edge of the bed. He was not quick enough and they were upon him at once. He tried to release their grip, but he did not have the strength. Before he knew what was happening, they had pulled his arms above his head and turned him on his stomach. His face fell into the pillow and he assumed they would smother him. Instead they moved the pillow away, and turned his head to one side. They pulled the covers down tightly against him to stifle his kicking.

"You're all right, Kon. I won't hurt you," he heard one of them say. "I promise I won't hurt you."

And then he felt hands on his bare back. He fought. He twisted. He struggled, but he could not break free. His ribs heaved against the bandages wrapped around him and he panted with the effort. It was all to no avail for he was powerless to prevent the hands from pressing into him. Suddenly, all the anger and fear he had been suppressing welled up in him and he began to scream and curse, overcome by the utter futility of his resistance. It hurt to struggle. It hurt to scream. It hurt to breathe, but his mental control had broken and he could not govern himself. He had no hope that anyone would hear him and come to his aid. He had no hope that they would release him. He had no hope at all. Even the sound of his own voice terrified him, for it was laden with despair.

He imagined they might turn the music up or throttle him, but they didn't. Finally between gasps he heard one of them talking to him. "That's it. Let it out! Let it out! Let it all out!"

He was exhausting himself, but he could not stop. Every muscle in his body was tense and he cringed against the bed. Ceaselessly the hands continued their work. They were rubbing oil into him. It was icy cold at first, but gradually it began to feel warm. The probing fingers were forcing his muscles to relax, even against his will. When he was out of breath from screaming, he heard a deep, calm voice. It was Paul, and he was chanting. Kon could not understand the words, but he seemed to absorb their meaning. Then he realized that interspersed between the words of the chant, Paul was repeating in English, French, and Italian, "Give in, Kon. I won't hurt you. Give in. I promise I won't hurt you."

This man has power, Kon thought, the power of healing. Somehow he knows exactly where to press, and how hard, and how long; as if he has a map of my pain.

He could resist the brutality, he could resist the pain; but this he could not resist. This was too good. This was a lifeline of relief in an ocean of misery. He listened to the music, and imagined that if falling snowflakes made a sound, it would be the sound he was hearing. He could almost feel them landing on his back, tiny pieces of light, at first cold, and then warm, deliciously warm.

His very cells began to relax and he could not hold the tension in them. His arms were released and they floated back towards his body. Someone unfastened the band around his ribs and the hands moved across his back.

"Take deep breaths, Kon . . . slowly . . . deeply," Paul ordered and he obeyed. The room was permeated with the fragrance of burning incense and he inhaled its beauty. The temptation to surrender was overpowering. He felt the hands moving lower and lower on his back and he yielded. He hated himself for submitting, but he had no will of his own. He had been turned to clay by the power of those hands. He gave one desperate sob, as he realized he was totally subjugated.

Jack stood in silent awe, watching Paul demonstrate the full range of his power. He had never seen him in this mood. Paul could break a man's neck with a flick of his thumb, but now he was the embodiment of peace. Not passive peace—a powerful peace that was almost tangible. This wasn't just Paul at work. This was a high priest or shaman performing a sacred ritual. Paul worked with his eyes closed, engrossed in concentration, trying to remember the thousands of pressure points he knew from Oriental medicine, ignoring all the arguments Occidental medicine had for why they wouldn't work.

Paul pulled the covers farther down and suddenly Kon felt helpless and exposed, lying naked on the bed. Fear resurfaced as he realized he was powerless to resist if they chose to violate him. He shivered, wondering what they might do to him. But the hands on him were not seeking anything from him. They were giving . . . giving comfort, and healing, and freedom from pain. The hands slid to his left thigh. How did he know it hurt there? Kon wondered. He felt the hands pressing on his hips, pressing a fiery bolt into his joints. Then he could not feel his legs. There was no longer any pain, no pain anywhere, only warmth. He wondered if death were really soft and warm, not cold and hard as he had always feared. And then they fastened the wrapping around his ribs again and rolled him onto his back. He did not fight them. He had no defiance left. They covered him for modesty sake and he marveled that they understood his need.

The hands moved over his shoulders and down his arms with the same skill and knowledge they had of his back. The same combination of oil and herbs was pressed into his flesh. It smelled sweetly medicinal. Again he experienced cold followed by penetrating warmth. At last they lifted him and pulled something over his head. It felt comforting and warm as it clung to his chest. He had never realized how tangible warmth could be, but he sank into it now, appreciating the softness of the blankets they wrapped gently around him. Then they left, and he was alone. They had stolen his will, and then they had left. He felt empty, abandoned. Even the music had stopped. Before he sank into despair, however, they returned. "I brought you some tea," the dark-haired one said.

The blonde one lifted his head. He felt the cup pressing against his lips, but he did not drink. The dark-haired one looked at him with sad eyes. "There is nothing in it, I swear," he said and pulling the cup back, he drank from it and offered it again. "Come on, Kon. You've got to take something. Please."

'Please' . . . how strange to ask his permission when they had total dominance over him. He could smell the drink. It was tea and his mouth watered. "Come on," the dark-haired one continued, "I sweetened it for you."

The cup was against his teeth and he felt the warm liquid running down his chin. He knew they would pull it away if he showed any eagerness. He knew they would laugh and slap him, but he wanted it too badly to resist. He unlocked his jaw and let the sweetness pour into his mouth. He gulped rapidly, hoping he could get one full swallow before they yanked it away. Mercifully it kept coming and he drank greedily until he took too much and choked.

"Take it easy, Kon. There's plenty more," the blonde one said. He wiped Kon's chin and raised him a little higher. Kon drank again, and when the cup was drained, Paul refilled it. Seeing Kon hesitate, he drank from it himself to show that it was safe. Kon drained the cup a second time and took a third cupful after waiting for Paul to sample the contents. "Do you want more?" Paul asked.

Kon shook his head. He looked into Paul's eyes. Such dark, almond-shaped eyes, in such a perfectly symmetrical face, he thought. His face is . . . beautiful. Men aren't supposed to be beautiful, are they? No, probably not. They aren't supposed to be black and misshapen either, but I've seen such a face . . . somewhere. He seems kind, but . . . but it must be a trick. It won't last. He's just pretending to put me off guard. I won't fall for his tricks.

"It's no use," Kon mumbled, "I can't tell you anything about Etienne Rubard. I don't know who he is."

"That's O.K. I won't ask," Paul answered.

"You don't understand . . . I don't remember. I don't remember anything . . . anything at all."

"Don't worry about it," Paul assured him. "We'll tell you whatever you want to know."

His eyes are so kind, I wish it wasn't a trick, Kon thought.

224

"Who are you? What do you want from me?"

"My name is Paul and this is Jack. We are your friends."

"My friends?"

"Yes. We won't hurt you."

Then Kon voiced the question that Paul had dreaded; but even as it confirmed his worst fears, it indicated that Kon was at last ready to trust his thoughts to him. "And who am I?" Kon whispered.

"Your name is Peter," Paul responded immediately, "Peter Kononellos, but your friends call you Kon."

"Kon?"

"Yes."

"Not Emile?"

"No, you were just pretending to be Emile. Your real name is Kon."

"I don't understand. Why would I . . . you're just trying to confuse me."

Paul took Kon's hand and pressed it. "I'll explain everything later. Get some rest now. Everything's going to be O.K."

Kon stared silently at Paul. What an incredibly simplistic appraisal of the situation, he thought. Well, why wouldn't, what's his name? Paul . . . yes, Paul. Why wouldn't Paul think that way. He isn't lying flat on his back trying to keep the pieces of his skull together. He even seems to know who he is. Is everyone as calm and confident? He is obviously in charge. The other one takes orders from him, and he has absolute control over me. It's strange, I should be afraid, but I'm not. Maybe that's the ultimate deception. I will have to accept his help. I can't even get to the bathroom alone. He pressed Paul's hand weakly. Please let this be real, he prayed. Merciful God, please let this be real. He fell asleep clinging to a single spark of hope.

"I think we've finally made a connection," Paul said wearily after Kon was asleep.

"Yeah," Jack agreed. "He seems ready to give up the idea that he's Emile. I don't think he's afraid of you anymore. What was it you were reciting?"

"Just something I had to memorize as a kid."

"Come on, it was a Thai poem or something, wasn't it?"

Paul was always reluctant to display his Thai heritage, but it was very much a part of him. He was not the typical kid from Chicago.

"Yeah. It's a long epic poem . . . must run hundreds of pages. My uncle made me learn parts of it by heart . . . said it was good for the soul or the mind . . . who knows? I figured it could put anyone to sleep." Paul laughed and swayed slightly.

"Are you O.K., Paul?" Jack inquired looking sharply at Paul.

"Yeah, I'm fine."

"How in hell did you slip Kon that sleeping potion? I saw you drink from that cup every time!"

Paul laughed. "I'm a chemist, Jack, not a magician! I had to . . . I had to drink the stuff. It was the only way I could get him to take it." Paul laughed again and swayed precariously. "I figured I could out last him, he's so weak and . . . ya know the stuff's got a real kick."

"Hey maybe you'd better sit down," Jack said going toward Paul.

"Yeah . . . I better . . . I better get down. I didn't think he would drink so damn much."

Paul laughed and staggered a few steps and Jack caught him. "Come on. I've got you."

Paul tried to walk, but even with Jack's help, he couldn't make it to the door. Jack lifted him in his massive arms. "You out foxed yourself this time, buddy."

"Yeah. I sure . . . God, you're a moose, Jack," Paul laughed drunkenly. ". . . glad you're on our side. You're a God damn moose!"

Paul could not stop laughing and Jack laughed too as he carried Paul out to the couch in the main salon. "You'd better lie down for a while. You really wiped yourself out with that stuff. How about some coffee and a sandwich?"

"Yeah . . . better get something in my stomach so I . . . so I can fight it off."

"O.K. just stay put and try not to fall off the couch. I'll be right back."

Jack hurried through to the huge kitchen and started a pot of coffee, extra strong. While it was brewing he put together a passable sandwich with the last of the roast chicken and some lettuce. When he carried the food back to the salon a few minutes later, he saw that

Etienne had wheeled himself into the room. Etienne was confined to a wheelchair because he couldn't manage crutches with his arm in a sling.

"What happened to Paul?" Etienne asked anxiously.

Jack set the food down and tried to rouse Paul, but he was sound asleep. "He knocked himself out working on Kon. You should have seen him. He was incredible!"

"He's good at taking care of people," Etienne replied faintly.

"Yeah. He's got a big brother complex. Wears himself out looking after everybody, including you, though God knows why. I'd better get a blanket. He'll be out four or five hours at least."

When Jack returned from the bedroom, he saw that Etienne had started eating the sandwich he had made for Paul. "Hey! Put that down!" he shouted. "You're not fit to eat Paul's food! You're . . . You'd just better pray that Kon comes out of this O.K."

Etienne jumped nervously and dropped both the sandwich and the plate. "I'm sorry. I didn't mean . . . You're right . . . I . . . I was just hungry."

"Then go fix yourself something! Jesus! What a nerve!"

"I'm sorry," Etienne replied meekly and moved away.

Jack spread the blanket over Paul and then carried the remains of Paul's sandwich into the kitchen. Etienne had managed to pull some cheese out of the refrigerator, but he could not reach the cupboard to get the bread. Jack watched him struggle for a few minutes. He knew that if Paul was awake he would fix something for Etienne. Paul is like that, he thought, he has to take care of everybody. Not me. I don't have any sympathy for Rubard. The little shit got what he deserved.

Jack saw Etienne pull himself up and finally catch the end of the bread wrapper, but the bread shot out of the cupboard and fell to the floor in a shower of crumbs. Shit! He'll make a mess of the place before he's done, Jack thought.

"Here, give me that!" Jack said, grabbing the cheese from Etienne. "It's damn near impossible to cut French bread with one arm."

Etienne tried to back away from the counter, but one of the wheels on his chair got caught on the handle of a cupboard and he had a hard time getting free. Jack was busy with the food and didn't notice

Etienne as he left the kitchen. When Jack carried the sandwich out to the salon a few minutes later, he was surprised to see Etienne sitting by the couch, holding his head in his hands. His shoulders were shaking and he was sobbing quietly.

"Now what's the matter?" Jack asked curtly.

"I can't do anything right!" Etienne wailed. "I couldn't do anything right before and now I'll never be able to do anything. I have to depend on other people for everything and everyone hates helping me. You all think I'm a criminal."

"Quit feeling sorry for yourself, Rubard. I'm not listening," Jack said, putting the sandwich down by Etienne.

"I never meant for anyone to get hurt, I swear. It was just a game until that little girl got hit. That made me sick. I wanted to quit, but look what happened. A lot of people got killed and my sister almost got kidnapped. Christ! the only people who ever thought I was useful turned around and tried to kill me. Now they hate me and so does everyone else."

"Oh come off it, Etienne. You must have known that what you were doing was wrong!"

"I don't think I really did, Jack. I think I was too stupid. Can you believe I never seriously thought about it? It didn't seem to be hurting anyone. Everyone in the group acted like I was a hero or something. I was always in and out so fast. I was good at it! For once I was good at something. There was never any shooting until that last time. Now what's going to happen to me? Even Trinette must hate me. She hasn't called or anything."

"Jesus, Etienne, stop whipping yourself! It's too late for that. What's done is done," Jack declared firmly.

"Maybe for you, but I'll be stuck in this chair for the rest of my life," Etienne cried in anguish.

"Hey is that what you're crying about? Forget it. You'll be able to get around better once your arm heals."

"Do you think so?"

"Sure. You've still got both legs. One is just going to be weaker, that's all. You can probably get a brace or something. Ask Paul when he wakes up. Hey, I've seen guys with a lot less accomplish fantastic things."

"But how will I make a living? My father will cut me off for sure and I never was good in school."

"Maybe you didn't apply yourself. There must be something you're good at besides robbing banks. Maybe some school in Canada will be better for you."

"Are they still going to send me away? I thought the deal was over since your friends . . ."

"No. No, it's still on. We've just been kind of busy with Kon and all. Come on, Etienne, pull yourself together. Eat your sandwich before it dries out. It's still our job to get you out of Paris."

"I guess I'm lucky that my father has a lot of money. He can afford to pay people to take care of me. You must hate this assignment, and me."

Jack took a hard look at Etienne. I certainly haven't developed a fondness for you, he thought. But seeing you so down like this doesn't give me any satisfaction. You're just one more stupid kid who's screwed up and needs help. That's my job, isn't it? Helping people to get straightened out. Well, I can help you get to Canada, but I don't have a magic cure for all your problems. It's kind of sad really . . . those terrorists shattered more than your leg, Etienne. Your whole being has suffered. Jesus, that's Paul's realm not mine.

"I don't hate you, Etienne," Jack said at last and realized it was true. "Look, I'm sorry if I . . . Why don't you see what's on T.V. and I'll get us some coffee."

This big brother stuff is really a drag, Jack mused, as he went into the kitchen. I don't know how Paul can handle so much of it. I wonder how my brother Frank put up with Dave and me. I guess Dave looked up to Frank. I was always the smartass who couldn't get along with either of them. Well, who wants to be reminded that they're the baby in the family. And besides, I'd rather fly my airplane than drive a tractor.

Maybe I should call Frank to see if he needs money or anything. Naw, he'd just start raggin' me about Linda again. He still blames me for that. I never could tell him that she ran out on me. Hell, why should I spend my nickel to hear him rant and rave about how irresponsible I am! Maybe I'll just call mom to let her know I haven't crashed into that damned mountain she always worries about.

Kon felt calmer when he awoke the next morning. He recognized Paul and answered when Paul spoke to him. He was relieved that for once everything had not changed while he was asleep. He still felt terribly confused, but he accepted Paul's offer of food and didn't hesitate when Paul held a cup to his mouth. It surprised him that the liquid was not tea, but a slurry of farina and milk. It was sweet, and he was grateful it didn't need to be chewed. He would have taken more, but Paul explained that it was best if his first solid meal in almost two weeks was kept small. His disappointment diminished somewhat when Paul administered a long, gentle back massage.

It was a welcome change not to have to resist, not to be afraid. He wanted only to lay quietly without thinking. It was too disturbing to plumb the void of who he was. He submitted when they fed him and enjoyed the comfort when Paul worked on his back. When Paul offered him the option of swallowing capsules of antibiotics instead of being stuck, he agreed. He didn't fight when Paul put drops of oil in his ear. Gradually he saw that all the things they did to him were the same things they had been doing for several days. Was it possible that they had been trying to be kind all along?

Geilla could not be put off any longer. She was feeling stronger and presented her case to Brad, insisting that she would file a missing person report with the police in Geneva and Paris if she was not allowed to see Kon. Brad knew that Geilla could be extremely stubborn and he tried to persuade Paul that it would be wise to yield to Geilla's demands. He reminded Paul that there was the outside chance that seeing Geilla would help restore Kon's memory.

Paul agreed that it was possible, but argued that he didn't want to risk harming Geilla's child in an ill-conceived experiment. Brad saw that Paul's attempt to shield Geilla was only upsetting her and causing additional stress for Paul. Paul's feelings for both Geilla and Kon were so strong that he could not bear the responsibility of permitting them to hurt one another. At last, asserting his authority as leader of the group, Brad ordered Paul to allow Geilla to visit Kon. He reminded Paul that Geilla knew full well how defensive and suspicious Kon could be.

Indeed, Geilla had known Kon longer than anyone else on the team. Following a chance reunion with Kon after her husband's death, Geilla had doggedly pursued him. She had traced him to the bank in Geneva, and deluged him with calls and letters. He had rebuffed her, however, falsely believing that she had betrayed him for another man. After months of fruitless attempts to make contact, she happened to see Kon's picture in an Italian newspaper. He had been a very reluctant witness in a trial involving several terrorists.

When she recognized Brad, who was standing next to Kon in the picture, she surmised that he was not the insurance investigator he had pretended to be when he came to question her about Kon. She contacted the newspaper and talked to the reporter who had snapped Kon's picture. Flattered by her interest, he in turn referred her to Sergeant Trigillio, the man who had worked closely with the team to capture the terrorists. Geilla set up a meeting with Trigillio and charmed Brad's name and address from him. The trail went cold when she contacted Brad, however, for Brad had promised Dr. Carlin La Monde that he would not let Geilla enter Kon's life again. Although Geilla repeatedly begged Brad for information about Kon, he had refused until the time he needed her help to track a foreign agent through the social strata of Rome.

Geilla had many valuable connections in Italian society due to her beauty, her diplomacy, and her close friendship with Nadia D'Allesandro, the pre-eminent hostess in the glittering eternal city. Geilla had demonstrated rare ingenuity at keeping suspects occupied while their private quarters or their business establishment was being searched. At first Brad permitted Geilla to work only as an adjunct to the team, carefully restricting her to roles where she would have little contact with Kon. She continued to pester Brad about a permanent place on the team, however.

Her opportunity finally came, not through Brad, but through Paul. He had watched Kon sink into another desperate period of heavy drinking following the sudden end of his love affair with a French actress named Lillian. Kon had been shocked to discover that Lillian was in truth a married woman. Worse yet, her jealous husband had caused a nasty public scene when he discovered his wife in a restaurant with Kon. After a brief verbal exchange, the man assaulted his unfaithful wife with a bottle. Unfortunately, a prowling reporter snapped a picture just as Kon moved to defend Lillian.

Kon's career at the bank might have been ruined if the powerful women in his life had not moved quickly to protect him. In Geneva, Charlotte Marneé let it be known that she would brook no discussion of the incident in her wide social circle; and in Rome, Nadia D'Allesandro ruled that the antics of a second-rate movie actress were beneath her interest. She spread the rumor that Lillian and her husband were nothing more than a pair of fortune hunters who preyed on wealthy young businessmen. Fortunately for Kon, just before the scandal broke he had concluded a series of remarkably successful currency trades. His rich, sophisticated clients might have raised an eyebrow in their private drawing rooms, but they were not about to cancel their business arrangements with such a talented young man.

Tired of seeing Kon entangled in unhappy romances, Paul became convinced that Geilla could provide the love that Kon was searching for. Without Kon's knowledge, Paul used his influence to secure her a place on the team. Kon had been furious. Initially he threatened to quit, but Brad had remained adamant. After he cooled down, Kon decided that his friendship with Paul was too precious to risk losing. Kon did not trust many people, but he trusted Paul implicitly. He envied Paul's wisdom and calmness, and relied on him to steady his own volatile nature. He stayed on the team, and Paul, Brad and even Jack learned to act as buffers between Kon and Geilla. Eventually, the emotional wall Kon habitually kept between himself and others was strong enough to permit him to deal with her presence. It had taken four more years and many more shattered love affairs, however, before Kon came to see that Geilla was the woman he needed.

Although Paul did not believe that Geilla should be allowed to see Kon, he was forced to bow to Brad's directive. He went to the hotel to see her and again cautioned her that Kon's behavior was unpredictable. He still appeared to have complete memory loss.

"Surely he will remember me," Geilla retorted when Paul expressed his doubts to her.

"I would hope so, but please don't get upset if he doesn't. Kon was so determined not to tell anyone anything about Etienne that he sealed off his mind. I believe that right now Kon is suppressing all his memories, the bad and the good."

"I know he distrusted me for years, but I thought that was over."

"I hope it is, Geilla, but don't be upset if it's not. Kon is very unsure of himself. It must be absolute hell not to remember who you are. Don't be surprised if he has nothing to give."

Geilla didn't answer. Paul's attitude about her seeing Kon was so negative, she thought he was overreacting. She couldn't imagine that staying away from her husband was the right thing to do. It seemed to her that this was the time he needed her the most.

"There's someone here to see you, Kon," Paul said as he stepped into Kon's room at the villa. He switched off the music that Kon had been listening to. He had brought the tapes and some of Kon's other personal belongings from the apartment Kon kept in Paris.

"Someone to see me?" Kon responded a bit anxiously. "Who?"

"Don't worry. She's a friend. Come on. Sit up and say hello," Paul coaxed, propping some pillows behind Kon. He was suddenly sorry he hadn't thought to give Kon a shave. He had done it twice while Kon was drugged, but had been ignoring the stubble since Kon had stopped fighting and was accepting nourishment. Between the beard, the eye patch, and the bruises, Kon definitely doesn't look his best, Paul thought ruefully. He motioned for Geilla to up to the bed.

As she saw Kon's battered face, she was afraid her expression would betray her pain. She struggled to control herself. After all, for years she had hid her feelings from Kon. That was supposed to have changed now that they were married, but here she was doing it again. It tore her apart not to rush to Kon, to hold him and try to comfort him, but she could see how leery he was. Swallowing hard, she tried to speak lightheartedly. "Hello, Kon. How are you feeling?"

Kon gave no answer to her question. He just looked at her for several minutes before asking, "Do I know you?"

His question stabbed her heart. She thought she had prepared herself, but his complete lack of response came as a shock. She felt that if she tried to speak she might give way to tears. Kon kept looking at her, but there was no warmth of recognition in his eyes.

Paul took her gently by the arm and smiled at Kon as though his question was totally rational. "Of course you know her, Kon. She's your wife."

"My wife?" Kon said in surprise. "No! I have no wife." And then, as if the word had awakened an unhappy memory, he mumbled, "The wedding was canceled. They said I wasn't good enough. They said . . . I wasn't after her inheritance . . . really I wasn't . . ."

"I know," Paul said soothingly. "That was a long time ago, Kon. This is Geilla, She's your wife now."

"No! She can't be!" Kon said defensively. "I would remember my own wife! A man does not forget his wife!"

Paul felt Geilla start to shake, but he continued to smile at Kon. "Usually a man doesn't forget . . . but sometimes if he has been beaten . . . you don't remember much about yourself, do you, Kon? You don't remember me and I'm your friend. I was best man at your wedding. I know Geilla is your wife. She's expecting your child."

Kon started. "My child! I . . . No! You're lying! I wouldn't forget my wife and child. What kind of man would I be? No! You're lying! You're just trying to confuse me! They said I wasn't good enough."

Paul could see that Kon was becoming distraught, but before he could say anything else, Kon cried, "Take her away! She can't be my wife! I've never seen her before! Leave me alone!"

Even as he shouted, Kon noticed the tears streaming down Geilla's face and he felt terrible. She looks so unhappy, so alone, he thought. What is the matter with me? I hate not knowing all these people who claim to know me. Are they all trying to drive me crazy? I think it's beginning to work. I just don't understand what's going on. I thought I could trust Paul, but maybe I can't. Maybe I can't trust anyone.

Paul whisked Geilla from the room, but returned immediately.

"It's all right, Kon. Calm down," he said going toward the bed. "You don't have to deal with her right now."

He tried to put his hands on Kon's shoulders, but Kon recoiled, snarling, "Leave me alone! Just leave me alone!"

"All right. Just take it easy. There's no need to get excited. Nobody's trying to hurt you, Kon," Paul said calmly. "Here, let me put the music on again," he continued, turning on the tape player.

"I'll be in the other room if you need anything. O.K.?"

Kon remained silent and defensive, and Paul feared that days of work in building Kon's trust had been lost. "Everything's going to be O.K., Kon. I promise," he said softly before he turned and left.

Jack, who was sitting on the sofa with Geilla, looked up as Paul came into the living room. "Is he O.K.?"

Paul shook his head. "Go keep an eye on him, Jack. Ask him if he wants the window open. Offer him a drink of water or some tea. Try to get him talking."

"Good idea. I'll see what I can do."

Paul sat beside Geilla on the long sofa. "I'm sorry, Geilla. I was afraid this might happen. I didn't want you to see him like this. They hurt him, Geilla. He's always been defensive but . . ."

"Oh, Paul," Geilla interrupted. "They've destroyed him. He wanted this child so much. What am I going to do?"

Paul patted her hand. Why hadn't she stayed in Geneva? It would have been much easier to lie to her if she hadn't seen how bad Kon was. He sighed. "You've got to take care of yourself and the baby. I'll work on Kon. He'll come out of it, you'll see." Paul rattled on, as much to bolster himself as to convince Geilla. "At least he spoke to you. He was so withdrawn and scared, he wouldn't speak at all for several days. He'll come out of it and he'll want the baby. Why don't you rest here today and then go back to Geneva."

Geilla, who had always been independent, suddenly felt overwhelmed. "I dread going back to face Charlotte and Edgar. They've been so kind since they learned about the baby. What am I going to tell them?"

"Tell them Kon needs to be kept quiet for a while. I'll call Carlin. He understands."

Geilla nodded and Paul forced himself to smile. "Do you want a cup of tea or anything? Why don't you take a nap."

"No. I'll be all right. Go look after Kon. I wish . . . maybe I could say good-bye to him tomorrow."

"Sure! He'll be calmed down by then," Paul promised airily. He quickly decided that one way or another, Kon would be asleep when Geilla left. At least then she could touch him and kiss him good-bye. She deserved that much.

Chapter Fifteen

Edouard's parents were no longer in Paris. Apparently they had departed for Cantois as soon as the story of Edouard's violent death hit the morning papers. Paul thought it strange that they hadn't even contacted the police to claim Edouard's body. Monsieur Sabasté had not been cooperative when Paul made the initial phone contact, but after Paul resumed his role as a GIGN agent, Sabasté agreed to see him. Paul was unhappy about being away from Kon and Edouard for a full day, but he had promised Edouard that he would try to bring about a reconciliation with his parents. Whatever their previous attitude had been, Paul felt confident that they would be relieved and happy to learn that their son was alive.

Edouard was clinging steadfastly to his resolve to overcome his drug habit. The medical treatment he was undergoing helped greatly to control his withdrawal symptoms, but it was Paul's faith in him and Paul's assurances that he had performed valiantly in rescuing Kon that sustained him. Edouard was desperately in need of approval and Paul did not withhold it from him. Edouard's compassion had been the deciding factor is saving Kon's life, and Paul was grateful. He sheltered Edouard from self-recrimination and nurtured his emerging independence. He understood that Edouard was trying to gain control over his life and he was willing to provide support.

Jack was worried about Paul flying to Bordeoux alone, but he knew he had to stay with Kon. Kon was still too uncertain and nervous to tolerate having a stranger stay with him. Jack cautioned Paul not to overdo as he drove him to the airport. They both felt fairly certain that the villa was secure, but they did not want to risk having any records of taxis coming and going from that address.

When Paul reached Bordeoux, he hired a car. Fighting the traffic around Bordeoux, he headed east to Cantois. The Sabasté estate was not a massive holding, but the house was extremely well-kept, and whoever had replaced Gaston as gardener was doing an excellent job. As soon as Paul saw the grounds he understood why Edouard had felt the need to surrounded himself with paintings of trees and flowers.

In answer to Paul's knock, an elderly maid opened the front door. She ushered him into a cheery sun porch that opened onto colorful flower beds. In the distance Paul could see row after row of grape vines. The room's charm and informality contrasted sharply with the reserved greeting Paul received from Monsieur and Madame Sabasté when they entered the room.

"Monsieur Martel, I am sorry you insisted upon coming all this way to question us about Edouard's activities," Monsieur Sabasté began after offering Paul a brief swipe of a handshake. "We were shocked to learn of Edouard's behavior and can offer no explanations. It is extremely painful to Madame Sabasté and I to even discuss the matter with anyone."

"I can understand your feelings," Paul said in a conciliatory manner. "The news of Edouard's death must have come as a terrible blow to you, but I have come in secret to assure you that the story is not true. Edouard is alive."

"Alive!" Madame Sabasté gasped. "But why . . . ?"

"The newspaper account was intended to deceive the Direct Action group. I felt it was necessary in order to protect Edouard from reprisals."

"Protect him!" Monsieur Sabasté responded. "You have destroyed his reputation and ours as well! I shall never be able to hold my head up in public again."

"I am sorry to cause you inconvenience," Paul said, trying to keep the edge out of his voice. "I thought Edouard's life was more important than his family's reputation. Surely the standing you have built up over a lifetime will not be shattered by the ill conceived actions of your son. These things happen, even in the best . . ."

"Perhaps in Paris, Monsieur Martel, but not in Cantois!" Monsieur Sabasté answered coldly. "How could he have let himself be tempted by drugs? How could he degrade himself by associating with kidnappers and murderers? I am ashamed to think that money I sent for Edouard's education has been used to support a terrorist!"

"Edouard's no terrorist," Paul objected. "He never hurt anyone. It's not in him."

"Are you telling me that Edouard did not take drugs? Why was he involved with this group? He must have known what he was doing! I think he has deceived you the way he has deceived us. He lied to us about being in school! He lied to us about wanting to be a doctor! He even lied to us about where he lived."

"He was going to school. He was doing very well, but the pressure to excel was too much for him. He was lonely and out of his element in Paris. You never went to see him. You never asked how he spent his time. Do you have any idea of how unhappy he was?"

"Unhappiness is no excuse for terrorism!"

"The group used Edouard. They exploited his dependence on drugs and blackmailed him into helping them. He was not an active member of the group. His weakness, if you want to call it that, is that he can't bear to see anyone, even a terrorist, suffer. He put his own life in jeopardy to save my partner."

"You talk as if you condone his behavior. Well, I cannot!" Monsieur Sabasté roared. "We gave that wretched boy everything and he betrayed our trust. He humiliated us before our friends. I have never understood Edouard and I want nothing more to do with him!"

"But he's your son."

"That may be, by an accident of nature, but no true son would behave in such a disgraceful manner."

"Edouard is very young," Paul began calmly. "Scholastically he may be brilliant, but socially he's extremely naive. He needs your attention and approval now as never before. He's trying to gain control of his life, but he needs guidance."

"Are you asking me to condone kidnaping and murder?"

"No. I am only asking that you forgive Edouard for being young and foolish and give him a little support now that he is trying to straighten himself out. He is very determined to overcome his drug addiction and . . ."

"I don't want to hear another word about his drug addiction! The papers are full of it! Everyone in the village knows all the lurid details."

"Please, Henri, don't say any more," Madame Sabasté suddenly cut in. She turned to Paul. "What will happen to Edouard now? Will he go to prison?"

"No, he won't go to prison. He will be given a new identity and sent out of the country for his own protection."

"So he will be hidden from us."

"It doesn't have to be that way. I can arrange for contact through an intermediary. I came here hoping that you would come to Paris to see him before he is . . ."

"We do not wish to see him," Monsieur Sabasté declared firmly. "He has given no thought to his position. I cannot forgive him."

"Is that your final position?" Paul asked.

"Yes."

"No!" Madame Sabasté dissented immediately.

"Silana! The matter is closed," Monsieur Sabasté insisted.

"No, Henri. Edouard is my son. I left the work of raising him to others, but he is my son. I cannot cut him off without a word." She turned to Paul. "Please wait while I write a message," she said and dashed from the room.

Monsieur Sabasté ran after her shouting, "Silana! Come back here! The matter is finished, do you hear!"

Paul stepped into the hall in time to hear Madame Sabasté shout, "Leave me be! He is my child, Henri! My child! For once in my life I must have the courage to act like his mother."

"I will not give that boy another sou. Do you understand? Nothing!"

"That is your choice, Henri. I will not turn my back on him. I have done that for too long and look what has become of him."

A moment later, as Madame Sabasté came rushing back into the hall, Paul heard Monsieur Sabasté call after her, "Silana! Come back! You will only encourage Edouard with your softness. He is no longer my son and heir. He's become a common criminal!"

Hurriedly Madame Sabasté thrust an envelope into Paul's hand.

"Please give this to Edouard. God has granted me a second chance. Perhaps this time I can fulfill my responsibility as a mother. I beg Edouard's forgiveness but . . . I cannot come to Paris. His father . . ."

"I understand," Paul answered. "I am grateful to have even a word of affection to bring him."

"Please . . . you must go now. Leave me to deal with Henri."

"Perhaps in time he will change his mind and help Edouard."

"I will pray for it, but Henri is very strong-willed. Thank you for bringing me news of Edouard. I am much relieved to know he is alive. I entrust him to your care. I can see you have sympathy for him."

Paul sensed she would have said more, but Monsieur Sabasté bellowed again, demanding that she return. It was obvious to Paul that Monsieur Sabasté dominated his wife as well as his son.

"I must go," Madame Sabasté whispered fearfully.

"I understand. I will send you word of Edouard."

"Yes. Please do," she begged and retreated, wiping her eyes with her hand.

Paul slipped the envelope into his coat pocket and headed down the hall. He opened the front door, but as he stepped through, the maid suddenly appeared behind him. She put her finger to her lips and pulled the door shut behind them with a loud click.

"I have only a moment before they call for me, Monsieur," she said in hushed tones. Offering Paul a small leather-bound book, she continued, "Please give this to Edouard. I fear he will have need of it wherever you send him."

Silently Paul opened the cover and saw that it was a prayer book. Several franc notes of small denominations had been stuffed between the pages.

"It's Edouard's," the maid whispered. "He used it when he was a child. When he left for university, they packed everything to go into the attic. This was all I could save." She looked tearfully at Paul. "In some ways I was more of a mother to him than she ever was. When he was sick, I sat with him. When he was dirty, I gave him a bath. She didn't know how and she didn't want to learn.

"Forgive me for talking of her this way. You mustn't blame her too much. She was just a child herself when Edouard was born. She was forced to marry Monsieur Sabasté at fifteen to avoid a scandal. She was not the first girl he had ruined, but her family was too powerful to be bought off. Neither of them wanted the child. Poor Edouard was like an orphan in his own home. It was the old gardener and I who brought him up."

"You did a good job," Paul assured her quickly. "You must not believe the stories you read about him."

"Oh, I never believed that Edouard could do all those wicked things. He was a gentle boy. His secret is safe with me. You see I tore the page that showed his name."

"I see that Edouard has one true friend here. May I ask her name?"

"Juliana, but he always called me 'Tullie'."

"I will remember you to Edouard, Tullie. He needs to know that someone thinks well of him. He . . ." Before Paul could finish, he heard Monsieur Sabasté calling Juliana's name.

"I must go. God speed!" the maid whispered and slipped inside the house again.

Paul limped to the car with a heavy heart. How can I tell Edouard that his father has disowned him? he wondered sadly. Perhaps he is better off without his father's money. He was cut off emotionally long ago. Paul looked around at the manicured lawns and beautiful gardens. It's a blessing for Edouard that he absorbed the goodness of this place and left the bitterness behind. Tullie and Gaston did well by him.

Paul's leg was throbbing painfully as he drove toward the airport in Bordeaux. Not daring to risk making himself drowsy with pain killers, he gritted his teeth, gripped the steering wheel, and hoped his strength would last.

Somehow he made it to the terminal and staggered to his seat on the plane. The stewardess gave him an unsympathetic glance as he downed two pain capsules without the benefit of water just before takeoff. She's probably worried that I'll be airsick, he thought vaguely and realized it was a distinct possibility given the fact that he hadn't eaten anything all day.

He knew his leg was swollen and Carlin's dire warnings of phlebitis rang in his ears. As he sank back against the seat, he was thankful for the extra leg room in the first class compartment. Some time later he heard the clatter of dishes, but no one bothered him about a drink or a choice of entrees. He wasn't aware of anyone bothering him at all until he felt someone pulling at his tie. He opened his eyes and saw several people leaning over him.

"Monsieur? Monsieur, are you all right?" a woman's voice asked. Someone laid something cold and wet on his forehead and he realized that his shirt was damp. He tried to move and noticed that he was strapped down.

"Monsieur? Can you hear me?" the woman asked again.

"Yes," he mumbled weakly, attempting to bring the woman's face into focus.

"You have to sit up, monsieur. The plane is about to land."

"Land? Where?" he questioned.

"In Paris, monsieur. Please . . . you must sit up."

Shit! I must have blacked out, he thought as he felt himself moving forward. Suddenly he was upright and it didn't feel good at all.

"Get a bag!" someone ordered. Everything started to spin and he swallowed hard. Oh God! Pull yourself together, Paul! Don't throw up in front of all these people. Focus! Focus!

He heard the rustle of paper as someone opened the air sickness bag, but he held everything down.

"The rest of you go sit down," the woman said. He heard the seat belt click on the seat next to him, then someone was rubbing his wrist and talking to him. "Stay awake, monsieur. Stay awake. We're almost down."

Don't lie to me, mademoiselle, my ears tell me differently, he thought. He was glad everyone had gone away. Focus, Paul! Focus! he told himself again. He began mentally repeating the words to the chant he had used to calm Kon, but he couldn't seem to get past the first two lines. He kept repeating them over and over until he felt the wheels bump the runway.

Someone wiped his face with a wet cloth, but he didn't open his eyes. He figured it was the woman, and he was too embarrassed to look at her. When he did look at her she smiled and asked, "Feeling any better?"

He nodded, "Yeah, a little, thanks."

"Would you like us to call a cab for you?"

"A cab? No. I'll be all right."

"Are you sure, monsieur? You don't look well."

"I'm sure. I'll be fine. I feel much better, really," he said aloud. The woman did not seem to agree. She kept looking at him.

I have to be O.K., he told himself. I don't want to attract any more attention. The last thing I want is for anyone to remember me on this trip. I should never have taken those capsules on an empty stomach. I should have let my damn leg hurt! I've got to catch the train to town like any other passenger. I'll call Jack as soon as I get near the villa.

At last the woman stopped staring at him. "All right, monsieur, if you insist. I must see to the other passengers now. Goodbye."

Paul nodded and she stood, straightened her skirt and moved to the passenger door. It was already open and the rest of the first class passengers were almost gone. Paul stood with difficulty and concentrated his will on getting off the plane without staggering. He moved forward slowly, gritting his teeth and trying not to wince.

Suddenly, his way was blocked by a family group who were giving the man in front of him a boisterous greeting. Paul knew he should move around them, but he couldn't summon the energy. He stood, ignoring the passengers behind him who began jostling to get past. When he turned to get out of the way, someone grabbed his arm.

"Paul! You look like hell! What happened?"

"Jack? What are you doing here?" For once he was glad that Jack hadn't done exactly as he was told.

"I got worried about you trying to take that train if it was crowded. You don't look too good, Paul. You'd better sit down while I bring the car around."

"I'm O.K. I don't need help."

"Oh sure! Your sweating, pal. And what's this?" Jack asked, pulling at Paul's coat pocket. "Looks like you've already had a go-round with the barf bag."

"No I didn't! I just . . . Someone must have . . . ."

"Come on. Let's go home. Nea's here."

"She's here?"

"Yeah, she called and I brought her along for the ride."

Paul groaned inwardly. He was embarrassed to have Nea see him looking so tired and washed out. Well, so what? I've got to stop seeing Nea one of these days. Maybe this is the perfect opportunity.

Paul was only dimly aware of the bustling crowd as Jack steered him past the ticket counter and down the wide hall, but he had no trouble spotting Nea as they reached the seating area. Even under artificial light her hair seemed to sparkle with fire. His mental daze dissolved in the glow of her smile. He was surprised at how glad he was that Nea was speaking to him again. When Geilla ended up back in the hospital after her visit to Kon, Nea and Mary at last understood why he had been so adamant about keeping them apart.

"Welcome back, Paul. I'm glad you're safe," she said warmly and kissed him lightly on the cheek.

The very nearness of her suffused him with energy, but for a moment he could think of nothing to say. Has she missed me as much as I missed her? he wondered. She doesn't seem to notice how bedraggled I look or maybe she doesn't care.

She took his arm and he felt her energy flowing over him. I shouldn't let her affect me this way, he cautioned himself. I mustn't become . . . I have to be stronger than everyone else. I have to be complete in order to give. I don't need anyone else, do I? It must be this damned medication. I'll be back to normal when it wears off. But right now . . . right now I'd better be careful. Just being with Nea feels so good I might say something I'll regret.

He just stood and smiled wisely, or so he thought; never realizing that his tongue-tied grin told her volumes about how pleased he was to see her. And then they were in the car. Jack had insisted that he sit in the back and put his leg up. He had even pulled his shoes off for him. Nea was in the front, but she turned and smiled at him so often he didn't feel alone. It actually made it easier for him to focus on Jack, telling him how disappointing the day had been, telling him that Edouard's father had disowned him. He wondered aloud how he was going to break the news to Edouard.

He found it easy to talk to Jack. He could even let Jack help him once in a while. Jack was his friend and Jack understood that he was in charge. Geilla had always understood. She had never complicated matters by making him feel that he needed her. After all, it was Kon who needed her. It was right and good that they should be together. That's what he had worked for. That's what he wanted, even if it meant that he was alone. I don't mind being alone, he told himself. I don't need anyone else. Everyone knows that. It's only Nea who doesn't understand.

"I'm sorry things didn't work out in Cantois," Jack was saying. "It was a really good day here. After you left, Kon started asking a lot of questions about you. He seemed so much better, I invited him to come out to the living room for a while. He seemed really surprised that he could leave the bedroom. I don't think it had really sunk in that he's not a prisoner anymore. Anyway, I showed him his clothes and he got dressed. Then he came out and sat and talked with me a bit until Etienne wheeled himself in.

"I didn't know how Kon would react, but he didn't panic. Maybe because Etienne is in a wheelchair, he didn't seem threatening. When I introduced Etienne, Kon recognized the name immediately. He seemed absolutely amazed that Etienne was alive. You know, I think that all the time he was a prisoner those guys were beating him in order to get him to tell where Etienne was and he never would tell. I bet that's why he kept insisting that he wasn't going to tell us anything. He's been protecting Etienne all this time. Even though he couldn't remember his own name, he was protecting Etienne. Ya got to hand it to him. He's got will power. He's just having trouble sorting things out right now. Meeting Etienne was a definite breakthrough."

"That's great, Jack!"

"Of course Etienne was really excited to have anyone take an interest in him. It was great to see them both so happy. I fixed some sandwiches and they were watching a soccer game together when I left."

Paul laughed. "I'm surprised you could pull yourself away, Jack! It'll be good for Kon to start getting out a bit more. I've been thinking about taking him to his apartment, but I didn't want to rush him. Meeting Geilla really upset him. I think a part of him is still angry with her."

"I don't know. I think he's mad at himself for not remembering his own wife and baby. He asked me a couple of times why her husband abandoned her."

"What did you tell him?"

"I didn't know what to say. I didn't want to make him feel bad. I finally said that her husband was just away for a while and that soon they would be together again. He accepted that. He feels really bad that he made her cry."

"How is Geilla doing, Nea? I've been so busy with Kon and Edouard I haven't been able to spend much time with her."

"Frankly, I'm worried. I guess you know that Dr. La Monde came back to Paris after you rushed Geilla to the hospital. He had them do a sonogram. The baby seems O.K., but Geilla is still bleeding. She won't admit it, but she's scared. It hasn't helped that there have been two stillbirths at the hospital since she arrived. She's just not going to get better until Kon does."

"Well, maybe now that he's up and around, we can take him to the hospital to see her," Paul said. "Even if we have to play along with his idea that she's someone else's wife, it might do her good to see that at least physically Kon is doing better."

"And who knows," Jack added hopefully, "He might remember her next time."

"He might," Paul agreed. "He'll come out of this. I know he will," Paul continued and suddenly realized that he had repeated that statement so often it was beginning to sound like a mantra. Well, that was how a mantra was supposed to work. You just kept repeating it until it became true.

Paul was feeling much better. Getting his leg up and his shoes off had really helped. He enjoyed being with Jack and Nea and was encouraged to hear that Kon was doing better. He was looking forward to getting back to the villa. Maybe they could pick up some Chinese food later and the five of them could enjoy a quiet evening together. It would be so nice to relax for a while the way they used to.

Paul's dream of tranquility was shattered abruptly as they reached the villa. The metal gates were wide open and two strange cars were parked in the driveway. He sat up quickly, jamming his feet into his shoes.

"What the hell is going on?" Jack sputtered as he raced the car through the gate and up the drive. "I left two GIGN agents in charge," he said in answer to Paul's silent question.

Jack and Paul jumped from the car as soon as it came to a stop, leaving Nea wondering if Paul would ever have time to spend with her. She watched them run toward the front door and saw it open as they reached it. Pienaar was standing in the hall looking as if he had been waiting for them.

"Ah, Monsieur Artier and Monsieur Barrons, we meet again."

"What's going on, Pienaar? Where's Rubard?" Paul demanded immediately.

"Monsieur Rubard is quite safe. It is your kidnap victim who has gone mad."

"What! What are you talking about?"

"He assaulted one of my men with a knife. He stole his coat, his wallet, and his gun. Then he forced him to unlock the gate so he could make his escape."

"Escape? He wasn't a prisoner here."

"Perhaps he thought differently. It is interesting that he waited until you were both gone to make his move."

"That's crazy!" Jack snapped. "I left two of your men in charge. They were supposed to watch things."

"And they did, Monsieur Barrons, they did. As soon as young Rubard called, they came. Your friend is very cunning. He hid until my men went looking for him and then he jumped one of them."

"Where's Rubard," Paul asked, pushing past Pienaar. "Something must have happened." He rushed down the hall and into the living room where he found Etienne sitting in his wheelchair by the couch. He looked frightened and was biting his knuckles so intently that he didn't notice Paul until he spoke.

"Are you all right, Etienne? What happened?"

Etienne looked up and gasped, "I'm sorry! I'm sorry! I just couldn't move fast enough! I hate this chair! I hate being in this . . ."

"Calm down, Etienne. No one's accusing you of anything. Just tell me what happened. Jack said you were watching a game."

"We were. We were just sitting here watching television when the news came on. The group has killed someone else! I don't know who. I didn't want to listen, but they went on and on. Then they started to talk about the raid on the apartment. They showed pictures of Michon, and George, and Sabasté. I was trying to ignore it and didn't notice Kon until I heard a crash. He had dropped his coffee and was just staring at the screen. I could see he was upset and I tried to turn the television off, but I couldn't get around the table fast enough. I hate this chair. I hate . . ."

"Stop whining, Etienne. It doesn't help," Paul said patiently. "Tell me what happened next."

"I finally got to the set, but by then Kon had run into the bedroom and shut the door. I called to him, but he didn't answer. I went toward the door, but before I got there I heard a loud crash. I didn't know what to do. I knew I couldn't help him if he were hurt, so I wheeled out to the front door. Jack had promised there would be someone on guard and there was. I told the man about the crash and he rushed into Kon's room. He came out a minute later and said that Kon had smashed the window and was gone. He started calling on his radio and the next thing I knew the place was full of GIGN agents. I'm sorry, Paul. I'm really sorry . . ."

"It's O.K., Etienne. You did the right thing to get help. He couldn't have gotten far. Did Kon have a knife?"

"I didn't see one."

"Did he go into the kitchen at all?"

"No. We were just sitting here. I'm sorry."

"O.K., Etienne. Relax. We'll find him," Paul said. He patted Etienne on the arm, then hurried into Kon's room.

Jack joined him there a moment later. "I searched the bushes but I couldn't find a knife. All I found was a long splinter of glass and a towel. I think that agent was imagining things."

"Did you talk to him? Is he O.K.?" Paul asked quickly.

"Yeah. I think he was so embarrassed that Kon got the jump on him, he embellished his story a bit."

"Jees! What the hell does Kon think he's doing?"

"I don't think he really knows who he is yet, Paul. He's still scared and groping for answers."

"Yeah, well now he's armed and scared. We've got to find him before one of Pienaar's trigger happy agents does."

Chapter Sixteen

Kon ran from the villa more in dread of his mental confusion than of the men who were chasing him. They were solid and he could hide from them. What he could not escape was the formless fear that pursued him relentlessly. Even in the supposed security of his room at the villa, he had suffered hideous nightmares. Frequently he had awoken to find Paul standing quietly by his bed.

Paul always uttered reassuring words, but Kon was still not sure whether or not it was Paul he should be afraid of. He couldn't remember Paul having hit him, but he hadn't remembered Michon and Georges either until he had seen their pictures on the television.

Kon hadn't really planned to escape. He hadn't thought it was necessary until he had seen those pictures. He was shocked that Edouard was dead and stunned to learn that he was a terrorist. He remembered only Edouard's gentle kindness. The images on the screen had jarred loose such a flood of memories that he felt more confused than ever.

As Kon ran he tried to focus on his immediate danger. He had to find a place to hide while he sorted things out, but everywhere he looked he saw only stone walls and metal fences surrounding villas very much like the one he had fled. He had to get off the street.

He slowed to a walk, figuring he would be less conspicuous. He was glad that Jack had offered him the option of wearing street clothes. As he walked he studied the gates carefully until finally he spotted an opportunity. On the gate of this particular villa the ornate metal bars did not reach all the way to the ground. Although the corner posts for the gate were massive, the paving did not extend out to the posts. Between the post and the driveway was a narrow strip of garden.

Kon noticed that on the left side, behind a cypress tree, the earth had been washed away. He guessed that the erosion had been caused by a faulty sprinkler head. Seeing a car approach, he slipped behind the cypress and dropped to his knees. In addition to erosion, the ground showed signs of having been dug away. Aware that he might have to face whatever had done the digging, Kon rolled onto his back and squeezed under the gate.

As he pulled himself up, he saw a huge evergreen on his left. He hurried for the cover of its branches and threw himself onto the soft ground. He was out of breath and his ribs ached. He couldn't remember how long it had been since he had done anything so vigorous. That was his biggest problem. He still couldn't remember much of anything.

At least I have escaped from the villa, he reasoned. He felt safe hidden in the old tree. He could see a two-story house through the branches, but no one was moving about. He settled back against the trunk and took stock of his situation. I have to think. I have to sort it all out. I thought things were beginning to make sense. I thought I could trust Jack and Paul. Now, I don't know. I just don't know.

Slowly, methodically he reviewed everything he could remember, trying to piece the bits of information together. The thing that was freshest in his mind was the pictures on the television screen. Thinking about them was not pleasant, but as he forced himself to do it, he became certain that they were the men who had hit him.

If Jack and Paul are my friends, why were they keeping me behind locked gates? he wondered. And why were men with loaded guns searching the bushes for me?

I've got to remember where I met Edouard. I recognized those others too. Why? Am I a terrorist? Maybe all that talk about not being a prisoner was just a trick to get me to talk. But they already have Rubard. What is it they want?

He tried to remember what Michon and Georges had been asking him, but all he could come up with was, "Where is Etienne Rubard?" He pushed himself to review everything he had heard them say and then he remembered. They called me Emile Breaux. So had Edouard. They thought I was a GIGN agent. Am I? Paul said I was a banker.

I've got to find out who I am or I'll go crazy. Maybe that's it. Maybe I *am* crazy. Paul said they might put me in a straight jacket. Maybe that's why I have those terrible dreams. Oh, God, maybe all the beatings and the questions are just hallucinations. He put his hand to his head in despair and it came to him. No, they were real. This cast is real. Paul said they beat me. He said that was why I couldn't remember anything. Maybe Paul is a GIGN agent. Maybe that guy at the villa was a GIGN agent. He had a gun. I took his wallet. There might be some identification in it, he thought and began searching.

It was after dark and still Kon had not been found. Jack and Paul were combing the city for him, the police were looking for him, and Pienaar had assigned every agent he could spare to the search. Pienaar was making his fourth trip to the coffee urn when one of his men called out "Have you ever heard of a guy named Breaux?"

Pienaar stopped in his tracks. "Breaux?"

"Yes. There's a guy on the phone who insists he works here. I told him I've never heard of him. Maybe he's at some other . . ."

Pienaar snatched the phone before the agent could finish. Silently he signaled that he wanted the call traced and flipped on the recorder.

"You are looking for Agent Breaux?" he said into the phone. "He's not here at the moment. Would you like to leave a message? I don't know exactly when he will be back. Could you leave your name? I'll see that . . . Damn! He hung up!" Pienaar growled, turning to the agent. "Did you get a location?"

The agent shook his head. "It was too short. Who is Breaux?"

"There is no Emile Breaux! That was Kononellos. I'm sure of it. The man's gone mad! He's running around Paris with a gun, looking for a man that doesn't exist. We've got to find him before he hurts someone."

I'm no further ahead, Kon thought as he hung up the phone. If I am Emile Breaux, I don't work in that office. What was it that Paul said? Yes, he said I was only pretending to be Emile. It doesn't make sense, but maybe it's true. The only things I am sure of are that it's cold and I'm hungry. That guy at the villa sure didn't carry much money with him.

Officer Cudran was sitting at his desk at the police station, sipping his coffee and logging in the calls; a purse snatching, a man exposing himself in the Metro station, a battered wife, the usual late evening fare. Then a call about a robbery came in. A young business executive who had been working late reported being held up in a parking garage by a lone gunman. There was nothing unusual about the story except that the description of the robber sounded vaguely familiar. The caller remembered him as a tall, thin man with his right hand in a cast and a bandage over his left eye.

The victim hadn't lost much money. The robber took only his smaller bills, some change, and his overcoat. "That's what made me mad!" he kept telling Officer Cudran. "It was a brand new coat—a present from my wife. When I objected, the bastard said he would return it and the money as soon as he could. How's that for a likely story?"

"Did he take your wallet?" Officer Cudran asked.

"No. He made me empty it onto the hood of my car and then he snatched the bills. He took my driver's license too."

"Did you see which way he went?"

"No. That part was strange. First he asked me to get on the floor in the back of my car, but when I opened the door he suddenly changed his mind. He started repeating that he wouldn't hurt me and asked me to turn around. For a minute I was afraid he was going to hit me over the head, but he just ran away. I don't think he's a professional. He didn't take my watch or my ring or the car."

"I don't think he was," Officer Cudran agreed, suddenly remembering where he had heard the description before. "We'll call you if we find him," he said and continued filling out the report form.

Kon decided to risk one last call from the phone in the Metro station. He was afraid someone might notice that he had been on the phone for over an hour, but he had a lot of calls to make. There seemed to be an endless listing under "banks" in the phone book and it took people a long time to determine if anyone named Peter Kononellos was on the staff. Everyone had been polite and helpful, but since he didn't know if he was trying to find the president or a clerk, he got transferred around a lot.

Methodically he ran his finger down the list and placed the next call. "Good morning. May I speak with Monsieur Peter Kononellos, please?" he said in answer to the formal greeting from the young lady who answered the phone.

"One moment, please," came back and he waited, visualizing a manicured fingertip sliding down a lengthy list of names. But instead of the now familiar, "Sorry, I don't see him on my list. What department does he work for?" another voice came on the line.

"Good morning. May I help you?"

Politely Kon repeated his request to speak to Peter Kononellos.

"I'm sorry Monsieur Kononellos is not here this morning. He's in Geneva this week. Would you like the number for that office?"

Kon almost dropped the phone in surprise. Paul had said that he lived in Geneva. Had he at last found a clue?

"Monsieur? Do you need the number?" the voice asked again.

"Er . . . yes. Yes, please," Kon stammered and quickly took down the number using the GIGN agent's pen.

Kon doubted that he had enough change to make the call to Geneva, but he decided to risk it. At the least he would learn what the charge actually was. With a mixture of anticipation and dread he pushed coins into the slot and dialed the operator. Following her instructions, he started dropping his precious stack of coins into the phone. The call was answered by a woman who sounded competent yet friendly, and Kon quickly repeated his request to speak to Peter Kononellos.

"Monsieur Peter Kononellos? Certainly. One moment please."

Again Kon felt his heart speed up. Someone had actually recognized the name. After a pause another voice came on the line, "Good morning this is Mademoiselle Flambert. May I help you?"

Kon hesitated. What if the real Peter Kononellos came on the line?

"Good morning. May I help you?" the woman repeated.

"May I speak with Monsieur Kononellos please?"

"May I tell him who is calling?"

Oh God, it must be someone else! What can I say? he wondered anxiously.

"May I tell him who is calling please?" the woman inquired again.

"Tell him . . . tell him . . ." Kon began hesitantly, but the woman cut him off. "Oh my God! Just a moment."

Before he could answer there was a click and he could hear the phone ringing again. He was startled and was about to hang up when suddenly a man's voice came on the line. "Peter? Peter, is that you? This is Edgar. Where are you? We were all so worried about you. Peter?"

"I . . . I . . ." Kon stammered. "I need to speak with Peter Kononellos . . . please. It's important."

"Oh my God! Don't you remember? You are Peter Kononellos."

Before Kon could respond the operator came on the line asking him to deposit more money.

"I don't have any . . ." he began, but Edgar cut in decisively, "Operator, this is an emergency! Switch the charges to my number immediately. And please, clear the line!"

Kon heard another click and then, "Peter? Are you still there?"

"Yes. You know me?"

"Of course I know you. This is Edgar. My God, what have they done to you?"

Even through the telephone Kon could feel the depth of Edgar's concern. He sounded very wise and kind. Kon longed to reach out to him to confess his confusion and find some answers.

"They kept hitting me, Edgar," he mumbled. "They just kept hitting me and asking questions. Paul said that's why I can't remember anything. Why were they hitting me, Edgar?"

"Oh, Peter! I'm so sorry they hurt you. They were trying to find out where a young man named Etienne Rubard was and you wouldn't tell them."

"Rubard! Yes, I met Rubard. He's alive. Why did they think I was Emile Breaux?"

"You were only pretending to be Emile Breaux. You were on an assignment with Jack and Paul. You were kidnaped, Peter."

"Only pretending," Kon mumbled. "That's what Paul said. I didn't understand."

"Peter, please tell me where you are."

"I'm . . . I'm in Paris."

"Where in Paris? We've lost you. We want you to come home."

"Home?"

"Yes. We miss you, Peter. Charlotte and the boys are worried. Carlin is worried. Geilla is worried. She needs you, Peter. Please come home."

"I can't come home, Edgar. I can't. I've got to find out why they killed Edouard. I thought he was my friend."

"Peter, listen to me! You must call Paul. He's looking for you. He wants to help you."

"You know Paul?"

"Yes. He's your friend. He can explain everything. Let me give you his phone . . ."

"Someone's coming, Edgar. I have to go!"

"Peter! Wait!"

"I've become a thief, Edgar. I'll be a prisoner again if they find me."

Edgar heard the phone drop, but he kept calling, "Peter! Wait! Call me! Call me, please!"

Paul was sitting in his car across from the bank. He and Jack had been swapping the duties of watching the bank and Kon's apartment. He knew that Kon was searching for his identity and felt sure that sooner or later he would show up at one of those places. It was just a matter of time, he kept telling himself.

It would have been easier to find Kon if they could have put his picture in the newspapers or on television, but once again, Paul was trying to keep the news of Kon's disappearance from Geilla. She was still in the hospital, so for the moment the news blackout was possible. Paul was wondering how to break the news to Geilla when Officer Cudran pulled his car in front of Paul's and got out.

Oh shit! I hope Kon hasn't pulled another holdup, Paul thought as Cudran came up to his car. Jees, Kon, if you had to pull a stickup, why didn't you take enough to last? God you're a lousy thief!

"Good evening, Monsieur Martel," Cudran began. "How are you holding up?"

"Is that supposed to be a pun?" Paul snapped.

Cudran smiled. "Sorry—poor choice of words. I have nothing new to report about your friend."

"He's really not dangerous. He's just . . ."

"I didn't come to hassle you. I only came to tell you something I thought you might be interested in."

"What's that?"

"I know you are following the recent slayings by the Direct Action group."

Paul nodded.

"Apparently your friend was not the only one who saw those pictures on the television last night."

"What do you mean?"

"A woman came into the station house this afternoon and asked for Nicolas Grenelle's body."

"What? Who was she?"

"Méline something or other. Here, I wrote down her name and address. You can't miss her. She's really unusual."

"Unusual? What do you mean?"

"You'll find out," Cudran snickered. "And stand upwind or the perfume will kill you."

"Thanks. I'm sorry if . . ."

"Forget it. You've got trouble."

Paul smiled wearily and pocketed the piece of paper. The local police have been very helpful, he thought as Cudran walked back to his car. I'd better ask Mary to keep watch at the bank while I talk to Méline. Poor Mary. You're really getting involved in this assignment.

No one answered when Paul first knocked on the door of Méline's apartment, but he thought he heard voices behind the door so he rapped again more loudly. He heard a crash then several loud noises as if someone were bumping into things. He kept knocking and eventually the door was opened by an older woman with frizzy, orange-red hair.

"What do you want? I don't have any, no matter what it is," she said, slurring her words.

"Are you Méline Aizenay?" Paul asked even as his nose told him the answer.

"Who wants to know?"

"Martel, from GIGN," Paul answered, holding out his fake I.D.

"In that case, Méline's not here!" the woman answered. She tried to push the door closed, but Paul was too quick and blocked the way.

"I think she is. I need to talk to you, Méline. It's about Nicolas."

"Nicolas! Don't you know he's dead? Can't you people leave him in peace?"

"I know he's dead. I was with him when he died. I promised him I would get the man who did it. We need to talk, Méline."

"Talking won't do any good. It was you people who killed my Nickie. Leave him in peace! Leave me in peace!"

"It wasn't the police who killed Nicolas. It was the man he was working for. Please . . . I need to talk to you. May I come in?"

"Why not?" Méline asked with hopeless resignation. "Méline never turns anybody away. Might as well not have the damn door!"

Paul stepped inside and closed the door. Méline appeared a bit disheveled, but her apartment looked as if it had been ransacked by burglars. "Did you have a break-in?" Paul asked.

"No. No. I was just looking for something. I wasn't expecting company."

Méline started for the living room, but lurched into a small table. Paul suddenly guessed what she had been searching for so frantically.

"What are you on, Méline? Heroin? Cocaine?" he asked without emotion.

"What do you care?"

"You're killing yourself with it. Why . . ."

"It's just a little morphine. It's my back that kills me without it. Nickie used to bring it for me. Now what will I do? Nickie was the only one who cared about old Méline."

She began to sniffle and Paul took her arm and steered her towards the couch.

"Come on, Méline. Pull yourself together. I need to ask you about Nicolas."

"Poor Nickie," she sobbed. "He looked so bad. Why did you have to shoot him? Why did you kill my poor Nickie?"

"Listen to me, Méline. It wasn't the police . . ." Paul began, but Méline didn't hear him. She began wailing and pulling her hair.

"Listen to me, Méline," he tried again, but decided it was useless.

He handed her his handkerchief and went to find the kitchen. It was messier than the sitting room and he felt sad that what could have been a cheerful room had fallen into neglect. Shaking his head, he began searching the cupboards.

Méline was still sobbing when he returned to the living room a short time later. "Come on, Méline, drink this," he said handing her a cup of tea. "I need your help to do one last thing for Nicolas."

"You want to do something for Nickie? Why? You're from GIGN. What did you say your name was?" she asked sipping gratefully.

"Martel."

"Why would Martel from GIGN want to do anything for my Nickie?"

"Because the bastard who shot Nico . . . Nickie beat my partner so badly he can't even remember who he is."

For a moment Méline looked at him and he hoped she might be calmer. "Listen, Méline. I know who got Nickie, but I need your help to find him. Did Nickie ever mention a man named Gérard?"

"Gérard? No. Nickie never told me what he was involved in. He said he didn't want the police to badger me any more. Nickie and me go way back . . . way back. He and my old man used to work together. I married Renaud, but I should have married Nickie. Renaud was a mean son of a bitch. Nickie used to get on him about the way he treated me. It was Nickie who came to see me after Renaud put me in the hospital."

"Where is Renaud? Would he know where Gérard is?"

"Renaud? No, he got himself killed while I was in the hospital. He and Nickie were on a bank job. Renaud got killed, but Nickie got away. I never told who Renaud was with. Nickie was real good to me. After I left the hospital, the doctors wouldn't give me any more morphine. They said I wasn't helping the police so they cut me off. Nickie came through for me though. He never did find another partner, but somehow he got into selling the hard stuff. He was making good money, but his kid brother got hooked real bad. He O.D.ed at fifteen. Nickie was real broke up about it. He quit selling the stuff. He got so hot . . . well, I guess it don't matter now. He took a couple dealers off the streets. Know what I mean? Christ! If he worked for GIGN, they would have pinned a medal on him. It just don't figure. Nickie was real down on drugs."

"Do you have any idea who Nicolas was working with? Can you think of anyone who might lead me to Gérard?"

"No. Nickie never told me what he was up to. I don't think he was happy with . . . you know, he did bring a young man here one day."

"Can you think of his name? Why did he bring him?"

"The poor kid was suffering real bad drug withdrawal. Nickie said he had to keep him off the streets and get him back in working order. I gave him some stuff just to get him back on track."

"Do you remember his name?"

"Let's see. It was something like Eric or Edmund."

"Could it have been Edouard?" Paul asked in surprise.

"Yes! That's it! A real young kid. Oh my God! He's the one they showed on television last night. I forgot all about him until just now. Nickie kept at him to kick the habit, but poor Edouard was too sick to give a damn. Oh poor Edouard! Poor Edouard! He was so young."

Méline started to sob again and Paul saw that he wasn't going to get anything useful from her. He was tempted to tell her that Edouard was alive and coming through treatment very well, but he doubted that Méline could be trusted with such a secret.

"Shh, shh, Méline. Don't cry about Edouard. Let's decide what we are going to do about Méline. When was the last time you ate?"

"Me? I don't know. I must have had something this morning."

"Why don't you go wash your face and I'll see what I can find in the kitchen."

"You would do that for me?"

"Sure."

"Why?"

Paul shrugged. How can I explain it to her, when I don't understand it myself. I just can't leave, knowing that she is sitting here alone, crying her eyes out over a thief and a drug addict. "I guess I just can't stand to see a lady cry," he said after a long silence.

"Me? A lady! Oh Monsieur Martel from GIGN, you're sweet. You're really sweet. How did you ever get tangled up with GIGN?"

"We're not all ogres, you know. It's just a job. Some of us have wives and homes and kids like real people."

"Real people huh. Do you have a home and a wife?"

"Me? No, but . . . What about you? Isn't there someplace you can go?"

"I have a sister in Nantes, but I haven't written in years. She and I . . . well, she doesn't approve of my life style. Can't say as I blame her when I see where it all ended. Maybe it would have been different if I had married Nickie."

"Have you thought of calling her?"

"My sister? No. She's got a nice little family—two kids, I think. She has no use for me."

"Are you sure? When was the last time you wrote to her?"

"Well . . . must be four or five years now. She invited me to her eldest daughter's wedding. She's real proud of that girl. I thought about going . . . Nickie said he'd give me money for the ticket."

"But you didn't go."

"No."

"Why?"

"Guess I was ashamed to let my sister know . . . I was always the pretty one. I had dresses and shoes, and men. I always had a dozen on the string. None of them were worth a damn, but I was popular. My sister was more serious. She married the boy who delivered groceries. He had a head for business though. They moved to Nantes and started a little café. She did all right."

"Maybe you should write to her."

Méline shrugged. "To tell the truth, I lost her address. I guess she gave up writing when I didn't go to the wedding."

"Maybe I could help you find her. I've got a few connections."

Méline smiled. "Oh, yes. I bet you do, Monsieur Martel from GIGN. Is that your real name? What do your friends call you? What does your girl friend call you?"

"My girl friend?"

"Yeah. You must have at least one—good looking man like you."

"Ah . . . umm . . . my friends call me Paul."

"No cute little nick-names? Are you always so serious?"

"I work for a serious outfit, Méline."

"Yeah, I guess shooting nice kids like Edouard can't . . ."

"I did not . . .! Go wash your face, Méline. I'll see if I can find something to eat."

Chapter Seventeen

It was early afternoon and Kon was on a bus that passed in front of the bank. He had ridden by four times before, but he hadn't dared to get off. He suspected that the police were looking for him. He knew it was risky to be in the area, but the only address he had was that of the bank. He kept hoping that something would look familiar. Unfortunately, nothing did until on the third pass, he spotted Paul sitting in a car parked across the street from the bank. When he saw him again on the fourth pass, he decided what he must do.

Kon rode two stops beyond the bank, then got off the bus. Walking over one block, he circled around and approached Paul's car from the rear. He hesitated in a doorway for a moment until no one was passing then dashed for the car. His heart was beating rapidly as he raised his gun and smashed the window on the passenger side. Instantly, he unlocked the door and yanked it open. Pointing his gun straight at Paul, he snapped, "Keep your hands on the wheel!"

Instead of showing surprise or fear, Paul immediately demanded, "Where the hell have you been? Every cop in Paris is looking for you! Half of them think you're a missing person and the other half think you're wanted for armed robbery. Jesus! Get in here before someone sees you with that thing!"

Kon was startled by Paul's response and even more startled by the sudden wave of anxiety that rose in him as he contemplated entering the car. It was the same feeling of near-panic that had struck him in the parking garage when he had tried to force a man into a car. He stared at Paul for almost a minute before he reluctantly got into the car. It seemed strange that even though he had the gun, Paul was giving the orders. He was scared, but Paul was his only link with reality. He seemed to have all the answers.

"You said I had an apartment in Paris. Take me there!" Kon barked, waving the gun at Paul.

"O.K. O.K. I'll take you," Paul agreed and started the engine. "Will you put that thing away!"

"No! Just drive!" Kon snapped, suddenly feeling frustrated that Paul did not appear to be afraid of him. Maybe it's all a trap, he thought anxiously. Maybe he's going to take me back to the villa. Maybe I don't work at that bank after all. Nothing seems familiar. Should I get out now? But where would I go? I have no real choice. I have to trust Paul.

"Are you all right? You look like hell," Paul commented. "Why did you run off like that? Do you know how worried we were? I was afraid Geilla would find out that you had disappeared again."

"Geilla? Who is Geilla?"

"She's your wife. Don't you remember? She came to visit you at the villa."

"I remember a woman coming. I shouted at her and . . . and made her cry. I didn't mean to make her cry. She was so beautiful and so . . . alone."

"She misses you, Kon. Don't you want to see her?"

"See her? I . . . I can't. I have to find out who killed Edouard."

"Is that what this is all about? Edouard is still alive, Kon. I can take you to see him."

Kon was stunned for a moment, but then became agitated. "No! You're lying! I saw those pictures. You're lying to me!"

"I'm not lying," Paul said quietly. "The pictures were meant to fool the men who might hurt Edouard. He is still alive."

"I don't believe you! It can't be true!" Kon snapped. "Just drive. I don't want to hear any more."

"Listen, Kon . . ."

"Shut up and drive! I don't want to hear any more of your lies," Kon snarled and pointed the gun at Paul again.

"O.K. O.K. Calm down. Jees! You may not remember who you are, but your personality sure hasn't improved."

Kon had been keeping his eyes on Paul and hadn't noticed where they were going, until suddenly it occurred to him that they had been past the same building twice before.

"Why are you circling?" he demanded. "Is this a trick?"

"It's not a trick," Paul answered calmly. "This is were you live and I'm looking for a parking place. Jees, calm down. Will you put that gun away."

"No!"

"All right. Will you at least keep it out of sight when we go in?" Paul asked as he slipped the car into a spot across from Kon's apartment building. "Your landlord thinks you're a respectable banker. It's a quiet neighborhood. Don't get your neighbors upset. They're nice people."

"How do you know my neighbors?"

"I've been coming here for years, Kon. Why do you think I have a key to your apartment?"

"You have a key?"

"Yes. Do you recognize anything?"

Kon hesitated and looked around. All the buildings appeared to be built of the same grey stone and none of them seemed familiar. Maybe I am crazy, he thought. I feel as though I am in the middle of another man's life. He noticed that Paul was watching him and was afraid to admit his confusion. "You go first," he finally said. "And remember, I'll have the gun pointed at your back."

"O.K. I'll lead the way," Paul agreed. He stepped out of the car and pocketed the keys. "It's across the street."

Kon nodded and followed after Paul wondering what he would do if Paul was leading him into a trap. Paul moved slowly and Kon saw that he was limping. He hadn't noticed the limp before and wondered how he could have missed it. He was close behind Paul when Paul took the steps up to the double doors on one of the buildings. Paul produced a key and quickly unlocked the door.

The lobby was small, but elegantly decorated with a large gilt frame mirror and a crystal chandelier. The room was attractive, it was just the tile floor that made Kon uneasy. After one quick glance, he decided to fix his attention on Paul's shoulders and not look down.

The elevator was ready and the door opened immediately when Paul pushed the button. Neither of them spoke as they rode to the third floor. When Paul stepped out and turned right, Kon followed without hesitation. Somehow he knew it was the way to go. He wished Paul would hurry as they headed down the hall. He was anxious to see if he would recognize anything in the apartment.

"This is it," Paul said when they reached apartment five. He too was eager to know if Kon would recognize the place. He sensed

Kon's nervousness as he fiddled with the key. "This damn key never has worked right," he remarked and then he heard the bolt click.

"Here we are," he said pushing the door open.

"You first," Kon barked.

"O.K.! Would you just relax!" Paul said and stepped through the doorway.

Kon hesitated briefly then followed. He was barely inside when something struck him in the back. He lurched forward and the next thing he knew he was lying on the floor clutching his wrist, and Paul was holding the gun. Jack was standing behind him.

Kon raised his hand to protect his head and waited for the next blow to land.

"Relax, Kon," he heard Paul say. "I told you we aren't going to hurt you."

"He's right, Kon," Jack added. "Look, I'm sorry I hit you, but you'd be really pissed at me later if I let you shoot your best friend. Here, let me give you a hand."

Jack extended his hand but Kon shrank away. He sat staring suspiciously at Jack and Paul.

"Leave him alone, Jack," Paul remarked and motioned for Jack to step away. "He just isn't ready to trust us."

"O.K." Jack said, pulling his hand back. "It's your place, Kon. If you want to cower on the floor, go right ahead. I prefer to sample some of your cognac before it gets any older." Without another word, Jack turned and walked away.

"Sounds good to me," Paul agreed and followed after Jack.

"Hey, are you hungry?" Jack asked a moment later.

"I'm starved," Paul responded eagerly.

"I could pick up something at that little market on the corner," Jack offered.

"That's a great idea! How about you, Kon? Have you had anything to eat? What would you like?"

Food? Kon thought. They're offering me food? This is crazy. First they throw me on the floor and then they offer me food. It's all so strange. They don't even seem angry that I had a gun. He sat up slowly, half expecting them to kick him. He saw that Paul was still holding the gun.

"The damned thing's empty," Paul sputtered. "You mean you pulled a stickup with an empty gun?"

"I . . . I . . ." Kon stammered. "I can't hold it very well with my left hand. I was afraid it would go off."

"God that was stupid! You're just lucky you're in Paris. If you tried that in Chicago you'd probably get your head blown off. You're a lousy thief, Kon," Paul concluded, shaking his head.

"That's good, isn't it?" Kon asked hesitantly. "I mean, it shows I don't do it every day."

Paul laughed. "Yeah. I guess it is a good thing. We're just glad you came to your senses and came back. Why don't you come and sit down over here. It's more comfortable than the floor."

Kon looked around slowly and then went to sit on the couch across from Paul.

"What would you like to eat?" Paul asked.

Kon shrugged. "I don't know. Anything. Is this really my apartment?"

"Yes. Does anything look familiar?"

Kon didn't answer.

"Why don't you look around while Jack gets the food. Take your time. Maybe something will register."

Left on his own, Kon found the shower and changed his clothes. He also discovered that Jack was right about the cognac supply.

Paul watched Kon down several glasses in quick succession while he studied the various photographs displayed on the book shelves. He seemed fascinated by the wedding picture of himself and Geilla. He was so carefree that day, Paul mused. He was torn between wanting Kon to relax and hoping he wouldn't make himself sick by drinking so much on an empty stomach. He was relieved when Jack finally returned with the food.

When Kon made no move to act as host, Paul went into the kitchen to find some plates and the three of them shared a meal in the living room. Kon didn't say much and Paul wondered if he recognized anything in the apartment.

"Do you still have the driver's license you took from that guy in the garage?" Paul asked after they had eaten.

"Yes. I . . . I took it for the address. I hoped to get his money and his coat back to him. I suppose the police won't see it as a loan."

"Well, I understand he was more upset over the coat than the money. Don't worry about it. I can probably get the coat cleaned or get him another one."

"What about the police? Will they arrest me?"

"I'll deal with them, Kon. Coat thieves aren't exactly high on their list of priorities. I can probably get the guy to drop the charges. He recognized that you're not a professional. I guess we should be getting back to the villa to check on Etienne. Do you want to come with us, Kon?"

"No! I won't go back there. I don't want to be locked up."

Paul shook his head. "You weren't a prisoner, Kon. You don't have to go back if you don't want to. It would just be easier if . . ."

"No! I won't go back."

"O.K. It's your life. This is your place. We'll leave you alone if that's what you really want."

"Yes. Just leave me alone. I have to think."

"O.K. I'm sorry you feel that way, but we'll go if that will make you happy. We've got a lot to do. Just give us a call if you need anything."

Paul stood and motioned to Jack to move toward the door. Kon nodded but remained silent. Paul turned to face Kon when he reached the door, but Kon turned his back.

"I don't think he remembers that apartment," Jack whispered when they had reached the elevators.

"Just give him some time. He'll come around," Paul repeated and realized how lame it sounded. Could a man be lost to his friends and family forever, just like that? Maybe so. What am I going to say to Geilla? Paul suddenly felt drained. He leaned against the wall and waited while the elevator made its way from the first floor. "What the hell's keeping it! I've got to go see Edouard," Paul muttered in disgust and Jack understood how disappointed he was. They rode to the lobby in silence. They were almost to the front door when suddenly the door to the stairs burst open and Kon rushed through calling, "Paul! Wait!"

He ran to Paul and grabbed his arm as if clinging to Paul meant clinging to sanity itself.

"Are you . . . are you really busy? Could you stay and talk to me?" Kon pleaded. "Please. I don't want to be alone."

Paul grinned, his fatigue erased. "Sure! What do you want to talk about?"

"Tell me about myself, the bank . . . that apartment . . . those people in the pictures. You're the only one who knows who I am."

"Sure, Kon. Whatever you want to know, just ask."

For the moment Kon seemed satisfied just to grip Paul's arm while Paul steered him into the elevator and back to his apartment. Kon noted that Jack had a key to his apartment also. Strangely enough it made him feel safer. Maybe Jack and Paul were his friends. They hadn't really hurt him and he knew they could if they wanted to.

"Is it true about Edouard? Is he alive?" Kon asked abruptly.

"He is alive. I can take you to see him if you want," Paul answered.

"Where is he? Why hasn't he come before?"

"He's still in the hospital. He had a concussion and now he's at a drug treatment facility."

"Drug treatment? What's wrong with him?"

"He got hooked on Demerol."

"Edouard's on drugs? Is . . . he is working for the men who . . . ?"

"Edouard's not a terrorist, Kon. He's just a mixed up kid they blackmailed into helping them. He was a medical student until he got on drugs."

Kon looked relieved. "He was kind to me. I don't know why, but he was kind."

"He's basically a good kid. Without his help we might not have gotten you back alive."

"And the others . . . are they still alive?"

"No. Michon and George are dead."

"So it's all over then. I was just looking for shadows out there."

"Not exactly . . . a man named Gérard did get away. We can't seem to get a lead on him and unfortunately he appears to be much higher in the organization than either Georges or Michon."

"Why were you keeping me at the villa. Are the police after me?"

"No . . . well, at least they weren't until you robbed that guy. We were just keeping you in a safe place until you could recuperate. You

267

weren't a prisoner there, Etienne was."

"Michon and George were after Etienne. That's what they kept asking me. They just kept hitting me and . . ." Kon shuddered. He wanted to know everything that had happened, but it was painful to remember the details.

"You never told them anything, Kon. Not once." Paul assured him.

Kon smiled briefly in response to the approval evident in Paul's voice.

"I feel like a coward," Kon blurted. "I feel so afraid and . . . and I'm not sure who or what I'm afraid of. Sometimes I'm terrified to even close my eyes for fear I'll disintegrate."

"It's normal to be afraid, Kon. They held you at gunpoint and beat the shit out of you. They broke your wrist, they cracked three of your ribs, they burnt you. You had every right to be concerned about what they might do next. I know you, Kon, and if there's one thing you are not, it's a coward."

Kon smiled shyly.

"Would you like to see Edouard. I could take you . . ."

"To the hospital? No! I don't want to go there. I was in a hospital, wasn't I?"

"Yes," Paul answered in a non-committal tone.

"They were keeping me tied down and I didn't like it very much. I don't want to go back."

Paul smiled. "That hasn't changed. You never have liked hospitals, Kon. I could bring Edouard to the villa if you like. He is still in my custody. I've got to keep an eye on him."

"I don't want to go back to the villa. I like it better here. This place feels better to me."

Paul sighed. Logistics were becoming a nightmare. Besides taking care of Kon, Etienne, and Edouard, he had been squeezing in visits to Arnot, Lorelle, and Detlief, and trying to keep Geilla calm. Things would be so much easier if Kon were at the villa, he thought. He isn't really ready to be out on his own yet. There's no chance of him understanding that though. He's as stubborn as ever.

"Well, maybe I could bring Edouard here for a visit," he said aloud. "Why don't I make some coffee and we can talk about it."

Kon nodded and Paul smiled, confident that when the coffee was ready the discussion would be over.

As Kon struggled to open his eyes, he heard someone ask, "Are you awake, Emile. How are you feeling?"

Oh God! It happened again, he thought in alarm. Everything has changed. I'm back to being Emile.

He sat up and looked around in confusion until he suddenly realized he was back at the villa and that it was Edouard who was talking to him.

"I guess it's really Kon, isn't it?" Edouard continued. "I'm so glad you made it."

"Edouard? What happened? How did we get here?"

"Paul said you wanted to see me and I guess I'm still under arrest. The police won't let me out of their sight, so Paul brought you here. You're not angry, are you?"

Kon shook his head. "No, Edouard. I'm really glad to see you." He seized Edouard's hand and pressed it. "How are you? Paul said you were in the hospital."

"I was. I'm better now. It was rough for a while, but Paul was great. He never gave up. He hung on to me even when I wanted to die and get it over with."

"I know what you mean," Kon agreed. "I'm so glad you're alive, Edouard! I'm so glad you're alive! Thank God! Thank God it's over and we're both alive."

Slowly the pieces of his life were beginning to merge into a single reality. There were still gaps in his memory, but the total picture made more sense. Jack and Paul, Etienne and Edouard, and himself were all parts of the picture. He could see that now.

"You saved my life, Edouard," Kon said gratefully.

Edouard craved approval, but Kon's gratitude made him uncomfortable. "I tried, Emile. I tried, but I could have killed you with that pentothal. I'm sorry. I didn't want to do it. I didn't think it would hurt you."

"Oh, God! That was you, wasn't it?" Kon gasped as another piece of the puzzle dropped into place.

"Yes," Edouard admitted, biting his lip. "I'm sorry. I'm so sorry. I didn't want to, but Michon . . ." Edouard expected Kon to withdraw his hand, but Kon only pressed it more firmly.

"It's O.K., Edouard. I understand. It was those eyes. There was no life in them . . . nothing. I dream of them even now."

"Yes, yes," Edouard agreed quickly. "Michon was like a machine. I hated being around him."

Suddenly the understanding of a fellow sufferer meant even more to Edouard than Paul's approval. And so the two sat, exchanging confidences about their fears and consoling one another for the torments they had endured. After their pain was laid bare, they saw the strength in one another and rejoiced that they had helped each other to survive. As they talked, Kon saw that his formless fears had a basis in forgotten facts and he felt more confident about his sanity. He put aside his haunting shame that he had tried to kill himself.

Kon spent the night at the villa and so did Edouard. In the morning Kon expressed no interest in returning to his apartment, seeming to prefer being with Edouard over being alone. When Paul brought more of Kon's belongings, particularly his wedding pictures, Kon spent hours studying them.

On the third day, when Kon came in from taking a solitary walk around the grounds, he saw that someone new had been added to the group. He recognized Geilla immediately as she sat and talked with Etienne and Edouard. At first, he thought to leave, but then decided against it. Instead, he went to the bookcase and picked up the now familiar photos. He studied them once again, stealing quick glances at Geilla from the corner of his eye. The others pretended not to notice him and continued their conversation. Geilla was telling Etienne and Edouard about various people Charlotte had introduced her to in Geneva and how they differed from the people she knew in Italian society. She spoke of the differences between the two countries, but assured Etienne that with a little effort he would learn to adjust to life in Canada.

Kon listened for a few minutes and then approached the group.

"Do you think it is possible to adjust to a life that is unfamiliar?" he asked, directing his question to Geilla.

"Yes," she answered, focusing her whole attention on Kon. "It may take some time, but I believe it is possible."

"And you have adjusted to living in Geneva?"

"I believe so."

"You never feel out of place?"

"Not really, but I get lonely when my husband is away."

"Why are you here and not in Geneva?"

"I came in search of my husband."

"What happened to him?"

"He was kidnaped and beaten and now he does not remember me."

"Is it his child you carry?"

"Yes, a child he wanted very much."

"Do you still love him?"

"Yes. Very much."

"Even though he has forgotten his wife and child?"

"I believe he wants to remember us. I believe his love is as strong as ever. It is only his memory that has been damaged."

Kon moved closer and stood before Geilla. He spoke slowly, deliberately. "Could you love him if he never remembered that you were his wife?"

"I would give him all my love if only he would come back and try to love me."

"Would you recognize him if he came back?"

"Of course, he is my husband."

Kon held out the picture he was holding. "Do you know the man in this picture?"

"Yes. It is my husband, Peter Kononellos. That picture was taken on our wedding day."

"They tell me my name is Peter. Do you remember me?"

"Yes. You are the man I married. You are the father of my child."

"Would you go to Geneva with me, knowing that I do not remember the day that is pictured?"

"Yes. I remember that day well. You were so happy. I have beautiful memories in my heart that I will share with you. I love you, Kon. I *am* your wife."

Kon hesitated and Geilla could feel the intensity of his thoughts, the longing, the hope, the doubt. As last he offered his hand. "Let us go then. Perhaps I will learn to be this man you love so much."

Geilla smiled warmly, but as she took his hand she understood the depth of his uncertainty. Although he looked the same, she realized that Kon was no longer the man she had married. Charlotte had warned her that Kon would not be easy to live with. And that was when he knew who she was and was set on marrying her despite Charlotte and Edgar's objections. She doubted that even Charlotte could guess what he would be like now. She hoped that at least a part of him still loved her.

"I will tell Paul that we are going home," Geilla offered, guessing that making decisions might be difficult for Kon.

"Yes," he agreed readily. "Perhaps he can arrange things. I have no money and I . . . I don't seem to know the address."

Paul was pleased to learn that Kon wanted to go to Geneva, hoping that resuming the normal rhythm of his life with Geilla would help restore his memory. However, he wondered as Geilla had, about Kon's capacity to deal with the unknown. In the end, since Geilla had been cautioned against air travel in her delicate condition, it was decided that Kon and Geilla would go to Geneva by train and that Paul would accompany them.

The following morning was chosen for their departure. As they set out, Paul mused that Kon and Geilla clung to each other, not as the amorous newlyweds they had been so recently, but as a very old couple who had seen their former security swept away. Kon had developed a profound aversion to entering vehicles, which he could conquer only if he opened the door himself and took a place in front.

Although Paul was quick to assure Kon that his anxiety was related to being kidnaped and would gradually fade, Kon viewed it as one more sign that he was inferior to Paul. In addition to doubting his sanity, Kon was beginning to doubt his mental ability. His confusion was heightened by the fact that he still could not hear well. He had managed at the villa, but in the large, crowded railroad station, normal conversation was lost and he had difficulty deciphering what Geilla and Paul were saying. It was bad enough to have to depend on Paul to arrange everything, but he was beginning to resent the way Paul took care of Geilla. They seemed so relaxed together, he felt like an outsider. It seemed strange and slightly disconcerting to be traveling to a place he did not know with a woman he did not remember. She claimed to be his wife, but Kon was suspicious. Perhaps she was really Paul's wife and it was all a plot.

Since Kon was too ashamed to express his feelings, he had no way to know that he was actually doing a good job at surmounting the fears and anxieties that plague kidnap victims. Facing the problems with an impaired memory was especially difficult.

Once they were on the train, Geilla sat close to Kon and clung to his arm. Her nearness was very pleasant and he tried hard to appear happy and relaxed. He avoided her eyes, however, fearing she would read the suspicion in them. He would have to trust her as well as Paul and, unfortunately, trusting anyone had never been easy for Kon.

Chapter Eighteen

Geilla had mentioned ice cream at dinner, and by God, Kon was determined to get her some. He had to prove to her that he was capable. Neither Carlin nor Edgar would let him return to work at the bank, and frankly he was not looking forward to it. He was not certain that he would remember what he did there. When he had gone in with Edgar one morning, no one had appeared glad to see him. Edgar had brought some files home for him, and he had made a few calculations; but the client list did not seem at all familiar. He wondered how he was going to handle the workload for banks in two major cities.

Geilla was still in the kitchen cleaning up from dinner. She liked everything put away just so and he couldn't remember the system from one day to the next. It annoyed him that he couldn't seem to remember the layout of their apartment either. Geilla said they had not been there long, but he was too embarrassed to ask how long it had been.

Slipping into the bedroom, Kon took some cash from the top of the dresser and headed for the door.

"I'm going for some dessert. I'll be right back," he called cheerfully to Geilla.

"Kon! Wait!" she answered anxiously then tried to cover with, "I'll go with you."

He was becoming acutely aware of everyone's attempts to control him and her pretense didn't work. "I can find the shop! We went there yesterday," he snapped.

Geilla looked hurt for a moment then nodded. "I know. Go ahead. I'll make more coffee." She knew her extreme anxiety annoyed him, but she couldn't help herself.

Kon turned and hurried down the stairs. He resented the fact that everyone was treating him like a child. He had not been left alone since he had returned to his apartment in Paris. He burst through the street door with a euphoric sense of freedom and started for the corner. Although it was still early, the shop was closed when he reached it. With one eye bandaged, had to turn his head like a bird to see things, but he finally noticed a small card on the door.

It was an apology from the proprietor explaining that he had left early because of a death in the family. Kon felt disappointed. He was about to turn back when a stocky woman with a shopping basket bumped into him from behind. Her large frame effectively blocked his way and he waited while she read the note.

"Death in the family! It's just another excuse! The man's a drunkard," she muttered in disgust. "It's a waste of time to come here. I might as well take my business to Westfield's."

"Westfield's? Where's that?" Kon asked, hoping to gain something useful from the encounter.

The woman turned and glanced up at Kon. She seemed startled to see his bandaged eye and looked him over critically. Unconsciously Kon tucked his injured wrist closer to his chest. She saw the gesture, however, inspected him even more closely.

Is she afraid I'm going to produce a tin cup and ask for money? he thought, feeling uncomfortable under her gaze.

"Three blocks down," the woman muttered at last, as if judging Kon unworthy of more explanation. Stepping backward, she turned and hurried away.

Kon suddenly felt self-conscious about being on the street alone. He ran his left hand through his hair and over his chin wondering if he had forgotten to shave. The woman's rudeness had spoiled his mood. He walked on quickly hoping he wouldn't run into her again at Westfield's.

He was beginning to think he had made a mistake in the direction when he saw a small sign in the distance. Westfield's was four blocks down, not three, and it was across the street. Kon stepped inside and noticed gratefully that the rude woman was nowhere in sight. The shop was crowded, however, and he had to wait a long time for service. He couldn't remember Geilla's having mentioned a particular flavor, so he settled on a quart of vanilla, hand-packed from a newly opened drum. The clerk put the ice cream in a paper bag for him and made change, patiently waiting while Kon counted out the money with his left hand.

As he stepped out of the shop, Kon spotted the rude woman coming down the street and impulsively he turned the other way. He intended to go around the block and head back, but when he reached the corner he was distracted by a group of boys who were playing soccer. He stopped and watched them until suddenly the ball came flying up over the curb. Without thinking, he kicked it back into play. The boys called out their thanks and he continued to watch them, their happy shouts bringing back vague memories. When at last he started again, he forgot to turn right.

Five blocks later he noticed his mistake. Nothing looked familiar and he realized with a sinking feeling that he couldn't remember his street name. He racked his brain, but all he could dredge up was 2753. He reached for his wallet to confirm the number, but his pockets were empty. Did I leave my wallet on the counter in that shop? he wondered. No! No! I was only going a block. I didn't bring it. Now what? Stay calm, 2753 has to be around here somewhere. But when he checked the house numbers they were six blocks off. That's it. I'm only five blocks away. I just turned the wrong way. He turned and walked swiftly north. After five blocks he still did not recognize the building. Number 2753 was an office complex not an apartment house. It can't be far, he told himself. I will just walk until I find the right 2753.

Seven blocks later, he was becoming discouraged when suddenly he spotted a building that looked familiar. Yes, the design on the plate glass doors was definitely familiar. He went up to the doors, but they were locked. Ah yes, I came out without my key. I will have to buzz Geilla. She will no doubt scold me for forgetting my key. I must start to be more careful about details. He glanced at the names above the mailboxes but Kononellos was not listed. It startled him until he remembered Geilla telling him that they had only recently moved in. I'll buzz the manager instead. He could picture the old man clearly, but he couldn't remember his name.

"Yes. How can I help you?" a man's voice answered to Kon's ring.

"Good evening, Monsieur. This is Peter Kononellos. Forgive me for bothering you, but I have forgotten my key. Could you let me in please."

"Who is this?" the man demanded impatiently.

"Peter Kononellos."

"There isn't anyone named Kononellos living here," the man answered after a moment.

Kon was taken aback but persisted. "I have just moved in. My wife and I . . ."

"I haven't had a vacancy for weeks. You must have the wrong address. Go away!"

"Wait! Please. My wife . . ." Kon stammered but the man didn't answer. Kon was stunned. He knew he had the right building. He was sure of it. He rang the manager again. "Please, you must let me in. My apartment is on the third floor. My wife is waiting. She'll be worried . . ."

"Look!" the manager shouted back at Kon. "I tell you you've got the wrong building. Stop bothering me or I'll call the police."

Something strange is happening, Kon thought growing uneasy. He must have a record of us. If he won't cooperate, I'll just ring all the apartments on the third floor until Geilla answers. Kon began ringing the apartments one by one, but everyone turned him away. In desperation he rang the manager again. "Please, you must let me in. I know I can find the right apartment if you'll let me look. Please . . ."

"Now you look!" the manager answered heatedly. "I've had enough! I'm calling the police!"

"I don't understand! I know this is my building!" Kon shouted into the speaker. Geilla's in there somewhere. And the baby, he thought anxiously. Oh God! Am I really going mad? Everything keeps changing. I can't stand it! I've got to get in.

Kon began to bang on the doors, but they remained closed. Suddenly above his pounding he heard a police siren. He glanced over his shoulder and saw the flashing lights. Oh no! If they lock me up they'll think I'm crazy. I can't even remember my telephone number. I can't let them take me!

Before the police car slowed to a stop, Kon was racing down the block. Without looking back, he swung around the corner and dove through the door of a shop. The thin man behind the counter looked up in surprise as the bells above the door clamored furiously. He stared at Kon for a moment before his face softened into a smile.

"Why, Monsieur Kononellos, what a surprise!"

Even in his excitement Kon noticed the marked Slavic accent to the man's French.

"You know me?" Kon panted.

"But of course. How could I forget my favorite customer. What brings you back to the old neighborhood? Don't tell me. The fruit is not as ripe over there, eh?"

"Old neighborhood? But I live here. I'm sorry . . . I've . . . I've been in an accident . . ."

"Oh dear God! Not again. Rachel! Rachel come quick! It's Monsieur Kononellos. Steady now. You look about to faint. Come in the back."

Before Kon could object the man took his arm and pulled him behind the counter and through a door he hadn't noticed before.

"Good heavens. Sit down! Sit down!" he heard a woman say in the same accent as the man. Someone guided him into a soft chair. He felt dazed and was barely aware that he was still clutching the paper bag with the ice cream. The contents had melted and were now dripping down his pant leg.

"My, my. Let me get rid of this," the woman said, prying Kon's sticky fingers open.

Kon was confused, but somehow he felt safe with this kindly couple.

"Now, tell me why you've come," the man asked gently in a voice that welcomed confidence.

"I . . . I live here. I mean, I live around the corner. I went to get Geilla some ice cream and when I came home I couldn't get in. My landlord, old Monsieur Denker . . . he wouldn't let me in and . . . and I kept banging . . . he called the police."

The man shook his head and exchanged knowing glances with the woman.

"Calm down, Monsieur Kononellos. You don't live here anymore. You moved away about four months ago. Your wife said you needed a bigger place because of the baby. We were sorry to see you go."

"I moved? Where to? I have to get home. Geilla will be upset. She didn't want me to go alone . . ."

"Yes. Yes. She's right, you know. You're not yourself, my dear," the woman said. "I'll make us some tea, and Abrim will ring up Monsieur Denker and see if he can find an address."

"But he didn't remember me. He wouldn't . . ."

"Oh that would be Donald, his son. He took over when his father retired last month. Not a nice young man at all. Now you just relax while we tend to things," she said and they both disappeared.

Kon sat, feeling like a stray cat, but grateful that the couple had not suggested calling the police. He heard snatches of whispered conversation and then the whistle of a tea kettle.

"How . . .? How do you know me?" Kon asked a few minutes later when Rachel brought the tea.

"You've lived here for years, Monsieur Kononellos. We've watched you grow up, so to speak."

"I'm sorry, I . . . I don't remember you."

"Well, you have these spells, my dear . . ."

"Spells? You mean I'm crazy, don't you?"

"Oh no, dear. No more than the rest of us. But you've been in an inordinate number of accidents. Sometimes you forget things for a while. But don't worry, you always come out of it."

"You mean this has happened before?"

"The memory loss? Well, that was only once. But you have been hurt a lot. I think it's something to do with your line of work."

"My work? But I'm a banker!"

"Well yes, so Monsieur Marneé says. But I think you do some other work on the side."

"Why do you say that? What other work?"

"Well, Monsieur Denker has told us a few things . . . it's not that we listen to rumors, you know . . . but your rather strange schedule does generate some curiosity. You're always hobbling in here after some 'accident' or other, and there's been other little signs . . ."

My God, Kon thought suddenly, does everyone know the details of my life better than I do? "What other signs?" he asked aloud.

"Well, one night several years ago a robber came in just before closing time and held a gun on us. You just happened by at the right time. Somehow you came in the back door which was locked and disarmed that thief in no time at all. It led us to believe that you must have had some training about these things."

Kon was at a loss. He couldn't remember the incident at all. He sat quietly racking his brain and sipping his tea until Abrim returned.

"Well, thank the Lord, things worked out just fine, Monsieur Kononellos. Monsieur Denker didn't have your new address but he gave me Monsieur Marneé's telephone number. He'll be here shortly to fetch you home."

"You know Monsieur Marneé too?" Kon asked in disbelief.

"Yes. Yes. Several times he stopped in to ask us to deliver some groceries when you were sick and he saw that your cupboard was bare."

"That certainly was thoughtful of him."

"He cares a lot about you, Monsieur Kononellos."

"So I am beginning to learn. I guess it's hard on everyone when I can't remember them. I'm sorry."

"Now don't you worry about it. You'll come around," Rachel assured him and refilled his cup. She sat silently smiling at him until they heard the bell over the door jingle merrily. "I bet that's Monsieur Marneé now," she said. She hurried out and Kon heard Edgar's voice in response to her questions.

"Thank you," Kon said awkwardly to Abrim and stood up. "I don't know what I would have done if . . ."

"It was no trouble, Monsieur Kononellos. No trouble at all. We're always glad to see you. I'm afraid your ice cream is spoilt, but you take your wife these," he said handing Kon a plastic bag full of large blue-black grapes. "She'll forgive your being late."

Kon dug in his pocket. "I don't seem . . ."

"Next time, Monsieur Kononellos. Your credit is always good here. And bring that pretty wife of yours along."

Before he could respond, Edgar came through the door. "Peter! I'm so glad you're safe."

"I'm sorry to bother you, Edgar. I thought I could do it. I really wanted . . ."

"It's all right. We all worry too much. I told Geilla you would be all right. Good evening Monsieur Neufeld. Thank you for calling me," Edgar added turning to Abrim.

"It was my pleasure, Monsieur Marneé. We're always glad to see Monsieur Kononellos."

Edgar led Kon out to the car, but made a point not to open the door or stand behind him. Instead, he got in quickly, unlocked the passenger door and busied himself setting and resetting knobs on the dashboard while Kon struggled with his fears about entering the car.

"You called Geilla? he asked when he was finally seated.

"No, she called me when you were late."

"I'm sorry she bothered you. She's over-reacting. I . . . I feel so stupid. Don't tell Paul. Please don't tell Paul!"

"I won't tell anyone, Peter. Stop worrying. You'll get better."

Kon was doubtful.

"That couple at the shop back there certainly were nice to me. They must think I'm crazy."

Edgar smiled. "Quite the contrary, Peter. They think very highly of you."

"Why? I made a fool of myself barging in there like a criminal."

"Peter, I believer Abrim and Rachel would do just about anything for you. You paid their son's way through engineering school."

"I did?"

"Yes. At first the boy thought he wanted to play the violin, so you paid for music lessons. But he had so little talent everyone agreed he should try something else."

"Where is he now?"

"He's in Zurich somewhere. Doing rather well I hear."

"I wish I could remember them. I wish . . ."

"You're doing fine, Peter. You're doing just fine."

Kon studied Edgar. He is so kind. How can I tell him it's all a lie? How can I tell him that I really don't remember him or his wife? They must have suspected when we went to dinner the other night. I had nothing to say. Perhaps Geilla warned them that I was nervous. She goes out of her way to shield me.

"Please don't tell Geilla that the landlord called the police," Kon said at last. "She thinks I'm hopelessly incompetent."

"Stop worrying, Peter. She was very upset when you were kidnaped. She's feeling a little insecure right now. Give her time."

"She's feeling insecure! What the hell does she think I'm feeling? I'm not even sure she's . . . I'm sorry, Edgar . . . maybe I should not have come to Geneva. I'm just not sure of anything."

"You're doing fine, Peter. We're all glad to have you home," Edgar said and parked the car.

Kon saw that his new apartment building actually wasn't far from where he used to live. Perhaps he was starting to get better. He had recognized his old apartment building and he had recalled Monsieur Denker's name. Maybe a trip to the old neighborhood had been beneficial.

Kon followed Edgar out of the car. Now that he was in front of his building, he remembered seeing it before. He just wasn't sure he could have picked it out from the others on the block. Edgar pressed the buzzer and Kon noticed that "Kononellos" was printed neatly above the button.

"Who is it?" Geilla asked a moment later.

Kon hesitated and Edgar whispered, "Go ahead. Tell her you forgot your key."

"It's me. I . . . I forgot my key."

"Oh thank God!" Geilla gasped with relief and immediately buzzed to unlock the door.

Kon and Edgar hurried in and got on the elevator. Kon was about to press for the third floor when he remembered that in this building he and Geilla lived on the fourth floor. Well, that was some progress, he thought proudly. When Paul brought us in, I didn't have the slightest idea where to go.

Geilla was waiting at the apartment door and seemed surprised to see Edgar.

"I ran into Peter at the shop and gave him a lift," Edgar said quickly. "He offered me coffee in exchange."

"Oh . . . yes. Why yes. Do come in," she began formally then turned to Kon. "Where have you been? I was so worried."

"I . . . I went shopping," he stammered shyly and offered her the plastic bag. "I hope you like grapes. Abrim said you liked . . ."

Geilla seemed a bit startled, but she smiled and took the bag. "They're beautiful! I love grapes. The baby loves grapes. Oh, Kon . . ."

She put her arms around him and nestled her face on his chest.

Kon was about to enfold her in his arms when suddenly he glanced over her shoulder. "What is he doing here?" he demanded as he recognized Paul.

"I called him. You were gone so . . ."

"Is he here to look for me? Or has he come to comfort you?" Kon asked, raising his voice.

"Kon!"

"We don't need you here," Kon continued pushing past Geilla. "We are doing quite well. And I'd thank you to stay away from my wife!"

"Settle down, Kon. I just . . ." Paul began calmly, but Kon cut him off.

"You just thought you've move in while the coast was clear. Well, I'm back! And I don't need any help taking care of my wife!"

"Kon! Stop it!" Geilla called. "What's gotten into you? You're acting . . ."

Kon wheeled to face Geilla. "I'm acting what? Crazy? Go ahead! Say it! It's what you're thinking. My husband, the village idiot! He can't be trusted to go out alone."

"Stop it, Kon. I never said that."

"Not to me, but I know you think it! I'm gone for five minutes and all of Geneva knows I got lost. Who else but an idiot would get lost? I'm so strange people stare at me in the street! People I can't remember tell me I have spells! The whole neighborhood must know I'm crazy. Is it in the papers too?"

"Peter! Control yourself," Edgar cut in, seeing that Kon was becoming upset.

"Control myself? How can I? Everyone else controls me! Poor Kon, he has to be protected. He isn't quite right, you know. He can't remember where he lives! He can't remember where he works! He can't remember people who claim to be his friends!"

"I know it's hard, Kon, but . . ." Paul started.

"How could you possibly know what it's like?" Kon snapped. "I have these terrible thoughts and I don't know if they are true or if I just imagined them. You say you are my friend. Then tell me the truth. Did you sleep with my wife? Is it your child she's carrying?"

Geilla gasped and Paul went white momentarily.

"Peter, really! This is absurd!" Edgar objected and took Kon by the arm as if to reign him in.

"Leave him be, Edgar," Paul called hoarsely. "Living with half a

283

memory is torturing him. He needs the truth."

Paul came closer to Kon and stood clenching his fist as if what he was going to say was physically painful. "Your memory is coming back, Kon, but not all of it. I am your friend and yes, I did sleep with Geilla. But only before she married you. I swear to you by everything I hold sacred, you are the father of her child."

Kon drew in his breath and stepped backwards, as if the weight of the truth struck him like a blow. "Oh God!" he groaned. "I'd hoped is was just another dream—another nightmare!"

"I didn't hide it from you, Kon," Geilla offered quietly. "You knew about it before we were married. I thought you understood."

"You told him about us? Why?" Paul blurted, suddenly feeling his trust had been betrayed.

"I didn't tell him, Paul! Do you think I would deliberately hurt him? Do you think I would hurt either of you. He knew about us all along."

Paul was dumbfounded for a moment then turned to Kon. "I swear I never meant . . . ."

Kon ignored him and turned to Geilla demanding, "Why did you marry me? Was it because I have more money?"

"No, Kon! It was because I love you."

"Love me? But why? You should have married Paul! He's the one who takes care of you, not me. I have nothing to offer. I can't even take care of myself."

"Don't say that, Kon. I love you. I've always loved you."

Kon looked intently at Geilla, but remained silent, torn by indecision.

"Look, Kon, if my being here upsets you, I'll leave," Paul offered as a conciliatory gesture.

Kon turned to face Paul. "Yes, go! Leave me alone!" Kon shouted at Paul and then turned to Geilla. "Go with him if you want. I won't stop you. I won't tie you to a promise I can't remember making!"

Geilla gasped as Kon wheeled around, stormed into the bedroom, and slammed the door.

Edgar looked from Geilla to Paul, but neither spoke until at last Geilla cried, "Oh, Paul, what's happened to him? He was never like this."

"I don't know, Geilla, but my being here is only pouring oil on the fire. Maybe he'll calm down after I'm gone."

"I'm sure he didn't mean to drive you away. He needs you, Paul."

"Maybe that's what's bothering him. He sure doesn't need me messing up his marriage," Paul said going to the sofa and picking up his coat. "I hate to abandon you, Geilla, but . . . my God! I never expected this. Call me when he calms down. Take care of them, Edgar. I've got to disappear for a while."

Edgar nodded and watched in helpless dismay as Paul hurried out. He felt embarrassed to look at Geilla. He was shocked to learn of her affair with Paul, but he was sorry that Peter had been so cruel to her.

"It would be easier to forgive him if I thought he really was crazy," Edgar said at last. "I apologize that I have been unable to teach him to control his vicious temper. Perhaps a father's duty never ends."

Without waiting for an answer, Edgar turned and walked to the bedroom door. He knocked twice and called out, "Peter, I know this is your house and you have a right to privacy, but I need to speak with you." When there was no answer, he called again. "Peter, it's Edgar. I'm worried about you. May I come in?"

Peter did not answer, but Edgar heard someone moving behind the door. "Peter, please . . ." he started, but the door suddenly opened a crack. He pushed it open further, stepped inside, and closed the door behind him. Kon was standing by the window with his back to the door. He did not turn when Edgar spoke to him.

"Peter, I've forgiven your actions because of your memory loss, but your behavior just now was inexcusable. I don't know what Geilla did before she married you, but she is your lawful wife now and she deserves respect. She has chosen you to be the father of her child. I have seen you chase after women who were little better than prostitutes, and I never interfered. I love you like a son, but I am ashamed to see you be so low and mean to your wife and your best friend. That man would walk through fire for you, and Geilla suffered terribly when you were kidnapped. It's your own evil thoughts that torment you."

"What am I to do, Edgar?" Kon asked without turning. "I've wrecked everything. I've hurt everyone. Maybe she'd be better off without me. I wish they had killed me. Then she would be free to go to Paul."

"Peter! Haven't you heard anything I've said? She doesn't want Paul. She wants you. Who can explain love. It just happens. Why can't you ever believe you are worth loving? You hurt yourself more than anyone with your suspicions. You have a home, a beautiful wife, and the beginning of a family. Don't throw it all away because of your irrational jealousy."

"Oh Edgar, I wish I could be sure. I have these terrible nightmares, and when I learn that some of them are true . . . Do you think I'm crazy?" Peter turned and hung his head, as if waiting for the verdict.

Edgar smiled and going to Peter, he put his hand on his shoulder. "No, Peter. I don't think you're crazy. I think you're just human and human beings make mistakes. We all feel stupid and small sometimes and wonder how anyone can love us."

"You are very kind, Edgar. Can you forgive me?"

"Yes, and I know Geilla can too if you ask her."

"I am ashamed, Edgar. I didn't mean to hurt her. I was just so angry that she told Paul I was stupid enough to get lost. I have been so dependant on him. He is so strong and so sure. I think I might have gone mad without his help."

"Paul is strong, but so are you. You just need to give yourself a little time."

"I hope you are right. I just feel so . . . so frustrated. It's as though my life is standing still. I will try to be calmer."

"If it's any consolation, Peter, patience has never come easily for you."

"That is one thing I am certain is true about myself," Peter agreed readily. "I guess I must apologize and go on. Is Paul still here?"

"No. He left. He did not want to upset you."

"Did . . . did she go with him?"

"No. Of course not. She's just trying to understand why you are so jealous."

"That's the word, isn't it? I am jealous of Paul. He's just so . . . perfect."

"I don't know whether or not he is perfect, but I do know he is a true friend to you and to Geilla. She needs you Peter. Go talk to her. She needs to know you want her and the baby."

"I do want them. I have no doubt of that. I just feel . . . I don't feel as if I deserve them."

"You do, Peter. You've waited a long time to be happy. Go tell her you're sorry."

Peter sighed. "I will try."

He came away from the window and went into the living room. Seeing that the room was empty, he wondered if Geilla had decided to follow Paul. He was suddenly seized by the fear that she had abandoned him. His heart sank until he heard water running in the kitchen. He hurried through the apartment calling Geilla's name, but she didn't answer. When he came up behind her, she seemed absorbed in scrubbing the counter.

"Geilla! I was afraid you had left."

Geilla turned slowly. "Oh, Kon, I don't want to leave. I never loved Paul. He does take care of me, but he takes care of you and Jack and everyone else. I never meant anything special to him."

He stepped closer and reached behind her to turn the water off. His hand brushed her arm and then suddenly his arms were around her and he was whispering in her ear. "Please don't leave me! I couldn't bear it if you left. I don't remember how we came to be together, but I don't want you to leave—ever! I'm sorry I was so horrible to Paul. I just went crazy when I thought he had come to take you away."

She listened to his words with growing joy and when she realized he was speaking Italian, she knew he was getting better. He had been very formal with her and had spoken only French since she had gone to the villa. Before, they had always spoken Italian when they were alone together. He had seemed hesitant to touch her and she had feared her growing roundness had repulsed him. Feeling his arms encircling her now was so good, so natural, the way it had always felt.

287

Chapter Nineteen

Paul paid the cab driver then stood watching until the cab disappeared around the corner. When it was out of sight, he started walking east. He had barely gone a block before he concluded that walking the last half mile to the villa was a bad idea. I should have called Jack from the airport, he thought. He's going to ask what happened in Geneva. He'll wonder why I didn't spend the night as planned. Poor Jack! He never did figure out what was going on between Geilla and me before she married Kon. Hell! maybe I never understood what was happening either. I thought I had everything under control. I thought I was helping her. I thought I was helping both of them. Maybe I just screwed everything up.

Paul was glad to hear a challenge when he limped up to the gate in front of the villa. It meant that GIGN was still on the job. He was doubly glad that the youngish agent recognized him. Switching roles from Artier to Martel was becoming a bother. It's no wonder Kon has trouble remembering that he's no longer Emile, he thought as he headed up the drive.

As he reached the main entrance, he saw Jack standing in the open door. For a moment he was surprised, but then it dawned on him that the gatekeeper would alert Jack to any and all visitors.

"Hey, Paul!" Jack exclaimed. "What brings you back so late? I didn't expect . . ."

"Yeah, well there was a change in plans," Paul answered sharply and immediately felt ashamed that he hadn't controlled his mood.

"Did you find Kon?" Jack asked, deliberately cutting to business.

"Yeah. He wandered back to his old neighborhood by mistake and someone called Edgar."

"Is he O.K.?" Jack asked, probing for the source of Paul's mood.

"Not really, Jack. Do we have to discuss it right now?"

"No. I was just concerned. That's all. Come on in and kick your shoes off. You look like you could use a drink. How's the leg holding up?"

"The damned thing still keeps swelling up on me," Paul grumbled. "Why don't you go into the study and I'll bring you a drink."

"O.K. Sounds good," Paul said and started down the hall. He went into the study and ignoring the formal, high-backed, leather arm chairs, he settled for the comfort of the couch. Jack seemed to be taking a long time to fix their drinks, but when he returned Paul understood why. In addition to a bottle of wine, Jack brought a plate of sliced meat and some bread. He too ignored the hard, leather chairs and threw himself heavily on the opposite end of the couch.

"I guess I'll have to get more supplies tomorrow," he mumbled almost to himself.

Paul helped himself to a glass of wine. He knew Jack was waiting to hear what had happened in Geneva, but he really didn't want to talk about Kon. He decided to pick a different subject. "How did it go today, Jack? Did you go to see Arnot?"

"Yes," Jack said after a pause.

"Did you learn anything?"

Jack shifted his weight slightly and suddenly Paul knew something was wrong. "What happened, Jack?"

Instead of answering, Jack put his hand to his mouth and bit his knuckles.

"Jack?"

"Ah hell!" Jack suddenly growled, jumping to his feet. "Everything turns to shit on this job! You might as well hear it from me."

"Just tell me what happened, Jack," Paul said evenly.

"I went to see Arnot this afternoon. You know how he has been worried that his mother would find out he's in jail?"

Paul nodded.

"Well, some dirty, slime-bucket went to see her and roughed her up. She has a weak heart and the little visit put her in the hospital. She sent word that she wanted to see Arnot and he was really shook up. He was crying and wringing his hands when I got there. He wanted to go see her, but he was afraid. He paced around his cell for about an hour trying to decide what to do. He was so desperate, I called Pienaar to see if I could get permission for him to go to the hospital. I thought maybe he would loosen up a bit if he saw that we really were trying to help him.

"Anyway, Arnot pleaded with me to go with him, and I just couldn't say no. There were four of us in the car with him. It was supposed to be a big secret, but everyone at the hospital must have known he was under guard. By the time we got there Arnot's mother was fading fast and calling for him. He told me he's an only child. His father died when he was twelve. Arnot begged us to take his handcuffs off so his mother wouldn't see his shame. He looked so damned miserable it got to me. Finally the police agreed to unlock the cuffs if I went in with him. I didn't really want to, but I said 'O.K.'

"Luckily for Arnot, his mother recognized him. She was so happy to see him. She held his hand and told him again and again what a good boy he was. She didn't seem to notice me and I was glad. Arnot never said a damn word. He just stood there and cried. When his mother finally noticed that he was crying, she reached up to wipe his tears away. She told him she was proud that he worked so hard and . . . then she was gone.

"Arnot just fell apart. He started sobbing so bitterly we had to lead him away. When we got outside, one of the officers went to bring the car around. We were standing there when the police car pulled up and stopped. I was behind Arnot and one of the police officers stepped forward to open the rear door. In the split second when his back was turned, Arnot grabbed his gun. I leaped forward, but I was too late. Arnot pulled the trigger and shot himself in the chest. I caught him but . . . Jesus! Point blank like that . . . by the time we got him inside he was dead."

For a moment Paul was silent, then he began to repeat, "I knew it! I knew it! I knew he was going to do something like this. I just knew it! God damn it! I should have been there! I was supposed to protect him. I promised him I would protect him!"

Jack turned, his own guilt magnified by the depth of Paul's remorse. "God damn it, Paul! Even you can't be in two places at once. Besides you promised to protect him from Gérard. No one can protect a man from himself. I was there and I tried. Damn it! I tried! He was determined. I don't think your being there would have made any difference!"

Paul suddenly realized that expressing his own sense of guilt had only added to Jack's burden. "I didn't mean . . ." he began. "Jesus, Jack, I know you did all you could."

Jack did not respond.

"Did the incident get any publicity?" Paul asked breaking into the silence.

"No. Thank God for that," Jack answered and returned to the couch. "I sent one of the young police recruits out to buy me a new shirt before I came back here. Edouard knew Arnot from the university. I figured he would be upset if he found out."

"Yes. And Etienne would start worrying about his family. We're going to have to close the case for Etienne."

"What do you mean?"

"We never have made an official statement about Etienne. We'll have to put out the word that he died as a result of the attack at the train station."

"What if no one picks up on it? The attack is old news by now."

"I'll see if I can convince Adrian Rubard to stage a mock funeral for his son. That would attract the attention of anyone who was watching the family."

"Yeah, I guess that would be the best thing to do," Jack agreed. "Jesus, I'm sorry, Paul. I wish I had been faster."

Paul was determined to get things moving for Etienne and the following evening the obituary columns of three major newspapers carried the news of the death of Etienne Rubard. The official cause of death was listed as complications from surgery. The funeral was scheduled for three days later.

Etienne's reaction to the obituary was to sink deeper into depression. Since the attack at the railroad station, Jack and Paul had been so involved with locating and rescuing Kon that they had had little time to interrogate Etienne to determine precisely what information he could offer to the French police in return for his freedom. Although his initial position had been weakened by the slaying of many of the terrorists he had known, he did have one strong card to play. He had not yet revealed how many weapons he had stolen from Direct Action or what he had done with them.

As Paul suspected, Etienne was much less reluctant to talk to him than to the men from GIGN. When it was put to him that it was at last time to deliver some information or face prison, Etienne finally confessed that he had gathered six Skorpians, eleven Colt .45s, and two M-16s from various caches throughout the city. He had packed them in book boxes and shipped them to Le Harve to be stored under a name and address he had picked at random from the Paris telephone book.

Recovering the weapons cache was a point in Etienne's favor, but Paul doubted that the French government would accept so little in exchange for Etienne's freedom. He began to pressure Etienne for specific details about the bank robberies.

"Who actually planned the jobs?" Paul questioned.

"At first I didn't know. I just went along to keep the people inside the bank under control. After I had done two or three jobs, they started shifting me around. Sometimes I drove, sometimes I collected the cash. But a guy named Janoff was always in charge. Maybe he was a trainer or something. I don't know. But after a while, maybe six or seven jobs, I never saw him again. One day I got a call to go to a certain house and I was given instructions about which banks we were going to hit."

"Were you the leader?"

"No. I was told to take orders from Cluree. I knew him slightly from some of the jobs we had done. I was a little surprised when we headed out because the group was much smaller, down to four from maybe six or seven and nobody on foot."

"Did you always work with the same people?"

"No, the people changed a lot. But Cluree was always in charge. Where is this leading? I already gave you the names of everyone I can remember! I'm not trying to hide anything!"

"I know," Paul responded soothingly. "I'm just trying to jog your memory, Etienne. The guys from GIGN are going to want hard facts and plenty of details. Where did you meet to receive instructions?"

"Usually some apartment. I would get a call or someone would pass me a message in the hall after class."

"Did you make friends with anyone particular in the group?"

"Friends? They weren't my friends, Paul. I worked with them and

. . . I guess I wanted their approval. After Catia . . . I wanted to attract her attention. You know, make her see she was wrong about me."

"Did you ever meet any of the group anywhere else?"

"A couple of times after jobs Clureé took us to a place on Rue Damrémont. His girl friend lived there."

"We checked that place. He's gone. Anywhere else?"

"No! I've told you everything I know. We always . . . well, one time Lescot asked me to pick him up at an office supply place."

"Office supply? What's it called."

"Bélidor's."

"Bélidor's? What's the address?"

"Haussmann Boulevard. I don't remember the number. It's in the book. They run a big ad."

"Did you ever meet anyone else from the group there?"

"No, just Lescot."

"Well, he can't tell us much, can he?" Paul remarked, referring to the fact that Lescot had been killed during the assault at the Gare de Lyon.

"Do you think anyone else might have known you came to the store?"

"I don't know. No one else ever mentioned the place to me. Do you think something was going on there?"

"I don't know, Etienne, but I think that's enough for now. Why don't you relax. Watch some T.V."

Paul let Etienne return to the sitting room while he went to question Edouard about the store where he and Kon had been held. Although Edouard racked his brain to remember something about the place, he couldn't come up with a name. Michon had punched him in the mouth to quiet him the night they took Kon from Georges' apartment, and he didn't remember anything except being yanked out of the car and shoved through a doorway. When he was hauled out again the next day, he had been too sick to notice his surroundings. After his brief chat with Edouard, Paul left Jack in charge and went to visit Lorelle.

Weeks of sitting in jail had made Lorelle more thoughtful. Almost everyone she had known in the group was either dead or in jail. No one had staged an armed breakout for her and the group had not bothered to send one of their lawyers. Her mother had come, but she couldn't afford much legal help. Paul was her only contact with Detlef, and although she tried to pretend otherwise, she looked forward to his visits.

She hadn't told Paul much about her involvement with the group, but this time when he asked for the name of the office supply store, she named Bélidor's without hesitation. She was tired of protecting the group. If she and Detlef had to sit in jail, she wanted the rest of them to know what it was like.

The rest was easy. Pienaar secured a warrant and a carload of GIGN officers began searching every inch of Bélidor's Office Supply. They soon discovered that five of the twelve boxes of heavy-duty staplers imported from Germany held enough parts to assemble six complete Heckler & Koch MP5 submachine guns. Monsieur Bélidor was arrested on the spot. Paul wished that Kon was available to help him sift through the import documents, but he was able to establish the link between the store and Lothar Berentson. Well, well, Paul thought as he showed the records to Pienaar. Etienne can start packing his bags for Canada.

Three days after the funeral service for Etienne, Adrian Rubard and his daughter Trinette took a cab to the office of the family attorneys. When they arrived in the building, however, instead of taking the elevator to the seventh floor, they were rushed out the back door and into another car. They were quickly driven to the villa that Jack and Paul were using as a base of operations. The visit had been carefully planned, but kept secret even from Etienne who was completely surprised when his father appeared.

"Father! I . . . I didn't expect you. Have you come to tell me in person what an abomination I am? You could have spared yourself the trouble. Everyone else has done it for you."

"I have not come to scold, Etienne, only to bid you farewell. I wanted to come before, but Monsieur Artier did not think it would be safe. He has at last worked out the details with the police."

"So am I to be exiled after all?" Etienne asked biting his lip.

"I'm afraid so," Adrian answered reluctantly. Hearing Etienne moan he stepped closer and put his hand on the boy's shoulder. "It is for your own good, Etienne."

"Oh, Father . . . ," Etienne gasped. "I am sorry I disappointed you. I should have made something of myself. Now it's too late. There is no time to make amends. I wish I had tried harder."

"Etienne! It is I who should beg forgiveness. As I walked behind the bier yesterday making a show of grief, I was struck by the thought that it could have been real. I came so close to losing you, not from bullets, but by my attitude. For the sake of preserving my pride, I have treated you unjustly. I never told you, but when you were born I was so proud to have a son. I wanted to give you everything and bask in the light of your triumphs. Later, when your mother left, I was so angry that she had made a fool of me. I put it all on you and that was wrong. It was too great a burden for a child. After your mother left, I doubted that you were really my son. I could not believe that a faithful wife would leave like she did. But now, when I see how easily you were led astray . . . there is so much of myself in you. I fathered you, Etienne, but I abandoned you as surely as your mother did."

"Father . . . I always thought you hated me because I was weak like my mother. I tried to please you, but after a while I gave up. I thought the people in the group were pleased with me. I thought I had at last found a purpose. I never questioned what they stood for. I have disgraced myself and you."

"No, No, Etienne. You have not disgraced me. I did it to myself. But I am determined to make amends, Etienne, if you will let me. You have a whole life ahead of you. You have a chance to start again in a new place."

"But I'm afraid, Father. I'm no good at my studies and I'm stuck in this horrible chair. I just don't have the strength."

"But you do! You had the courage to leave that group once you saw what they stood for. You had the wisdom to escape before they made you into an unfeeling creature like themselves."

"But I don't want to be alone, Father. I am no good at making decisions. I'm not even sure I can tell right from wrong anymore. What if I am like my mother?"

"It is not always easy to decide what is right, but I have faith that you will be wiser in the future. As for your mother, I no longer believe she was wicked. She was just very young. I should have realized that at the time."

"But it will be so hard. I won't know anyone. I won't know the customs."

"Ah, but you won't be alone. Monsieur Artier tells me there is a young man here who could go with you as a tutor and a companion."

"Who? You mean Edouard?"

"Yes, I believe that is his name."

"But he's in as much trouble as I am."

"I understand, but Monsieur Artier has explained the circumstances. He believes it could be arranged if you would agree."

"Agree! I would jump at the chance. Edouard's really been great. He fixes my food. He helps me get around. And he doesn't act like I'm a criminal. Could he really come with me? I know he needs a job."

"I think I could arrange to pay him to look after you. Perhaps then I could get a report on your progress from time to time."

"I promise I will write. I never thought you cared what I did. I will try to learn . . . something. I have no idea . . . will I ever see you again, Father?"

"I don't know, Etienne. I am an old man to make such a long journey. Perhaps Trinette could go someday. You will have to ask her."

"Is she here? Has she forgiven me after all? I thought she was too ashamed of me to come."

"No. No. She has pestered Monsieur Artier, day and night for weeks about seeing you. You always were her hero, Etienne. You allowed her to have fun and took the blame for any wrong she did. I don't know how you kept from being jealous. I was always more lenient with her."

"She believed in me, Father. She thought I was kind and brave. I let her down too."

She does not hold your mistakes against you, Etienne. She helped me see how badly I have treated you. Now I must let her in or I shall never hear the end of it."

296

Two days after Etienne said good-bye to his father and sister, Jack and Paul drove him and Edouard to the airport. It is not unusual for young men to feel uncertain when leaving home, but the knowledge that they could never return to their families hung like a weight on Etienne and Edouard's spirits. Paul was glad that Adrian Rubard had taken his suggestion to send Edouard as a companion for Etienne. Etienne still needed help to get around and Edouard showed him more kindness than he had ever received at home.

Edouard was relieved to have any way to support himself and caring for Etienne gave him a sense of purpose. Having to be strong for Etienne kept him focused. His immediate goal was to stay off drugs and out of prison. Although he had no money to enroll at McGill University with Etienne, Paul had given him the name of a chemistry professor and made him swear that he would contact him. After the horror of his involvement with Direct Action, Edouard was looking forward to returning to the quiet life on campus, if only as a tutor. He was also looking forward to working with Etienne, having discovered that Etienne was really much brighter than his father suspected.

Several agents from GIGN were at the airport, and after the last farewells had been said, Pienaar approached Paul. He indicated that he wanted to talk with him and Jack in private. Paul nodded and started after Pienaar, but when Jack began to follow along, Paul stopped abruptly and declared gruffly, "The oil light in the car is flashing, Jack. You need to check it before we drive back to town."

"Oh . . . sorry. I must have missed it," Jack apologized and retreated, silently blessing Paul's quick thinking that would spare him the boredom of a discussion with Pienaar.

As Jack headed toward the car, however, he was intercepted by David Falcon, one of the GIGN agents that had participated in the raid to rescue Kon.

"I need to talk to you," Falcon began earnestly.

"Yeah. What about?" Jack asked.

"I never had a chance to thank you and Artier for saving my ass at the agency. Pienaar . . ."

"So it was you! Look, I don't need to know all the details. It wasn't your finest hour, but . . . what the hell . . . forget it."

"It's not something I can easily forget. Listen, Barrons, I have some news I thought you might find interesting."

Jack gave Falcon a quizzical look, but remained silent.

"Lothar Berentson was arrested this morning."

Jack was suddenly all attention. "Arrested? Where?"

"At the border crossing between Colmar and Breisach am Rhine. They nabbed him coming across with high-powered weapons hidden in a truckload of furniture."

"Christ! The group must be getting desperate. He may give us a lead on Gérard. How did you find out about it?"

"I have a contact at Interpol. I told Pienaar, but he said it's out of his jurisdiction. I was tempted to tell him to go to hell and get over there, but I'm on thin ice. I can't afford to tick Pienaar off right now, but you . . . I think you want to get Gérard as bad as I do. Jesus! Maybe it *is* an obsession, but it's all I've got left. I'm still having a hard time keeping it together. Are you interested?"

"Of course I'm interested."

"Look, if I give you the name of my contact in Interpol, will you promise not to mention it to Pienaar?"

"Pienaar who?" Jack asked innocently.

Falcon smirked and handed Jack a card. "Tell Brian thanks for the tip, but I can't leave Paris right now."

"Sure. I'll tell him you're doing better," Jack promised.

Falcon shrugged. "Yeah, why not? Who wants to hear the truth anyway?"

Chapter Twenty

The whole blasted trip to see Lothar had been a waste of time. Lothar showed no interest in disclosing any information in exchange for leniency for Detlef. He voiced only contempt for him, insisting that he was through helping an incompetent weakling. As far as he was concerned, Detlef was just the result of an unlucky fuck on the part of his aging parents.

Jack was sorry the French had captured Lothar instead of the Germans. He felt confident that if the GSG-9 antiterrorist group had interrogated Lothar, he would have "volunteered" more information. Jack saw that it was useless to attempt to change Lothar's attitude, but it was difficult for Paul to accept the fact that Lothar cared nothing for Detlef. Looking after his brothers was a cardinal rule in Paul's life. In fact, it seemed to Jack that Paul collected people to look after.

Before they were even on the plane back to Paris, Jack could tell that Paul had "adopted" Detlef as another little brother. Thank God Etienne and Edouard are safely dispatched, he mused. Paul is wearing himself out gathering the discards from the Direct Action group.

A pre-trial hearing for Lorelle Chalandon, Detlef Berentson, and Philippe Garday was scheduled for 10 a.m. Paul had been visiting all three of the young prisoners regularly and on his last trip Detlef had begged him to come to the hearing with him. Lorelle seemed indifferent about her future, and Philippe's parents would be in the courtroom to plead on his behalf. Only Detlef appeared desperately in need of moral support. Paul realized that his presence would have little effect on the outcome of the official proceedings, but he could not ignore Detlef's pleas.

The police had decided to transport the three terrorists in the same van and began loading at 9:20 a.m. in order to allow ample time for moving the prisoners who were handcuffed and shackled. The police had agreed to allow Jack and Paul to accompany the prisoners, but they were not permitted to ride with them. Space in the van was at a premium and was reserved for four heavily-armed guards.

Jack was granted a place in the back seat of the escort car, and the officers in the second van reluctantly let Paul squeeze in with them. Word had come down from Pienaar that Jack and Paul were to accompany the group, but sensing the resentment of the individual officers, Paul regretted that he had not approached Cudran to request the favor.

The ride from the jail to the courthouse was short, and Jack bounded out of the car as soon as it reached the curb. He stood waiting while the two vans positioned themselves behind the escort vehicle. A large group of reporters and curious spectators had gathered outside the courthouse and they hurried to crowd around the vans as they pulled up. Police officers from the escort car began to direct the bystanders as the men in the second van climbed out and took up positions around the first van. Only after they were in place did the officer-in-charge radio the guards inside the van.

Paul and Jack were standing on the curb side of the first van as the doors opened and two armed guards stepped out. After several moments, the officer-in-charge shouted an order and one of the officers stepped forward to assist the prisoners who somehow had become hopelessly entangled in their chains. After some barely audible cursing and a lot of clanking, Lorelle stepped down, followed by Detlef and Philippe. Seeing the prisoner's dejected, frightened expressions, the crowd fell silent for a brief moment and the police were able to clear a path to the curb. As Lorelle started to move, however, one of the more eager reporters pushed his way forward. Another reporter shouted his objection and instantly the crowd was transformed into a raucous, jostling mass of arms, all waving cameras and microphones.

The police guards struggled to form a protective ring around the prisoners, but as Paul tried to join them a woman suddenly lost her balance and fell directly in front of him. He stooped to save her from being trampled by the crowd. As he placed her safely on her feet, he looked up to see two masked figures racing across the plaza on a motorbike. He drew his automatic and began to fight his way toward the prisoners. Just as he arrived at the ring of guards, a blast of machine gun fire rent the air and the screaming started. He tried to fire at the people on the motorbike but he could not get a clear shot through the fleeing crowd.

The police did not return fire immediately for the same reason and the gunmen charged toward the prisoners unchecked. Paul saw Detlef leap in front of Lorelle to shield her. He jumped forward to push them both to the pavement, but a police officer misjudged his intention and swung the butt of his automatic into the side of Paul's head. Paul swayed, dropped his gun, and fell on his hands and knees. When he reached to retrieve his gun, the officer struck him on the back. As the officer raised his gun to hit Paul a third time, Cudran suddenly appeared screaming, "Enough! Jesus! He's with us, you fool!"

Cudran grabbed Paul's arm and pulled him to his feet. "Martel! Are you O.K.?" he yelled into Paul's face.

Paul tottered for a minute then instinctively swung at Cudran with his free arm. The blow had no force, however, and Cudran caught his wrist.

"Relax, Martel. It's Cudran. Christ! If I had known you were coming I would have introduced you to the men."

Paul stood blinking and shaking his head, but he could not see clearly or get his mind in gear to speak. After a moment, his gaze focused on the ground behind Cudran. Someone was lying on the pavement in a pool of blood and Lorelle was hunched over the body, screaming hysterically.

"Detlef!" Paul gasped. He tried to stagger forward, but Cudran held him back.

"Take it easy, Martel. Get in the van!"

"No!" Paul said and reached a hand up to hold his head. "I've got to . . . I've got to help him. He begged me . . . ."

Cudran stared at Paul, watching the blood trickle down the side of his face. "This is personal, isn't it?" he said at last.

Paul nodded.

"Get his gun," Cudran said over his shoulder to the man who had struck Paul. Without a word the man picked up the gun and handed it to Cudran.

"O.K. . . . . It's your head," Cudran muttered. He tucked Paul's gun back into its holster. "Just remember, you're a cop, not a social worker," he advised and released his grip on Paul.

Paul lurched forward, staggered toward Lorelle, and dropped to his knees beside her. He tried to pull her away from Detlef, but she slapped at his hands and continued calling Detlef's name.

"Let me see him, Lorelle! Let me help him!" Paul shouted, but Lorelle ignored him.

"It's too late! He's dead! He's dead!" she wailed.

When Paul finally managed to pull her away, he saw that she was right. Detlef had taken several hits in the chest in his effort to protect Lorelle. "Oh God!" Paul groaned and put his hands to his head. Then he noticed that Philippe was sitting on the ground beside Detlef, still chained to his body. Philippe's face was colorless, his eyes glazed with fear. His coat was splattered with Detlef's blood and his arm was bleeding. Mechanically Paul pulled his tie off and slowly wrapped it around Philippe's arm. Philippe didn't move, but sat gaping at Detlef's body.

"You'll be O.K., Philippe. Have courage. You'll be O.K." Paul said softly and put a hand on Philippe's shoulder.

Philippe let out a strangled cry and seized Paul's right arm. "It's O.K., Philippe. It's . . ." Paul began, but suddenly Lorelle jumped at him and began pounding on his left arm screaming, "He shouldn't have died like this. Not like this! He was sweet and gentle. He was the only decent man I ever met."

Paul tried to catch her wrists with his free hand, but his movements were too slow. "I'm sorry, Lorelle. I'm so sorry," Paul repeated several times, but Lorelle didn't seem to hear.

She pounded Paul a few more times and then suddenly put her head against his shoulder and hid her face.

"You don't know!" she cried. "You just don't know! I loved him! I loved him!"

Paul reached his arm around her and pulled her toward him. "He loved you, Lorelle. He gave his life to prove it."

"I never told him, Paul. I never told him," Lorelle sobbed. "I didn't realize until now how much he meant to me."

"He knew, Lorelle. He knew. I told him," Paul assured her, although at the moment he couldn't recall what he had told Detlef.

Paul knelt holding Lorelle against him, feeling her shake as she sobbed uncontrollably. He felt empty, but he knew he must shelter Lorelle and Philippe from fear and despair. It was his duty. He heard sirens wailing and then Jack was beside him, asking anxiously, "Paul! Are you O.K.?"

Paul turned and Jack saw the bloody gash. "Christ! Were you hit?"

"They got Detlef, Jack! The bastards got Detlef! I couldn't . . ."

"I know. I know. We got both of them. Are you O.K.?"

"Yeah . . . I'm . . . I'm O.K. . . . Get help for Philippe."

"O.K. I'm going to see what's keeping those damned medics! Just hang on," Jack ordered and moved away.

Paul looked around slowly and realized that the plaza was littered with shattered bodies. Two armed guards lay dead on his right and a T.V. crewman lay on his left. There was no more screaming, only muffled sobbing and moans. The woman Paul had saved was nowhere to be seen. She had fled without thanking him. Now, in the anguish he felt at having failed Detlef, he did not remember that he had delayed only long enough to help her.

A few minutes later several ambulances arrived followed by two carloads of police. Two policewomen came and pulled Lorelle away from Paul using a mixture of authority and sympathy. She did not look back at Paul as they led her away and he remained mute. He grieved for her, but he felt he had no right to promise protection to anyone.

Paul was only vaguely aware that while the policewomen were talking to Lorelle, two men from the ambulance had come to treat Philippe. They had tried to put him on a stretcher but had been hampered by the fact that he was still shackled to Detlef's body. There was some confusion about who had the keys and the police went to search the pockets of the dead guards. Jack was still helping to administer first-aid to several of the bystanders who had been wounded.

Paul was sitting on the ground beside Philippe, keeping him company while he waited to be freed, when Philippe's parents rushed up. They had gone to the courthouse early to avoid the reporters and had been barred from leaving when the shooting started. As they spoke to Philippe, he came out of his stupor and began to moan softly. After a minute, he started to pant. He looked around with wild eyes and then began to laugh a mirthless, hysterical laugh.

"It happened again! It all happened again! They won't stop. They'll just keep killing until we're all dead . . . every one of us!"

Paul moved to comfort Philippe, but Monsieur Garday blocked his way. "Stay away from him! Why must you persecute him? He's been punished more than enough!"

Paul drew back, stunned by the remark. He must be confusing me with someone else, he thought. I tried to help him. I tried to help all of them. I always try . . .

"O.K., buddy, it's your turn," Jack said, breaking into Paul's thoughts. "This time you're going in the ambulance."

"I don't need . . ."

"Oh yes you do!" Jack countered decisively. "I'm not falling for that story again. Now shut up and get in or I'll throw you in!"

Paul looked up. He had never doubted that he could best Jack. Although shorter and lighter than Jack, he was exceptionally fast and far more skilled in martial arts. At the moment though, his world seemed to be out of focus and moving in slow motion. Jack appeared incredibly large and immovable as he bent over him.

"O.K., Jack. Have it your way," he mumbled. "But you're making a molehill . . . I mean, mountain . . . mountain out of a hellhole . . . er, molehole . . . you're making a mole . . ."

"Ah shit! You really are out of it, Paul," Jack said and carefully lifting Paul to his feet, he helped him to the nearest ambulance.

The doctors bandaged Paul's head, held a basin under his chin while he vomited, and declared that he had a concussion. They wanted to keep him under observation for twenty-four hours, but Paul adamantly refused. Jack took over holding the basin and arguing with Paul, but he finally gave in and drove Paul back to the hotel. He realized that Paul was really down about Detlef's death and sensed that he needed to be alone for a while to contemplate or meditate or whatever the hell he did when things got to him.

Jack was in the mood to numb his low spirits with a steady supply of stiff drinks, but limited himself to two in order to keep an eye on

Paul. It was his responsibility to stay sober enough to detect whether or not Paul's confusion was getting worse. After about an hour, Jack complained, "You know, it's damned hard to detect slurred speech patterns in a man who refuses to talk." At the risk of making Paul angry, he asked him the usual series of questions about who he was, where he lived, and what year it was.

Paul didn't get upset, he just answered. He was down, but he knew what Jack was doing. He was glad that Jack was there to take care of things. He felt guilty about sitting, but he was dizzy and couldn't summon the strength to take care of anyone, including himself.

Paul felt as though he had been in a daze for hours when Nea arrived. He didn't think to wonder how or why she had come. He was just glad she was there. She has a way of appearing when I'm at my worst, he mused, but things always seem to get better once she comes. He wanted to return the smile she gave him as she took his hand and sat beside him, but his face remained a frozen mask. He pressed her hand and let his eyes drink in her beauty.

After a moment she slipped away and swirled around the room, filling it with bright flowers and soft music. He let her peel his bloody shirt off and permitted her to guide his arms into a sweat shirt. Once again he tried to smile, not realizing that his feelings never made it to the surface.

She sat beside him and coaxed him to sip some tea. It wasn't the strong English tea with milk that she preferred, it was a clear, soothing herb tea. Rose hips, his analytical mind categorized, with maybe a bit of licorice bark. It seemed that before he had fully recognized the ingredients, he was lying on the sofa with his head cradled on her lap. She was rubbing his chest and it felt wonderful.

She was so full of life and love her warmth seemed to banish his lingering visions of death and sorrow. Her presence alone dispelled darkness. She asked nothing from him yet he wanted to give. Not from a sense of responsibility, not from duty, only as a means of drawing closer to her.

Get up, Paul! Get up now! he told himself. You're losing control. You've got work to do. You've got responsibilities. You're the caretaker. You're the strongest. They're all relying on you now, Paul, all of them. Don't let them down. Don't fail them like you did Arnot and Detlef. Don't fail them like you failed your father. He jerked and tried to sit up, but Nea pressed him down.

"It's O.K. now, Paul. Just relax," she whispered. "Everything's taken care of. Just rest."

Everything's taken care of? No. How can it be? he wondered. There is always something else I have to do, always someone else to take care of. It's all my responsibility now that my father is dead. They told me it was. My mother and my uncle told me over and over again. It is my duty, my role, my burden. They never say it, but I understand. It's my only hope of forgiveness for being a bad son.

"Shh . . . shh . . . Everything's O.K. now. Just relax for a little while," he heard Nea say again. She seems so sure. Maybe things have changed. Maybe I've been forgiven, he thought dreamily and let himself relax. He smiled and this time it registered on his face. I never meant to let him down. I never meant to ruin my mother's life. I never meant to shatter their world, never. The last thing he remembered was looking up at Nea's beautiful smile.

Brad had chosen to remain in the hospital in Paris rather than be transferred to London in order to be available for consultations with Paul. Mary had agreed, knowing that he would rest better if he could be kept up to date on the Rubard case. Since Etienne had been safely dispatched to Canada and the team had no further leads on Gérard, Brad decided it was time to return to England. Jack had assured him that Paul was recovering from his concussion and that he would continue to keep an eye on him.

Nea stayed behind when Mary and Brad left. She told Mary that she wanted to visit the fabric outlets, but Mary suspected that Nea hoped that once his assignment was finished, Paul would at last succumb to the fabled romance of Paris.

Late in the afternoon on the third day after Detlef was killed, Jack received a phone call from the police letting him know that Philippe was asking to see him. Philippe had been treated and was back in his cell. He would have been sent back sooner, but the doctor who treated him noticed his hysterical behavior and gave him a strong sedative.

When Jack arrived at the jail, he discovered that Cudran had left orders that he was to be shown in to Philippe right away. Philippe had worked himself into a nervous state again and was barely able to sit still. He eagerly accepted the cigarette Jack offered, but dropped it twice before Jack could light it for him.

"Calm down, Garday," Jack advised. "Pull yourself together."

"I can't," Philippe sputtered. "He means to kill us! He means to kill us all!"

"Who? What are you talking about?" Jack asked calmly.

"Gérard. It was Bernon at the courthouse yesterday. I think Gérard sent him. He wants us all dead! We're too big a risk to him. You've got to stop him, Jack!"

"How can you be sure it was Bernon?"

"I saw his body for Christ sake! They took me there this morning. I didn't let on that I recognized him, but it was Bernon all right. He was a link to Gérard. He used to send me to deliver things to Gérard."

"What kind of things?"

"Papers and . . . I'm not sure, but it must have been weapons."

"What makes you think it was weapons? Did you actually see them?"

"No. The cases were always locked. But they were heavy, really heavy."

"What kind of cases? Where did you take them?"

Philippe hesitated, looking around uneasily and biting his lower lip.

"Have you got another cigarette?"

"Sure," Jack answered easily. He tapped a cigarette out of his pack, but closed his hand around it when Philippe reached for it. "Tell me about the cases first. Where did you take them?"

Philippe stood up, folded his arms across his chest and gripped his shoulders.

"Come on, Garday. If you've got something to say, spill it!" Jack said bruskly.

"O.K.! They were metal cases—the kind used to carry camera equipment."

"Where did you take them?"

"Brussels. I always took them to the same camera shop. I . . . I used to take the train. If I left on the early train, I could deliver the stuff and get home before I was missed."

"How often did you go?"

Philippe sat down again and drummed his fingers on the table.

"Can I have the cigarette now? Please!"

"Alright, here. Hang on to it," Jack said opening his hand. Philippe grabbed the cigarette and put it between his lips. Jack lit it for him and waited while Philippe took two desperate drags and appeared to relax slightly.

"How often did you go to Brussels?"

"Initially it was only once or twice a month. But after Rubard disappeared, I was sent more often. Sometimes I had to pick up cases and bring them back."

"Did you ever meet Gérard?"

"No. I just left the stuff with the owner at the shop."

"What was his name?"

"Leverett."

"And you always dealt with him, no one else?"

"Yes. It was always Monsieur Leverett."

"What does he look like?"

Philippe shrugged. "Nothing out of the ordinary. Medium height, running to fat around the middle, dark hair, thinning a little on top. He had a moustache. What's to describe? He looked like an ordinary clerk!"

"Yeah. And you look like an ordinary student."

Philippe shot Jack a quick look and lowered his eyes.

"Can you identify the man who was with Bernon?" Jack asked.

"Yes," Philippe answered without looking up.

"Well, who was it?"

"Some guy named Cluree. I saw him a couple of times at Catia's"

"And you haven't told the police about them?"

"No! For God's sake no! I'm scared, Jack. I haven't told the police a damned thing and I almost got killed. Gérard's not finished with me. You've got to work a deal for me, Jack. Help me get out of here. I know I screwed up. I'll go to prison if I have to, but I don't deserve to wind up dead."

"You should have cooperated before, Garday. You could have

saved everybody a lot of grief."

"Look, I'm sorry. I thought if I just kept my mouth shut everything would be O.K. I didn't think anybody would bother with the likes of me. I'm a nothing—a nobody in the organization."

"Somebody picked you for the attack on the railroad station. Why was that?"

"That was an accident. I was at Catia's place with a few others when Michon came by to get some recruits. I had never done anything like that before. I just went along. I thought I would be safe in the group. I thought Michon and some of the others would look out for me. You know, solidarity and brotherhood and all that other shit they preach. It sounded pretty good while we were sitting around smoking and trying to impress one another. But it sure fell apart fast out on the street. Nobody told me what to do or where to run. So maybe I *was* new and too stupid to bother with, but nobody stopped for Catia either and shit, everybody knew Catia."

"That's what I've heard. She must have been quite a girl."

"She was, you know. Just totally wild. She didn't take discipline from anybody. She even talked back to Michon. We all admired that. We . . . well the guys anyway . . . we used to vie to get her attention. It was sort of an initiation ritual. If you hadn't screwed Catia, you were a nothing. Not that she had any discrimination. She slept with everyone, even two or three at a time. She broke all the rules. She was so free."

"All that so called freedom ended on the sidewalk. Did you admire that too?" Jack demanded sharply.

Philippe lowered his gaze and turned away silently.

"I'll be honest with you, Garday," Jack said slowly. "I don't know what I can do to help you, but if you want me to try, you'll have to fill me in on everything you know about Gérard—everything!"

Chapter Twenty-One

Physically Paul was feeling better and, at least on the surface, he appeared to have absorbed Detlef's death. He had called Detlef's parents and attempted to explain that what the police and the press were saying about Detlef was not true. It had not been easy. They wanted to blame someone and since Paul was the only identifiable target, he got blasted. After the call he got clearance from Pienaar to pack up Detlef's few personal belongings. When he went to tell the landlord that Detlef was dead, he was forced to endure a lecture on the irresponsibility of youth and ended up paying Detlef's overdue rent.

He shipped Detlef's possessions back to Germany holding back only a small volume of poetry as a memento for Lorelle. Pienaar had offered to send one of his men to take care of all the details, but Paul had refused. He felt it was his duty. The only part he didn't do was to deliver the book to Lorelle. That was another duty, but he wasn't ready to face her. First he had to see Meliné.

Paul had tried to call ahead, but there had been no answer at Meliné's apartment. He had stopped by to see her several times and knew she stayed close to home. He figured that by the time he drove over she would probably be back. He was eager to give her the good news. In the midst of all his other work, he had managed to track down her sister. He had even called Nantes and talked to her. As Meliné had mentioned, her sister was fairly secure financially, but she was lonely. Her husband had recently died of a heart attack and her daughters had married and moved away. In short, she was receptive to the idea of having Meliné come and live with her. There was plenty of room in her house now, and she really didn't want the headache of renting out the extra rooms.

As Paul parked the car and went into the apartment building, it struck him that the place was even more run down than it had been a few days before. Perhaps he had been in more of a hurry the last time, but he didn't recall seeing the battered sofa that was now almost blocking the hall on the third floor. The seat cushions were missing and two springs were protruding from the back. Paul heard dogs yapping as he came up the stairs and thought how much better off Meliné was going to be in Nantes. He wasn't sure he had the clout to push the paper work through the French system, but he had investigated the possibility of getting Meliné some disability payments. Having seen the way she walked, he was sure she wasn't lying about having a bad back.

Paul rapped firmly on the door to Meliné's apartment, but there was no answer. He rapped again and called out, but still no answer. He leaned close to the door and listened intently. He could not hear anything, but suddenly he noticed a peculiar odor as if something was burning. Gas! he thought, suddenly recognizing the smell.

He stepped back, turned 90 degrees and snap-kicked the door with his foot. Instantly he whirled around and kicked twice more until he heard the door frame crack. One final kick separated the fasteners on the chain lock from the frame and the door burst open. As the smell of gas flooded into the hall, Paul dashed through the apartment and raced into the kitchen. Spotting the blackened pot on the stove, he snapped off the burner and yanked the window open. Hurrying back to the living room he quickly threw open all the windows.

"Meliné? Meliné?" he called aloud several times before rushing into the bedroom. The room was dim, but he could see daylight showing under the drapes. Pushing them aside, he unlocked the window and struggled to raise it. He had to strike the sash several times before the window finally opened. Turning from the window, he suddenly drew in his breath. Meliné was lying on the floor in the narrow space between the foot of the bed and the dresser.

"Meliné!" he cried, jumping forward. Her eyes were closed and there was no sign of life. Kneeling to feel her pulse, Paul groaned as he saw the needle stuck in her arm. He thought to pull it out, but changed his mind. "Damn it, Meliné, why? Why now? You were so close . . . so close."

As he stood he noticed a bag of white powder on the dresser. He picked it up and it suddenly dawned on him that this was not suicide. Meliné had cleaned herself up and was heating some soup. Her death was a stupid accident.

Mechanically Paul went to the phone and dialed the police. He reported Meliné's full name and address, gave the cause and estimated time of her death, but hung up as the dispatcher asked his name.

Then he sat on the couch and covered his face with his hands. Oh God, three in a row, he thought bitterly. First Arnot, then Detlef, and now Meliné. I was supposed to help them. They were depending on me and I failed. I failed. I failed.

Paul was still sitting on the couch when Officer Cudran and the ambulance crew arrived. Cudran didn't speak but went straight to the bedroom. He returned a few minutes later shaking his head. He threw himself into the chair to the right of the couch asking, "You the one who called?"

Paul nodded, but did not uncover his face.

"Guess she figured she didn't have much to live for now that . . ."

"It wasn't suicide!" Paul snapped looking at Cudran. "She was fixing lunch. She's had a bad back for years. Nickie used to see that she was comfortable. She must have gotten some new stuff."

"What were you doing here?"

"Me? I came to tell her the good news," Paul said bitterly.

"What good news?"

"I located her sister. I came . . . I came to tell her everything was set. I had it all worked out. Everything all taken care of. Well, I sure as hell took care of things, didn't I?"

"Hey, take it easy, Martel. She was a junkie. This could have happened anytime."

"But it didn't! It happened now, while I was trying to arrange things. If I had been here an hour earlier, she would still be alive. What the hell am I going to tell her sister?"

"I don't know. Tell her you tried. Tell her, her sister's bad habits finally caught up with her. It's not your fault, Martel. Don't take it personally. Look, in our business we see people die all the time. We can't be there for all of them."

"Maybe not all of them, but I was supposed to be there for Meliné! That's what I'm supposed . . ." Ah hell, he just doesn't understand, Paul thought breaking off and covering his face again. I'm supposed to take care of people. It's not just a job, it's . . . it's just the way it is. People depend on me. I have to be strong. I've always been strong.

"For Christ sake, Martel! Who put you in charge of the world?"

312

Cudran suddenly asked. "I don't know how it is with GIGN, but for me it's just a job. I do the best I can and then . . . "

"Then what?" Paul snapped. "Forget about it? Jesus, Cudran . . ."

"Look . . . you just can't let it eat you up like this. Come on, you need a drink. You need to get your mind off it."

"I don't need anything!" Paul snarled, burying his face again.

"Sure! You're just gong to sit here and brood about things. Pull yourself together, Martel."

"You're right," Paul sighed a moment later. "There's not a damned thing I can do for her now."

"That's true. Just let me call the station," Cudran said and left the apartment.

Paul sat alone until Cudran returned a few minutes later. He wasn't particularly eager to go with Cudran, but he gave in to his persistence.

"I'll drive," Cudran determined. "We can pick up your car later."

Cudran's car was unmarked which told Paul that he probably held the rank of detective or higher. He didn't bother to ask. At the moment he flat didn't care. Cudran didn't make conversation while he drove, but he stole a few furtive glances at Paul out of the corner of his eye.

"This is as good a place as any," he said several minutes later as he parked the car. Paul followed Cudran inside. He was relieved that the place was quiet and decidedly more genteel than the exterior indicated. He was glad to be away from the shabby neighborhood where Meliné had lived.

Cudran signaled to someone in the back as they entered and steered Paul to a corner table. They were barely seated when a waiter appeared with two glasses and a bottle. Cudran poured.

"Come here to relax," he said leaning his chair back against the wall.

Cudran was full of stories and related them with surprising skill and wit, but try as he might, Paul just could not pick up on Cudran's good humor. He just sat and drank and listened. He knew Cudran was trying to take his mind off Meliné and he wanted desperately for him to succeed. He listened attentively and asked questions, but in the back of his mind the thought that he had failed continued to smoulder.

Cudran talked on, the drinks kept coming, and gradually Paul lost track of time and stopped counting. Self-control and discipline seemed a useless waste of effort. He just wanted to stop caring about anything for a while. Cudran was about to launch into another story when suddenly he looked at his watch and stopped short. "Christ! Where has the time gone? I've got to get home to supper."

"Supper? What time is it?" Paul asked, feeling too out of focus to check his own watch.

"It's 5:30. My wife has a fit when I don't show up on time."

"5:30?" Paul asked in disbelief.

"Yeah. I guess I really got wound . . . "

"Ah shit!" Paul mumbled. "I was supposed to meet someone for lunch."

"Well, you missed that one, friend. Maybe you'd better call and explain."

"Yeah, I better call," he agreed and stood up. He noticed his legs felt numb, but after the trouble they had been giving him lately, the sensation was not all unpleasant. He picked his way carefully between the tables and found the phone. He dialed the number for the hotel, but when he asked for Nea's room, the clerk informed him that she had checked out.

"Checked out? When?" he asked, suddenly feeling his senses snapping to attention.

"About 3:15, sir," the clerk replied.

"Look, this is Martel from GIGN. Did she leave any messages? Where did she go?" he asked anxiously.

"Just a moment, sir," the clerk responded, and Paul heard the phone cut off. He waited with growing dismay until the clerk came back on the line several minutes later.

"She didn't leave any messages, Monsieur Martel, but one of the porters heard her ask the cab driver for the airport."

"The airport! Oh . . ." Paul answered feeling stunned.

"I hope we did the right thing, sir. No one told us . . ."

"No. It's all right . . . She has a right to leave. It's just . . . I'm just surprised she left without . . . Thank you. Thank you very much. Everything's fine." Paul said abruptly and hung up.

"Don't tell me! You're in trouble with the wife!" Cudran said

314

lightly as he came up beside Paul.

Paul glanced at him and wondered if his dismay was obvious to everyone.

"I don't have a wife," he blurted. "She's just . . ." He stopped. Just what? he asked himself. A friend? Friends don't leave just because . . . Because what? Because you can't seem to find the time for them. Well, friends are supposed to understand these things.

"Don't worry about it," Cudran said, breaking into Paul's thoughts. "You can call and apologize later. Send her some flowers. That always works."

"Yeah . . . flowers . . . she likes flowers . . . orchids," Paul mumbled suddenly realizing that the empty feeling he had been trying to dispel had only deepened. "It doesn't matter," he said more to himself than to Cudran.

"That's the best way to look at it," Cudran said lightly. "You look done in. I'll drive you home and send someone for your car later."

Paul didn't object and Cudran half-led him out to the car. "I should have called, but she knows I'm tied up on this job. I thought she understood that."

"Well, sometimes women don't pick up on what we are trying to tell them," Cudran answered. "Where are you staying?"

"What?" Paul mumbled absently.

"Where are you staying, Martel?"

Paul didn't answer. He suddenly felt confused about his role as Martel. Martel is supposed to solve problems and save the world, he mused. It's Artier who keeps screwing things up. It's Artier who lets everyone down. Well, one of them sure as hell is drunk. It couldn't be Artier. He never gets drunk. He's too perfect. I've got to explain that to Nea.

"Where are you staying?" Cudran repeated, tapping Paul on the arm.

"What? Oh, Le Dauphine."

"That's better. Are you O.K.? I didn't overdo the happy hour routine, did I?"

"No. I'm O.K."

"Good. Get some rest, Martel. You're working too hard."

"Yeah, I am. That's my job. That's what I do. She has to

understand that."

"Don't worry about it," Cudran advised. "Call her later."

"Yeah . . . better not to worry."

Cudran stopped in front of Le Dauphine, but when Paul made no move to get out, he double parked and went around to open the door for him.

"I don't need help!" Paul snapped when Cudran took his arm.

"Oh, I can see that," Cudran responded jovially. "I just want to see what the lobby looks like. Thought I might send some friends here. Careful! Watch you head!" he continued, pulling Paul from the car.

"I'm O.K." Paul insisted. "I don't need help. I don't need anyone."

"As you say," Cudran continued, steering Paul into the hotel.

"What's the room number? I'll get the key."

"The room?"

"Yes, what's the number?"

"561 . . . No that's her's . . . 563."

"O.K. wait here."

Cudran got the key from the desk clerk and handed it to Paul. "Get some rest and don't worry about your car. I'll see that you have it by tomorrow morning. Give me the keys."

"Keys? Oh, right . . . good . . . Thanks," Paul mumbled. He dug in his pocket and handed several keys to Cudran, who quickly fished out a ring with car keys. He slipped the others back into Paul's coat pocket and watched as Paul headed for the elevators.

Paul had some trouble with the key when he reached his room, but the door finally opened. He struggled to remove his coat and hung it over the back of the chair by the small desk. He checked his watch—6:17. I'd better call Nea, he thought, picking up the phone. Nea didn't answer, but he left a message on her machine. Then he sat and waited, trying not to think about Meliné, but not able to get her out of his mind. She had ended up so alone. He had never minded being alone. In fact, he sought solitude as an escape from the burdens of looking after people. At this particular time, however, being alone did not appeal to him. He wished that he and Kon had parted under different circumstances so he could call without feeling that he was intruding. He wished that Jack was back from Brussels so they could go for a meal. But most of all, he wished Nea would return his call. It surprised him how badly he wanted to speak with her. I'm just concerned whether or not she got home safely, he told himself, but he knew it wasn't true. He wanted to hear her voice, wanted her to tell him that the world wouldn't come apart if he relaxed for a few minutes.

He placed another call at 6:45 and one at 7:15. Where could she be? he wondered. She left at 3:15. He called room service and ordered a bottle of scotch. He was worrying needlessly. He needed a drink to steady himself. He couldn't let her know how anxious he was. That would never do.

The scotch came, but the phone didn't ring. At 7:52 he called again, but didn't leave a message when the machine came on. He poured himself another drink to keep his mind from conjuring up morbid possibilities as to why Nea had not returned his call. At 8:06 he couldn't stand the waiting and put in a call to Mary.

"Mary? It's Paul."

"Good evening, Paul. I'm glad to hear you got back all right. Nea said you got tied up on some mission."

"You talked to Nea?"

"Yes."

"When?"

"Oh, shortly after 5. She said she had just gotten in."

"She called at 5 o'clock? Did she say where she was going?"

"No . . . actually she said she was going to stay home and tidy up her apartment."

"She's home?"

"Well, I can't be sure. Is something wrong, Paul?"

"No. I just . . . Was she upset about my missing lunch? I tried to call. I've been apologizing to her blasted machine since 6:30."

"Oh dear. Do you want me to call her and then call you back?"

"No . . . that won't be necessary. I . . . I think I get the picture. I'm just a little surprised. I'm sorry I bothered you, Mary. I thought she understood my job and all . . . why should she be any different? She just fooled me, you know."

"Have you been drinking, Paul?" Mary asked.

"Drinking? No . . . well, maybe a little. I'm not really Mr.

317

Perfect, Mary. But you always knew that. I never fooled you."

"No one expects you to be perfect, Paul."

"Oh, but they do, Mary. They do! And when I'm not, people die."

"What are you talking about? Who died, Paul? Paul? Are you there?"

"Yeah . . . I'm here . . . but I wasn't there when they needed me. First Arnot, and then Detlef and now Meliné . . . all dead."

"Arnot killed himself, Paul. That wasn't your fault."

"But I promised him . . . I promised all of them. They were depending on me. Everyone depends on me. I can't do it any more, Mary. I just can't . . ."

"What happened, Paul? Who is Meliné?"

"An old woman . . . just a lonely old woman that nobody will miss. That's what's so terrible. She didn't have anybody but Nickie and I watched them both die."

"Oh, Paul, you can't be responsible for everyone. You take on too much. Where are you now, Paul?"

"At the hotel. I came back to call Nea. I thought she would understand, but she doesn't. It was just an act. I shouldn't have fallen for it. I never let women get to me. She just put on such a good act."

"It wasn't an act, Paul. She does care about you."

"Don't lie to me, Mary! I don't want to hear any more lies. I'm fed up! I'm just fed up with everything."

"Listen to me, Paul. It's not like you to be so down. I think you've been working too hard. You need to get some sleep. Where's Jack? Let me talk to him."

"He's not here. He went to Brussels. I stayed behind to fix things for Meliné. She was so close, Mary . . . so close. If only I had gotten there sooner, everything would have worked out. I let her down. I let all of them down. Maybe I let Nea distract me. I've never let a women distract me before. I just thought she was different."

"Listen to me, Paul!" Mary cut in. "You haven't let anyone down. You're just pushing too hard. You need to get some rest."

"Rest! Hell no! I've got to find out where Meliné got the stuff that killed her. I've got . . ."

"Paul! Stay out of it. Let the police do it."

"I can't, Mary. I let her down."

"Paul, you're not listening to me."

"There's no time, Mary. I've got to go," Paul said and hung up.

The chair fell over as Paul yanked his coat off the back of it, but he didn't stop. He was suddenly angry with himself for not realizing before that he had to do this for Meliné. He lurched out the door and took the elevator to the lobby. He was three blocks from the hotel before he realized he should hail a cab. He couldn't remember the street number and gave the driver only the name of the nearest major cross street.

When the cab arrived at the intersection, Paul had more than a little difficulty determining which way to go. After a brief argument he decided to go on foot. He was sure the cab driver had overcharged him, but he didn't care. The man had been surly and had regaled him with tales of having been robbed twice in this part of town. Paul wanted to get away from him as quickly as possible.

After two false starts, Paul found Meliné's street and set off down the block. He had gone only a short distance when he spotted his car. There were two men by it and they appeared to be intently engaged in removing the tires on the driver's side. Paul was suddenly furious.

He ran forward, grabbed one man from behind and tossed him against the rear door of the car. The man bending over the wheel called out and started to stand up, but Paul kicked him in the ribs and sent him sprawling. Paul turned in time to see the first man produce a tire iron. Instantly he spun, lashed out with his leg and sent the tire iron flying. Paul spun to kick the man again, but before he completed his turn something hit him in the back.

Suddenly he was surrounded by a group of assailants all swinging clubs and fists. He blocked their attack with his arms, he swept their feet from under them, he threw them over his shoulders, but still they kept coming.

He whirled like a crazed top, kicking and striking, all the while letting forth ear-piercing cries as wild and blood-curdling as any that had echoed through the streets of Paris in its long history of war and revolution. But there were too many assailants and the blows they struck sapped Paul's strength until at last he went down and they were on top of him like a pack. He tried to count their faces as they stared down at him, but they were spinning too fast.

Chapter Twenty-Two

Kon was sitting in Paul's room at the Le Dauphin Hotel. He felt slightly guilty and slightly amazed that he had been able to open the door so easily. He had been surprised when Geilla had called him at his apartment in Paris and asked him to break into Paul's room. She had been absolutely convinced that he had the tools and could do it and she had been right.

He had come to Paris alone to discover for himself if he truly was a banker. He realized that the old couple at the corner shop had been right about his strange array of skills. And then there was the knife. He had been aghast when he first saw it in a drawer in his apartment. But the instant he held it, he knew it was his.

Several officers at the bank had appeared to know him when he had gone there in the afternoon. They had shown him to an office they claimed was his and were careful not to embarrass him with too many questions. Undoubtedly, they had been coached by Edgar to be polite. Actually, he liked the staff in Paris much better than the group in Geneva. They came forward to shake his hand and their questions about his health had a ring of sincerity he had not detected from the people in Geneva.

The Paris staff seemed to regard him as somewhat of a hero for having survived being kidnaped. At first, he was startled that they knew, but he soon realized that Edgar had been wise to tell them part of the truth. Many of them were in a position to be targets themselves and it made them feel better that he had been rescued alive without impoverishing his family.

The truth also helped them to show understanding after he had leaped to his feet screaming obscenities when a secretary accidentally spilled hot coffee on him during a meeting. The poor girl had been deeply offended until a senior secretary who had been taking minutes explained that his outburst was an expression of suppressed anger and should not be construed as a personal insult.

Kon had been upset about his violent outburst, however, seeing it as further proof that he did not have himself under control. He secluded himself in his office and brooded about the possible mental implications of his breach of etiquette until he remembered the incident of Michon throwing coffee at him. Reassured that his lapse of good manners did not indicate that he was losing his mind, he succumbed to a long established habit and called Charlotte Marneé for advice. Charlotte's solution of requiring Peter to present the young lady with a formal apology and a small box of chocolates cleared the air and enabled everyone to concentrate on more important matters.

Kon was roused from his musings by a sound at the hotel door. He regretted that Paul had returned before he had rehearsed his long overdue apology for having practically thrown him out of his apartment in Geneva. He stood, getting ready to explain his unannounced visit by referring to the call from Mary that had upset Geilla. But when the door opened a moment later, Kon fell speechless at the sight in the hall.

A tall, broad-shouldered man with greying hair was supporting Paul by holding Paul's left arm around his neck. Paul looked so dazed and battered that Kon stood immobilized with shock until the tall man shouted, "Either give me a hand with him or get the hell out of the way!"

Kon obeyed instantly. Putting Paul's right arm over his shoulder, he helped carry him into the room and lay him on the bed.

The tall man was panting from his effort.

"Who are you? What are you . . ." he demanded impatiently. Then he noticed Kon's wrist. "Hell, you must be Breaux, the one who was kidnapped. Only it isn't really Breaux, is it?"

"No. How badly is he hurt?" Kon asked anxiously, wasting no time on explanations.

The tall man gave a disgusted grunt and shook his head. "Not seriously. They checked him at the station. He's more drunk than hurt."

"Who are you? How did this happen?" Kon demanded.

"Detective Cudran. The damned fool tangled with what he thought were a couple of guys stealing tires. Only it turns out they were a professional gang who strip cars and pedal drugs. My men showed up just as he finished wiping the street with the them. He was so damned drunk he started in on my men. He was kicking and punching everything in sight. . . screaming like a banshee the whole time! He was so riled up, he snapped a baton over his knee. You should see my men. They'll he black and blue for weeks. Jesus, he's a mean son of a bitch when he's drunk!"

"But Paul doesn't get drunk! I've never seen him get drunk!" Kon objected and somehow he knew he was right.

"Well, he was practicing mighty hard this afternoon and he sure as hell is stinko now! If he wasn't with GIGN, I'd have left him locked up for the night. I wish both of you would just clear out of Paris and leave me in peace!" Cudran concluded and grabbed the phone.

"Is this the front desk?" he shouted into the receiver. "Good. This is Detective Cudran, Paris Police. I want some ice sent up to Room 563 immediately. Yes, I realize that it's late, but you don't have to saute it and you don't have to put parsley on it. Just get it up here! Now! Thank you. I appreciate your cooperation," Cudran concluded more calmly and slammed the receiver back into the cradle.

"I shouldn't have started him drinking, but he was so down this afternoon, I thought it might take his mind off things. He was out of it when I brought him back. I thought he would be sensible and go to bed. Something must have set him off. He sure was spoiling for a fight when he hit the street."

"That just doesn't sound like Paul. I can't imagine . . . oh, shit! That's what the phone call was about."

"What are you talking about?"

"I'm sorry . . . look, this is a private matter. Paul doesn't discuss his personal life . . . "

"You mean like the woman he forgot to meet for lunch?"

Kon bristled. "This is no joke, Cudran."

"Relax! I understand. Look, now that you're here I don't have to hang around. Just be sure you put some ice on that eye of his."

"Don't worry. I'll take care of it right away. Thanks for bringing him home. It's really not like him to get upset about things."

"That's damn lucky for the rest of us," Cudran said with a smile. "Well, here's the ice," he added as he opened the door. "Good evening to you," he said pleasantly and slipped down the hall.

Kon mumbled 'thanks,' snatched the bucket of ice from the bellboy, and quickly closed the door. Hurrying into the bathroom, he gathered up a wash cloth, several large towels, and the plastic waste can. Then he turned on the light by the bed and sat beside Paul. He dipped the cloth into the melting ice and pressed it carefully against Paul's face. He repeated the routine several times before Paul's eyelids flickered open and he groaned, "Christ! What hit me?"

"It was more a 'who' than a 'what'," Kon answered. "It seems you took on a gang of car thieves and half the Paris police force."

"Police? No! It was car thieves . . . after my tires . . . the cab driver told me it was a bad neighbor . . . oh God, I feel rotten. Did they kick me in the head?"

"I don't think so. Cudran said you'd been drinking. What happened?"

"Drinking? Yeah, I guess I was."

"How come? That's not your style."

"Well, it's not my style to screw everything up either, but I've sure been botching things lately! It's like everything's coming apart at once. I can't seem to do anything right anymore. I'm sorry you found out about Geilla and me. It was all before she married you, Kon, I swear. I was just trying to keep her from getting lonely and running off with some jerk. She never wanted me. It was always you."

"It's O.K., Paul. I was an idiot to get so upset. I've been meaning to apologize but . . . hey, lie still!"

"Cut the nursemaid act . . . oh Jees! My ribs are caving in!"

"Just take it easy, O.K.? If it makes you feel any better, Cudran said the other guys are in worse shape than you are."

"Oh that's really good to know!" Paul remarked with heavy sarcasm. "What the hell are you doing here anyway?"

"Mary was worried about you so she called Geilla. I just happened to be here on business so I said I would check on you."

"Mary called?"

"Yes. Something about your lunch with Nea."

"Oh yeah . . . look, it's just that . . . hell, you're more of an expert about these things than I am. Why the hell do they do it? I mean, why the hell do women act all sweet and concerned and then just when you think you can rely on them, they kick you in the balls and act like you're shit. Why? I just don't get it, Kon. I just don't get it."

"I don't know. Maybe they don't mean to. Maybe they don't understand how much it hurts."

"Don't give me that crap! They enjoy it! It's like some sport. I watched Alyce do it to you, and Linda ground Jack into little pieces! They get you all excited and then wham! And I fell for it! Jesus! What a jerk! How could you stand it, Kon? All those times . . . I never really understood how you felt. It was always so easy for me. Take it or leave it . . . no strings. And just when I thought Nea was different, wham! Don't tell me she didn't enjoy it, the lousy bitch! She probably kept score to see how many times I would apologize to her stupid machine. Stupid bitch, she . . . oh God . . ."

"Settle down, Paul. Shit! At least try to aim," Kon ordered, pushing Paul's head over the waste can.

"Agh. I can't believe this," Paul moaned after he had vomited. "How come you never get sick, Kon? You just pass out and get it over with."

"Judging from the quantity of liquor I keep around, I would say I've had a lot more practice being drunk, Paul. I've never seen you get drunk."

"Well, I sure as hell am now. Me . . . Mr. Perfect . . . drunk as a slunk, er skunk . . . drunk as a skunk, sick as a dog. Can't you hold that damned thing still!" he complained leaning over the waste can.

"I am holding it still. You're the one who's weaving all over the place!"

"Jesus . . . why didn't you just leave me in the street to get run over by a truck. It's got to be a quicker way to go."

"Hang on now. It'll all be over tomorrow."

"Tomorrow! Oh God! Brad's going to be bloody annoyed with me, Kon . . . bloody annoyed . . . I'm supposed to meet Jack in Brussels . . . bloody annoyed . . . hold that damn bucket still, will you!"

"O.K.! O.K.! Keep it off the bedspread for God's sake!"

"Jack's not going to believe this, Kon. Me, Mr. Perfect, getting the crap knocked out of me in a street fight. Oh God . . . don't tell him . . . please don't tell him. I'll never live it down!"

"Relax, will you. I won't say a word. I'll make some excuse. What's Jack doing in Brussels?"

"He got a lead on Gérard. We have to get him back to Paris. Oh God, how could she do this to me? I just can't believe . . . she fooled me . . . ya know. Just when I thought . . . Stinking bitch . . . lousy stinking bitch. . . " Paul's voice faded to a mumble and he slumped forward onto the bed.

Kon set the waste can down, pushed Paul back onto the bed, and started to unbutton his shirt. It grieved him to see Paul so battered both physically and emotionally. He realized how wrong he had been to be jealous. Even though he judged Paul to be smarter and better looking than himself, he was the one the Geilla had chosen. He was the one who had a wife and a child on the way.

Kon pulled the covers back, but as he rolled Paul over, Paul started to mumble again. "Don't tell Jack, Kon, please. Don't tell . . ."

"I won't. I won't. I promise," he assured Paul and then he made his decision. He was still not certain how he was involved with Paul and Jack, but he knew that the old couple was right. He was more than an ordinary banker.

"Where are we supposed to meet Jack?" he asked casually as he untied Paul's shoes and pulled them off.

"Where?"

"Yes. I . . . I can't remember the address."

"Ambassador Hotel . . . ask for Erick Hendricksen. Tell him I was delayed."

"O.K. I will."

"Good . . . good . . . supposed to take him that case of equipment . . . guy always brings enough gear for a God damn platoon."

"I'll take care of it, Paul. Get some rest," Kon said gently. He finished pulling Paul's clothes off and rolled him under the covers before he went to call Geilla.

Chapter Twenty-Three

Mary didn't usually spend much time at the dress boutique that she and Nea ran in London, but she decided that this was the right morning to check the inventory. At least that was the excuse she offered Nea when she appeared at the shop just before lunch time. Nea was in the back at her drawing board, apparently inspired by her recent trip to Paris. Mary knew she was not concentrating on her work, however, for she showed Mary around the shop and let herself be persuaded to accompany Mary to lunch.

"Did you get any new ideas while you were in Paris?" Mary asked as they sat down at the table.

"Do you mean for dress designs?"

"Yes . . . or about anything else."

"If you mean about Paul . . . it's just not going to work. I'm not ready for this, Mary. It's too soon, or maybe he's too much like Keith. He's always running off to help someone and I'm left to wait. At least Keith would call me once in a while. Paul hardly ever does. You call me, or Jack calls, but not Paul. I'm sick and tired of chasing him. I'm just a convenience to have around when he has nothing better to do."

"That's not true, Nea. He cares deeply about you."

"Well, why can't he say it, or show it? When I throw myself at him he is so tender it's wonderful. But as soon as he goes off, he forgets all about me."

"He doesn't forget about you," Mary objected. "Paul has a lot of responsibilities. He gives to everyone. He's not used to receiving and I think it makes him uncomfortable."

"Perhaps you are right. Why do I keep getting mixed up with men who give to everyone but me? Keith was bent on saving everyone. His ultimate high was carrying a baby from a burning building. He gave to everyone too, and in the end it killed him. I can't go through that again, Mary. We had so much planned, a house and children. It's like he gave himself away and I was left with nothing."

"I know it was rough, but you can't go on grieving forever. It's been two years. You need to start seeing people again."

"I know. I know," Nea sighed. "But that's the problem, Mary. I never get to see Paul. He's always working."

"But isn't Paul's caring nature what attracted you in the first place? You can't ask him to stop being what he is."

Nea stopped with her fork in mid-air and then smiled. "You're right, Mary. Paul cares about everyone. I only wish he would focus on me once in awhile."

"You need to be patient. I know Paul cares about you. He's never spent so much time with anyone as he has with you. He's just very involved with his work. They're all like that, Paul and Kon, Jack and Brad. Brad goes off for days and I'll lose track of him, but when he comes home . . . If you love him, you put up with it. Could you love a man who didn't care about the terrible things that go on in the world?"

"I suppose not. I don't know how you do it, you and Geilla. Maybe you're stronger than I. I suffered with her, Mary. She's still suffering because of Kon. He treats her like a stranger."

"Kon's behavior right now is not a true reflection of how he feels about Geilla. I suspect he pretends to remember things, but he doesn't. He's still confused and afraid. Geilla needs to be patient too. She knows Kon does not like to be smothered and controlled, but she keeps doing it to him. He was just starting to adjust to being married when he was kidnaped. He'll get over this."

"But what if he doesn't? Where does that leave Geilla?"

Mary hesitated. Then she smiled and said with a twinkle in her eye, "She'll find herself married to an exceedingly handsome, mysterious stranger who is sure to fall in love with her all over again."

Nea laughed in surprise. "That could be interesting. At least she got a ring before he forgot who she was. I think Paul's forgotten me already. I'll never get a commitment from him. He's married to his job."

"He hasn't forgotten you. I know he hasn't. He's just about as confused as Kon right now. He's having a terrible time accepting that he needs anyone. If you think he's worth having, you'll have to do the chasing for a while."

"I don't know if I have the patience, Mary. He is fantastic though. And much more mature than Keith ever was."

"Paul had tremendous responsibilities thrust upon him when he was seventeen. He's handled it well, but it left him little time for himself. He still sends most of his money home to his mother and his brothers."

"He takes care of Kon and Jack too."

"Yes, but he chose to do that and it's different with them. They don't demand things from him and burden him with guilt the way his family does. And they take care of him too, as much as he will allow. The team is like a family. If you take one you get the others thrown in. They take care of each other and they'll take care of you too if you really need them. They won't let you down. You saw how they arranged for Brad to have the best care possible. I don't worry as much about Brad when I know he's with the team."

"Is that why Jack tries to play matchmaker? He can be so funny and so obvious. Paul still hasn't caught on. What a dear Jack is for trying though."

"Jack just wants Paul to relax and have some fun out of life."

"Yes, that would be good for him."

"Well, what do you say?" Mary coaxed. Will you give him another chance?"

"I suppose so . . . but he has to make the first move. I'm tired of throwing myself at him."

Since Jack and Paul had not been able to get a word out of Lothar, Plan B was put into action. With Bélidor Office Supply Shop shut down and Lothar under wraps, Paul reasoned that Gérard had to be getting desperate for weapons. Pienaar had been reluctant to cooperate at first, but when Paul pushed him, he agreed to supply enough weapons to bait a trap.

Jack chartered a plane to Stuttgart then boarded a train for Brussels. Sitting still for hours was not Jack's style, but he figured he should trace the route he would have used if he actually was delivering weapons from Germany. He was to make the preliminary contact at the camera shop and then wait for Paul. Although Jack was anxious to get started, Paul wanted a positive I.D. on Gérard before they set up a deal.

Jack was feeling cramped by the time he got off the train and rode the Metro into town. Garday was right, he thought as he walked up the street searching for the right number. There is certainly nothing distinctive about the shop. One glance at the single display window told you the clientele was more practical than chic. The merchandise was arranged on faded black fabric with more military precision than artistry.

No cheery bell sounded when Jack entered through the door to the right of the window, but he noticed the complex arrangement of dusty mirrors. Obviously, whoever was in the back did not want to be taken by surprise. The shop appeared to be empty, but by the time Jack strode to the counter and hefted the metal case onto it, a short, middle-aged man appeared.

"Good-day, sir. How may I help you?" the man began in French.

"I have some sophisticated equipment I want to sell, Monsieur Leverett," Jack answered in French. "I understand you might be able to connect me with a buyer."

The man looked slightly startled to be addressed by name, but replied only, "That is possible, but I must be sure of its quality. Where was it made?"

"Germany."

"I see. How much do you have to sell?"

"Not as much as I'd like. The company had some trouble getting customs clearance and the main lot got delayed at the French border."

"I see," Leverett replied cautiously.

"Perhaps you would like to examine the sample I have brought and give me a call. My number is in the case."

"Yes. Yes. I believe that is the way to proceed."

"Very well. I will be expecting a call," Jack concluded. He nodded, flipped a key onto the counter, and left.

Jack felt restless confined to his room at the hotel, but he had to stay close to the phone in case Gérard or Leverett called. When he heard a knock on the door, he hurried to open it and was definitely surprised.

"Kon! What the hell are you doing here? I thought you were in Geneva."

Kon smiled shyly. "I was. Then I went to Paris and now I'm here."

"How did you know where I was? Where's Paul?"

"Paul has the flu," Kon offered.

"The flu? When did that happen? He was fine yesterday."

"Ah . . . it came on very suddenly. Probably one of those 24-hour things. He's been working pretty hard lately. He was aching and throwing up so badly he asked me to come."

"He sent you? But I thought . . . no offence, Kon, but are you sure you are up to this?"

"Yes. I'm feeling much better . . . really. I . . . I have to do this, Jack. I have a personal score to settle with Gérard."

"Maybe that's the very reason you should stay out of it."

"No! I'm here and I have to do this. I'm still looking for answers."

"Are you sure Paul knows you're here?" Jack asked, giving Kon a closer look.

"Yes. How else would I know where to find you? He asked me to bring you this equipment."

"Well . . . O.K.," Jack agreed reluctantly taking the metal case from Kon. "I guess it's all right." He knew Paul would forbid him to do the job alone. Having Kon's help allowed him to continue. "Maybe I should call Paul."

"Don't . . . er . . . he might be asleep. Don't wake him. He was sick all night."

"O.K. I'll leave him be. You might as well make yourself comfortable. I'm still waiting to be contacted. This is the worst part—just sitting and waiting. I'm glad for the company, but if the phone rings, don't pick it up. I'm supposed to be alone."

"I won't get in your way, Jack," Kon said taking off his coat.

And so they waited, making small talk. Jack could tell that Kon didn't know the details or remember some of the key players in the case. He was both victim and investigator, but he did not remember enough to make him 100 percent effective in either role.

Finally, at quarter to three, the phone rang. Kon waited anxiously, trying to piece together the conversation from Jack's few grunts. At long last Jack put down the phone.

"That was Leverett. It's on for 10:30 tonight."

"Where?"

"In front of Coudenberg's fish market."

"Outside? How am I going to spot him at night?"

Jack seemed unconcerned. "No problem," he answered, slowly letting a sly grin spread across his face. "Despite what Paul says, I don't carry all this gear around just to build up my arm muscles."

Kon watched in silence as Jack hefted the metal case he had brought onto the bed and snapped open the clasps.

"I had a feeling these would come in handy," Jack said handing Kon a pair of binoculars. "The light magnification on these babies is fantastic! You'll be able to observe everything from a block away."

"You really think of everything, don't you," Kon said with admiration. He suddenly realized that he had underestimated Jack.

Jack looked at his watch in disgust. It was after eleven and still no one had shown. He wondered if he was in for a series of false starts to test his reliability. The cold weather combined with the light drizzle made standing around more than just a nuisance. Jack blew on his hands and rubbed them together briskly wishing he had worn gloves. Only a few cars had passed and he was beginning to get angry about being left waiting in the rain.

Suddenly he thought he heard rapid footsteps and he turned to face the store window as instructed. The footsteps became louder and less hurried, but he did not turn until he heard a man ask in French, "How many have you got? And where can I pick them up?"

"Fourteen. And you'll have to come for them yourself," Jack answered.

"Are they all like the sample?" the man asked, referring to the submachine gun that Jack had left with Leverett.

"Yes. All Heckler and Koch MP5s," Jack answered.

"I want them, but I want them delivered to Paris."

"No deal," Jack said bluntly.

"Why not? I'll pay."

"Like the way you paid Lothar?"

"What do you mean? Lothar never delivered the stuff!"

"Quit playing games! Somebody set him up. He never got past the border!"

"That wasn't my fault," the man objected.

"So you say. I say you'll have to come to Germany for them."

"Lothar always handled shipping. That was part of the deal!"

"Well, Lothar won't be around for a while. Things have gotten more difficult!" Jack shouted.

"All right! I'll come to Germany. Maybe Leverett can arrange something. He has some contacts."

"I won't work with Leverett," Jack objected. "You'll have to arrange it yourself."

"Listen!" the terrorist countered. "I don't have time to set this up. If you want to deal, you'll have to make the stuff available. How do I know you didn't set Lothar up so you could take over?"

"Are you accusing me of something?" Jack snarled."

"Maybe I am and maybe I'm not," the terrorist replied. "Let's just handle one thing at a time. I said I would come to Germany. How can I get you to work with me on this? What's your price?"

"It's going up by the minute standing out here in the rain," Jack grumbled.

"Screw the rain! What's your price?"

"11,000 D-Marks each."

"11,000 D-Marks! Where the hell are they coming from?"

"They're all brand new, equipped with silencers and still in crates."

"Jesus! I don't give a shit about the crates. I still have to arrange delivery. 8800 is all I'll give."

"Then there's no deal," Jack said coldly. "We lost some people getting these!"

"I don't give a damn!" the terrorist shouted.

Jack did not answer. He turned his back as if preparing to leave and suddenly the terrorist reconsidered. "O.K. O.K.! 9500."

"140,000 D-Marks for the lot," Jack snapped, setting the price at approximately 4,000 U.S. dollars each. "Who else can get you so many at one time?"

"Alright 140,000. But you deliver in Paris!"

"No!"

"Then there's no deal!"

"Look," Jack said as if he had succumbed to the offer. "What if you agree to bring them to Paris with me. That way we can keep an eye on each another."

The man turned away nervously before mumbling, "I really don't want to be in Paris right now."

"Well, I really don't want to drive across the border alone with a truck full of MP5s. Either you come with me or the deal is off!"

"You're driving me into a corner!" the terrorist shouted.

"Look! I'll drive you into hell if you pay me enough, but I'm not going across that border alone," Jack said decisively.

"All right! We'll go across together. But there better not be any slip-ups!" the terrorist growled, suddenly pulling a Browning automatic from his shoulder holster.

"There won't be," Jack said firmly. "Meet me in Stuttgart next Tuesday."

"Where?"

"Call this number when you get in," Jack said reaching into his pocket and pulling out a card. "Someone will give you instructions."

"I'll be there," the man said coldly and shoved the automatic back into his holster. Without further comment he turned and walked away.

Jack watched him for a few minutes. I wonder if Kon was able to get a clear view of his face, he thought peering across the street. He scanned the shadows expecting to spot Kon, but he couldn't see any movement. It had started to rain harder and it was difficult to see much of anything across the street. He glanced back at the terrorist and suddenly noticed a slight figure moving furtively through the shadows. He didn't have to think twice to know it was Kon.

Shit! He's going to follow the guy, Jack thought. If he's spotted he'll blow the whole set-up. Christ! I shouldn't have let him come. I should have locked him in his room at the hotel.

Jack stood still. He dared not make any move that would attract the terrorist's attention. When the terrorist was at the end of the block, he paused to light a cigarette. Jack guessed he was signaling someone that he was ready to be picked up.

As the terrorist lowered his hands, Kon suddenly sprung from his hiding place and seized him by the throat.

Jesus! Kon must have recognized Gérard! Jack thought in alarm. He has no idea that Gérard is armed or maybe he's too mad to care. He drew his gun and tore down the street after Kon. Jack had never been able to run as fast as Kon, but he felt driven now. Kon was struggling frantically with Gérard and Jack hoped he could reach them before Gérard got to his gun.

Suddenly Gérard struck a savage blow on Kon's fractured wrist. Kon cried out in agony and Gérard managed to wrench himself free. Instantly he raised his arm and rammed Kon in the temple with his elbow. Kon staggered backwards, lost his balance, and fell.

As Jack charged forward, he heard the sound of tires splashing along the wet street. He saw Gérard draw the Browning, then a car skidded to a stop by the curb. He despaired that he could prevent Gérard from shooting Kon and making his escape. He fired into the air as he ran hoping to distract Gérard.

Suddenly, to Jack's horror Kon rose to his feet and charged at Gérard. "No! Kon! Don't!" he screamed as several shots rang out. In one desperate lounge Jack leaped forward, shoved Kon aside, and turned to face Gérard with his gun raised.

Gérard was holding the Browning, but he didn't fire.

"Drop it, Gérard!" Jack ordered, but Gérard just stood until a moment later he fell forward.

Seeing a man step from behind the car, Jack fired over his head, calling out, "Freeze!"

"Don't shoot, Barrons," the answer came back. Jack's mouth fell open as he recognized David Falcon.

"I couldn't let him get away," Falcon continued coming closer. "Are you both O.K.?"

"I think so," Jack said turning to help Kon who was struggling to get up. "Are you O.K., Kon?"

Kon didn't answer. He just stood looking from Jack to Falcon and then to Gérard.

"Kon? Are you O.K.?" Jack asked again.

"It was Gérard," Kon mumbled. "I wasn't sure at first, but it was him. When I saw him with that cigarette . . . I . . . I don't know what happened. Things started coming back to me . . . crowding in on me, almost suffocating me . . . fear and anger."

"It's O.K. now, Kon," Jack cut in. "He's dead. Just forget about him."

"I can't. He made a coward of me, Jack. I hated him for that. I've never hated anyone like that!"

"It's over, Kon. Let it go."

"You don't understand . . . the nightmares . . . "

"I do understand!" Jack suddenly shouted. "Will you just cut it out about being a coward! Just because he beat you physically does not mean you're a coward. Believe me, I've met a few cowards in my life and there's no way you qualify. If Paul or I even suspected that you were a coward, you wouldn't have been on the damned job in the first place. You didn't get kidnapped because you were acting like a coward so just shut up about it!"

Kon stared mutely at Jack. Paul's assurances about his character had been comforting, but Jack's vehement denial of any cowardice was even more powerful.

When Jack followed up forcefully with, "I am getting through to you?" Kon nodded.

Jack knew it would take a while for Kon to get over being kidnapped. He wouldn't crowd him. It had taken him a little while to get over 'Nam. He turned back to Falcon. "How did you know Gérard was here?"

"I beat it out of Leverett."

"But why? And who told you about Leverett?"

"Garday told me everything. Pienaar sent me to escort him to a hearing. The kid was terrified of leaving his cell. He kept screaming that Gérard was going to kill him. He told me that you were going after Gérard and begged me to let him stay where he was until you told him Gérard had been taken care of. He's watched so many people get gunned down he was crazy with fear."

"But why didn't you just let us handle it?"

"I almost did. I went to Pienaar and told him what Garday had told me. He said you were going to handle it and that it was out of his hands. But this afternoon I learned that Lothar has escaped. I was afraid Lothar would tip off Gérard and you would walk into a trap. I went to the camera shop and . . . and . . ."

Suddenly Falcon seemed overcome with emotion. He threw down his gun. "God help me, I almost beat Leverett to death I was so angry. I think I would have, but his wife came into the shop. I couldn't kill him in front of her. Not after . . . I know what it feels like. They've taken everything, even my self-respect. I lost control with Leverett the way I lost control in Paris when I shot your friend. I have negated everything I stand for, law and order and due process."

"What about justice?" Jack cut in. "Gérard was slime! Do you think he gave any due process to Kon or to those people at that restaurant?"

"But I will be thrown off the force. I don't have any jurisdiction here."

"So what's the big deal?" Jack shrugged. "You're just a few miles away. He was about to shoot my partner so you got him first."

"But how can we prove it? With my record and your friend's here, who would believe us? He's not even wanted for anything in Belgium."

"Well, he is now! God you're thick, Falcon! Do you think I would come all this way to set this up and not record it. I've got the whole thing on tape."

"You do?" Falcon asked in surprise.

"Of course. I wasn't sure Gérard would agree to meet me in Germany and I wasn't about to let him off the hook. Don't be so hard on yourself, Falcon. With Lothar on the loose, we need men like you."

Falcon stared at Jack for a moment then straightened himself and retrieved his gun. "I'll call the police," he said with determination. "You'd better take Kononellos back to his family."

Chapter Twenty-Four

It was February and Paul was sound asleep in his London apartment until he was jolted awake by the raucous ringing of the phone. Not again, he thought wearily as he rubbed his eyes and tried to read the clock on his nightstand. Three-ten in the morning! Jees. I told mom I can't come running back to Chicago every time someone stubs their toe. They've got to learn to stand on their own two feet. I can't keep solving all their problems for them. I can't do it anymore. I just can't!

"Hello!" he growled, snatching the receiver.

"Paul! You've got to come!" he heard a familiar voice plead. "It's Geilla. She's started labor early. Hurry!"

"Kon?" Paul asked, forcing his sleep-clouded brain to shift gears.

"Yes. You've got to help her, Paul. It's too soon. It's five weeks too soon!"

"O.K.! O.K.! I'll come. Calm down, Kon. Where are you?"

"At the hospital. We've been here for three hours. We've walked up and down a million times. I rubbed her back. Nothing seems to be helping. You've got to help her, Paul. I don't know what to do. She wants this baby so badly. I can't face her if it dies."

"Listen to me, Kon!" Paul said firmly. "The baby isn't going to die. Call Carlin and then get back to Geilla. She's the one who has to do all the work. You just have to hold her hand."

"Carlin is here. He keeps telling me not to worry, but I think he's lying."

"Stop imagining things, Kon! When has Carlin ever lied to you?"

"I don't know . . . it's just that they're all trying to protect me. I know I still can't remember things, but I'm not incompetent, Paul."

"No one thinks you're incompetent, Kon. They're your family. It's natural for them to want to protect you. Carlin would not withhold information from you. If he says the baby is O.K., you have to believe him."

"But why is the baby so early? There must be something wrong!"

"Not necessarily. Stop worrying. Carlin knows what he's doing. Now pull yourself together before you upset Geilla. You can do this, Kon. I know you can. Just stay calm and do what Carlin tells you. I'll be there as soon as I can."

"I'll try," Kon answered shakily. "Hurry, Paul, please."

"I will. Stay calm, Kon, stay calm," Paul urged again.

Sure, he thought, hanging up the phone. Stay calm. Fat chance, knowing you. Why the hell is the baby so early? I wonder if Carlin is keeping something from Kon. Jees! I wish my family would try to protect me once in a while instead of dumping all their garbage on me. Stop it, Paul, he told himself. If you hadn't screwed up dad might still be alive to take care of them.

Well, I'm sorry. Haven't I paid enough? I never thought joining the Green Dragons at sixteen would wreck so many lives. I wasn't any brighter than Etienne and Edouard about joining the wrong organization. I'm just glad I got them out before they hurt someone besides themselves.

He reached for the suitcase he kept packed. I'll have to take a charter flight, he mused dialing for a cab. Well, Jack's friend Dean is always eager to make a little extra money. What a time for Jack to be off to Dartmoor for another hiking trip. Ha! Hiking, my eye! You've got something going down there, buddy. You're the only guy I know who polishes his shoes before he goes hiking. And you've become worse than Kon for keeping secrets lately. Honestly, sometimes you guys are more trouble than all my brothers put together!

The weather was cold but clear when Dean landed in Geneva. He had called ahead and a waiting cab rushed Paul to the hospital. Paul was shocked to find Kon sitting in the waiting room, flanked by two heavy-weight orderlies. Kon looked white and shaken.

"Kon! What happened? Why aren't you with Geilla?"

Kon leaped to his feet and grabbed Paul's arm. "I was. I tried, Paul. I really tried, but I got . . . I got upset and they threw me out."

"Upset? What happened? Did you pass out?"

"No . . . I . . . er . . ."

338

"Well? What? Did you throw up?" Paul demanded. He looked questioningly at the two orderlies, but they ignored him.

"No! It all happened so fast . . . I was with Geilla and she was trying to be brave . . . but . . . she couldn't help it . . . she started to groan and I couldn't take it. I started swearing at the doctor to do something. He told me to be quiet. He said I was upsetting his patient! That set me off, Paul. I shouted that he was killing my wife and . . . and I think I took a swing at him. Geilla started screaming and then people were leaping all over me and they dragged me out. I tried to get back in, but they said they would have me arrested if I didn't sit still."

"Jesus, Kon! Leave it to you! Where's Carlin?"

"He's with Geilla. You've got to get in there, Paul! They won't let me in. She's dying in there, Paul, and they won't let me in! My mother died in childbirth! What am I going to do when she's gone? I'll kill myself, Paul. I swear I'll kill myself without Geilla."

Paul suddenly seized Kon by the shoulders and spun him away from the orderlies. "Will you shut up about dying," he said calmly, as if the whole idea was ridiculous. "Nobody's dying, Kon," he continued, lowering his voice. "This is just the way childbirth is. It hurts and women scream. It doesn't mean they're dying. And punching the doctor doesn't speed things up one damn bit! Now take a deep breath and get a hold of yourself."

Kon struggled to follow Paul's advice and Paul released his grip. "I'm sorry," Kon said dejectedly. "I let her down. I just wasn't ready for the screaming. I was O.K. up until then. I just can't stand screaming, Paul."

"I know. I know. No one ever talks about that part. But it's normal. Women claim it's worth the pain to get a kid. If it helps Geilla to get through this faster, let her scream, for God's sake."

"I'm sorry. I'm so afraid of losing her. I know how to handle a broken leg or a bullet wound, but this baby business makes me feel so damned helpless!"

"Your job is support on this one, Kon. It's like the team. We all do our job with more confidence when we know someone is covering us."

Kon nodded.

"Now . . . I'm going in to say 'hello' to Geilla and talk with Carlin. When I come out, I'll brief you and then you go in. Agreed?"

"What about those two?" Kon asked, gesturing toward the orderlies.

"Don't worry about them. You just get ready to provide support to Geilla. Pretend the screaming is just a bad soprano at the opera. No matter what happens, the story has a happy ending when the baby comes. O.K.?"

Kon smiled weakly. "O.K."

"Good," Paul answered and disappeared into the delivery room.

Kon paced anxiously under the watchful eyes of the orderlies until Paul emerged a short time later.

"How is she?" Kon asked, rushing up to Paul.

"She's doing fine," Paul said lowering his voice to a whisper. "But she's worried about you and it's distracting her. She's got a lot more work to do so you'd better get in there."

"What about the doctor? Will be object?"

Paul shook his head. "I told him I shot you so full of tranquilizers nothing would phase you. Now don't make a liar out of me."

"O.K." Kon agreed and moved toward the delivery room door. Immediately the two orderlies were on their feet calling, "Hey! You can't go in there!"

Before they could take another step, Paul jumped in front of them, pulling open his coat so that they could see he was armed.

"Gentlemen, please . . . sit . . ." he said fixing them in a cold stare. "I think family values are very important. Don't you agree?"

Kon slipped inside feeling confident that, as usual, Paul had the situation under control. If only I could learn to be more like him, he thought going up to where Geilla lay clutching Carlin's hand. He looked Carlin in the eye, silently giving his word that be would not cause another scene.

Geilla was panting and obviously working very hard, but she quickly released Carlin's hand and reached gratefully for Kon's. "It's taking longer than I thought," she gasped. "Is everything O.K.? Why is Paul here?"

Kon bent to kiss Geilla's forehead. "Everything is fine, my love. Paul just came to handle the two goons who were keeping guard on me out there. I'm sorry I lost my head. You win the prize for bravery."

"I'm glad you're back. I was afraid . . . oh . . . oh damn!" Geilla winced. "I was afraid I would have to post bail so that you could visit your son. You really are impossible, Kon. There's no getting around it."

"I'm sorry. I'm sorry. Please don't call me impossible. I'll behave myself. I promise."

Geilla suddenly gripped his hand as another contraction began.

"I hope you do," she said sharply as the pain subsided. "If you're going to act like an idiot when I need you, you can forget your house-full-of-children idea."

"I'm sorry. I won't let you down again," Kon promised and threw his arm around her. "I love you so much. It was torture sitting out there alone. I won't leave you. I'll never leave you!"

And Kon kept his word. He held Geilla and encouraged her to relax. He rubbed her back very gently thinking that his efforts were clumsy and awkward compared to Paul's techniques. He remained so calm outwardly that Geilla never once suspected how extremely frightened he was. He was also secretly gratified that through all the pain Geilla never once called for Paul.

Finally, as Kon felt he was close to losing control again from watching Geilla suffer, the baby's head emerged. Kon's heart sank when he saw how gray and lifeless it looked. Merciful God, he prayed, after all this effort, let him be alive. Please let him be alive! He clutched Geilla's hand tightly.

"What's happening, Kon? Is everything all right?" she asked quickly.

"Yes, my love. Everything is fine," he said numbly. That's what you're supposed to say, isn't it? Even if you are scared to death that it isn't true.

After a few more contractions the baby was fully visible. Kon reached for it, but Carlin caught his arm. "Stand aside, Peter," he said gently.

Kon froze. He knew he was not imagining things. There was definitely something wrong. Dr. Brekke and Carlin were hovering over the baby, but it was deathly silent in the room. Kon was conscious of the seconds ticking by until suddenly he heard the cry. Feeble at first, but then it became louder and stronger.

"Congratulations Madame Kononellos! It's a boy!" he heard Dr. Brekke announce.

Although Kon had known for months that the baby was a boy, a suddenly wave of euphoria washed over him. There were tears in his eyes as he leaned to kiss Geilla's smiling face. The ordeal was over and he was a father. A father! My God! Geilla will be a good mother, but me, a father? I've always wanted a son, but somehow I envisioned I would be stronger and wiser when it happened.

Dr. Brekke suddenly broke into Kon's reverie asking, "And what is the child to be named?"

Kon and Geilla both responded immediately, but as Geilla answered, "Edgar", as she and Kon had agreed, Kon responded, "Paul!" Geilla was surprised, but she nodded, and Edgar Paul Kononellos was officially registered as the first born son of Peter and Geilla.

Kon's sense of relief evaporated when he looked at the baby, however. Although the child did not have slanted eyes as he had feared, Kon was sure that the tiny, shriveled child with bluish hands and feet and paper-thin skin was too frail to live. He hid his despair and smiled as Geilla cooed in pleasure. Truly mother love is a miracle, he thought, for Geilla didn't seem to care how ugly the child was.

Paul and Carlin came to congratulate him, but his pleasure was gone. He felt numb, exhausted. He had hid his fear that Geilla would die and leave him alone and now he hid his trepidation that his child would not survive. He stood clutching Geilla's hand until Carlin pulled him away, saying that Geilla needed to sleep. She smiled wearily at him and he heard himself promise to visit her later. Someone pulled him into the hall and he saw that the orderlies were gone and that Charlotte and Edgar had arrived. Edgar pumped his hand and patted him on the back, but Kon remained speechless.

It was Charlotte who first noticed that Kon was disturbed about something. "Peter, dear, tell me what's wrong?"

Kon looked at her. Doesn't she know? he thought. Is she trying to protect my feelings? Why are they all pretending to be happy?

"It isn't Geilla's fault. It's mine," he mumbled.

"What's your fault, Peter," Charlotte asked, taking his arm.

Suddenly he could not hold back any longer. Charlotte is so wise about everything. Maybe she can explain what is wrong with my son.

"The baby . . . he's so small. Is he going to live?"

"Oh, Peter, of course he's going to live! There's nothing wrong with him. He'll grow," Charlotte assured him.

"But he's so tiny and so blue? There must be something the matter with him! Don't lie to me, Charlotte. I can't stand it when people lie to me."

"I'm not lying, Peter. Please calm down. There is nothing wrong with the baby. I think you need to talk to Carlin."

Seeing Kon's utter misery on what should have been one of the happiest days of his life, Paul hurried to find Carlin. Together they took Kon to the nursery and showed him the other newborns. Carlin explained patiently that little Edgar Paul's color was not unusual for a premature baby.

"But why is he so small?" Kon persisted.

"Peter, four pounds, nine ounces is not abnormal. He's perfectly formed. He'll grow. Give him time."

"I will pray that you are right, but . . ."

"Stop worrying, Peter. You don't know how lucky you are. Geilla came close to losing the baby several times."

"He's right, Kon," Paul cut in. "Why would you expect a big baby? Geilla's tiny and you're thin as a rail."

"But why did he come so early if there is nothing wrong with him?"

Carlin shook his head. "I don't know, Peter. Sometimes it just happens that way. Perhaps he has no more patience than his father!"

Kon was startled by Carlin's answer, but then he smiled guiltily. "After my performance in the delivery room, I can offer no argument. Dio mio! I hope the baby has more sense than to take after me!"

Paul laughed. "You're in for it now, Kon. Maybe you'll appreciate just how difficult it is to keep you in line."

Chapter Twenty-Five

Charlotte was happy to at last be hosting a party for little Edgar Paul. She had wanted to hold a celebration earlier, but Kon kept putting her off. He pleaded that Geilla needed more time to recover and that the baby was too fragile to be brought out in the bad weather. His arguments seemed wise and logical and not even Paul suspected that Kon still doubted that his child was normal. Kon had hired a nurse to look after Geilla and the baby, but the woman had little to do since Kon had taken time off from work after the baby was born. Whenever Geilla slept, he would hold the child and fight his fears that it was going to die from some mysterious ailment.

The situation might have continued for months if Georgio Vittorini, a long-time friend of Kon's, had not shown up unexpectedly when he was in Geneva on one of his trucking runs. He knew that Geilla was expecting and as the father of eight he was experienced enough to calculate when she was due. Knowing Kon as well as he did, he suspected something was wrong when Kon did not call to announce the birth of his child.

Kon had been upset and embarrassed when Georgio suddenly appeared at his apartment. Although he recognized Georgio, he could not dredge up a name to fit his face. Since he wasn't sure of his relationship to Georgio, he did not know how to respond. Charlotte's strict training in etiquette stood Kon in good stead, however. He invited Georgio in, showed him to a chair, and excused himself politely before he ran to find Geilla.

Geilla saved the day by greeting Georgio by name and asking so many questions about his business and his family that Kon was finally able to recall who he was. Little by little Kon's memory had been returning, but he was often embarrassed when caught off guard. He found it humiliating to tell people that he had been kidnaped and had not responded to the pile of letters on his desk. Even some of his closest friends still did not know what had happened to him and attributed his slow response to his busy schedule.

Once he was confronted by Georgio's presence, he realized that he could not go on sheltering his child from the harsh judgement of the world. But to his amazement, Georgio did not appear disappointed when Geilla presented little Edgar Paul for inspection. Georgio poked and tickled the baby with exuberance and announced that he was bello! bello! bellissimo! Even when Kon apologized that his son was so tiny, Georgio's approval did not fade.

"He's a bambino, Peter. What do you expect? Look at his legs. He's going to be tall like his father, maybe not such a bean pole, but tall. And see the hair. It is just like yours, running both north and south at the same time. Congratulations, Peter!"

Kon smiled at Georgio's enthusiasm. He suddenly saw his son in a new light. Georgio certainly knows more about babies than I do, he thought. Maybe Edgar Paul is going to be O.K. He's not as small as before and he's not blue anymore. He can grip your finger as though he means to keep you from escaping, and he doesn't cry much. In fact, he's really very healthy, Kon concluded. All of a sudden Kon agreed with Charlotte that they should have a party to celebrate Edgar Paul's arrival.

Once Charlotte had Kon's permission, she was quick to arrange the event and invited all of Peter's friends. What better way for him to get reacquainted with them than at a happy occasion where she and Edgar and Carlin would be on hand to smooth things along for him. Geilla had agreed and had called a number of the people herself, quietly explaining the situation to them. Everyone had been relieved that Kon was recovering and promised not to be upset if he didn't recognize them straightaway.

"It's good to see you up and about, Brad," Carlin said coming up to greet Brad, Mary, and Jack when they arrived at the Marneés.

"Where's Paul? Didn't he come with you?"

"No. He was delayed at the last minute, something about having to wire money to his brother. He'll he here shortly."

"I hope it's nothing serious," Carlin remarked.

"Naw. It's just the usual you've-got-to-help-him story from his mother," Jack put in. "I wish they'd leave him alone. They don't understand how busy he is."

"They make him feel guilty about things that were not his fault," Mary added. "I wish he could recognize it and get out from under. He's just too soft hearted."

"He is that," Carlin agreed. "It's a shame they take advantage of him. But you certainly are looking fit, Brad. Much different from the last time we met."

"Yes. Yes. I've been back at work for weeks—much to Mary's displeasure."

"I know you wouldn't have it any other way, but do try to set an example of moderation for the others, especially Peter. He tends to drive himself."

"I'll try, but you must understand that I have very little influence over Peter. You must have been working on him lately. I hear he has agreed to go for counseling about the nightmares."

"Ah, yes, but I can't claim credit for his decision. I've been after him for years, but he only becomes upset when I mention them. No, it was little Edgar that made Peter change his mind."

"The baby? But how?"

"When Peter woke up screaming the other night he found the baby crying. He was so horrified that he had frightened his son, he called me in the morning and pleaded for help. When he asked for sleeping pills, I knew he was desperate. He rejected the idea of counseling at first, but he agreed that he could not use sleeping pills every night until his son was grown. He finally said he would talk to Paul before making a final decision."

"Any of course Paul encouraged him to seek help."

"Most definitely. Paul has known about the dreams for years. He even promised to find a therapist with a high-level security clearance."

"Who did he finally recommend?"

"Dr. Krejci. Quite the opposite of a classic scholar, but with an extremely broad background in psychology and sociology. Very competent man. He's done some work for NATO in Athens and speaks passible Greek. I'm sure that's why Paul chose him."

"Yes, if Kon is ever going to express what's troubling him, it will have to be in Greek. That's his core of feelings. Everything else is just a veneer."

"Yes and he's never fully come to terms with it."

"Did Kon go to see Krejci?"

"Yes, but it was very difficult. I went with him to make introductions and instill confidence. Peter told me afterwards that it was the hardest thing he had ever done. He couldn't even bring himself to sit down. He paced for the entire hour, barely getting beyond his name and the reason he had come. He was exhausted afterwards, but the most promising thing is that he agreed to go back twice a week."

"Well, it's not like Kon to give up on something once he makes up his mind. I truly hope the sessions help him."

A little while later when Paul arrived, Mary greeted him warmly. "Hello, Paul. Is everything all right back in Chicago?"

"Yeah . . . I guess so, until next time. I don't want to talk about it anymore."

"I was just concerned. I'm glad you didn't get held up for long. I've been anxious to tell you that I've received a letter from Trinette."

"Good! How is she doing?"

"Oh, she's fine. She asked me to tell you that she's found homes for two of Edouard's cats. She kept the little gray one herself. She says it has the sweetest disposition."

"That great. I'll be sure to let Edouard know."

"Please do. Trinette also reported the splendid news that Vérèna has recovered and is back to work!"

"That's wonderful. She was so bad I was afraid she would quit the force."

"No. She is as determined as ever. She was in the hospital for weeks and then was restricted to a desk job, but she's back in the field once again."

"That's terrific. She's a fine officer."

"Have you heard anything about that other lad—the one who set you on to Gérard?"

"Yes, that was Philippe. We got him off and sent him to Lausanne under a witness protection program. Unfortunately, once his parents had to face the fact that he was not a victim of police persecution, but was deeply involved with the terrorists, they withdrew their support.

Philippe just couldn't cope on his own and had a mental breakdown. Jack went to visit him. The doctors said it had such a positive effect Jack is trying to get him transferred to London so that he can visit him more often."

"So after everything Jack says about not getting involved, he's playing big brother himself. That's splendid. And how are you, Paul. I noticed you've been avoiding Nea. Are you still angry with her?"

"I'm not angry with Nea. I was never angry. I was just . . . disappointed, I guess. It doesn't matter anyway," he concluded shrugging his shoulders.

"But it does matter. Stop punishing yourself, Paul. You don't have to be alone all the time."

"I don't mind being alone. I don't need her! I don't need anyone."

"I know you don't absolutely 'need' anyone, Paul. Think of her company as a luxury. You always look after everyone else. It's time you indulge yourself a little."

"I won't crawl, Mary. It's over."

"My, my! And you talk about Kon being stubborn. You don't have to crawl. Just walk over there and say 'hello'."

"You think it's that simple?"

"Yes. Nea is still interested in you, Paul, but you'll lose her if you don't cultivate that interest. Don't you at least want to know if it could work?"

"I don't know, Mary. I don't seem to know what I want. Maybe that's why I never get it."

"Well, you seemed very hurt when she left Paris without telling you."

"I was. I'll admit it. But I'm over it."

"Are you absolutely sure?"

Paul looked at Mary for a brief moment then studied his hands. "Why is it I can never hide anything from you?"

"Go talk to her, Paul," Mary urged, taking a hold of his arm. "Do something for yourself for once."

"Alright! Alright! You and Jack insist upon playing matchmaker."

"I'm not trying to start anything. Just go say 'hello' and see where it leads."

"O.K. I'll do it, but don't think . . ."

"Go," Mary ordered with a smile.

Paul shook his head, and turned to look for Nea. She was talking with Charlotte, but before he could cross the room, Charlotte was called away.

He stood awkwardly for a moment before saying, "Hello, Nea. How have you been?"

He thought she looked startled, but she answered slowly, "Oh, fine. Fine. Keeping busy. And you?"

"Busy. I like it that way," he said coolly. This is stupid, he thought to himself. I'm supposed to be Mr. Perfect. Why can't I think of something brilliant to say?

"I see you finally got back from Paris," Nea put in. "Has there been any news from Etienne?"

Paul suddenly felt a rush of pleasure that she remembered the details of the case. Maybe she had been interested. "Yes, I got a letter a few days ago. He still needs his wheelchair, but he's been measured for a leg brace. I'm hopeful that he'll be able to get around by himself one day."

"Is he back in school?"

"Yes, and doing very well. Edouard's got him studying biology and botany and he's soaking it up. In fact, his father is so impressed by the change in him that he has promised to finance Edouard's return to school later this year."

"That's wonderful!" Nea beamed. "What is he going to study?"

It was a simple question, but her response had been suffused with such genuine enthusiasm that Paul felt himself drawn to her. I can't blame it on medication this time, and I don't have a concussion, he analyzed. It's got to be something else.

I haven't felt this way about anyone except Geilla, but she only came to me when she was longing for Kon. She never knew how much I longed for her. She's better off with Kon. They both want stability and kids and all that. I need more freedom. But then it might be nice to have someone waiting for me when I got back from an assignment. Nea seems interested in me even when I'm not all dressed up and spending money. Is she really attracted to me or am I a substitute for Keith? I sure don't want to go through that again.

Paul finally noticed that Nea was waiting expectantly for an answer. "Oh, right. Edouard's determined to try med school again. Working with Etienne has reawakened a childhood dream. He wants to be an orthopedic surgeon."

"Oh, I'm so glad for him. He really is bright."

"Yes he is. Etienne's father has taken both boys under his wing. He's decided to put his money to good use instead of hording it."

"That's wonderful. Tell me," Nea started. She slid over and indicated that Paul should sit beside her. "Have you heard anything about Lorelle?"

Paul smiled and sat. "As a matter of fact, I have. After the incident at the pre-trial hearing, Pienaar requested that the proceedings be moved to Marseille. I didn't get down there, but I understand the trial got very little publicity. Lorelle got off with two years and she is serving her time there. Her mother hasn't been able to get down to see her, but all in all, it's a lot safer for her there.

"I think she's fed up with being a terrorist and is trying to improve society on her own. The last I heard she volunteered to teach some of the other prisoners how to read."

"That's great! You seem to be keeping in touch with everyone. It must make you feel good to know that you helped turn so many lives around."

"Getting people straightened out is my job."

"Yes, and you do seem to thrive on it."

"It takes a lot of time. Look, I know I'm very involved with my work. That's the way I am, but . . . well . . . maybe . . ."

"Yes," Nea urged expectantly.

"Well, maybe I *could* arrange . . ." Paul hesitated and then suddenly took her by the hand. "I've missed you, Nea. More than I ever imagined I would."

"I've missed you too, Paul."

"Maybe we could sort of start over."

"No, let's not go back to the beginning. I want to get beyond all that. Let's try to go forward. I promise I won't interfere with your work if you promise to save a little time for me."

"That sounds good. Even I must have a little spare time. Would . . . would you like to go somewhere now? Just to drive around and kind of . . . talk."

"Sure. I'm not flying back until tomorrow."

"Great! Just let me talk to Kon for a minute. Don't go away."

"I'll wait, Paul. I promise."

Paul laughed and squeezed her hand.

"O.K. I'll be right back," he said hurriedly and looking around quickly, he made a beeline to where Kon was sitting with Georgio. "Ah, Kon . . . er . . . could you . . . er, that is . . . could I possibly borrow the Ferrari for a few hours?"

Kon grinned. "The Ferrari? My very own precious Ferrari? What's the occasion?"

"Oh, nothing special. I just thought I might take Nea for a drive."

"Oh, I see," Kon said knowingly. "She's off the shit list. Good move, my friend." Kon reached in his pocket and pulled out his silver key ring. "Here, take the car, but do us both a favor. Don't let things stall this time."

Paul looked at Kon in surprise. "I wasn't the one who slammed on the brakes."

"Well, be careful. Just keep her purring along and she'll take you a long way. And don't hurry back. My family and I are spending the night here."

Paul noticed how Kon lingered over the words "my family" and he smiled. God it was good to see Kon enjoying the life he always wanted. Who knows? Maybe I'll finally figure out what it is I'm looking for.